baptism

in

blood

———

jane haddam

BANTAM BOOKS
NEW YORK · TORONTO · LONDON · SYDNEY · AUCKLAND

BAPTISM IN BLOOD

A Bantam Book

Bantam paperback edition / December 1996

ISBN 0-553-57464-7

Published simultaneously in the United States and Canada

Bantam Books are published by Bantam Books, a division of Bantam
Doubleday Dell Publishing Group, Inc. Its trademark, consisting of the
words "Bantam Books" and the portrayal of a rooster, is Registered
in U.S. Patent and Trademark Office and in other countries. Marca
Registrada. Bantam Books, 1540 Broadway, New York, New York 10036.

PRINTED IN THE UNITED STATES OF AMERICA

OPM   10 9 8 7 6 5 4 3 2 1

baptism

in

blood

Dear Gregor:

I have been thinking all morning about the things you said last night, and running around trying to get you the things you said you'd need. I don't understand it, exactly, but here they are: all the clippings from the local paper here and the bigger one up in Raleigh-Durham; a photocopy of the report the state police did right after the storm; the only picture of the body I know for sure is in existence. I looked at the picture for a long time, trying to make it be familiar. I didn't manage it. Corpses are not what I expected them to be. They're nothing at all like the people who once inhabited them. Looking at dead flesh makes me think that all those philosophers who believe that there are two entities, soul and body, might have had more to go on than just wishful thinking. Looking at dead flesh makes me want to drown my life in very expensive bourbon.

I'm including a few pages of notes on what I saw and did that day, too, just the way you asked me to, but I'm afraid they aren't going to be much help. Everything I remember is very impressionistic, very mundane. The first time I knew that there was something wrong was when I saw the blood in the water, and I just thought it was the storm. Hurricane Elsa. I remember the wind getting so strong it bent the trees sideways along the edge of the beach, and took the roof off Rose MacNeill's high-towered Victorian house. An old bum named Cary Deckeran drowned in a puddle of water in the crawl space under his front porch.

He'd gone there to get out of the rain and had fallen asleep with drink just as the water started rising. Four people in town died that night just from the wind and water, and forty more were injured. There was blood everywhere.

I couldn't tell you now why it was I knew that the blood I saw was different, but I did know. When she came out of the trees a few minutes later, all cut up and wild, I was almost expecting her. I wasn't expecting what I found later—all the candles and incense, that strange ritual circle with its oils and perfumes, and the body lying there on top of the table, not only dead but cut into. Maybe that is what has always bothered me most. The body was cut into, Gregor, with little blood-traced lines all over it, as if it had been ripped apart and stitched together again like a crocheted quilt or badly made lace. I remember asking myself frantically when it had been done, when the body was dead or when it was alive. I asked the police about it, too, the first chance I got, but I didn't get anything like a satisfactory answer. The attitude around here seems to be that I am the stranger in this place, and the atheist, and that it's probably all my fault one way or another anyhow. I don't mean that anybody suspects me of murder. They don't. Here they think on a much more cosmic level than we're used to thinking in New York.

Anyway, here it all is, and I hope it does you some good. Clayton Hall tells me he will be glad to have you here, and will write and tell you so himself. I have a feeling that the state police are less glad, but they aren't saying so at the moment. You must be used to that.

It's like I told you on the phone. Everything is a mess here, and nothing is getting done, and we're making the papers in Los Angeles and New

York for all the wrong reasons. Everybody's edgy and nervous. No matter how many times we all tell ourselves that it has nothing to do with us, not really, it's all those people up at the camp— everybody is half expecting another body to show up, or worse. And she—*well, you've seen her. Talking to Connie Chung. Talking to Barbara Walters. Going on and on the way she does with that big dumb bigot always at her side, never smiling, perpetually grim. I know he has nothing to smile about. I know it was his tragedy, too. I hate the man anyway.*

See what I'm turning into? Good old logical me, the one who always and everywhere brought reason to bear on even the smallest problem, and I'm talking like a spiritualist with the spooks. The next thing you know, I'm going to be seeing ghosts on Main Street and the devil in Town Hall. The big dumb bigot sees the devil everywhere, even in church.

What I need, Gregor, is for you to get down here, right now, as fast as you can, and bring me back to myself. At least get enough of this straightened out so that I can think about something else for a while. My house wasn't hit too badly by the storm, in spite of being on the beach. You can have the back bedroom and a desk to work at in the library. Don't pay too much attention to the way I sounded on the phone last night. This is a lovely place, with lovely people in it. They don't mean to get worked up the way they have. This is just the kind of thing people get worked up about, even me.

Blood in the water, that's the point. So much blood in the water, it couldn't all have been hers. Blood shot through the white foam of the caps stirred up by the storm. Blood splashed across the smooth round rocks that fanned out from the front door of the lodge up at the camp. Blood on the black tablecloth that covered the makeshift altar where the body was found. There have been rumors down here ever since it happened that in order to worship the devil you have to shed blood, your own as well as somebody else's. I don't believe that anyone worships the devil. I don't believe in the devil. Still, you know how people get. I don't like the way the air feels around here these days. I worry about how frightened everybody is.

So. Pack your bags. Send our friend Bennis off to Paris or Palm Beach or someplace else she's likely to be able to stay out of trouble. Tell Tibor that I still haven't had a conversion experience and that I still don't want one, although I'm still interested in a little poker anytime he wants to visit me for a game. Say all the normal things, Gregor, and then just get here.

I think I'm getting desperate.

David

prologue

———

hurricane elsa

1

For David Sandler, Bellerton, North Carolina, had always been a place of rest. Bellerton was where he came on the long spring vacations when his students were in Fort Lauderdale or the Bahamas. Bellerton was where he came in the summer, with his books packed into liquor boxes in the back of his ancient Volvo station wagon and his class notes stuffed into the glove compartment. What had made him decide to come down here on his sabbatical, when he would have to do real work, he didn't know. He had the house on the beach now. It was the only house he had ever really owned. He liked walking through Bellerton's small town center. He liked the flat-roofed brick buildings that held the little stores that lined Main Street. He liked the tall-columned Greek revival houses that sat back on broad lawns for the four or five short blocks with sidewalks on them that made up "town" before the country started. He even liked Bellerton's six mainstream churches—which was funny, really, because David Sandler was the man *People* magazine had called "The Most Famous Atheist in America." David didn't know if he was famous or not, but in Bellerton these days he was noted. People left Bible tracts under his windshield wipers while he was picking up milk at the grocery store. People stuffed brochures into his mailbox: glossy four-color advertising flyers with headlines that said *Have You Accepted Christ As Your Personal Savior?* People even tried to talk to him, awkwardly, as if they hated to intrude. David had a bright silver decal on the back of his car: a fish with legs and the word "Darwin" written inside it. People walked around that as if it could jump off the metal and go stomping around on their feet.

On the day of the hurricane, David stood on the deck of his house looking out at the sea and thinking that he didn't like Bellerton's *other* churches at all. The other churches were in storefronts and shacks and private houses out along the access roads off the interstate. They had names like The Good News Full Gospel Assembly and the Bellerton Church of Christ Jesus. They also seemed to have all the parishioners. Something had happened to the country in the thirty years since David had first started teaching. It was as if no one was interested anymore in what was really real. They preferred to shout at each other instead. They preferred to shout at *him*. What was worse, the more they shouted, the more they seemed to come into money.

The sea was choppy and dark. The sky was a mass of black clouds. The little portable radio David had set up on the empty deck chair was urging everybody to board up their windows and head for higher ground. It was October and it was colder than David had thought it ever could be, this far south. That was what came of spending his life in New York City, of making Columbia University his only serious home. When the article had appeared in *People* about his getting a grant to write a book in favor of atheism, at least two dozen people had written in to ask what else they could have expected, since Dr. Sandler was a professor at a secular humanist communist Jewish place like Columbia. Actually, David was the son of a Presbyterian minister—but that was a story he didn't go into often, and then only if he had to.

"The National Weather Service is reporting winds over a hundred twenty miles an hour off Hilton Head," the radio said. "If you live on the beach, get off now. This is the biggest storm we've seen in fifteen years. You're not going to be able to ride this one out."

David went through the sliding glass doors into the house. The big square living room with its twenty-foot ceiling was empty. David heard typing coming from the study and the singsong giggle that told him that Ginny Marsh's baby Tiffany was awake and in need of attention. Ginny

Marsh was the young woman from town he had hired to type up his notes. David was surprised she was still there. With all the talk about the storm and the way the baby was fussing, he had assumed she would have gone an hour ago.

David went to the door to the study and looked in. Ginny was sitting at the word processor with her back to him, typing away. Tiffany was enthroned in a blue plastic baby seat, covered with a tiny eyelet quilt. The baby's eyes were big and dark and very solemn. Ginny's work station was littered with objects: a cross on a stand; a picture of Jesus with his arms stretched out to receive the multitudes; a pile of brightly colored pencils with pictures of angels smiling on the sides of them and the words *"Jesus Loves YOU."* The pencils were for sale in town at Rose Mac-Neill's shop, along with lapel pins that said *"My Boss Is a Jewish Carpenter"* and coffee mugs that said *"Jesus Is Lord."*

David coughed. Tiffany turned her head to look at him and smiled. Ginny looked back over her shoulder and then swiveled her chair around to face him.

"Oh," she said. "Dr. Sandler. Is there something I can do for you?"

David walked into the room and took Tiffany out of her chair. Tiffany was the first baby he had ever known, and he liked her enormously. When he picked her up, she curled against him, soft and warm and breathy.

"All the weather news is bad," David said. "You shouldn't be here this late. Even I shouldn't be here. There's going to be a hurricane."

Ginny waved this away and turned back to her typing. Her hair cascaded down her back in a curling ponytail. Her hands were full of rings, so full that her only real one—her wedding ring—seemed to get lost.

"There isn't going to be a hurricane for hours yet," she said confidently. "I know. I've been through them. I've got plenty of time to get this done before I have to head into town."

"I'd still feel safer if you headed into town."

Ginny tapped impatiently at the computer. "Besides," she said, "you know what I'd have to do if I left here now?"

"No."

"Go up to that camp," Ginny said. "That's what I'd have to do. I promised that Miss Meyer. Ms., she wants to be called. My husband says they're worshipping the devil up at that camp. Did you know that?"

"No," David said. "I didn't know it. I don't think it's true, Ginny. They're not devils up there. They're just a lot of middle-aged women whose lives haven't worked out so well."

Ginny wrinkled her nose. "They won't let me put my pictures up out there," she told him. "My cross and the picture of my Lord. They won't even let me use my own pencils because they have Jesus' name written on them. Their hearts are hardened against the Lord."

"Their hearts are hardened against a lot of things, I expect."

"They're lesbians, too," Ginny said. "They say so right out. They don't care what anybody else thinks. Homosexuals are an abomination in the sight of the Lord."

"Somehow, I have a hard time thinking of Zhondra Meyer as an abomination. A nag, maybe, but not an abomination."

Ginny looked back over her shoulder again and grinned. "I know," she said, giggling. "They're just like a bunch of old maids up there. It's terrible. But Bobby's the one who went to Bible college. He's the one who knows. So he must be right about it, don't you think?"

Bobby was Ginny's husband. David shifted Tiffany from one shoulder to the other. Tiffany was asleep.

"Right about Zhondra Meyer?" he asked. "Well, Ginny, I don't know. By now you must realize that I don't put much credence in—"

"Put what?"

"That I don't believe in God," David said.

"You just say you don't believe in God," Ginny said

quickly. "It's Ms. Meyer who really doesn't believe in Him. You let me keep my pictures up. You even let me listen to the PTL Club when I stay late. They don't even have a television up there at that camp."

"They probably can't afford one."

Ginny turned back to the terminal screen and frowned at it. "Bobby says it's a dangerous thing, denying God and worshipping Satan. He says it can get out of hand and start affecting everybody. And I know what he means. I went to college myself for a while. Out at North Carolina State. I went for two years."

"You should have stayed."

"I saw it in some of the people I met out there," Ginny went on. "It's a terrible thing, to lose your faith in the Lord. People get—crazy."

"People get crazy with the Lord just as well as without him, Ginny."

Ginny shook her head. "Bobby says people don't really think about Hell anymore. That's the problem. If we really thought about Hell, if we really understood what it meant, we'd never do anything wrong. We wouldn't want to risk for even a second going down to the fire. The fire that lasts for all of eternity."

"Ginny—"

"But some people actually like Hell. Bobby says that's what most people don't understand. Some people get committed to Satan, and then when they do they like Hell, it makes them happy, and it makes them happiest to see souls in torment, you know, souls that haven't been saved but haven't been committed to Satan, either. Do you see what I mean?"

"I see that this baby needs changing."

"You've got the kind of soul that ends up in torment," Ginny went on. "You only think you don't believe in God. I read this stuff you give me to type. It's just silly, Dr. Sandler. All this stuff about how old the rocks are. Nobody can know how old the rocks are. That's just a lot of silliness they taught you at your college, and now you think the Bible isn't true. But the Bible is true. It's God's word from beginning to end. And it's trying to talk to you."

"Ginny, the baby needs—"

Ginny reached out and took the baby. "It's not the same as what goes on up there at the camp," she told him seriously. "They hate everything about God up there. They hate everything God does, especially saving people. They want everybody on earth to go to Hell with them and keep them company. They're bad people, Dr. Sandler. I know. I spend hours and hours up there, typing for Ms. Meyer, even though Bobby wants me to quit. It's a job and we need the money."

"I know you do."

Ginny took the baby over to the couch and laid her down on the black leather cushion. Her face was turned away from him. He couldn't see her eyes. She found her tote bag on the floor and began to take out diapers and wipes.

"There's something else," she said. "Something I haven't even told Bobby about. It worries me."

"What's that, Ginny?"

Ginny shuddered slightly. "They're doing things out there, Dr. Sandler. I wasn't supposed to see them, but I saw them. They're doing things in the woods with candles."

"Candles?"

"Stark naked, too," Ginny went on. "Sitting in circles in the leaves. I thought they were, you know, doing something private, but then I heard them chanting. To the goddess. I don't know which goddess. It sounded like hundreds of goddesses. There were so many names. They were calling up the spirits of the earth. I heard them say it. And they had knives."

"Knives?"

"Big long ones. I didn't see what they did with them. I got out of there as fast as I could. I didn't want them to know I'd been there. But I've been thinking about it. Calling up the spirits of the earth. I figure that has to be the same as the Prince of This World. Don't you?''

David cleared his throat. He didn't know where to start with this. ''I don't think so,'' he told Ginny carefully. ''I think the idea is, they believe that God is in everything and everything is God, even rocks and trees, so the whole earth is holy, even the leaves and the ground—''

''But the earth isn't holy,'' Ginny argued. ''The earth has been corrupted. That's what happened at Adam's fall.''

Tiffany was twisting and turning on the couch. Her clean new Pampers looked shiny along the waist. Her eyes were bright and round and curious, taking the world in. David wanted to pick her up and take her somewhere where she wouldn't be taught this kind of nonsense before she could even read.

Instead, he went to the window of the study and looked out. The sky looked even worse than it had when he was on the deck. The wind was doing hard, erratic things to the weather vane that sat on the roof of the next house down the beach. The world looked cold and dirty and wet.

''It really is getting bad out there, Ginny,'' he said. ''I'm going to go into town now. You ought to go, too. Once this storm hits, there's going to be a mess.''

''I'll be praying for your house, Dr. Sandler. I'll be praying that the Lord preserves this house intact. You remember that when the storm is over and it's still standing.''

''I will remember it.''

''Maybe that will be the miracle that brings you to the Lord.'' Ginny had been kneeling on the floor beside the couch. Now she stood up and brought Tiffany with her. ''You were destined to be saved,'' Ginny said fervently. ''I knew that the minute I saw you. You were destined to be saved, and no matter what you do, the Lord is going to get you in the end. So you might as well give up and come over right now.''

''I'll think about it, Ginny.''

''You do that,'' Ginny said.

Then she stomped away across the study, to get her

pocketbook, to pack up her cross and her pencils and her picture. David watched her move, with that funny bouncy lightness so many of the young women down here had. Her ponytail shivered and jumped. Her eyes seemed to be looking at nothing at all. If she had been born in the North instead of the South, David thought, she would have believed in cheerleading and therapy instead of God and Christ Jesus.

Ginny put Tiffany into her Snugli carrier and slipped the carrier on her back.

"You take care now," she told him. "I'll see you in the morning."

It was morning, but David didn't bring that up. It was barely eleven o'clock. He watched Ginny leave the study and all the while he was wondering what fool nonsense Zhondra Meyer and her band of merry ladies were getting up to up at the camp.

2

The temperature dropped sharply at just about eleven o'clock, but Rose MacNeill didn't notice it. Rose MacNeill was having a hot flash, the worst she'd had yet, and to make sure nobody caught her at it she had locked herself in the little storage room that had once been the kitchen pantry of her big Victorian house. It was the only Victorian house in all of Bellerton, North Carolina. All the other big houses in town were pre–Civil War Greek revival. There was a little square window in the pantry that Rose could look out of, down Main Street to the old Episcopal Church. She could see the trees being bent by the wind. She could see Maggie Kelleher nailing boards across the plate glass windows of her bookshop and Charlie Hare folding up the plywood display tables he usually kept feed and fertilizer on. Rose had known both of these people all their lives, and most of the rest of the people in town as well, and it suddenly struck her that she hated them all with a passion.

There was a plaque hanging on the wall next to the little square window that said: *Jesus Loves You*. Out on the street, Jim Bonham stopped to help Maggie Kelleher with her boards. Bobby Marsh went by without talking to anybody. Rose closed her eyes and pressed her forehead against the wall. Her head hurt. Her whole body was hot. She could feel rivers of sweat running down the sides of her spine. She had spent her entire life in Bellerton, North Carolina, and all she had ever really wanted to do was get out. Even back in high school, when she was president of the best school sorority and the steady date of the nicest boy in town, all she had been able to think about was other places, other people, going north to live in New York City or out over the ocean to stay in Paris. Instead, she had stayed here to be safe. She had learned to wear very high heels with very tight skirts and to pin her blond hair into a French twist. She wore enameled tin pins on her dresses that said things like *Let Go and Let God*.

She was supposed to be safe.

Once she stopped feeling hot, she was suddenly cold. She stepped away from the window and squinted through the glass. Maggie Kelleher was mostly done with her window. Bobby Marsh was gone. Jim Bonham was talking to Charlie Hare. Rose wondered where all the rest of them were. Had they all taken care of their places early, and ridden out to stay with relatives inland? And what about those women up at the camp? They didn't have any relatives. That was why they were up at the camp. That was what the paper said. Rose thought for a moment of the women up there. Then she tried to think of what they did with each other, and her mind went blank. Lesbians. The word was a hard crystal rock in Rose's head. There didn't used to be lesbians in places like Bellerton, North Carolina. Rose had been nearly forty before she even knew what the word meant. There were lesbians here now, though, and an atheist, too, and with all the publicity they got, Bellerton was getting to be famous. For all the wrong things.

There was a sharp rap on the pantry door.

"Rose?" Kathi Nelson asked. "Are you in there? I need to talk to you."

Kathi Nelson was Rose's assistant in the shop. She was seventeen years old and not very bright—and not very popular, either. Rose would have preferred to hire the kind of girls she had been herself at seventeen, but those girls didn't come asking for jobs in a Christian gift shop. Those girls took cram courses for the Scholastic Aptitude Test and went away to Chapel Hill for college. Things had changed a lot since Rose's day, when a girl who wanted to go away to college was assumed not to want to get married at all, ever, no matter what.

"Rose?" Kathi asked again.

Rose pulled herself away from the little square window. She was surrounded by shipping boxes: one thousand blue enamel angel pins; thirty-four engraved brass desk plaques reading *Christ Is the Only Answer You Need;* forty-two copies of a book called *Help, Lord! The Devil Wants Me Fat!* Rose shook her head, hoping to clear her eyes. She didn't want to rub them, because she had makeup on them and she didn't want to smear it.

"I'm here," she called out to Kathi. "I'll be right out."

"Are you feeling okay, Miss MacNeill? Is there anything I can get for you?"

"I'm fine."

"Lisa Cameron came in here just a little while ago and bought that great big angel statue to take to her niece's christening—can you imagine? In this weather. In my church, we don't believe in people getting baptized until they're all grown up and know what they're doing. I mean, what does a little baby know about resisting the snares of the Devil?"

Rose's eyes went to the Methodist Church on the other end of Main Street. They baptized little babies there, and teddy bears, too, if someone wanted them to. Women wore good dresses and little hats. The organist knew how to play

Bach. It was the most liberal church in town, and Stephen Harrow was the most liberal minister.

Rose smoothed her hair again, opened the pantry door, and went out into the hall. Kathi was standing in the dim light, wearing a denim overall jumper and a T-shirt. She was plump and overeager, like a badly trained dog. Rose could hear the roof creaking above her head and the whistle of the wind. If it was like this now, before the storm had really started, it was going to be a very bad day.

"We should lock up and head over to the high school," Rose told her. "This is going to be awful."

"Oh, I know," Kathi said breathlessly. "I know. I've been packing things away in cupboards all morning."

"Good."

"It seems like everybody in town has been working and working," Kathi said. "Boarding up windows. Do you think we ought to board up some windows?"

"I wouldn't know how to start."

"These windows are small compared to the ones at the bookstore. And the feed store, too. That has—what do you call it—plate glass."

"That's what you call it."

"I wish we could board up the stained glass windows, though. It would be a shame to lose those. They're so pretty."

There was the sound of bells in the air—inside bells, tinkling like fairy queens, the bells that rang every time anybody opened the shop's front door. Rose and Kathi looked up at once.

"I wonder who that could be at a time like this," Kathi said. "It couldn't be anybody wanting to buy something."

"Put the books in there up on higher shelves," Rose said. "I'll go see who it is myself."

"Oh, you don't have to do that, Miss MacNeill. I'll just run on out—"

"I'll go see for myself," Rose repeated. Then she turned her back on Kathi and walked swiftly away, down the hall, toward the sound of someone walking around the front rooms, picking things up and putting them down again. The walking made her feel a little better—a little lighter, a little less old. The movement of air across her face made her feel dizzy.

When she got to the door to the front rooms, Rose stopped and looked through the spy hole. Then she closed her eyes and counted to ten. The woman wandering around the framed pictures of Christ on the cross and guardian angels standing watch over the beds of children was no one Rose knew, but she was certainly someone Rose recognized. She was one of those women from up at the camp. Unless they'd just arrived that morning, Rose knew every one of the camp's residents by sight.

A heavyset woman with hair cropped short and freckles on her nose. A sloppy woman dressed in a frayed blue cotton shirt and tight synthetic-fabric shorts in very bright red. Rose wrinkled her nose in distaste. It only went to show you. Men were necessary for women. Without men around, women let themselves go all to hell. You could see it in those women from the camp. You could see it in those *lesbians.*

A sudden vision of Zhondra Meyer came into Rose's mind: the tall thinness, the high cheekbones, the big dark eyes. Rose pushed the vision away and opened the door to the front rooms. The woman in there was wandering around among the displays, looking dazed. She stopped in front of a pile of pastel kitchen tiles with the Mother's Prayer printed on them and blinked.

"Excuse me," Rose said. The woman jumped. "Is there anything I can do for you?"

The woman looked down at the Mother's Prayer again. Then she turned away. She really was a homely woman, Rose thought. Her skin was terrible. Her hair was like straw. Now she was blushing, sort of, mottling up and looking strained. Rose had a sudden urge to shake her by the shoulders and put her on a diet.

"Oh," the woman said. "Yes. I was looking—for a baptism, you know—for a—"

Most of the women who came into Rose's shop were looking for something to buy for a baptism. Either that or they wanted Christian books and didn't think they were going to get to Raleigh-Durham anytime soon to shop in a real Christian bookstore. There were stories all over town about the kind of baptisms that went on up at the camp, though. Rose didn't know whether to believe the stories or not. She went behind the checkout counter and picked up a little stack of bookmarks with the face of Jesus printed on them, preserved under laminate that could be cleaned with a wet sponge.

"You can't want to buy something for a christening now," Rose said. "Don't you realize there's a storm coming?"

"Storm," the woman said stupidly. "Oh, yes. Yes. I was in the library, you see—"

"The library is open today?"

"It was. For a little while this morning. And I'd heard about the storm, of course, but I didn't think, you know—"

"Hurricane Hugo knocked out a third of the South Carolina coast," Rose said. "We had a storm down here a couple of years ago that took down half the houses on the beach."

The woman's skin mottled again. "That was the kind of thing they were saying at the library. The woman there, the one with the lace collars and the green glasses, she told me—"

"Naomi Brent."

"Excuse me?"

"Naomi Brent," Rose repeated. "That's the name of the woman at the library who wears the lace collars and the green glasses. Naomi Brent. She tried out for Miss North Carolina the year she was eighteen, but she didn't make it."

"I wanted to buy a gift," the woman said. "For a

baptism. I wanted to buy one of those pictures, you know, with the mother and child—"

"A Madonna."

"—and I thought you'd have one. A big picture in a frame. That you can hang on a wall."

"Are you a Catholic?" Rose asked.

The woman looked startled. "Catholic? No. No, of course not. Why would you think that?"

"That's who mostly wants Madonnas," Rose said. "Catholics. It's a kind of Catholic specialty."

"Oh."

"Regular Christians want pictures of Jesus. Either that or they're grandmothers, and then they like angels, especially for granddaughters. You shouldn't buy a Madonna for a regular Christian."

The woman's face seemed to close off. "I want one of those pictures of a mother and child," she said. "One that can hang on a wall. With a frame."

Rose moved around from behind the counter. She didn't have many Madonnas. There were more Catholics in North Carolina now than there had been when she was growing up, but there still weren't a lot. She went over to a shelf along the west wall and took down what she had: four different pictures in four different frames, ranging in size from a three-by-five card to a cabinet door. The woman reached immediately for the one the size of the cabinet door. It was the most sentimental one Rose had, with a baby Jesus that looked like he had just eaten all the icing off a cake.

"How much is this one?" the woman asked.

"Fifty-four fifty."

"Oh." The woman stepped back. "Well."

Rose put her hand on the next size down. "This one is thirty-four fifty," she said. "The next smallest is twenty-nine ninety-five. The little one is fifteen dollars."

The woman looked at the little one. It was a murky picture, hard to see anything in. She picked up the next size larger, the one that would cost twenty-nine ninety-five, and turned it over in her hands.

"I'll take this one," she said.

"There'll be sales tax on it," Rose said. "It'll come to—"

"I know." The woman was turning out the pockets of her shorts. The shorts seemed to be full of money, dollar bills, loose change. The woman went to the counter next to the cash register and laid the money out next to the bookmarks and enameled pins. Rose went to the counter, too.

"Thirty sixty-eight," she said.

The woman counted her money out again, and pushed it across the counter with the flat of her hand.

Five minutes later, Rose was standing at the shop's front window, watching the heavyset woman walk back up Main Street. Kathi had come out from the back and was watching, too, her hands full of prayer books with thick gold crosses etched into their fake white leather covers.

"What do you think she really wants it for?" Kathi asked. "Those people don't get their children baptized, do they?"

"I don't think she has any children," Rose said. "I don't think any of them do, up at the camp."

"Ginny Marsh says they worship a goddess up there. They sit around naked in a circle and call out to spirits. Ginny saw them."

"Ginny is a stupid little fool and so are you if you believe them. Let's get moving here. Can't you hear the wind?"

Kathi pressed her face against the small pane of glass. "I wonder what she really wants with that picture, Rose. I wonder what she's going to do with it. Doesn't it make you feel creepy, just thinking of what she might have had to get it for?"

Rose pushed Kathi away from the window and started to close the interior shutters. There were exterior shutters, too. She would have to go around front and get those when she was done inside. She tried to think of the plain, heavy woman doing something evil with a picture of the baby Jesus. Instead she got a picture of Zhondra Meyer again, a picture so clear she could almost touch the curling tendrils of that thick dark hair.

There's a storm coming, Rose told herself sternly. Then she started to hurry, to hurry and hurry, because if she didn't hurry she would think, and if she thought she would go crazy.

She was already going crazy, and she thought it might be killing her.

3

Stephen Harrow saw Carol Littleton come out of Rose MacNeill's big Victorian house, carrying a flat brown paper bag, but the vision didn't register. Stephen was standing on the sidewalk in front of the Methodist Church, looking up at the bell tower and worrying. The wind was whistling and rattling in the trees. The few thin strands of sandy hair that were still left on his head were jerking violently across his scalp. In spite of the fact that he was only thirty-two, Stephen felt very old and very stupid. This wasn't the first time he had wished that he belonged to a denomination whose ministers wore backwards collars. Sometimes it didn't make any sense to him, being any kind of minister at all. When it got very dark at night, he would try to remember how he had made his decision. He would see himself, all alone in the attic bedroom of his parents' house in Greenville, Massachusetts. If there was a God, Stephen Harrow had never met Him. If Christ had really risen from the dead, Stephen didn't think there would be so many different Christian denominations now or so many people who didn't believe in Him. This was the kind of thing that was understood implicitly in Massachusetts. At the seminary where Stephen had trained, there wasn't a single professor who would have argued for the literal divinity of Jesus. It was different down here. All of his parishioners in Bellerton believed that Jesus Christ was really and truly God incarnate. All of them believed that there would be a last day of judgment with the righteous taken bodily into Heaven along with their immortal souls. Half of them believed in a literal interpretation of Genesis. When Stephen preached a sermon that mentioned evolution, or used it as a metaphor for the spiritual life, he always got a dozen phone calls, complaining about his lack of commitment to the inerrant Word of God. God, these people seemed to think, was a ghostly CEO, dictating letters to His tireless secretaries, wearing out the girls in the typing pool, insisting on His words being accepted without correction. Stephen couldn't remember when he had started to hate it here, but it was soon after he came. If it hadn't been for his wife, he would have left months ago. By now he even hated the accents these people had, and the way they walked down the street. He wanted to go home.

The parsonage was a big white farmhouse-style house right next to the church itself. As Stephen stepped back to the curb to look at the bell tower's roof, the parsonage's front door opened and his wife walked out onto the porch. She was wearing one of those thin flowered dresses she had taken to as soon as they moved down here. If she had had a hat with flowers on it, she would have looked like one of the garden party ladies in *The Manchurian Candidate*. Her name was Lisa, and back when Stephen was in the seminary she used to wear short skirts with lace panels on the sides of them and thick black tights. She would come to the room he had rented and spend the weekend. She would drink Tequila Sunrises until her lips were red with cold. Stephen had had no way of knowing that this was not the person she really was.

Lisa turned to look up Main Street and then came across the porch and down the steps to the sidewalk. She came close enough to him to be heard but not close enough for him to reach out and touch her.

"Is that Carol Littleton I see with the brown paper bag?" she asked. "What did she want in this weather?"

"She wasn't here." Stephen went back to looking at the bell tower. "She was at Rose's. I think she bought something."

"Now?"

"Rose seems to be open, Lisa. If Rose is open, Carol Littleton can buy something."

"You'd think they would all have left town by now, for God's sake. Why do you think they stay? It can't be comfortable for them here."

"Maybe they have nowhere else to go."

"Carol Littleton might not have anyplace to go to, but Zhondra Meyer does. She's rich as Croesus. She's only here to bother us. She wants to enlighten the poor benighted yokels."

"Enlighten us about what?"

"Gay rights. Tolerance and diversity. All that kind of thing. You know: We've all been colonized by a white male culture. We have to throw off the chains that bind our imaginations and remythologize our lives into paradigms of true equality. That kind of thing."

"Really."

Lisa made a face. "She talked to the library reading group last week. That was Maggie Kelleher's idea, of course. God, but she's been a strange woman since she came back from New York. I wonder what happened to her there."

"Probably the same things that happened to you in New York," Stephen said. "I met you in New York."

Lisa gave him a sideways look. "You may have met me in New York, but I didn't change in New York. Maggie *changed* in New York. She changed a lot. I remember her from when she got accepted at that silly college of hers. She was all ruffles and charm bracelets. She was the kind of girl people's mothers always called 'sweet.' "

"You must have been in the cradle."

"I was eight."

Eight, Stephen thought. That must make Maggie— what? Forty? He squinted in the direction of the bell tower roof. This was the kind of thing he ought to talk to Lisa about. She was the one who was born here. She was the one who ought to care. The Methodist Church was the oldest building in Bellerton. It was the only one still standing that had existed at the time of the American Revolution. Everything else had been destroyed one way or another: burned down in skirmishes during the Civil War; gone to rot; bulldozed for the newer and shinier and brighter and smaller mock–Greek revival places everybody here preferred to live in. The truth about Lisa was that she would bulldoze it all and put up split-levels if anybody ever gave her a chance. Lisa had no sentimentality at all and no feeling for history.

"You ought to come inside," she said now. "We've got to pack a few things up and go to the high school. They say that storm is going to come right through the middle of town."

"I'm worried about the church," Stephen said. "About the tower. It's such an old building."

"You can't take the church to the high school, Stephen. It won't fit into the car."

"That isn't what I'm trying to say."

"You can't stay here, either." Lisa tapped her foot against the pavement, impatient. "This is a major hurricane we're talking about. It's already done I don't know how much damage. If you get in the way of it, it will blow you right to China."

"I was thinking that maybe we could put something on the bell tower roof. Plywood boards. Something to protect it."

"If you were going to do something like that, you would have had to start days ago. It's too late now, Stephen. Let's get our things and go."

"I will go. In a minute. I just want to stay here and—think for a while."

"Think," Lisa repeated. She turned on her heel and started to walk away from him, back across the front lawn, back to the porch. She didn't turn around and tell him to be careful. She didn't even tell him to hurry up again. She just went.

Once, Stephen thought, he spent all his time imagining what Lisa was like without her clothes on. He sat across from her in restaurants and thought of the way her small breasts swelled as they hung, light and active, under the curve of her shoulders. He sat next to her on buses and thought of the way her thighs flowed into her hips, smooth and restless and very clean. Now he imagined her locked in closets and shut away in cardboard boxes, tied up and gagged, silent, sexless, free of him.

Stephen turned to go back into the house himself, but as he did he saw Ginny Marsh coming down the sidewalk at him, bouncing along with Tiffany in her Snugli sling. Ginny was not one of Stephen's parishioners—like half of everybody else, she went to one of those big fundamentalist churches on the outskirts of town—but he knew her to talk to from seeing her around town. He knew the baby, too, because she was a good baby to play with for a man who felt uncomfortable around infants. He was worried that they were both going to be as blown away as Lisa said everybody would be. He had never been in a hurricane before, but he could feel the badness of it in the wind. The air around him was so full of water, he found it hard to breathe.

"You should be home," he said, flagging Ginny down. "Or at the high school. There's going to be a storm."

Ginny stopped and adjusted Tiffany on her front. "Hello, Mr. Harrow. We'll be all right. We're headed up to the camp."

"The camp?"

"That's got to be the highest place in Bellerton," Ginny said. "I don't think they're going to get any water at all up there. Unless the Lord is sending a flood."

"I think the Lord promised Noah not to do that again. I think it's supposed to be the fire next time."

The quote meant nothing to Ginny. "Our pastor says

God can do anything He wants to do, and that makes sense to me. Doesn't it make sense to you?"

"Of course."

"I'm not worried about drowning up there, Mr. Harrow. I'm worried about those women. And you would be, too, if you realized."

"Maybe they don't seem so strange to me, Ginny. Since I'm from the north myself."

Tiffany was fussing. Ginny adjusted her again, not really paying attention. "Sometimes what I really worry about is bringing Tiffany up there. You know. Because lesbians are homosexuals, aren't they? And you never know what homosexuals will do."

Right, Stephen thought. This was not a conversation he wanted to get into. His roommate his first year in the seminary had been gay, although in those days nobody got up and shouted about it. Stephen had never understood why so many people made such a noise about homosexuality.

"I just saw Carol Littleton headed up that way," he told Ginny. "If you hurry, you might be able to catch up to her. Carol doesn't move very fast even when the weather's good."

"My pastor says the Lord wants us all to accept Christ as our personal savior. That's the important thing. But the Devil gets to some people and he just won't let go."

"Is that what it is?"

"Like those people who bombed that building in Oklahoma City," Ginny went on, talking automatically now. This was like a tape she'd heard so many times, she had it memorized. Stephen couldn't tell if she actually understood what she was saying. "It's all of a piece, that's what my pastor says. Sin is all of a piece. It's not like there are big sins and little sins. There's just one sin. Disobedience to the will of God."

"I guess that would cover it," Stephen said.

"I'm going to try to bring Tiffany up so that she never has to worry about any of that, Mr. Harrow. I'm going to try to bring her up right in the heart of the Lord."

"I guess that's a good idea, Ginny."

Ginny backed away. "I've got to go now," she said. "I've got to get up to the camp. I've got some typing to do and we need the money. And she wants me to come."

"Zhondra Meyer does?"

"That's right. I called her from Dr. Sandler's house and said maybe I ought to forget about it today, with the weather, but she wouldn't hear of it. She's a very driven woman, Ms. Meyer. It's like work has hold of her and just won't let her go."

"Well, maybe it's something important she's got for you to do. Maybe it's something that just won't wait."

"When the Lord breathes upon the face of the earth, everything can wait, Mr. Harrow. It has to."

Tiffany had closed her eyes and laid her head down on Ginny's breast. She looked achingly sweet there, soft and round and warm, the perfection of innocence.

"Hurry on up to the camp, then, if that's where you're going," Stephen said. "You don't want to keep that baby out in the rain."

"Oh," Ginny said. "Oh, no. I don't. She'd catch a cold."

"That's right."

"It's a terrible thing, when babies have colds. They hate it."

"Say hello to Ms. Meyer for me. Say hello to Carol Littleton, too. Carol should have stopped."

Ginny started to back away up Main Street. "See you later," she said. "You get yourself to someplace safe, too."

Someplace safe, Stephen thought. He watched Ginny make her way in the wind, past the storefronts, past the Greek revival houses, past the churches. Tiffany seemed to have woken up again and started looking around. Stephen went up his walk and up the steps to his porch, listening for the sounds Lisa made when she was packing, the humming, the cursing, the slamming of doors.

Lisa didn't want children. She didn't want sex any-more, either. Lisa wanted to live here, in Bellerton, where she had grown up. There was a church coming open in Minneapolis next summer. He'd seen the notice about it in the newsletter the national organization sent out. He had even sent a letter and a vita. He didn't think Lisa would stand for it. He saw himself at the head of a congregation full of people who believed the way he did, who loved science and art and music, who read something besides Scripture when they wanted to know how the world worked. Lisa saw herself in the cold among a lot of people she didn't know and probably wouldn't like. Feminists. Goddess worshippers. Liberals. Gays.

Lisa came to the front door just as Stephen reached the top of the porch steps.

"What were you doing out there all this time?" she demanded. "What could you possibly have been thinking of?"

Stephen had half a mind to tell her what he'd been thinking of.

Divorce.

4

Maggie Kelleher knew that she shouldn't allow herself to be impatient with people like Carol Littleton. Carol couldn't help it if she was such a square, stolid, graceless sort of woman—or if she was so timid, either. As far as Maggie could tell, none of the women up at the camp could help anything about themselves. They had all led really terrible lives, full of abuse and betrayal. They had been beaten and raped, imprisoned and deserted, left on their own in honky-tonk bars, and dumped out of slowly moving vehicles. Zhondra Meyer could go on and on about what had happened to the women who stayed with her, and Maggie could listen—but that was different from actually having to listen to Carol Littleton, who was here in the store with her eyes full of tears and her hands full of a picture of the Madonna and child. Maggie wanted to shake her, or at

least push her out of the way. The store was in an uproar.
The storm was coming and they had barely gotten the ply-
wood nailed over the big plate glass window. Now Joshua
Lake, Maggie's assistant, was throwing books into boxes
and throwing the boxes on top of the highest bookshelves.
Serious water damage could wipe them out, and there was
likely to be at least serious water over the next few hours.
This was simply not the time.

"There was a story about it in the paper," Carol Littleton was saying. She had a hitch in her voice and a wet
smear of tears running down the right side of her face.
Maggie found herself wondering, absurdly, why the smear
was only on the *right* side.

"I got the library to subscribe to the papers," Carol
was going on. "My newspaper from home, you know.
They'll do that if you ask them."

Maggie knew that the library would do this if someone asked. She was the one who had talked Naomi Brent
into instituting the policy. It was a small part of the project
Maggie had set for herself since coming back to Bellerton
from New York. It was time to modernize this place a little.
It was time to drag Bellerton into the new multicultural
universe. It was at least time for the people of this town to
accept the fact that half of them were now transplants from
somewhere else, settling in a town that was both small
and within reasonably commuting distance to Raleigh–
Durham–Chapel Hill.

Maggie brushed wiry black hair off her forehead and
felt the line of sweat there. The motion made her oddly
aware of the thinness of her arm and the fluid way it arched
in the air: dancer's movements, because Maggie had been a
dancer once, good enough to get work but not quite good
enough to get any more than that. Maggie had been part of
Martha Graham's dance company in New York, a very
small part, not a featured principal. She had been on half a
dozen television commercials, including one that was still
running five years after it had been made, sending her nice
but not spectacular residuals. She had even had a small part

on *General Hospital* for a while. Always almost but not quite, Maggie decided, whenever she thought about it. She had come home exactly three hundred sixty-three days before her fortieth birthday. She could read the writing on the wall, so to speak. There were dozens of women like her, almost but not quite, good but not good enough, singing in second-rate lounges and doing off-off-Broadway plays, staying in the city, staying active, going down for the count. Maggie had decided that she didn't want to be one of them.

Joshua Lake was trying to get all the volumes of the Ignatius Press edition of the works of G. K. Chesterton into a single box. It wasn't working. Carol Littleton was turning the picture of the Madonna over and over in her hands, and staring at it, as if it were the picture of someone she knew. Maggie went to help Joshua.

"I don't mean to be rude," Maggie said over her shoulder, "but there's a storm coming. We've got work to do."

"I don't think you're being rude," Carol said.

Maggie got a flattened packing box from the pile next to the front desk and popped it into shape.

"The thing is," Carol said, "it was in the paper. You know. The announcement about the christening. And it made me feel so awful, because I never saw anything about the birth."

"This is your daughter Shelley you're talking about," Maggie said.

"Shelley Littleton Wade." Carol made it sound like a title. President of the United States. Supreme Pontiff. Boss of all Bosses. "She was pregnant the last time I saw her, but not very pregnant. Four months along. I remember thinking, in the middle of that awful fight, I remember worrying that she'd give herself a miscarriage, and then that would be my fault, too. But she didn't."

"She must not have," Maggie agreed.

"But I didn't see the birth announcement," Carol continued. "I read every word of that paper every day, and I didn't see it."

"Maybe there wasn't a birth announcement," Maggie said. "Not everybody sends one to the paper."

"Maybe she didn't send one because of me. Maybe she was afraid I'd try to send something to the baby. Or even come to see her. It's a girl she's had, did I tell you that?"

"I think you did."

"Melissa Jeanne. She didn't name her after me. Not that I would have wanted that. Carol is such an—an ordinary kind of name."

"We should have talked to old man Martin upstairs," Joshua Lake said. "That would be the best way to do this. Move all the stock up to the second floor."

"Martin would go through all the titles and reject the ones he thought were full of atheistic humanism," Maggie said. "He thinks Charles Dickens is full of atheistic humanism. Just pack, Joshua."

Carol sat down in one of the beige metal folding chairs that were scattered around the center of the store. She still had the Madonna in her hands, and her shoulders hunched.

"I wouldn't try to see the baby when she didn't want me to," she said. "I wouldn't just go to the hospital and visit when I knew Shelley didn't want me to see her. I'm really not a person like that."

"I'm sure you're not," Maggie said.

"It's what I have such a hard time explaining to Shelley about all of this," Carol said. "That I'm not different than I ever was. That I haven't changed. Because I haven't changed. I just understand some things about myself now that I didn't understand before."

"I'm sure it will work out, Carol. You have to give it time."

"I could understand her reaction if she was religious or something. If she went to church and believed in God. I remember from Catholic school that God wasn't supposed to like lesbians."

"I think he's supposed to like them well enough,

Carol. I think he's just not supposed to like what they do in bed with each other.''

"Whatever. The thing is though, she's not religious at all. I mean, she's having this christening, but it's at some church I've never heard of. Congregationalist. We were never Congregationalists.''

"Lots of people have their children christened who don't even believe in God, Carol. It's a ritual. A rite of passage.''

"I know,'' Carol said eagerly. "That's the point. She's having this christening, but she really isn't religious, and so I don't understand. Why she's so upset about all this. About me. Why she hates me for it.''

"Are you sure she hates you for it?''

"She won't talk to me, Maggie. She won't answer my letters. She won't even open my letters. The last one I sent to her came back stamped 'addressee unknown.' But I know that isn't true. I know she hasn't moved. Her address was in the christening announcement. It's the same as it always was.''

Maggie got a box filled with paperback copies of Agatha Christie mysteries and started to tape it shut. "Maybe you ought to just let it go for a while, Carol. Maybe you ought to give Shelley a little time to get used to the idea. To get used to you.''

"It's been months, Maggie. Months.''

"I know.''

Carol looked down at her hands. Like everything else about her, they were heavy and graceless and shapeless and dull. Maggie turned her attention to her books, forcing herself not to notice.

"Anyway,'' Carol said. "I bought this picture. For my granddaughter. For Melissa.

"But I was thinking,'' she went on, "that if Shelley knows it's from me, she'll just send it back, and that won't be any good at all. So I thought there might be a way to send it without anyone knowing it came from me. If you see what I mean.''

"Not really."

"Well," Carol said. "I thought you—you know. You go up to New York every month practically. You could maybe take it up, all wrapped and everything, and mail it from there."

"Does Shelley know anybody in New York?"

"No. No, I don't think so. But she knows I'm not in New York. She knows I'm here. I'm in touch with—with her father."

"Are you really? That must be interesting."

"We have to stay in touch. It's very complicated when you've been married for twenty-five years. There are considerations."

"Move out of the way a little, Carol. I've got to get at the Linda Lael Millers."

Carol got up and pushed the folding chair along the carpet. Then she sat down in it again. She put the Madonna back in its brown paper bag and put the brown paper bag across her lap.

"You wouldn't have to do anything about it," she said. "I would wrap it up and address it and all that. On a typewriter, so that Shelley can't recognize my handwriting. I'll be very careful. It's just—you know. She's my granddaughter. I want to do something for her. I want to give her something just from me. I wish they'd had a picture of her in the paper."

"Can't you get your ex-husband to send you one? Or are you worried that Shelley wouldn't like that, either?"

Carol blushed. "My husband wouldn't help me. My husband is with Shelley on all of this. He goes around and tells people I left him for another woman."

"And did you?"

"Of course I didn't. I didn't even meet Zhondra until after the divorce. He's the one who left me."

The Linda Lael Millers were all packed away. Now she had to put the historical romances into something. Maggie brushed the palms of her hands against the front of her apron.

"All right," she said. "I'll do it."

Carol brightened up. "You will? But that's wonderful. Thank you."

"But I won't do it today," Maggie said. "I don't have time. And I can't take the picture today, either. Not with all the things I have to do. You've got to take it back up to the camp until the storm is over with."

"Of course I'll take it back up to the camp. I have to package it. I told you."

"Yes. Well. Whatever. Take it back up to the camp. Then bring it down to me tomorrow or the day after that and I'll put it in my suitcase for New York so I won't forget it when I go. I'll drop it in the mail at Grand Central Station."

"That would be wonderful."

"Go back up to the camp, Carol."

Carol stood up. She held the bag as if what was in it was easily breakable. She held her body as if it were already broken.

"Well," she said. "Thank you. Again. You don't know how much I thank you."

Maggie could imagine having a daughter like Shelley, and what she would do about it. Carol was folding up her metal chair and putting it neatly against a wall of now-empty bookshelves. Outside, the wind was the strongest it had been all morning. The trees were beginning to look as if they were under siege.

Carol went to the door of the shop, opened it, and looked out onto the sidewalk. Maggie couldn't tell what was out there, because the window was boarded up and the door was a plain wooden one.

"Well," Carol said. "I suppose I'd better go."

"I'll see you tomorrow, Carol. Or the day after. Depending on the damage."

"I hope there isn't any damage. I hope it all just goes away. I hate the idea of a hurricane."

"I'll see you tomorrow, Carol."

Carol nodded quickly and scurried out into the street, letting the door swing closed behind her.

Maggie popped another packing box into shape and brushed hair out of her face. Joshua Lake, up on a ladder and too close to the ceiling for comfort, looked down.

"Strange lady," he said. "They all that strange up at the camp?"

"I don't know," Maggie told him. "I only know about three people from up at the camp. How are you doing up there?"

"Getting along."

"We better start taking some of these boxes into the back room. There isn't going to be space enough for all of them up there."

"Anything you say."

Anything I say, Maggie thought.

Then she started to throw American Indian romances into the empty box, one after the other, without bothering to look at the titles. She had nothing to say these days. That was the problem. She had nothing to say to people like Carol and nothing to say to herself. The world seemed full of grief and loss and pettiness and hate, and there wasn't a single damn thing she was able to do about it.

If Maggie Kelleher had believed in God, she might even have welcomed the hurricane, as a kind of cleansing water, a second flood, to wash the sin and sorrow all away.

5

Zhondra Meyer had always been very, very rich, and for a time in her life she had been ashamed of it. She could get a clear picture of herself, even now, at the age of fifteen, walking across the broad green quad at the Emma Willard School in Troy, New York. She was wearing a Villager skirt and sweater set, just like everybody else, and behind her was a plump blond girl from Atlanta named Mimi Dobbs.

"Shhh," Mimi was whispering to her friends, under a waterfall of sharp little giggles. "Shhh. You know what she is? She's a *filthy rich New York Jew*."

Zhondra's mother, who had been an active Zionist, would have worried about the anti-Semitism of it. She had wanted Zhondra to stay in the city and go to Brearley, where there was less of that kind of thing. Zhondra had a hard time (then) thinking of "Jew" as a category she belonged to. It was her history, and her religion, but it was being rich that really seemed to peg her. Up in her dorm room, she had a dozen cashmere sweaters and six pairs of shoes custom-made for her at a specialty shop in London. At the end of the term, instead of going to the train station in a cab like everyone else, she would be retrieved by a uniformed driver in an enormous Rolls-Royce Silver Shadow, and he would tip his hat at her. Girls watched the way she walked and what she wore. Sometimes their resentment was as thick and slick as butter on her skin. She imagined her father losing all his money, and being reduced to selling apples on the street.

Today, with the storm rising outside and the heat acting up in the west wing again, Zhondra was worried less about being rich or being Jewish than she was about what they would do if the utilities went out because of the hurricane. The designation "lesbian" didn't occur to her at all. This house had been built by her great-uncle Samuel back in the 1920s. It had two wings and a thick central core, seventeen thousand square feet in all, with thirty bedrooms and a ballroom big enough to serve as a wedding chamber for the Unification Church. It had been Samuel's "hobby," because he was a younger son without much money, and because he had no ambition to make anything of his life. What he had done with his life was to collect art, almost all of which Zhondra sincerely hated. Tintoretto. Titian. Raphael. The painters were good, and expensive. It was the subjects that drove Zhondra wild. All those fat Madonnas and fatter children. All those round little cherubs and heavenward-gazing saints. The first thing Zhondra had done, after coming down here from New York, was to call Sotheby's and put the whole mess up for auction. Then she'd bought art that suited her.

Now a very modern painting by an artist named Kalla Havila hung in the hall where a Titian Madonna once had, and right inside the front door there was a sign on a tripod that read: *Bonaventura Camp. A Retreat for Gay Women*. There was a sign like that down by the gate, too, in full sight of the road. Zhondra was convinced that you had to approach all this very directly. She had to be on the offensive. You couldn't let your guard down no matter what. This was the Bible Belt, after all. It might be a little better than Alabama or Mississippi, but Zhondra didn't think it was better by much. Every time she turned on her radio, the air was full of preachers. Every time she went to town, she had to pass a dozen of those big new concrete Evangelical churches. Town had the Episcopalians and the Baptists and the Methodists and the United Church of Christ. If there had ever been a synagogue in Bellerton, North Carolina, it must have been burned to the ground in a pogrom.

Zhondra opened one of the big metal front doors. Uncle Samuel liked to do everything he could in etched and molded brass. She stepped onto the broad platform at the top of the steep rose-marble front steps and looked around. Alice was coming out of the trees on the left, her short-cropped bright orange hair looking painted onto her skull. Ginny Marsh was trudging onto the drive through the front gate, baby Tiffany strapped to her like a cartoon papoose. Bobby Marsh really ought to get his act together and let that woman have a car, Zhondra thought. The thought left her immediately, because Bobby Marsh would never get his act together. Bobby Marsh was the walking definition of someone whose act was not together.

Alice reached the front steps and shook her head a little, to get some of the water out of it. It wasn't raining yet, but the air was wet. Zhondra felt it against her skin like a soaked washcloth.

"I've tried and I've tried," Alice said, sitting down on

a step as close to Zhondra as she could get, "but they won't listen to me. Maybe you ought to go out there and talk to them."

"Maybe they'll hurry it up a little," Zhondra told her. "We've probably got half an hour to forty-five minutes before the storm hits."

Alice shook her head again. "I don't think so. They're just setting up out there. They haven't even started yet. They're waiting for Carol to get back."

"Where's Carol?"

"In town."

"What for?"

Alice shrugged. "You know Carol. Walking around. Feeling sorry for herself. Sitting on park benches and bursting into tears."

"When is she expected to get back?"

"She's expected to get back when she *gets* back." Alice sounded near explosion. "Listen, Zhondra, you've got to do something. I can't talk any sense into them. They're out there with all these trees that are thin as toothpicks and they're stark naked, too—"

"—Oh, Lord—"

"—although, really, why you have to be naked to worship the goddess is beyond me. And Dinah's saying that litany about pubic hair or whatever and the rest of them all have their eyes closed and Carol might not get back before the storm at all, and then you know what that would mean, they'd all be rained on and probably killed in the storm."

"I'd hope they had sense enough to come in out of the rain," Zhondra said.

"I wouldn't count on it." Alice was grim. "I told you back in New York. Religion is an evil thing. I don't care if you worship Jehovah or the Goddess Sophia or the elderberry bush in your backyard. It makes people crazy. And I don't like the knives they use."

"I don't think they'd hurt anything with them," Zhondra said. "They're all for being at one with the earth and that kind of thing."

"They're going to hurt themselves, that's what I think," Alice said. "They do everything with their eyes closed. And I refuse here and now to go into the emergency room with them when they do and try to explain it all to the doctors. Especially here."

Ginny Marsh was better than halfway up the drive now. Zhondra ran her hands through her thick hair.

"Look," she said. "Here comes our visiting Holy Roller—"

"Oh, God," Alice moaned.

"—and we don't want her getting wind of this. Remember all the fuss she made last time? Go back out there and tell them I said to cut it out. Tell them I said I'd go make them cut it out if they didn't come back in right away. See if that works."

"What's Ginny doing here today, anyway?" Alice asked. "Shouldn't she be hiding in her basement or whatever you do in a hurricane?"

"Basements are for tornadoes," Zhondra said. "I don't know what she's doing here. She should have called me. I would have told her not to bother."

"Maybe she needs the money. That husband of hers can't make a dime."

"Maybe she just wants to be safely out of the storm," Zhondra replied. "We're the highest ground around here. Go out and talk to them, Alice, will you? I'll come out as soon as I get Ginny settled."

"You mean you're going to give her something to do?"

"Why not? She's here. And I can't send her back into town with the storm this close. I couldn't do that to the baby."

"It's a cute baby. Too bad it doesn't have better parents."

"Go, Alice."

Alice stood up, stretched, and started down the steps. "You be careful," she said. "I don't trust that woman. Baby or no baby."

"She's harmless," Zhondra said automatically. "She's stupid."

"Stupid is never harmless." Alice shoved her hands into the pockets of her jeans. "I'll do what I can, Zhondra, but then it's going to be up to you. They never listen to me, you know. They just tell me I'm blind to the feminine forces of spirituality in the universe. I keep wanting to give them all copies of *The Case Against God*."

Then Alice was gone, and Ginny was there, starting up the steps, smiling that bouncy queen-of-the-cheerleaders smile she had—that all of them seemed to have, all the women in this place. Zhondra came from a place where women were shrill and sarcastic and nasty, but never too eager to please. All this sweetness and light made her distinctly nervous.

"Hello, Ms. Meyer," Ginny sang out. "Here I am now. Ready to get to work."

Right, Zhondra thought. Tiffany gurgled in her carrier. All the molecules in Ginny Marsh's body seemed to be bouncing around at random, like the balls in the demonstration chamber of an old Mr. Wizard show. Zhondra turned around and headed up the steps again, saying nothing at all.

Less than five minutes later, Zhondra and Ginny were standing together in the large west wing study. Ginny was putting Tiffany in a plastic baby seat to one side of the computer on the broad oak desk. Zhondra was thinking that the big chandelier looked dirty and ought to be cleaned. All around them, velvet wall hangings fought with aggressive modern art, and both sides seemed to be losing.

"Well," Ginny said, checking the strap on Tiffany's baby seat one more time. "There we are. Do you have a minute to talk to me now, Ms. Meyer? There's something I have to bring up."

"Is there? Maybe we can talk about it later, Ginny. There's something I have to do."

"Well, I don't want to hold you up any, Ms. Meyer. But this is very important. It's about my going on working here after today."

"Do you mean that you have to be leaving us? I'm sorry about that, Ginny." Zhondra wasn't really. Not exactly. "You've done a very good job."

Ginny fiddled with the computer keys. "It's not that I have to leave no matter what. It's about . . . about our agreements here. My husband is putting his foot down."

"About what?"

"About my not being able to put my picture of the Lord up on my desk when I work," Ginny said. "Bobby doesn't mind it about how you won't let me listen to the radio. He says a lot of bosses don't let their workers listen to the radio at work. Although why not, I'll never know, Ms. Meyer. I mean, I type a lot faster when I'm praising the Lord with all my heart. But Bobby says that's all right."

"Does he." Zhondra's tone was dry.

Ginny wasn't paying attention. She was fooling with the computer keys. She was squinting at the fine print on the bottom of the screen. She was touching Tiffany's bootie-clad foot with her fingertip.

"The thing about the picture, though," she said, "is that it wouldn't bother anybody. It wouldn't make any noise. Nobody would even see it unless they came in here."

"But what if they did come in here?" Zhondra asked.

"Well, it wouldn't be bad for them if they did. It's a picture of the Lord I keep next to me, Ms. Meyer, not some rock star. Maybe someone would come in here and see that picture and feel called, you know, called to Christ."

"Most of the women who are here have been Christians in their time, Ginny. Most of them don't think it was a very pleasant experience."

"That's just the Devil talking," Ginny said. "The Devil does those things to people. He counterfeits. He makes you think he's Christ, and then he ruins your life, and you think Christ has done it."

"Maybe."

"But once you've been really and truly born again,

there's no going back," Ginny said confidently. "Once you've been baptized in the Holy Spirit, you're a child of God forever. God wants us to be His children, Ms. Meyer. He wants us to be saved."

"I don't want that picture up on your desk, Ginny. I don't want the PTL Club on the radio—"

"The PTL Club isn't on the radio. It's on TV."

"Whatever. I don't want that kind of thing, here. Most of these women feel they have been very damaged by patriarchal religion. They didn't come here to be reminded of it."

"I asked Bobby what that meant," Ginny said. "*Patriarchal*. Bobby said it meant 'of the fathers.' There's nothing wrong with fathers, Ms. Meyer. God is our Father."

"I know you think so, Ginny. I think God is a fiction that men made up to keep women down."

Ginny tapped a single finger against a single computer key. "If I can't at least put my picture up, Ms. Meyer, I'm not going to be able to work here anymore. I have a right to freedom of religion. Just like anybody else."

"There's no such thing as having a right to freedom of religion in somebody else's house."

There was the sound of something hitting against the side of the house: a stray branch, a piece of lawn furniture somebody had forgotten to bring inside. Zhondra and Ginny both turned toward the noise at the same moment. Ginny turned away again almost immediately. Zhondra watched her fiddling with the keys again.

"Well," Ginny said. "I'm very sorry about this, Ms. Meyer. But I do have to make a point of it."

"I'm afraid I have to make a point of it, too, Ginny."

"I'll just finish up here today," Ginny said. "And then I won't come back again. I'd appreciate it if you had my check for me when it was time for me to leave."

"I think I could manage that, Ginny, yes."

"I don't mean to be mean," Ginny said, "but it's a

matter of principle. That's what Bobby says. It's a matter of principle and a test of my love of the Lord.''

A test of my love of the Lord, Zhondra thought—and then she got a perfect vision, in Technicolor and three dimensions, of a scene from one of those bondage and discipline magazines, complete with whips and chains and leather straps to hold the woman still. Lord and master. Ball and chain. Zhondra stepped back a little, startled.

''Ms. Meyer?'' Ginny asked.

''Yes,'' Zhondra said. ''Never mind. I just thought of something. I have to go now, Ginny. It's like I said before. I have something I have to do.''

''Oh, yes, Ms. Meyer. That's all right. You'll have my check for me today?''

''I'll have it.''

''That's fine, then.''

Zhondra didn't know if it was fine or not. She just knew she wanted to get out of this room, and away, before her mind came up with any more sexist filth. Sometimes it seemed as if all there ever was in her mind was sexist filth, but that was another story.

One of the good things about being very, very rich was that Zhondra didn't have to deal with anything she didn't want to, and she didn't want to deal with this.

6

Naomi Brent began to have trouble with the computer at fifteen minutes to twelve. By then, the Bellerton library was as secure as it was going to get. The first-floor windows had been boarded over with plywood. The first-floor books had been moved to higher shelves. The first-floor computer equipment had been brought up here, to the tall-ceilinged old rooms where the Linnet family had once slept and made love and worried about sick children. Naomi liked to imagine herself back in 1925, with a picture hat and gloves that matched her shoes. She liked to think of herself romantically, in a sense too old to apply to those nasty books they sold down at the drugstore, books with names like *Passion's Furious Flight*. She was only thirty-five years old, but she was already a cliché, and she knew it. Old-maid librarian. Repressed southern spinster. Gothic horror story waiting to happen. Every morning Naomi Brent got up and looked at herself in the mirror. She counted the lines on her face and the dark circles under her eyes. She told herself that hope was useless and there was no point in going on. Then she took a shower and made herself up and forgot entirely about the fact that she had been married three times.

Of course, she had also been divorced three times. When Naomi got to thinking about her marriages, she got to thinking about her divorces, and that made her feel worse than thinking of herself as a dried-up old virgin who had never been touched. Actually, virginity was not Naomi's strong suit. She had slept with her first boyfriend when she was fifteen years old and had just made the Bellerton High School junior varsity cheerleading squad. She had slept with her latest boyfriend just ten days before this storm. In between there was a blur of faces and bodies, hands and lips and rough-skinned backs, all rimmed round with a glow of frustration. Naomi Brent had no idea what people were supposed to feel when they had sex. She only knew she couldn't be feeling it, because by and large she felt nothing. She got into bed with some man and let him pump and pump away at her. She closed her eyes and counted the number of stockings she remembered hanging on her line at home, or tried to pin down a piece of dialogue she'd heard at the movies and hadn't quite understood. Her last husband had been emphatic: Naomi was a cock tease, or something worse. Naomi remembered thinking at the time that he had hair growing out of his nostrils, and how was she supposed to be attracted to that? Men always seemed to shrivel into moldy old prunes as soon as you married them. Men always seemed to end up being men. Naomi thought of her mother, married thirty years without a break. She couldn't understand it. She especially couldn't understand it with her father, who smelled of beer and bellowed, who was cruel in a heavy-handed, relentless way that was really a desire to kill.

On the screen of the computer, Naomi had this:

> *Hello! to everyone in the BHS class of '79. This is your class correspondent, Naomi Brent, and boy, do I have a lot to report!*

Thunder and lightning rolled across the sky outside. The screen flickered. Naomi gnawed her lip. She did have a lot to report, but for the moment it all seemed silly. Cheryl Donners Cray was having another baby. Delia Caberdon was finally getting married. Mostly, Naomi reported on the girls who had been in her high school sorority, Gamma Alpha Mu, or in one of the two other high school sororities that counted. Births. Deaths. Marriages. Graduations. The only really exciting thing that had happened to anyone in the Class of '79 had happened to a girl named Julia Morrissey, who hadn't counted at all. Julia Morrissey was now a United States Congresswoman from the state of Virginia.

Naomi swiveled her chair toward the window. They hadn't boarded anything up up here, although they probably should have. Naomi could see right down Main Street, past Maggie Kelleher's bookstore, past Rose MacNeill's Victorian-housed shop. Everything was boarded and dead-looking. The sky was absolutely black. Only the rain hadn't started yet. Naomi didn't think it would take long.

There was a sound of footsteps on the stairs. Naomi turned her chair to look at the open door to the room. She heard Beatrix Dean say, "Oh, hell," and relaxed a little. A moment later, Beatrix was there, all five feet eleven inches of her, looking faintly ridiculous. Beatrix always looked faintly ridiculous. She had never really accepted the fact that she was tall. She had never really stopped trying to hide it.

Thunder rolled again and Naomi's computer screen went blank. She cursed at it, then sighed.

"I know I shouldn't be trying to do this," she said. "I know we're going to lose the power."

"I can't believe you're still here," Beatrix told her. "Don't you want to go home? Don't you have cats to worry about?"

"I used to have cats," Naomi said, "but they all ran away on me. Like men. Maybe they were tomcats."

"Oh," Beatrix said.

"I think I'm going to ride out the storm right here," Naomi said. "My house isn't on any higher ground. And what would happen to me if I left now? I'd probably get caught in the rain. I'd probably get electrocuted by a downed power line. With my luck, I'd probably get hit by lightning."

"You could come with me to my church," Beatrix suggested. "I'm meeting a van out on Main Street in fifteen minutes. We're driving all the way out on the Hartford Road. We won't get any seawater out there."

"I'm sure you won't."

"Besides, Naomi. I think it would do you good. To see the inside of a church for once."

"I've seen the insides of churches, Beatrix. I got married in three of them."

"Reverend Holborn says this hurricane is a judgment. Like that bombing out in Oklahoma City. Like that thing with the World Trade Center. Reverend Holborn says America has sold its soul to the Devil and now the Devil is having his way with us."

"Reverend Holborn," Naomi said carefully, "thinks hangnails are a judgment from God."

"Well, Naomi, maybe they are. I know you don't take religion seriously, but maybe you should. I mean, look at what's happened to this place. To Bellerton, for goodness sake. Lesbians. And atheists. It's like we're turning into a spiritual sewer."

Naomi had her pocketbook sitting next to her swivel

chair on the floor. She picked it up, put it in her lap, and riffled through it for her cigarettes and slim gold lighter. Most of the time, Naomi didn't smoke in the library building. She had gotten used to the new rules that said even a whiff of secondhand smoke could instantaneously give old ladies terminal lung cancer. Still, she needed a cigarette now, and she thought she deserved one.

The gold lighter was from Dunhill. One of her husbands had given it to her on their first anniversary. If Naomi remembered right, that marriage hadn't lasted another six months. She put a Virginia Slims menthol into her mouth and lit up.

"Spiritual sewer," she said through a haze of smoke, "I presume, is a direct quote from the saintly Reverend Holborn."

Beatrix frowned. Naomi was suddenly struck by how aggressively ugly the woman was—not just unattractive, like most of those women up at the camp, but *ugly*. It was something that went beyond Beatrix's weight, which was monumental. It was something that had settled into her features, like indelible grime.

"I think you should think about things more carefully," Beatrix said. "I think you should think about the complications. Like with the school."

"Which school?"

"All the schools. The high school. Even the elementary school. They're moving in on them, you know."

"The *they* in question being the women up at the camp?"

"That's right. You wouldn't believe how many of them have children. Though I don't understand how a lesbian gets children, do you?"

"Maybe they aren't all lesbians all of the time."

Beatrix blushed. "But it isn't only them," she went on. "It's him, too. That man with the house out on the beach."

"Dr. David Sandler."

"He's not a real doctor. Not the kind that does operations. He's just a college doctor. And he has that thing on the back of his car that, you know, says he worships Darwin.''

Naomi sighed. Her cigarette had grown a long column of ash. She tapped it carefully into the palm of her hand, winced a little at the heat, and then dumped the ashes in the empty wastepaper basket. Here was a library, full of books—and as far as she knew Beatrix hadn't read a single one of them. Beatrix said she read the Bible, but Naomi doubted it. What Beatrix did—Naomi knew this because she had done it herself, during her holy phase, when she was married to her second husband—was to open the book at random and read stray passages from it. It was a form of divination for people who didn't believe in divination. Open the book at random and it will speak to you. Close your eyes and put your finger on a passage and that will be the answer to your prayers.

"Look," Naomi said. "There's nothing wrong with David Sandler. He doesn't worship Darwin—''

"He's an atheist.''

"Lots of people are atheists, Beatrix, including me more than half the time. You shouldn't go around saying things like about how people worship Darwin or the Devil or whatever. It's dangerous.''

"You mean because I might get sued? I wouldn't care if I got sued. I'd think of it as a trial I was undergoing on behalf of the cross of Christ.''

"I think that's very nice, Beatrix, but it's utterly beside the point. David Sandler isn't going to sue you, for God's sake—''

"—I wish you wouldn't take the Lord's name in vain—''

"—why would he bother? Now Zhondra Meyer might sue you, just out of mean-spiritedness, because she's a world-class bitch—''

"—Naomi—''

"—but to tell you the truth, I don't think she's interested, either. But it's dangerous nonetheless, Beatrix, because talk like that gets out of hand. Talk like that can hurt people."

Beatrix waddled over to the window, the lines set in her face, furious. She pressed her face against the glass and closed her eyes.

"Nothing can hurt *them*," she said angrily. "They don't even have to obey the law. They aren't like the rest of us."

"Which is supposed to mean what?"

Beatrix pulled herself away from the window. "A couple of us from church went to the child welfare people. About the children up there, you know, at the camp. With all those lesbians. It isn't a wholesome situation. And that's what the child welfare people are supposed to be for."

Naomi's cigarette had burned to the filter. She put it out against the metal side of the wastepaper basket and got another from her pack.

"I can't believe this," she said. "I can't believe I'm hearing this."

"They just said they'd already checked into the camp, and there was nothing there for them to concern themselves over, there wasn't any abuse and neglect or anything like that—but what do you call bringing little children up around all that smuttiness? Isn't that abuse and neglect?"

"No," Naomi said.

Beatrix was oblivious. "Later on we found out that they had a lawyer, that Zhondra Meyer had hired a lawyer, a famous lawyer from New York. And the child welfare people were afraid of the lawyer, because everything is so clean up there and everybody is so rich. They were afraid of it getting in the papers and making them look silly."

"Good," Naomi said.

Beatrix was nearly in tears. "I wish you'd come to church with me, Naomi, I really do. I wish you'd accept Jesus Christ as your personal savior. Because we're in the last days, you know. And in the end you're going to have to choose."

"That's your van waiting out on Main Street," Naomi said. "Maybe you'd better pack up and get ready to go."

"I'm all ready to go. All I have to do is leave. I just wish I could make you listen. I like you, Naomi. You've been good to me. I don't want to see you go to Hell."

There is no such thing as hell, Naomi wanted to say. Instead, she stood up and began shooing Beatrix in the direction of the door.

"You'd better hurry now, Beatrix. You don't want to miss your ride and get stuck out here with me."

"I wouldn't mind being stuck out here with you if I knew I could convert you. I'd do anything to convert you."

"Go."

Naomi nearly shoved Beatrix out the door and onto the second-floor landing. Beatrix moved with stubborn leadenness, a prehistoric, dinosaur-sized donkey with a mind of her own.

"Go," Naomi said again.

Beatrix went down a few steps and looked back sorrowfully. Naomi thought she was going to cry.

"Please," Beatrix said. "Please think about it. You don't know what will happen to you, if you don't get born again. You don't understand. And the forces of good always need help. They really do."

"You'd better hurry, Beatrix. It's getting later by the second."

Beatrix hesitated, a mass of fat and bone. Then she turned and began to head on down the stairs again.

A few seconds later, looking down on Main Street, Naomi saw Beatrix come through the library's front door and make her way to a big white van. The van had a gold cross painted on the side of it and the words JESUS CHRIST IS LORD painted in red. The side door slid open and hands reached out. Beatrix hoisted herself upward and disappeared into the dark.

The cigarette in Naomi's hand had burned down to the filter again. She had forgotten she was even holding it. She pitched the butt into the wastebasket and sat down. Her computer screen was blank. Thunder and lightning had finally put her system down.

Hello! Naomi thought. *This is your class correspondent, Naomi Brent!*

She put her hand up to the gold chain she wore around her neck and fingered it. She had been given the chain, and the plain gold cross that hung on it, when she was twelve. She had worn it ever since without thinking about it. Half the time these days, she didn't even realize it was there.

Well, I realize it now, Naomi thought.

She put her hands around to the back of her neck and undid the little spring clasp.

Then she dumped the whole thing, chain and cross, into the wastepaper basket.

7

Bobby Marsh was supposed to take the church van out to Dedham Corners, pick up old Mrs. Michaels and her husband, and drive on back to the church on the Hartford Road. This was the little green van, the wimpy one, not the big white one with JESUS IS LORD painted on the side of it. Bobby used to drive bigger trucks than that van could ever be, but he'd had a few accidents, and the Reverend Holborn didn't like to trust him. Nobody trusted Bobby much anymore. He knew that. Less than five years ago, when he'd still been in high school, he'd been a real comer. He hadn't been "college material," as the guidance counselors liked to put it. He hadn't been one of those guys who was being packaged like a gift sausage and sent away to Vanderbilt or Chapel Hill. Even so, he'd had a lot going for him. Bobby could remember, with perfect clarity, all those late fall afternoons of his senior year. The rich girls sitting in their open-topped cars in the parking lot of the Burger King out at Dedham Corners. The sharp knobs of the hooks on Jerri Lynn Carver's bra as they wrestled in the back of Bobby's father's Ford pickup, parked in the trees out on Caravansary Lane. Bobby Marsh had been a good-looking boy at seventeen, good-looking enough so that even girls like Jerri Lynn Carver, who was going away to Sweet Briar after graduation, wanted to make out with him. In the years since all that had ended, Bobby had decided that there wasn't much else those girls had wanted of him. He still saw them sometimes, on Main Street, when they were at home visiting their parents. They had big gold wedding rings on their fingers and the kinds of clothes you saw in magazines and they pretended that they didn't really know him. That was why he had come to trust so much in the Lord. There didn't seem to be anyone else he could trust in. Once his life had been all sex, sex, sex, and it had made him miserable. Now his life was all praise, praise, praise, and it made him—

—angry.

Dedham Corners was right ahead, a big splash of concrete and asphalt and mock-brick facing. When Bobby Marsh was a small boy, Dedham Corners hadn't been anything but a wide place in the road with a gas station. Now there were three gas stations, a Burger King and a McDonald's, a 7-Eleven, a Kmart, and more. All the plate glass windows were boarded up, but all the lights were blazing. The sky was dark and the rain was coming down in slanting assaults, like electrons bombarding an atom in one of those educational in-school movies. Bobby couldn't remember what had made him so angry. Maybe it was everything and nothing at all. All he knew was that ever since he had joined the Reverend Holborn's church, ever since he had met Ginny and married her, something inside him had been bubbling up, getting ready to explode. It was crazy, really. He loved Ginny. He loved Tiffany. He loved the church, too, which had given him the only sane life he had ever known. Bobby Marsh knew that his growing up would have been much different—much better—if either of his parents had managed to get religion. Instead, his father got beer and his mother got laundry. His father worked until he was so drunk they had to fire him. His mother worked without ceasing, like a slave woman, carrying big plastic baskets full of dirty clothes up and down the side streets of Bellerton, driving out to Conover to buy her own clothes at the second-hand stores. They had a small place on a dirt road far out in the country, away from the sea. The roof leaked and the porch sagged and the yard was littered with pieces of dead machines. Jerri Lynn Carver's family had a big Greek revival right in the middle of town. Suellen Chambers's family had a split-level in a new subdivision right off the highway. It had all been rigged from the beginning, and Bobby Marsh knew it. He just didn't know what to do about it.

(Jesus is Lord, he thought now, half frantically, the words pumping through his brain like polished ball bearings, hitting each other and making his skull shake. *Jesus is Lord. Jesus is Lord. Jesus is Lord. Take me now Jesus because I'm falling right into the pit of sin.)*

Old Mrs. Michaels was standing under the roof overhang near the side door to Burger King. Burger King was closed, but there wasn't anywhere else on the strip for her to stand where she would be protected, even a little, from the rain. Bobby pulled into the parking lot and cut his engine. He could barely see through the windshield, the rain was that bad. Now that he was this close, though, he could see old *Mr.* Michaels, huddled behind his wife, blank-eyed and frightened. Mrs. Michaels was one of those big-stomached women who looked like they'd swallowed a basketball. She was wearing a bright orange sweat suit with the words CHRIST IS COMING BE PREPARED printed on the back of the sweatshirt. Mr. Michaels looked like he was wearing prison garb or pajamas. He was so thin, everything he put on his body sagged.

Bobby opened the door of the van and slid out. His thick-soled shit-kicker boots landed in the middle of a puddle and spattered water everywhere. He had water in his face, too, where the rain was hitting it. He put his hand up to shield his eyes and ran over to where the old people were standing.

"Praise the Lord," Mrs. Michaels said, when Bobby reached her. "I thought you'd been drowned in this storm, I really did. I thought we were going to be stranded here forever."

Bobby looked back at the van. "Maybe I ought to go get the side door open. Then we can run him right in and he won't have to stand around in the rain."

"It's been the Devil's own problem, keeping him out of the rain today," Mrs. Michaels said. "Every time I take my eyes off him, he just wanders off. I've been driven to distraction."

"Mmm," Bobby said.

"I talked to the reverend about it," Mrs. Michaels said, "but there wasn't much he could tell me. Alzheimer's disease, they call it nowadays. We just called it getting senile, in my time. That's what it is. Just getting senile. He won't ever get any better now."

Bobby looked dubiously at old Mr. Michaels. His eyes were vacant. His hands were limp. He was staring at a blown-up picture of a Double Whopper.

"Maybe you could go to a healing," Bobby said. "You know. Like they had down in Charlotte a couple of months ago. Maybe that would do him some good."

"I don't think so," Mrs. Michaels said. "I been to healings when I was younger. Those preachers never did seem to like people who were going senile. No percentage in it, I'd expect."

"Percentage?"

"Well, you couldn't make them better, no matter what, now could you?" Mrs. Michaels was matter-of-fact. "Better to get those other things, the cancers and the ulcers. Nobody knows if they're healed or not at the end of the night. Things work out better that way."

"But God can heal anything." Bobby felt confused. "You just have to find somebody He's given the gift of healing to. Then Christ will heal you and you'll be whole."

"Will you?"

The rain was getting worse by the second. Bobby felt

himself getting worse, too, angrier and more agitated. He had always thought of Mrs. Michaels as one of the most solid members of the church. Now it seemed she wasn't any such thing. She didn't believe in healing. She didn't believe in miracles. She was standing here telling him there were some things God just couldn't do. Or she seemed to be telling him that.

Bobby looked her over one more time and decided he just didn't like her. She was too bright and hard and cynical. Her jaw was slack and there were lines on both sides of her face, slashed into the skin like wounds, set off by big blue tinkling earrings bought at the jewelry counter of a five-and-dime. Bobby didn't like Mr. Michaels much, either, but that was just . . . reaction. It was hard to like somebody who drooled when you talked to him.

"I'm going to make a run for the van," Bobby said. "I'll get the door open and be right back."

"That's very good of you," Mrs. Michaels said. "Mr. Michaels and I would be much obliged."

Bobby put his head down and ran across the parking lot. Lightning split the sky over his head, making him wonder whether he was grounded or not, whether he would get hurt if he was hit. He landed in puddle after puddle, sending waves of wet up the insides of his legs. When he got to the van, he suddenly couldn't find his keys. He had searched all five of his pockets before he remembered that he had hooked them onto one of his belt loops.

"Crap," he said, out loud, into the wind. The wind was high and wild and strong. Nobody was going to hear him.

Bobby got the van's side door open and looked in. The interior was very clean. Reverend Holborn always kept the things that belonged to the church clean. Bobby took a thick cotton blanket off one of the seats and started back across the parking lot to Mr. and Mrs. Michaels.

"Can the old man run?" he asked Mrs. Michaels. "It's very wet out there."

"Maybe you could bring the van closer," Mrs. Michaels said. "Maybe that would work out better."

"If I bring it closer, we won't be able to get him in," Bobby pointed out. He kicked at the trapezoid concrete blocks that were lined up at the edge of the overhang. Lots of fast-food restaurants had them, but he had never understood why. Probably to keep people from doing just what Mrs. Michaels wanted him to do now.

"We could make him run," Mrs. Michaels said finally. "Not very fast, but a little. He's very weak."

"I don't think I can carry him," Bobby said. "He's too tall for me."

"Of course you can't carry him, dear. Let's just run him out there, together. That ought to work as well as anything. And then once we've got him in the van, we can make him warm and cover him up."

Bobby thought of the cotton blanket. "Right," he said. He grabbed one of Mr. Michaels's arms and tried to guide the old man to the edge of the overhang. Mr. Michaels seemed to be resisting.

"He gets very stubborn these days," Mrs. Michaels said. "He gets an idea into his head, and there isn't a thing you can do with him."

Bobby held old Mr. Michaels's arm even tighter. The door to the van was still open. Bobby was sure rain was pouring in there, getting the carpets soggy. Reverend Holborn always took such good care of all the things that belonged to the church. Bobby could hear him already, chiding gently, criticizing gently, in that super-Christian tone of voice that always made Bobby's head ache.

"Come on," Bobby said. "Let's move him. On the count of three."

"Oh, dear," Mrs. Michaels said.

Bobby locked his grip in place, put his head down, and began to run forward. He felt as if he had to drag both of them along with him. Mrs. Michaels was holding back. The run across the parking lot seemed to last forever. His socks got soaked through. His baseball hat blew off in the wind. The rain plastered his hair to his skull and made him very cold.

"Here we are," he said when they drew up close to the van. Old Mrs. Michaels seemed to be panting. Bobby pushed Mr. Michaels through the van's side door and let the old woman climb in after him. Old Mr. Michaels immediately sat down on the van floor and curled into a fetal position. Bobby slid the side door shut and ran around to climb into the front bucket seat.

"We've got a problem," Mrs. Michaels said as Bobby started the engine. "He's gone into one of his frozen periods. I can't get him moved."

"That's okay," Bobby said.

"But it isn't okay," Mrs. Michaels said. "There's that law about the seat belts. He can't be wearing a seat belt if he's curled up like that on the floor."

"It's all right, really. I don't think some cop is going to stop us to find out if we're wearing our seat belts in all this mess. The cops are going to have better things to do."

"Well," Mrs. Michaels said. "If you say so. But I'd think this is when they would want to know if you were wearing your safety belts. In a mess like this."

Bobby began to ease the van out of the parking lot. He went very, very slowly, because it was raining so hard now that the windshield wipers were virtually useless. He had the heat turned way up, too, because it was suddenly very cold, as cold as he could ever remember it being in North Carolina. He thought it was a good thing he would have to stick to the access roads and stay off the interstate to get where he was going. He wouldn't want to be in front of somebody who thought the best thing to do at a time like this was to hurry.

"Well, now," Mrs. Michaels said. "I almost forgot. Where's that sweet little wife of yours this morning? Are we meeting her at the church?"

"I don't know," Bobby said, suddenly uneasy. "I hope so."

"You mean you don't know where she is at a time like this? What about the baby?"

"The baby's with Ginny," Bobby said. "It's not that. She went to work this morning. I don't know if she got back down in time or if she got stuck up there."

"Up there?"

Bobby felt himself blushing furiously. "At the camp. You know. She does typing for that Ms. Meyer up there—"

"At the camp," Mrs. Michaels echoed. "My, my. I wouldn't like that, if it was somebody I loved. Aren't you worried about her? Don't you get anxious that they'll do something to her? Or to the baby?"

"She keeps her Bible with her. She puts on the honor of the Lord like an armor, like Reverend Holborn said."

"Yes, yes, I know. But *those* people." Mrs. Michaels shook her head. Bobby saw it in the rearview mirror. "It's just that you hear so many things. And you know what people like that are like. No discipline. No respect. Absolutely anything might happen."

"She just goes up there to type," Bobby said firmly.

"There was a case in Tennessee just a couple of months ago," Mrs. Michaels continued. "It was a horrible thing. Worshipping the Devil. Having sexual intercourse with babies. Eating flesh and drinking blood. The world isn't what it was when I was young."

"No," Bobby said.

"If I were you, I'd put my foot down just as soon as she came home. You know what young girls are like, especially young wives. They want to help so much, they think they can do anything. They don't believe they can ever get into trouble. If I were you, I'd tell her right out, you don't really need the money she makes in that place. You can do without it as long as she stays at home."

"Yes," Bobby said dully, and then thought: But we can't do without it; we can't afford to have Ginny stay home. How would we ever pay the rent?

He had gotten to the junction of the Hartford Road. He pumped the brakes lightly—anything more definite and they would have spun right out and landed in a ditch—and eased the van into a left turn. There was no one around anywhere, no other traffic, no sign of life in any of the small brick ranch houses that lined both sides of this street. Bobby let himself pick up a little speed.

The camp, the camp, the camp, he thought.

And then it was crystal clear to him, really, what he had been so angry about before, what he had been trying not to remember. He never stopped worrying about Ginny when she was up there. He never stopped wondering what happened to her, if any of them ever tried to touch her, if she ever thought about touching any of them. The horrible thing was that it excited him, all this thinking about women. It made him big and hard and dizzy all at once.

The Devil is a good psychologist, the Reverend Holborn was always saying, and Bobby had to agree. The Devil was a hypnotist, that was it, and any minute now he was going to drag Bobby Marsh down into Hell with him. It was going to happen as sure as this storm was going to be over tomorrow—unless he did something about it.

What Bobby Marsh hated most was feeling as if he were paralyzed. That was the way he felt when he thought about jobs or the way his money went out before it had come in. That was the way he felt when he recalled trying to learn things while he was still at school.

There was no need for him to feel paralyzed here, though. There was no need for him to feel helpless about the camp. He was a soldier of Christ, and armed with his faith and the glory of the Lord, he could stop the Devil himself in his tracks.

I'm going to do that, too, Bobby decided, as soon as this storm is over.

I'm going to go right on up to that camp and have it out with that Meyer woman once and for all.

I have been washed in the blood of the lamb, Bobby told himself.

And suddenly realized he was grinning.

8

The Reverend Henry Holborn couldn't remember when he'd taken off his jacket and tie. It must have been hours ago, when they were first getting the kitchen in the basement ready to feed a couple of thousand people. He couldn't remember what he'd done with his jacket and tie, either. They had to be floating around somewhere in the main room, where there were four thousand three hundred fifty seats. The seats radiated out in graduated arcs from the central core of the altar—except that to Henry Holborn, it wasn't really an altar. It was a stage. Henry Holborn had been brought up Catholic. He didn't believe in all that any-more—the Real Presence of Christ in the Eucharist; the Mass as the re-presentation of Christ's sacrifice on the cross—but it still seemed silly to him to call by the name "altar" what was really only a platform, with nothing much on it. The altars of his childhood had been elaborate affairs, made of marble, holding vessels of silver and gold. Maybe if the Catholic Church had stuck with that kind of thing, Henry Holborn would have stuck with the Catholic Church. Instead, the Catholic Church had gone all Protestant-y. The marble altars were exchanged for plain wooden tables. The Mass was rewritten until it sounded like a text-book for social workers. Nobody kneeled at the Commu-nion rail anymore, even if there was still a Communion rail to kneel at.

Looking around at this church sometimes, Henry was surprised at how well it had all gone. He could remember getting his call—lying in the back bedroom of a trailer just outside Greensboro, staring at the ceiling and thinking he ought to kill himself, he really ought to, because he'd been out of work for eight months and what was coming up looked like more of the same. His wife had left him and taken their one-year-old daughter with her. His parents hadn't talked to him since 1976. He could hear the voice now as clearly as he had heard it then—first as a tickle and a whisper in his ear; then growing stronger and deeper and more definite. He could see the face of Christ as clearly as he had seen it then, too. He knew it was the real Christ because it didn't look like the face of any other Christ he'd ever seen. It wasn't a long-suffering mask of self-pity. It wasn't a blank stare under a halo of gold. It was the gnarled, broad-boned face of a Middle Eastern Jew, with dark hair going to gray and a film of sweat along the line of the jaw. The face had filled up every molecule of air in that back bedroom. It had lifted him off the bed and into space. He had felt as if he were floating in water. And water, he knew, was what he needed.

Washed in the blood of the lamb.

Baptized in the Holy Spirit.

Born again.

Now he wiped sweat off his own jaw and surveyed this big open room one more time. His wife, Janet, was seeing to a couple of little old ladies back near the literature rack by the center doors. There were many more people here than actually belonged to the church. There were many more people here than attended services on Sunday, although Henry got a pretty good crowd. He filled all four thousand three hundred fifty seats more often than not. There were people downstairs in the basement and parceled out in the classrooms in the Sunday School wing. There were black people as well as white people, too. It was incredible to Henry how many of his neighbors lived in what were not much better than shanties. Of course, they didn't look like shanties. They looked like new brick ranches and builder's colonials. The problem was, they hadn't been built very well. The Lord only knew how many of those things were going to be washed out in this hurricane.

Janet raised her head for a moment and looked in his direction. Henry motioned to her. He remembered getting her back, after she had left, after he had been born again. He remembered sitting on the bottom step of the porch steps of her mother's house in Charleston, twisting his baseball hat in his hands, telling her what he would do if she would only give him one more chance. He still had that baseball hat, up in his bedroom sock drawer. It had a Yankees logo on it, as if, along with everything else he'd done wrong, he'd decided to be a traitor to the south.

Janet was a small, thin woman with lots of pale blond hair and very big blue eyes. Henry had always been glad that she didn't have that taste for makeup that so many born-again southern women had.

"What is it?" she asked him, when she reached him. "I'm dead on my feet. The old ladies are frantic."

"Not surprising."

"No," Janet agreed. "Not surprising. Bobby just brought in the Michaelses. He's having a very bad day."

"Bad bad?"

"Bad enough that I was thinking we might have to restrain him."

Henry rubbed the flat of his palm against the back of his neck. "Did you ever get in touch with David Sandler? I tried myself a couple of minutes ago, but the phones are out."

"The phones were out when I tried, too. Maybe it's just as well."

"Why?"

Janet shrugged. "He is an atheist, Henry. He's a very effective atheist."

"So?"

"So, you've got a church full of old people, not very well-educated old people. Half of them think that this hurricane is being caused by the Devil. They've told me so."

"I think this hurricane is being caused by the Devil," Henry said. "In a way."

"With the old ladies, there's no 'in a way' about it." Janet was firm. "I don't think I could live like that, Henry. Afraid every minute that any little thing that went wrong was the wrath of God. Afraid of Hell and trying to pretend I wasn't afraid of it."

"That's why we try to teach them to know that they're saved. To really know it. If they really know they're saved, they have nothing to be afraid of."

"Maybe. But it doesn't seem to work, does it? Not with a lot of them. You talk about the love of God and it makes me feel—inspired. But then I look out at the congregation and I see all those closed faces, and all that fear. Why is there so much fear?"

Henry thought about growing up, about walking to Mass along a dusty highway, about shoes with holes in them and a nun who told him that wearing shoes like that to Mass showed disrespect to the Lord.

"They've never had much of anything, most of these people," he told his wife. "They're always on the verge of losing what little they've managed to put aside. They aren't respected. The regular churches don't want them. Nobody on earth wants them but us."

"I wonder if that's true anymore," Janet said. "The regular churches don't seem to be doing very well."

"It's hard to do well as a Christian church when you don't even believe Christ rose from the dead. Do we know about the Harrows, Janet? Have they got a safe place to be?"

"I talked to Lisa Harrow right before the storm started. They were going in to the high school. I was surprised she didn't say they were going up to that camp."

Henry laughed. "I don't think even Stephen Harrow would push it that far. I'm sorry you couldn't find David Sandler, though. Atheist or no atheist. Living out on the beach like that. Remember what happened at Nag's Head."

"Oh, I know. But he's an intelligent man. He must have sense enough to get out of there and onto some high ground. Especially since he doesn't believe in life after death. He wouldn't want to be blotted out forever. I've got to go," Janet said. "I've got at least another dozen old ladies to see to. And I've got to help cook. Sarah Drake says we've got a freezer full of spare ribs left over from the Fourth of July picnic, so we're going to use those."

"Sounds good to me."

"I only hope there's enough for everybody. I've been thinking all morning that the Mormons have a point. Always keeping enough food on hand to last for a year's siege. We could use that kind of food around here today.''

''We wouldn't have had anyplace to keep it.''

Janet patted his arm and pecked at the air near his cheek. She wasn't tall enough to kiss him without jumping up to reach him.

''I've got to go,'' she said again. ''I'll talk to you later. Are we going to have a service while all this is going on?''

''I thought I'd wait until it was over. When we know what the extent of the damage is going to be.''

''Good idea.''

Janet kissed the air in the direction of his cheek again and then disappeared. Henry caught sight of her a couple of seconds later, her blond head bobbing among the gray ones, moving vigorously where all other movements were halt. Many of the people Henry saw were just what he had told Janet they were: poor and displaced, the sort of people who never seem to have any luck at all. Some of them, though, were an element that had begun to make even Henry uneasy. He believed without question that all people were called to live in Christ, and that God could perform miracles through the power of His Son. He believed without question in the reality of inner conversion, too. No matter how evil a man was, he could be born again and become a new creature. He could put on Christ and be forever afterward good. The Bible, Henry knew, was true down to the last dot and comma. Christ was really and factually born of a virgin in Bethlehem. He really and factually died on the cross, condemned by Pontius Pilate. He really and factually rose from the dead on the third day. He really and factually had called all men and all women to follow him.

The problem was, some of these people didn't seem so much interested in following Christ as they were in finding an excuse. They took ideas out of context. The Bible said all homosexuality was an abomination. Henry knew that was true. It was a sinful and disorderly way to live. There was no excuse for it. That wasn't the same as saying that you should—what?

Henry was an intelligent man, but he hadn't been well or even extensively educated. He knew that the Devil was up there, at that camp. He knew that was the only way the camp could exist as long as it had without collapsing under the weight of its own evil. He wondered what David Sandler thought about it. Just because you were an atheist didn't mean you were mired in filth and perversion. And it was filth and perversion, dangerous filth and perversion, it was just that he didn't want anyone to—what, what, what?

There was a roll of thunder across the sky. The rain hit the roof in waves. There were no windows in the tabernacle space itself. The walls were made of painted concrete and were blank. They could have been on a submarine.

Henry made his way across the stage/altar to the doors at the back, where the choir and everybody else came through when they were having services. He went through the choir room with its dressing stalls and its pale blue robes hung on brass wall hooks. He went out another door and into a back hall. Nobody had thought of using these spaces to house people or set up beds. The back hall was absolutely empty.

At the end of the back hall there was a spiral staircase, leading dangerously upward to the squat square space where the bells were kept. Normally, nobody had to come up here. Everything was done by computer these days. You punched your instructions into the program and the machine took care of the rest. The right bells rang at the right times. The right songs played for the right moments of spiritual uplift and conviction of sin. Sometimes the bells had to be fixed, though. The next time, Henry thought, they would have it all computerized, with hymns on tapes that could be played automatically, with no bells to fix.

Henry stopped at the landing at the top of the spiral staircase. He searched around in his pockets until he found the big brass ring of church keys. He opened the bell room door and let himself in. It was dark up here and very noisy.

There were no real windows in this room, only shutters that had to be screwed off the wall. The shutters were closed now, as they were whenever there was no service going on downstairs.

Henry put his keys back in his pocket and started to unscrew the set of shutters he was closest to. The bells felt like big hulking things with wills of their own. Henry hadn't felt this nervous since he was a small boy and believed that a monster lived in his bedroom closet. He got the shutters open just as the wind changed direction in a sudden gust. He got a face full of rain and a head full of thunder, rolling and crashing and hiccuping in bursts. Then the sky was filled with lightning and thunder again. It was only when the flash spots had cleared from his eyes that Henry realized that it wasn't really dark. The sun was up there somewhere, straining to get through. The world was full of a steady gray glow.

What Henry had hoped to see was the beach, but he'd made a miscalculation. He'd opened the wrong set of shutters. He was looking not eastward, toward sloping ground, but north. The land rose steadily but shallowly and it receded from his vantage point. There was a stand of trees and then, in the distance, the peaked roof of the camp's main lodge. Camp, Henry thought. Lodge. That place up there wasn't either thing. It wasn't even a mansion. It was a palace, and the woman who owned it thought she was a queen.

He was about to close up the shutters and go downstairs again—What was he doing here, anyway? What good would it do anybody if he could see David Sandler's house on the beach?—when he caught a movement on the lodge's roof. For a moment he thought it was nothing but the storm. Maybe the wind had blown a few of the shingles loose up there. Then he realized that what he was seeing was a woman, walking carefully along the catwalk.

Dear sweet Lord, Henry thought. His stomach turned over. He wanted to be sick.

She's going to fall.

But she didn't fall. Whoever it was—not Zhondra Meyer; somebody shorter, somebody heavier—inched along the catwalk with what seemed like studied deliberateness. Henry realized that she had to be holding on to the rail, at the very least. She got to the kink where she would have to turn a corner and stopped. Then she seemed to scrunch into a ball and rock back and forth. A second later, Henry saw that she'd disappeared. She hadn't fallen. He would have seen that. She had simply disappeared.

Into where?

Into what?

What if witches really did exist, and whoever it was had just taken off, become discorporeal, called on her God the Devil, and been made spirit right in front of Henry's eyes?

Henry stepped away from the window and slammed the shutters closed across it. He twisted the first of the screws in so savagely it tore against his hand. He could feel an ooze of blood where the edge of the screw handle had cut into his palm. He put the other three screws in more gently and turned toward the spiral stairs.

Of course, he told himself, whoever it was probably hadn't become discorporeal. She had simply lowered herself through some kind of trap door. If there were ways onto that catwalk there had to be ways off. It would be insane to design the thing any other way.

Henry let himself back out onto the landing and closed the bell room door behind himself. He got his keys out again and locked up. He couldn't remember when he had last been this shaken, if he had ever been.

What was it that Saint Paul had said? *The Devil is prowling among you like a raging lion.*

And yes, Henry thought. Yes, he was.

9

In the end, David Sandler made the kind of decision he had promised himself never to make—based on emotion, with all the reason left out. He should have stayed in the beach house. The water was bad, but the house was built on pilings. It was the sturdiest structure on the beach for miles. Instead, he went out onto his deck and looked at the waves coming at him. They were enormous, black and tall and as solid looking as a wall. He kept remembering the television photographs of all those houses on Nag's Head falling into the sea during the last hurricane. He saw the splintering wood. He saw the cracking porches. He saw them collapsing like sticks into the water.

Crazy.

He put on his bright red L.L. Bean rainwear—pants as well as jacket and hood—as if that would make a difference. Then he dug an old silver flask out of the pot cabinet in his kitchen and washed it out with the water he had left standing in the master bath. The flask had belonged to his father. The old man had taken it to football games, back in the days when people actually went to football games, instead of watching them on television. David filled the flask from a nearly full bottle of Johnnie Walker Red that sat on a shelf in the living room bar. He almost never drank liquor. It made his head fuzzy and left him unable to read. At the last moment, he took a long swig out of the bottle itself, before he put the cap back on it and put it back. He wasn't going to be reading anytime soon. He felt he needed—courage.

Crazy.

He went out the front door and stood in the little sheltered entry. The scene outside was even crazier than the way he was thinking. There were trees down all along the beach road. They were big trees, too. The trees that were still standing were bending almost sideways in the wind. There were power lines down, too, but no live wires touching the ground as far as David could see. A few years ago, there would have been wires everywhere. Now the wires were mostly underground. It was only out here, where the summer people lived, that the power company hadn't gotten around to the conversion.

David took the flask out of his back pocket and took a swig. The Scotch burned going down. He thought about going back into the house and forgetting this whole thing. He thought about Nag's Head again. He put the flask back into his pocket and started off. He was a coward, he realized. A coward about water. He hated the thought of himself drowning in a black and choppy sea.

As soon as he was out from the shelter of the entry, the wind hit him. He felt it like a dozen hands pummeling him. When he hadn't been subject to it, it had looked fairly far away—up on the road, maybe, high in the trees. Now he realized there was nothing on the beach to save him from it. He turned his back to it and tried to go forward without stumbling.

The sand was wet and slippery. The little incline up to the boardwalk was impossibly steep. David pushed against it and pushed against it, whatever it was, something coming at him, something strong. He suddenly realized what it was people saw when they thought they saw God. The world around him seemed very much alive to him, full of conscious intent and purpose. He thought of it as a grinning, angry man, bent on destroying David Sandler in particular, singling him out.

He got to the boardwalk, scrambling. He stumbled across to the road and then across the road to the start of Beach Street. The houses there hadn't been as lucky as his own, in spite of the fact that they were farther from the water. Two of them had their roofs blown off. All five of them were missing glass from their windows. These were the houses that belonged to summer people. None of them had been boarded up. David went between two of them, to get out of the worst of the wind. That was when he felt water rising up around his boots. He looked down and saw it snaking up on him. Water from the sea.

Jesus Christ, David thought, making himself move faster. He looked back at his house, but it seemed to be safe. Waves were coming up over the deck now, but nothing was wobbling, nothing looked unstable. If the water came in much farther, though, these houses he was walking among now were all going to fall.

David wove in and out of yards—yards of houses where people lived year-round now; most of the windows boarded up—and finally stumbled out onto Tolliver Road. It seemed to be deserted. Everybody must have gone up to the high school, David thought. There were soggy pieces of paper and old tin cans everywhere. Somebody must have forgotten to take in his garbage cans. There were roof shingles everywhere, too. Some of the houses had had all their shingles on one side ripped off. A big pinewood doghouse had been lifted up and deposited in the middle of the street. It had lost most of its roof shingles, too.

David made his way between two half-house cottages and then out onto Main Street finally. The rain was coming down so hard it blinded him the second he stopped shading his eyes with his hands. Rose MacNeill's turret was sagging. Something had smashed into the side of it and cracked a support beam. The bookstore's door was open and paperback books had spilled out, as if they were liquid, too. David saw the bright cover of a romance novel about American Indians. Only the library looked as if it had been kept reasonably safe, and how long could that last? The wind was rising again. The rain was coming harder. I should have stayed in the house, David told himself again. Then he pushed himself into the partial shelter of the hardware store's doorway and reached for his flask.

Now that he had gotten this far—and, maybe, now that he had drunk this much—reason had returned to him. He really, really should never have left the house. What he was doing was insane, and very dangerous. At the moment, however, it made no sense to try to go back. The sea was getting worse and worse. He would only end up getting swept off the boardwalk. The radio this morning had been telling everybody to get up to the high school. That was what he was going to have to try to do.

He put the flask securely back into his pocket and went out into the wind again. It really was getting worse. It was pushing so hard at his back that he kept threatening to fall on his face, splat, slapped against the concrete like a pesky bug. He turned down a side street to get away from it. He couldn't tell which side street, because the rain was so heavy he couldn't read the street sign. He wasn't even clear about which buildings he was passing, or which direction he was going in. The wind seemed to curl in on itself, to make eddies and waves, to sneak up on him from behind.

The side street did not look familiar. It must have been, because David had walked every street in Bellerton, North Carolina, a million times, but the houses all looked blank and odd. The lawns looked alien. The street was full of debris.

David didn't know when it was he lost all sense of where he was or what direction he was going in. Away from the wind, that was all he was sure of. There was so much water in his eyes, they stung. He was wet to the bone even under his rain gear. He just kept pushing ahead, pushing ahead, away from the wind, away from the slanting direction of the rain. There was water in the street at least an inch and a half deep. He slogged through it as if he were wading on the beach.

He turned a corner and then another corner. The houses got less and less familiar. The damage got worse and better and worse again, a random scattering of disasters. The torn-off shingles were ubiquitous. Other things—dolls; dinner plates; furniture—seemed to have been chosen without sense by imps or gremlins, small sly creatures who hated people as a profession.

I'm losing my mind, David told himself.

And then he was clear of it all, the houses and the wreckage. He tried to see in the rain and got only asphalt and dirt. He thought he had to be out on Route 152. That was the closest two-lane blacktop to town. The gutters here were full of water, but he was far enough away from the worst of the storm so that there wasn't as much broken and trampled on the ground.

Left, David told himself. If I go left I go north and if I go north I get to—the high school? the camp? He couldn't remember. He wished he could get another swig at the flask, but he knew it would be impossible in all this wind and rain. He would just get his eyes and nose filled with water, tilting his head back the way he would have to.

His head was full of rhythms. Go on, go on, go on. Walk fast, walk fast, walk fast. Keep at it, keep at it, keep at it. Walking this way, the rain was falling against his back. It got under the collar of his jacket and ran across his neck, cold and slick.

Up ahead of him was the Bellerton Full Gospel Church—was that in the right direction? The church was as boarded up and blank as the houses in town. It wasn't one of Bellerton's bigger churches, not like that complex Henry Holborn had out on the Hartford Road. The Bellerton Full Gospel Christian Church had lost the cross that used to sit on the peak of its roof. The cross was lying in the road, split in two, the edges jagged. David wondered, irrelevantly, what it had been made of, and why it hadn't been protected. Maybe, being a religious person, the pastor here had thought that Christ would protect His own.

David made his way past the church and then around its parking lot to a wider, more open space. The trees here were planted more thickly together. They seemed to be protecting each other. Not so many of them were down. Not so many were bent double with the force of the blow.

There was a shortcut through those trees to the high school. David was sure of it. He just couldn't remember exactly where the shortcut was or which way it went. The ground was starting to rise. He had to be going in the right direction. The ground rose and rose and then it got to the high school. Then it rose and rose some more and got to the camp. That was the only high ground in town. Everything else for miles around was dead flat.

David started to search the trees, for a break, for a path, anything. He was finding it hard to breathe. He hadn't gotten this much exercise in years. It couldn't be good for him. He tried to take a deep breath and choked on rainwater. He turned toward the trees as he started to cough—and then he saw her.

For a second or two, with all the insanity of the storm, he thought it was just a branch or a piece of junk being thrown around by the weather. It kept coming and coming and finally he recognized it. Her. He stood up and stared, oblivious for a moment to everything that was happening around him.

Her.

My God, he thought.

Ginny Marsh.

She was reeling through the trees as if she were dead drunk, and she was covered with blood.

From the Raleigh *News and Observer*, October 26—

BABY MURDERED BY SATANIC CULT

Devil Worship Motive for Baby's Death, Mother Says

BELLERTON—Satanic rituals and deals with the devil provided the motive for the murder of Tiffany Ann Marsh. So says the infant's mother, Virginia Leland Marsh, who is charging today that devil worshippers based at Zhondra Meyer's Bellerton women's retreat killed the child as a sacrifice to Satan during a "Black Mass" that was held on the grounds of the retreat during the early October onslaught of Hurricane Elsa. The child's body was discovered lying near a circle of stones in the retreat's back garden just after the hurricane passed through Bellerton. Her throat had been cut, and marks had been made in the infant's chest and abdomen, apparently with a kitchen knife. Mrs. Marsh says she was held immobile and forced to watch the proceedings by two women, only one of whom she recognized. The women involved in the ritual had their faces painted, thereby rendering them unrecognizable to Mrs. Marsh, who knew none of the residents well.

Robert Marsh, the baby's father, says that there have been rumors in town for many months that Satanic rituals were being practiced at the retreat. Local police authorities, however, say that no evidence of such practices has ever been found until now. An investigation following the discovery of the infant's body revealed pentagrams, candles, and a book with the pre–Vatican II traditional Latin Mass printed backwards, supposedly the method by which Satan worshippers celebrate their ritual. Church leaders in Bellerton, who have long been opposed to the camp because it is known to accept residents who are openly homosexual, are now calling for its closure at least until the death of Tiffany Ann Marsh has been definitively resolved. Zhondra Meyer, who owns and runs the camp, has said that she sees no reason to close, and does not believe that any of the women residing there have ever practiced Satanic cult rituals. Ms. Meyer is a direct descendant of the famous nineteenth-century robber baron, Isaac Samuel Meyer.

Bellerton local police and North Carolina state police are both said to be actively investigating this matter. Funeral services for Tiffany Ann Marsh were held yesterday at the Bellerton Church of Christ Jesus, the Reverend Henry Holborn presiding.

*part
one*

_____

one

1

Ever since Gregor Demarkian had come to live on Cavanaugh Street, he had spent a lot of time worrying about his best friend, Father Tibor Kasparian—but he had never been afraid for him, until now. The problem had started late on the afternoon of April 19, the day of the Oklahoma City bombing, when the reports first started to drift in that the bomber might not be an Islamic fundamentalist with ties to Iran, but someone more banal and domestic. It had gotten worse after Timothy McVeigh was arrested and everybody was sure. Gregor knew that Father Tibor had had a terrible life: arrested and imprisoned in the Soviet Union when the Soviet Union was still a power; suffering through God only knew what until he could make his way overland and underground, first to Israel and then to the United States. Tibor's wife had died in a Russian prison. Tibor himself limped slightly, and had only partial use of his left arm. Once, in the dark of a long night spent watching *Jaws* on videotape in the living room of the tiny rectory-apartment behind Holy Trinity Armenian Christian Church, Tibor had told Gregor the most frightening thing Gregor thought he had ever heard: that blood is the color of dirt, really, once it dries; that there are people who like the way corpses look, especially covered with dust and laid out on the ground.

"It's not," Gregor Demarkian told Bennis Hannaford,

one early morning in late October, months after the rest of the country had lost interest in Oklahoma and gone back to obsessing about the Simpson trial, "it's not as if I were an unsophisticated man. I spent most of my career chasing serial killers. I've seen a lot of blood and badness in my time. I've been depressed as hell about it. But this is different."

"Mmm," Bennis Hannaford said.

Gregor looked at Bennis's thick black hair and perfectly almond-shaped, enormous blue eyes, and sighed. Bennis was beautiful and Bennis was bright and Bennis loved Tibor, but she had quit a two-and-a-half-pack-a-day cigarette habit less than a month ago, and lately she just didn't seem to be mentally home. They were sitting facing each other in the window booth of the Ararat Restaurant. Gregor could look through the tall pane of glass at a bright, hard, cold fall day. It was only five minutes after seven. By seven-thirty, they would no longer be alone. Half the single people on the street ate their breakfasts at the Ararat. Half the married people did, too, when they were fighting with their spouses or not up to cooking anything or just in the mood to see people early. At night, the Ararat was Cavanaugh Street's main tourist attraction. It got written up in the restaurant section of the *Philadelphia Inquirer*. Tourists from Radnor and Wayne came in to see what "real Armenian cooking" was like. In the daytime, the Ararat resembled a diner with eccentric furniture. Hard vinyl floors and inexpensive green wallpaper clashed with tasseled sofa cushions and hand-crocheted antimacassars. As far as Gregor knew, the Ararat was the only restaurant of any kind, anywhere, that used antimacassars on the backs of straight-backed aluminum chairs.

"Bennis," Gregor said.

Bennis dragged her eyes away from the window. She looked unfocused. As far as Gregor knew, she hadn't done a single hour's work since she threw her Benson & Hedges menthols in the trash. Even unfocused, she was beautiful. Heading toward forty, she still had not a single wrinkle on her face. Her bone structure was extraordinary: fine but strong, sharp-edged and well defined. She was also a very successful fantasy novelist, but somehow Gregor never attached that to her, as part of her identity for him. Her apartment was full of papier-mâché castles and plastic unicorns. Her head was full of knights in shining armor and crones with magical powers. Gregor tried not to think about it, the way he would have if she had had something wrong with her that he thought she would find it embarrassing for him to notice.

"Bennis," Gregor said again, louder this time.

Bennis blinked and shook her head. She had a cup of coffee in front of her, barely touched. It had been sitting there barely touched for over half an hour.

"I'm sorry," Bennis said. "Excuse me, Gregor. Yes. I know. Tibor. It is worrying."

"It's more than worrying. It's downright terrifying. We've got to do something about this, Bennis."

Bennis took a sip of her coffee and made a face. It had to be stone cold. "I thought you'd already decided to do something about it," she said. "I thought you'd decided to take him with you down to North Carolina. To investigate this child murder case."

"I've decided to ask him, yes. I haven't talked to him about it yet."

"I wonder if he even knows it's happened," Bennis said. "I mean, you'd think, with all the publicity, he could hardly have failed to notice."

"Trobriand Islanders know about Ginger Marsh," Gregor said.

"Still," Bennis went on, "the way he's been—Maybe he has noticed it, and it's only made everything worse."

"I wouldn't know. I haven't talked to him about it. I haven't talked to him about much of anything in weeks."

"There was the Susan Smith case, too," Bennis said. "But that was different. And maybe I'm just overreacting here. That didn't seem to bother him much. Not like the Oklahoma thing."

Linda Melajian came out of the door at the back of the room. Gregor waved to her and Linda nodded, holding up a Pyrex pot of coffee with steam coming out the wide open top of it. People were getting used to Bennis's drifting off. They had started to make allowances for it.

"I don't think Tibor sees individual cases like Susan Smith and Ginger Marsh as having the same—gravity as what happened in Oklahoma City," Gregor said. "They lack the political element."

"There was a story in *Ms.* about the politics of motherhood," Bennis said. "They've got that kind of political element."

"These days, everything's got that kind of political element. That's not what I meant, and you know it."

Linda Melajian had arrived with her pot of coffee. She gave Bennis a new coffee cup and filled it. Bennis didn't notice.

"Bennis," Linda said.

"Oh." Bennis looked up. "Oh, Linda, hi. Could I have another cup of coffee? I let this one get cold."

Linda took the cup of cold coffee off the table and looked at the ceiling. Bennis didn't notice that, either.

"It's not that I think Tibor will be interested in the Ginger Marsh case," Gregor said. "It's that I don't like the idea of going off and leaving him for what could be a solid month. I don't like the shape he's in."

"I don't blame you."

"And it's not like I can count on the people around here looking after him," Gregor said. "Not lately. Lida's always off in California—what does she do in California, anyway?"

"Maybe she likes it there."

"And you're the next thing to useless these days. If you don't mind me saying so."

"Mmm," Bennis said.

"And old George is much too old to take on this kind of responsibility. He doesn't get around well enough." Gregor drummed his fingers against the table. "I don't really know what I ought to do here. It's not that I think the Ginger Marsh case will interest Tibor. It barely interests me. If David Sandler hadn't written me directly, I don't think I would have paid any attention to it at all."

"Satanism and witchcraft and child sacrifice?" Bennis looked up, her attention caught at last, frankly surprised. "You must be kidding. It got everybody else's attention. I'll bet the trial is going to be enormous."

"The trial is going to be a nonissue. Give it a couple of more months. They'll look into all their leads. They'll do the conscientious investigative probe. Then they'll arrest Ginger Marsh and she'll plead guilty."

"You really believe that."

"The only difference between Ginger Marsh and Susan Smith is that Ginger Marsh has a more elaborate sense of the theatrical. Pentagrams and candles and a bloody knife beat a phantom carjacker any day. But they're just as bogus. And they're just as cheap. That woman murdered her own child."

"I don't think I can remember you being this cynical before."

"It's not cynicism. It's experience. I was in the Federal Bureau of Investigation for twenty years. I know these people."

"Which people?"

"The Ginger Marshes of this world. The Susan Smiths. The Terry McVeighs. There really isn't much difference, you know. It's all the same—attitude, I guess you'd call it. The same arrogance. And if you don't mind my saying so, Bennis, I think that in my old age, I'm getting tired of it."

"You're not old, Gregor. For God's sake."

"I'll be sixty-one on my next birthday. Any day now, they'll stop talking about how I'm in early retirement. And like I said, I'm getting tired of it. More tired than you know."

"Then why do it? You're not obliged to go down there. The case will go on without you."

"I know it will."

"So?"

Gregor shrugged. "David Sandler is a friend of mine. He hasn't had much experience. He thinks there's something mysterious in what's happening down there. If I do what he's asking me to do, it might ease his mind."

"Right," Bennis said.

"And then there's Tibor, too. Maybe getting him away from here will help. Maybe if he has something else to do with his time besides sit around and brood about domestic terrorism and the disintegration of the American soul, he'd snap out of it and be Tibor again."

"He's got an entire church to run," Bennis pointed out. "And he's running it. He's got a school to run, too. I know he's been depressed, Gregor, but he really hasn't withdrawn from the world. He's been right in there the way he always has been."

"No." Gregor shook his head. "Not the way he always has been."

"I think you're kidding yourself," Bennis said. "I think this has less to do with Tibor than it has to do with yourself. I think you're using Tibor as some kind of cover."

"As a cover for what?"

The plate glass front door of the Ararat swung open. Bennis and Gregor looked up. Old George Tekemanian was limping in on unsteady legs, followed by a bustlingly important Hannah Krekorian and an over-made-up Sheila Kashinian. Hannah was gray-haired and plump and dowdy and downtrodden looking, in spite of the fact that she had to have at least a couple of million dollars. Sheila was wearing a three-quarter-length mink coat dyed into candy pink and lime green stripes, God only knew why. God only knew why Sheila Kashinian did anything. Old George looked embarrassed to be with her.

"That's an interesting outfit," Bennis Hannaford said, sipping at her coffee at last. "I wonder where she managed to find it."

"Maybe she had it made custom."

"Sheila doesn't do custom. It takes too long. If we ask old George over here, do you think we'll get Sheila, too?"

"We'll probably get Sheila no matter what you do."

"True."

Bennis swung her legs out of the booth and stood up. She was a small woman, no more than five four and no heavier than a hundred and five pounds, but sitting down she had a more commanding presence. Gregor watched her stride across the restaurant and stop where old George was standing just inside the front door. Hannah and Sheila crowded in, wanting to hear—whatever.

Out on Cavanaugh Street, the sunlight looked brittle, like cheap glass. Gregor could see the front of Lida Arkmanian's big five-story town house, its front door sporting a wreath of pink and blue ribbons in spite of the fact that Lida was away and likely to stay away for a while. Mara Kalikian had just had a baby, and Bennis and Donna Moradanyan were having a party for it after its christening next Sunday. *Her,* Gregor thought. A party for her. The baby was a girl. Maybe Bennis was right to say that this whole thing about going to North Carolina was really about himself, and not about Tibor. Sometimes these days, he seemed, to himself, almost as distracted and out of focus as Bennis.

Once, years ago, in the month when his wife Elizabeth had started the last serious agony of her dying, Gregor had stood at the edge of a ditch on the side of a road in rural Massachusetts, looking down at the bodies of five small boys. The picture was more clearly in his mind now than anything he could make himself look at: the arms and legs twisted and entwined; the reinforced toes on the shoes of the Massachusetts state policeman who had driven him out from Boston. While it was happening, it had all seemed very far away. Elizabeth was dying. That was what had been at the front of his mind. Elizabeth was dying and there was nothing they could do about it anymore, no way left to save her, no way left to lie to himself that it would finally turn out all right. He had been, at that moment, the head of the Federal Bureau of Investigation's Department of Behavioral Sciences. His job was to hunt and find and capture serial killers. A serial killer had killed those boys—and would probably kill more, given time, given freedom, given opportunity.

Up at the front door, Bennis had finished talking to Hannah and Sheila and old George. She was leading them across the room, toward the window booth and Gregor. Gregor rubbed the side of his face with the flat of his hand and took a deep breath. He had never caught the man who had murdered those boys. Nobody had. Gregor didn't know if he was still out there killing someplace, or if he had died, or if he had been jailed for something else, or if he had gone dormant, as some of them sometimes did. Donna Moradanyan's son Tommy was now about the age those boys had been. Watching Tommy flying down the sidewalk on Cavanaugh Street, it struck Gregor every once in a while that he might be in danger.

Of course, Gregor thought now, scooting over on the bench to give old George room to get in, everybody was in danger, all the time. That was the lesson of Oklahoma City. It was the lesson learned daily on every city street in America. There was no real safety and there never would be—not even on Cavanaugh Street.

Old George piled onto the bench and Hannah came after him, shoving Gregor all the way to the window, so that his arm was pressed against the glass. Sheila got in on the other side of the booth next to Bennis, shrugging her mink coat off her shoulders and letting it spread out around her. Bennis kept looking at the coat, as if she wanted to touch it, but was afraid to.

"Guess what I heard," Sheila announced, waving frantically for Linda Melajian. "Helen Tevorakian's niece Marissa is going out with a Muslim, and now they both want to convert to Buddhism and get married in a temple in Salt Lake City."

Gregor thought Salt Lake City was where the Mormons were—but he let that go. Religion made his head ache, and Sheila Kashinian made it ache even worse. He wanted to go over and find out how Tibor was, but it was too early. It wouldn't have been, in the old days, but lately Tibor stayed up all night watching CNN. Gregor had a terrible feeling Tibor stayed up all night talking to himself, too, but he couldn't prove it.

I should have made the world safe when I had a chance, Gregor thought, and then flushed bright red. Had he ever thought anything quite so stupid before in all his life? He didn't think he had.

Linda Melajian held her Pyrex pot of coffee over his cup and raised her eyebrows, but Gregor shook his head.

The way this day was going, the last thing he needed was more caffeine.

2

Half an hour later, Gregor was standing in the small courtyard behind Holy Trinity Armenian Christian Church. He could see a light shining through the vines from Tibor's front window. That, he knew, would be the light in the foyer. Tibor must have gone to bed without doing his usual spot check of the house. Maybe Tibor hadn't gone to bed at all. Gregor could just imagine how it had been: the darkened living room full of books; the television flickering; the icons propped up on the bookshelves and the fireplace mantel, looking down on it all in that blind wall-eyed way all icons seemed to have.

Gregor shook his head. The sun was hot and hard, even though it was still low on the horizon. He could hear faint sounds of traffic in the distance. He was still right in the middle of the city of Philadelphia, even though it didn't look like it here. He walked up to Tibor's front door and knocked. There was no answer. He knocked again. When there was no answer a second time, he got his keys out of his pocket and searched through them for the big clunky old-fashioned one that fit Tibor's door. He kept telling Tibor how important it was to get some kind of modern security put in. At the very least, in the middle of the city like this, Tibor ought to have a deadbolt and a chain. On matters of security, however, nobody on Cavanaugh Street listened to Gregor Demarkian. He was only the man who was supposed to be the expert.

He shouldn't have worried about Tibor sitting alone in the dark. It wasn't only the foyer light that was on. Through the archway, Gregor could see all four lamps in the living room, all lit. He could see the television, too. That wasn't lit. He moved carefully through the apartment, holding himself in so that he wouldn't brush against anything. He was a big man, six four and carrying more than twenty extra pounds. The halls in Tibor's apartment were narrow and their walls were lined to the ceilings with paperback books. Aristotle's *On Nature,* in the original Greek. Mickey Spillane's *The Body Lovers.* The new *Cathechism of the Catholic Church,* in the Vatican edition, in Latin. Judith Krantz's *Scruples.* Here and there, Gregor found a lightweight book club edition of something or other, mostly steamy sex novels of the throwaway variety. Bennis had given Tibor a membership in the Literary Guild for his birthday.

The living room was empty. The seats of the chairs were all full of books, as usual. The books had dust on them, which they never used to do, before Oklahoma City. Gregor went to the television set and ran his hand along the top of it. That was thick with dust, too. Tibor was supposed to have a housekeeper who came in every couple of weeks or so—the church paid for one—but either she didn't come or she'd given up trying to make the apartment livable. Tibor being Tibor, he probably sat her down at the kitchen table with a cup of coffee, got her to talk about all the problems she had ever had in her life, and never let her get any work done at all.

Gregor opened the door to the kitchen and looked in. The lights were all on in there, too, both the overhead and the small ones built in under the cabinets to make it easier to work at the counters. The kitchen table was covered with books, except in one small corner, which had a plate and fork on it, both clean. The sink was clean of dirty dishes, too. There was a straw basket full of apples on the counter next to the stove. The apples looked new and shiny. The basket looked full, as if it had been delivered as a gift and not touched since. Gregor took a deep breath and counted to ten.

"Tibor?" Gregor said finally.

There was a grunt from the direction of the pantry. Gregor had to make himself take a deep breath again. He didn't know what was wrong with him these days. He was always imagining disasters—and he had never been like that, never, not even in the worst of Elizabeth's dying. Now he was imagining Tibor flat on the pantry floor, out cold, the victim of a stroke or a heart attack. Gregor was a much better candidate for either than Tibor would ever be. Still, Gregor could see it. The dark pantry. The shelves of canned corn and sacks of flour. The smell of carrots and potatoes, still not washed clean of the dirt they grew in.

"Tibor?" Gregor said again.

"I am coming," Tibor said again, in a perfectly clear and normal voice.

Gregor felt himself blushing for the tenth time that morning. He went over to the pantry and looked in. There was an overhead light, and it was on. There was also a clip-on extension lamp on the table Tibor had set up to work on, the only table in the house that was not so thoroughly covered with books as to be unusable for any other purpose. What this one had on it was a brand-new IBM PC with a four-color display screen and a host of attachments Gregor couldn't begin to comprehend. Tibor was tapping away and humming a little under his breath. He had a Sony Walkman plugged into one ear. The other earplug was dangling, and through it Gregor could hear the thin sounds of Gregorian chant. He looked at the display screen again. He didn't know much about computers—in fact, he didn't know anything; he had been very, very happy to retire from his job before everybody at the Bureau had been required to know how to run one—but he knew expensive when he saw it, and this was very, very expensive.

"Where did this come from?" he asked Tibor.

Tibor took the headphone off his head and laid it down next to the keyboard. "Bennis got it for me. It's much easier to use than the one in the church office, Krekor. I have no problems with this one at all."

"That's good. What are you doing with it?"

Tibor pointed at the screen. "There are things called bulletin boards, Krekor. And discussions. People from all over the world share information. Even people from places like China, where they aren't supposed to. It's a wonderful thing."

"I'm sure it is. What are you sharing information about?"

"Sometimes I talk to people about religion. There is something called CR NET. It is for traditional believing Catholics who want to know more about the Church. I talk on that sometimes."

"And?"

"There's a thing called Dorothy L. It's about mystery stories. Sometimes I talk to people on that, too."

"And?"

Tibor looked down at the screen again. It was glowing, just like computer screens glowed in science fiction movies. Under the harsh light of the overhead, it looked too oddly, too intensely blue. Tibor looked enormously tired. He was a small man, wiry and much too thin. Years of living badly fed and badly treated had taken their toll on him. Gregor could see the lines in the sides of his face, deep and straight, and the white-skinned scars that wove their way through them. Tibor's face always looked, to Gregor, as if it should hurt him. Tibor's body always looked as if it had been wrung out like a piece of laundry by a giant's hand, and never quite unwound again.

"Who else do you communicate with on that thing?" Gregor asked again.

Tibor's shoulders gave a mighty shrug. "Yes, yes," he said. "There are here other people who are interested in the bombing. That is the case. I know you don't approve of it, Krekor."

"I don't think it's good for you."

"I don't think it's good for anybody, Krekor. How could a thing like this be good for anybody?"

"That's not what I meant."

"Yes, I know. I know. It isn't what you think, though, Krekor. It is not an unhealthy obsession."

"There was a week back in May where you didn't eat for three days straight. At least."

"That was back in May. I will admit, Krekor, when it first happened, I was distraught. I had reason to be distraught."

"You were nuts."

"But that was a long time ago, Krekor. I'm not like that now. I'm just . . . interested."

"Did you get any sleep last night?"

"Yes, Krekor. Of course I got to sleep."

"In your own bed?"

"I fell asleep on the couch. I was reading something. I often fall asleep on the couch, Krekor. I was doing that long before there was a bomb in Oklahoma City."

"What were you reading?"

Tibor's arms fluttered in the air. "It was only a periodical, Krekor. It was nothing important."

"It was about the bombing. Or about the militias. Or something. You were at it again."

Tibor tapped something into the keyboard, then stood up. A small white marker began to pulse in the lower left-hand corner of the screen.

"I think you make too much of this," he said. "You worry about me without need. I am concerned, yes, I am worried, but so are a lot of people. It isn't anything strange. It's you who are beginning to be strange."

"Why?" Gregor asked. "Because I care about what happens to you?"

"I am going to make some coffee now, Krekor. You should sit down with me and have some. And I have some *yaprak sarma* in the refrigerator that we could heat up in the microwave. Hannah Krekorian brought it over last night. You should relax a little, Krekor. It is you who are beginning to be distraught."

"I came to ask you to go someplace with me," Gregor said. "To North Carolina. I've been asked on a case."

"You've been asked on a case? And you want me to go with you?"

"That's right. There's a lot of religion in it. The case, I mean. I thought you could be a kind of expert witness."

Tibor swayed back and forth on his legs. "You never want any of us to go with you on a case. You never consider it safe. Why do you want me to go with you now?"

"I thought it would take your mind off—all this," Gregor said. "I thought the change of pace would be good for you."

"Krekor, if I want a change of pace, I will go to the Bahamas with Lida. When are you supposed to leave for this case?"

"Tomorrow."

"Tomorrow," Tibor said. "Krekor, I am responsible for the church here. For the services on Sunday. For baptisms and funerals. For weddings and religious instruction. I can't just pick up tomorrow and go off. I would have to make arrangements."

"You've done it before. It's not that hard to make arrangements."

"On less than one day's notice, it's impossible. Krekor, Krekor, you are not making any sense. You have not made any sense for weeks. It is you I think who needs to see the doctor."

"Don't be ridiculous," Gregor said.

Tibor grunted. "I will go now and make something to

eat. I will make you at least a cup of coffee. I am being serious when I say I think you should see a doctor, Krekor. I do not think you have been very well for weeks. I have been worried about it.''

''*You've* been worried about it,'' Gregor said.

But Tibor was gone. Gregor could hear him in the kitchen, rummaging around in the books and the utensils. There was that breathless rush that meant that the gas on one of the gas burners had been lit. It hadn't occurred to Gregor that Tibor would refuse to come with him to North Carolina. What was he supposed to do now?

Crash. Splatter. Whoosh. Tibor was making coffee. Tibor was making coffee so awful, no human being would be able to drink it, although Tibor would. Tibor could do this even with instant coffee. Gregor wasn't sure how.

Gregor looked down at the computer screen. The pulsing white in the lower left-hand corner of the screen said *downloading*. The machine was making absolutely no sound at all.

I'm perfectly fine, Gregor told himself. I haven't felt this well for years.

He rubbed the back of his neck reflexively and stretched. He was tense, but he was sure it was just that he was so worried about Tibor. He was jumpy, but that was worry about Tibor, too.

If he had been having nightmares lately, full-scale and out of control—well, there was nobody in the world who knew about that but him, and nobody who was going to.

two

1

It wasn't easy to get to Bellerton. There was an Amtrak train to Raleigh—making it unnecessary for Gregor to fly—but after that you were on your own. There were dozens of numbered highways on the map, two-lane blacktops, probably. They were useless if you didn't drive, which Gregor didn't. There were dozens of little towns, too. Some of them had names like Hendersonville and Cary and appeared on the map in bold black type. Others had names like Sallow Bridge and Lee Hollow. Were there really places with names like that? Gregor Demarkian was an urban man. He was so urban, in fact, that he had spent almost none of his time in the Federal Bureau of Investigation working in the South. The South was traditional seasoning territory for new special agents, too—or it had been, in those days. There had been a lot of prejudice back in the days when Gregor had first joined the Bureau. You were supposed to be Anglo and Protestant, a "real American," to qualify. There he had been, huge and hulking, with his odd name and his college degrees. He still had a strongly physical sense of what it had been like to sit in J. Edgar Hoover's office on the afternoon of his final interview. He could still see the two special agents who had brought him into the Great Man's presence. The agents were tall and slim in that maddening North European way. Even their bones were elongated and fine. Hoover was something else again. Gregor had known immediately that the man was a raving psychopath. The odd thing was that nobody else seemed to know it. The two special agents had kept their eyes trained on a point somewhere behind old J. Edgar's head. Gregor had kept his hands folded in his lap, hoping nobody would see how badly his palms were sweating. At that moment, he had wanted to be a special agent more desperately than he had ever wanted anything in his life. He was scared to death that that crazy old man would take it away from him.

Gregor was sitting in first class on the Amtrak train—why, he didn't know. Normally, he didn't like to go to that extra expense, even though he could afford it. First class was almost deserted. There was an old woman with a powder blue cardigan over her shoulders playing solitaire on her tray table. There were two very young women, dressed up in leather that had been studded with metal things. Gregor had both seats in his row to himself. He had the empty seat on the aisle filled with books and papers. Every once in a while he would look at it, annoyed and vaguely upset, and realize he was expecting to see Tibor in it. He had been hatching the plan to take Tibor with him to North Carolina ever since David Sandler's second letter arrived. Now he felt bottled up and frustrated. It wasn't just that Tibor wasn't here, when he ought to be. It was that Gregor himself needed somebody to talk to. He had all these maps and clippings that David had sent him, and these books on abnormal psychology and child abuse he had bought at the University of Pennsylvania bookstore. He had a book called *The Myths of Motherhood: How Culture Reinvents the Good Mother,* by Shari L. Thurer, which he thought was going to tell him how mothers felt about their children, but didn't, quite. He had no idea why he was going to such great lengths to do research for a case he was sure would end up being open-and-shut. He didn't know why he kept looking out the train window and thinking how flat everything was. When his wife was still alive, he had let her drive them down to Florida every couple of years or so, for what was supposed to be a vacation. He had always been able to tell exactly when they had crossed the state line from Virginia into North Carolina. The land seemed to flatten out. The air seemed to change color. The houses on the side of the road definitely got poorer and more rickety and more forlorn. There hadn't been many houses like that this time, Gregor had noticed, although there had been one or two. These days what appeared on the roadsides were small brick ranches with curving front windows. He supposed that was an improvement. Had things improved down here, since the days when he had prayed not to be assigned here because he didn't want to have to deal with racial problems and running guns? Bible thumping and ATF agents. Backyard stills and really murderous hate. Gregor didn't have a wonderful vision of the American South. Still, he thought, this was said to be the up and coming place. People were moving down here in droves. Surely they wouldn't do that if the South were as awful and backward a place as he had always assumed it to be. That was the problem with getting what you knew about something from television, especially television that was twenty years out of date. He could still see the dogs and the Federal marshals in Birmingham, George Wallace in his wheelchair, old Strom Thurmond switching parties so he wouldn't have to be in the one that was hell-bent on helping the . . . Negroes.

Gregor looked down at the mess he had made in the seat next to him. The map was spread out across most of it, green and blue and red, showing the route Interstate 95 took south from Richmond. Gregor stood up and brushed past it all into the aisle. He was so big, the aisle felt too narrow, although it wasn't. The ceiling was definitely too low. There was a bar and snack stand one car back. Gregor headed for that, even though he wasn't hungry. None of his thoughts would settle into a pattern. At the coupling between cars, the doors felt too heavy for him. He was so used to being a big man with powerful muscles, he was surprised.

The problem with this little favor he had promised to

do for David Sandler, Gregor realized, was that he hadn't taken it seriously even yet. His picture of the South was so firmly fixed in his mind, he kept expecting the whole thing to turn out like a *Beverly Hillbillies* episode. Virginia Marsh would turn out to be itching to run off with her husband's brother. The baby would turn out to have been the product of incest between Virginia and her own brother. The whole thing would blow up and land on *Sally Jessy Raphael,* which he would watch in stupefied amazement, unable to understand how anybody could be this dumb.

There was a drunk in the car, but Gregor ignored him. He was a drunk with a Yankee accent, which at least did nothing to excite Gregor's prejudices. He asked for a diet Coke and paid nearly two dollars for it. He looked out the window behind the bartender's head and saw rolling flatlands, as gentle as the waves on the surface of the water in a protected inland. Everything was green and bright and warm. True fall hadn't come to North Carolina yet. The cars on the road all seemed to be very new and bought from Ford.

"Raleigh coming up," the bartender said suddenly. It was as if one of the figures in a wax museum had started talking.

"Excuse me?" Gregor said.

"Raleigh coming up," the bartender repeated. He had a soft southern drawl, like the ones Gregor had rarely heard outside the movies. "It'll be less than five minutes. I'd go back to my seat if I had any luggage."

"Oh," Gregor said. "Yes. Thank you."

"They're going to cut this run, did you know that?" the bartender said. "The Republicans. Everybody votes Republican down here these days. My granddad would have died first. You a Republican?"

"I'm not an anything," Gregor said, thinking that right now he would sooner admit to being an extraterrestrial.

The bartender was cleaning his counter with a rag. The drunk had gone to sleep.

"What I notice," the bartender said, "these days, everybody up North is a Democrat, and everybody down here is a Republican. Opposite of what it used to be. You see what I mean?"

"I think so."

"It's the fault of the liberals," the bartender said solemnly. "The liberals ruined the Democratic party. It was much better when it was full of people like us."

"I think I'd better go back to my seat," Gregor said. "I think I'd better pack up my books and get ready to go."

"Nobody down here would vote for Jesse Helms if there was a decent Democrat running," the bartender said. "I don't think there's been a decent Democrat running since Harry Truman."

The bartender didn't look like he was much more than twenty-five years old. How much could he possibly know about Harry Truman?

"Yes," Gregor said, backing up. "Well."

He turned around and headed for the coupling of the cars, hurrying. There were windows open in the bar car. He could feel the warm outside air fighting against the frigidity of the air-conditioning. The drunk was snoring next to his beer. Gregor went through the coupling and back into first class. The woman who had been playing solitaire had packed up her cards. She was now half-curled in her seat, reading a book called *How to Have a Wonderful Sex Life at Any Age at All.*

Gregor scooped up his maps and his books and his newspaper clippings and sat down in the aisle seat. The train had begun to shudder and rattle, the way trains did when the tracks under their wheels got complicated. Outside, Gregor could see the start of a small industrial center, the smokestacks and metal-sided buildings, the warehouses and big flat parking lots full of heavy trucks. Gregor got his briefcase off the floor and stuffed the mess into it. Then he got the still unopened diet Coke out of his pocket and decided he didn't want to drink it after all.

Really, Gregor thought. I don't know anything at all

about the New South. I don't know anything at all about North Carolina. It's not only wrong to judge by stereotypes, it's stupid, especially when you're involved in a murder case.

Out beyond the tracks, the warehouses gave way to billboards. Some of them advertised HBO and termite extermination services. More of them advertised cigarettes and Jesus Christ. It was as if the only way to save your soul was to die of lung cancer while praying.

I *have to stop this,* Gregor told himself.

Then he stood up and began to get his luggage down off the overhead rack. The train was swaying so much, he nearly fell twice.

Out on the tracks, a billboard with Jesse Helms's face on it appeared out of nowhere, fat and round and big enough to swallow Detroit.

2

The first thing Gregor noticed about North Carolina was that the women there dressed in brighter colors than the women in Philadelphia. Where train stations in Philly were full of brown and black and beige, this one was overrun with pastels and primaries. Gregor saw a woman in a lemon yellow suit and lemon yellow shoes, and another in a dress that must have been fuchsia. She had fuchsia shoes on, too. Then there was the hair, and the makeup. Bennis Hannaford went weeks without wearing makeup. Gregor didn't think Donna Moradanyan had ever worn any makeup at all. These women all seemed to have eye shadow coordinated with their nail polish—and their nail polish wasn't chipped, either. How did women learn to do things like this to themselves? What did it mean that they did? Gregor threaded his way carefully through them, realizing, after a while, that he had started to be much more polite, and much more tentative, than he usually was around women. Maybe that was supposed to be the point, but he didn't think Bennis Hannaford's thoroughly feminist soul would like it any.

David Sandler was waiting for him at the place where the platforms spilled their passengers into the main concourse. It wasn't much of a concourse, not like the one in Philadelphia, but it was bright and clean and cheerful. Even David Sandler was cheerful. Gregor was used to him in his Columbia University professor mode: tweed jackets, dark ties, dark slacks, black leather shoes. This David Sandler was wearing a pair of battered-looking chinos and a bright orange T-shirt. He was carrying a sky blue windbreaker in his hands. Obviously, Gregor thought, whatever it was about colors that had infected the female half of the North Carolina population had infected the male half just as much.

Gregor excused himself to a young woman in a green-and-white-striped skirt and three miles of curling dark hair and waved to David Sandler with the hand he was holding the briefcase in. David held out his own hand and captured the briefcase.

"There you are," he said to Gregor. "I didn't recognize you. You look depressed as hell."

"Thanks a lot," Gregor said.

"I'm the one who's supposed to be depressed as hell," David said. "I guess I am, most of the time. But it was a good ride up here. North Carolina is a beautiful place."

They were headed out of the terminal into the parking lot. All Gregor could see were cars and billboards.

"Is Bellerton far from here?" he asked. "I tried to look it up on the map, but all I got was confused. You get down to the coast and it looks like you run out of road."

"You do, sort of. Bellerton's not on any kind of main thoroughfare. It's on the water."

"I know that, David."

"Yeah, well. There are advantages to being out of the way like that. Things you wouldn't necessarily think about. Like drugs."

"Drugs?"

"Right." David was leading them across the parking lot, threading them through cars and pickup trucks. "The two big drug routes on this side of the country are 95 and 301. Anyplace with access to either of those highways tends to be absolutely full of dope. Why not? You're going to run a shipment up to New York, you might as well stop off in a few small towns on the way and make a fast buck or two. Drugs."

"And Bellerton doesn't have drugs," Gregor said carefully.

David snorted. "Of course Bellerton has drugs, Gregor. Two-bit elementary schools in Montana have drugs these days. Bellerton doesn't have as many drugs as, say, Raleigh itself. Or Chapel Hill. Anyway," David said, "it isn't only the drugs. It's the tourists. We get tourists. We get a lot of tourists. I started out down here as a tourist. The thing is, we don't get the kind of crowds you get in places like Hatteras. It's quieter that way."

Gregor thought of all the clippings in his briefcase. "I wouldn't think it was very quiet now. With the Oklahoma City thing on hold for the moment and nothing new happening to O.J., you people seem to be the biggest game in town."

"I know. I find myself wishing that something awful would happen to somebody else, so I wouldn't have to watch the media invade Rose's gift shop anymore. But there you are."

"Is Rose one of the people I'm supposed to meet?"

"You'll have to meet everybody," David said. "Small towns are like that. And this small town is an absolute hotbed. It makes *Peyton Place* read like children's literature."

"You didn't put any of that in your letters."

"I didn't want to. Christ, Gregor—and I use the word 'Christ' advisedly—you wouldn't believe the kind of thing that goes on. Even I didn't know about most of it until all this happened and people started talking to me."

"I would believe it," Gregor said. "But what kind of thing are you talking about? Sex?"

"Of course I'm not talking about sex. Sex would be normal."

"Sex isn't always normal."

"In Bellerton, sex isn't always sex," David said. "But it isn't sex I'm talking about. It's religion."

"Do you mean cult religion? Like these devil worshippers the Raleigh paper is always talking about?"

"I mean religion, Gregor. Plain old ordinary religion. Christianity, just like we all grew up with, except people who are lucky, like Zhondra Meyer, who grew up as Jews."

"I think there are several hundred thousand Moslems in the country now," Gregor said, straight-faced.

David Sandler stopped dead in his tracks. "Gregor, listen. I have spent my life campaigning against religion. I don't believe in God. I do believe that most of the worst things that have happened to the human race have been the result of believing in a God who isn't there, because there isn't any God anywhere and we all know it if we're honest with ourselves. I've written articles full of scare stories about the religious right and felt I was doing the right thing. But do you know what, Gregor? I thought I was exaggerating. I thought I was *exaggerating*."

"And?"

"And I wasn't. Hell, I was understating the case. I'm telling you. You absolutely won't believe what's going on down here. You couldn't have the faintest idea. This is the car," David said.

David put his hand down on the hood of a purple Ford pickup truck. Gregor felt the bottom drop out of his stomach. The bed at the back of the truck was filled with lumber and fertilizer. Gregor didn't think he had ever ridden in a pickup truck before.

"Where's your car?" he asked David, trying not to sound panicked. "You don't drive this thing in New York."

"I don't drive anything in New York. I can't get insurance I can afford. I've got a regular car down in Bellerton, Gregor, but I had some things I had to pick up. You're not worried about riding in a truck, are you?''

Gregor was silent.

David got his keys out of his chinos. "I've got one of those Darwin magnets for the back of this thing, but I took it off to come up and get you. They're always telling you how suffocating and intolerant small towns are, Gregor, but I tell you, I'd much rather be driving around with that thing on my car in Bellerton than here. No Christian Nazis in Bellerton.''

Gregor didn't think David should call anybody a "Christian Nazi" while he was standing in the middle of a parking lot in the Bible Belt. Gregor put his foot up on the silver steel footboard and tried to haul himself up. It didn't quite work. David took the luggage.

"You've got to grab on with your hands and pull," David said. Then, instead of helping Gregor in, he went around the front of the truck and got in himself.

Gregor grabbed onto the sides of the doorway and pulled. He tried to remember what it had been like to climb into a tank when he was in the army, but he had only done that once, and the experience wouldn't come back to him.

"You all right?" David asked him.

Gregor knew David didn't really want an answer. The truck's engine was already humming. Gregor leaned halfway out of the cab and slammed his door shut, and as soon as he did the truck began to back out of its parking space. Gregor fumbled frantically for his seat belt. The sides were tangled up in each other.

"It's a nice ride down to Bellerton." David spoke over the roar of what Gregor thought must be a defective muffler. "You wait and see. I'm going to move down here permanently when I'm ready to retire.''

Like talking about "Christian Nazis" in the parking lot, Gregor thought this was probably a bad idea. City boys did not move easily into the country. Gregor knew that from his own experience. David was something more exotic than a simple city boy, too. He was a true intellectual, one of the last in existence. Heresy was a necessary ingredient in the very air he breathed.

They were out of the parking lot now and bumping along an in-town potholed back road. The road was lined with billboards, almost all of them about cigarettes. The Marlboro Man had taken up residence right next door to Joe Camel. In the distance, Gregor could see crosses lit up with neon, glowing red even in the clear light of day.

"I don't know," he told David Sandler. "Somehow, this wasn't the way I'd imagined you'd want to retire."

3

Actually, it got more and more like a place Gregor could imagine David retiring to the farther and farther they got from the Raleigh–Durham–Chapel Hill triangle. Commercial buildings and tightly packed housing developments gave way to open country. Closely crowded billboards gave way to well-spaced ones that appeared like surprises in a birthday cracker along the sides of the road. There was something comforting about the gentle flatness of it all, and the temperature that was neither too hot nor too cold, and the breeze that blew in through the windows of the truck, never too sharp or grating or strong. What was really surprising was the utter emptiness of it all. Sometimes the billboards were the only signs of life for miles. What houses there were were few and far between and very small. Gregor never saw any people in them. There were very few other cars on the road, too, and those there were all had out-of-state license plates. This was one of the main routes to Orlando and Disney World. People came through with their car packed solid and their children crying in the backseat.

After about twenty minutes, David turned off the main road onto a two-lane blacktop. Gregor looked right and left and saw, finally, the South he remembered from so many years ago. There were a few of those solid-looking new brick ranch houses he had seen from the train, but there were also the wooden shacks with their swaybacked roofs and their sagging porches, the washes hung out on lines, the cars missing tires in the side yards. Every once in a while, he saw children, but not many of them. It was the middle of a fall day. The children would be in school. Every once in a while, he saw an old person, sitting on a porch step. These old people were almost always male. David leaned forward and turned the truck's radio on to a country station. A singer Gregor didn't know was singing something apparently called "Pickup Man."

"I was beginning to think all that about the New South was true," Gregor said. "This certainly looks like the old South to me."

"All that stuff about the New South is true," David said. "It's just that it applies where it applies and it doesn't apply where it doesn't apply. I doubt if half the people who work in the Research Triangle even know all this stuff is here."

"Don't they have to drive through it every once in a while?"

David shrugged. "Maybe. They probably just don't pay attention. Why should they? Take a good look at it, Gregor. This is the real dung heap of history. All that high-tech stuff in Raleigh is the future."

"If that's really true, I'm not going to qualify for the future," Gregor said. "Is Bellerton like this?"

"This poor, you mean? No. It never was. It was turned into a kind of resort by old Meyer the Robber Baron, if you know who I mean. It's always been a kind of upscale stopping point for weary society people. That's how we ended up with Zhondra Meyer and her women's retreat. Which is what started all this, as far as I can tell."

"Zhondra Meyer is the woman who runs a camp for lesbians," Gregor said, trying to make certain he had it all sorted out in his head.

David made an exasperated gesture in the air. "She's

playing radical hostess to a bunch of women who are more sinned against than sinning, if you know what I mean. I mean, some of them may actually be lesbians in the classic sense, by which I mean they were born with a sexual orientation in that direction, but most of them are just worn out. Their husbands beat them or threw them out. Their children have no respect for them. They don't have much education and they haven't got much in the way of employment records. Stray cats.''

''And Zhondra Meyer collects stray cats?''

''Something like that. I think it makes her feel good about herself, which is what everybody's after in life these days.''

''Do these stray cats actually practice Satanic rituals?''

David Sandler blew a raspberry. ''Gregor, the stray cats are a bunch of weary-looking middle-aged women who wouldn't know a Satanic ritual from a coconut custard pie. They're perfectly harmless. If Zhondra Meyer hadn't gone around telling anybody that she was making a 'safe place for gay women'—which is what she said on the radio when she first opened up the place—there wouldn't be all this nonsense going on now. The problem with Zhondra Meyer is that she not only wants to do good, she wants to let everybody know she's doing good, and get them all upset about it. Don't let all the hype and hoopla take you in, Gregor.''

''No,'' Gregor said. ''Of course. I wouldn't.''

Still, he thought, a woman who not only wanted to do good but wanted to get other people upset about it was not what he would call harmless.

three

1

When Rose MacNeill first heard that Gregor Demarkian was coming to Bellerton, she did absolutely nothing about it. That was right after the hurricane, when there was so much to do and all that trouble with Ginny Marsh on top of it—not that that trouble with Ginny Marsh had ever eneded, not to this very day, because it hadn't. Rose MacNeill hadn't known the baby, Tiffany, and for that reason she had a hard time thinking of it as real. When she tried to focus on Tiffany, what she saw was a package in a harness on Ginny, with no eyes or nose or mouth to distinguish it. She got a much better picture in her mind of Zhondra Meyer, and what Zhondra must have looked like when the baby was discovered dead. She could have seen Zhondra's face at the time, since she was up at the camp getting out of the storm herself, but she had been otherwise occupied. It was the storm Rose really fixated on, no matter how hard she tried to think of other things. Rose had been in hurricanes before, but never anything like Elsa. She had come roaring in on them all at once, all wind and water and battering debris. Rose remembered standing in the doorway of her shop and watching the wind slice the roof right off of Lisa Cameron's house on Ellerver Street, and that was before the real trouble started. That was at the very beginning, when Rose had decided that going to the high school wouldn't be enough. She would have to get to even higher ground. The wind was battering against the windows of the shop, making them rattle. The rose petal stained glass window in the pantry hall shook itself to pieces. All along Main Street, the power lines were down. Telephone poles were snapped and twisted and hanging sideways. The thin black cables for the cable TV were ripped off the sides of houses and twisted into snakelike coiling heaps on the ground. All the people had disappeared—and that, Rose had found to her surprise, was a wonderful thing. There was something truly magical about Bellerton with no people in it.

The second time Rose MacNeill heard that Gregor Demarkian was coming to Bellerton, she was standing in Charlie Hare's feed store, buying a packet of seed for the basil she liked to grow in pots on the ledge over her kitchen sink—and then it struck her. By then it was all over, theoretically. The plywood had come off the windows of the stores on Main Street. Maggie Kelleher had even put out a little display stand full of paperback books, horror novels with cutout covers and silver foil letters and pictures of the Devil glaring through fiery eye sockets that had nothing in them but flames. Still, there was no way to ignore the fact that Something Had Happened, the Something at the time being represented not by the debris still scattered over Main Street itself or the number of houses without roofs that could be seen by standing on the front steps of the library, but by the CBS News truck parked in front of Town Hall. Something had happened, all right, and that something was Ginny Marsh and her dead baby and what might or might not have gone on up at the camp while the storm was going on everywhere else.

"It was David Sandler's idea," Charlie Hare told her, as he put her seed packet into a small brown paper bag. Rose's mother used to put her school lunches in paper bags just like that one, when Rose was in elementary school. "Sandler knew him from somewhere. Clayton Hall says it's okay for him to be here, too, because with a case like this, it's good to look like you're doing everything you can."

"Oh, yes," Rose said. "I suppose it would be. Why is the name so familiar to me?"

"It's familiar because it's in *People* magazine all the time," Charlie said. "The Armenian-American Hercule Poirot. That one."

Something went *click* in the inner recesses of Rose MacNeill's brain. She looked down at the paper bag with the seed packet in it and caught her hands instead, long-fingered and beginning to go rough.

"The thing is," Charlie continued, "what's got a lot of people worried, is that if Sandler is an atheist, maybe this Demarkian is an atheist, too. And it's like Henry Holborn is always saying. You don't want an atheist mixed up in a case like this."

"What?" Rose said.

Charlie's face went round and bloated with self-satisfaction. The little gold cross he wore on a chain around his neck gleamed in the light from the fluorescent patch above his head. "Atheists don't believe in God, do they?" he asked her. "And because atheists don't believe in God, they've got no resources against the Devil. And you have to admit it, Rose, no matter what you think about religion. The Devil is what we've got here, one way or another. The Devil pure and simple."

Rose snatched the paper bag out of Charlie's hand. "Don't be ridiculous," she snapped. "And don't you go around talking like that, either, Charlie Hare. It could cause a lot of trouble."

"We've already got a lot of trouble. We've got a baby dead. We've got a baby with its throat slit and its skin carved up. That's what the paper said that came down from Raleigh."

"You shouldn't believe everything you read in the paper," Rose snapped. "And you shouldn't believe everything Henry Holborn tells you, either, that old snake oil salesman. He's just like one of those preachers my grandma used to go to hear, and your grandma, too, if you're honest about it, and you know it."

"There's nothing to be said against the way my grandma practiced her religion," Charlie said stiffly. "She was a good woman. She was a holy woman by the time she died. They knew how to give their lives to the Lord in those days."

"All Henry Holborn knows how to give to is himself. He's been stirring up trouble against that camp since the day it opened, and you know why? Because it scares the pants off the local yokels, that's why. Half of them don't know what a lesbian is and the other half would just as soon try it. And as soon as Henry has them all worked up, they just dump their paychecks in his lap."

"Henry Holborn is a man of God," Charlie said, even more stiffly. "You ought to watch yourself, Rose MacNeill. You ought to get yourself born again. The way you're going these days, you're going to end up in the arms of the Devil yourself."

"You're going to end up in the asylum," Rose said furiously. "What's gotten into everybody these days? People used to know better."

"People used to worship God and obey His commandments," Charlie said, "and now they don't anymore. You ought to do some listening instead of talking someday, Rose. We're living in the End Times. Henry Holborn's been saying so for years. We're living in the End Times and God is calling us all to choose up sides."

Rose's head had started to throb. "If we're living in the End Times, I won't need a packet of basil seeds," she said, throwing the paper bag down on the counter in front of Charlie. "The Rapture's likely to start and lift me up into Heaven when I'm in the middle of planting."

"The Rapture's not likely to lift *you* up anywhere," Charlie said.

"The Rapture's more likely to lift me up than the Devil is to appear up at Zhondra Meyer's camp," Rose spat out—and then she couldn't take it anymore, she just couldn't. She left her seeds on Charlie's counter, turned on her high stiletto heels, and marched back onto Main Street.

The air was muggy and thick with water. The street was full of strangers—not just CBS News, but all the rest of them. NBC. ABC. CNN. Writers for papers as far away as San Francisco and Portland. All of this, because of Ginny Marsh and her silly story, her evil story, her—

Rose marched back down Main Street to the big Victorian house and let herself in the side door. She could hear Kathi Nelson in the front room, waiting on a customer. The customer had a funny voice, like a tourist's. Since there weren't any tourists in Bellerton this time of year, Rose presumed the voice belonged to one of the media people. Rose went into the kitchen and sat down at the little table in the corner where she had her computer set up. There were people who seemed to be resisting the information age with every cell in their bodies, but Rose wasn't one of them. She'd gotten herself on the Internet within a week of the first time she ever heard of it, and by now she didn't know how she had ever lived without it.

"That will be twelve ninety-five," she heard Kathi Nelson say to somebody.

Rose poked her perfectly manicured, perfectly scarlet fingernails into her high pile of dark hair. Today she had stood in Charlie Hare's store and defended those lesbians up at that camp. That was what she had done. She had no idea why she had done it. Even right before the storm, she would have said she hated those people up there as thoroughly as she had ever hated anybody in her life. She still thought she did.

"Have a good day," she heard Kathi Nelson call out. Rose made a face, and the little strip of cowbells on the front door tinkled.

It was better when everybody said, "Y'all come back now, hear?"—except they didn't anymore, because ever since it had been on that commercial, everybody thought it was hick.

Rose tapped a series of input numbers on the keyboard, waited for the system to get into form, and wrote:

GREGOR DEMARKIAN
GLOBAL REQUEST

Then she sat back and waited to see what would happen. Usually, nothing did happen, not at once. It took at least half an hour, or sometimes more. This time she must have caught the system just as somebody useful was logging on to it. In no time at all, a blizzard of words appeared on her screen and her printer began to whirr.

Rose had expected that the information she got would be more or less along the lines of the information she'd heard—the Armenian-American Hercule Poirot; the darling of *People*—but instead what came up on the screen was all about the Federal Bureau of Investigation and serial killers. Rose MacNeill bit her lip.

Really, she thought. This might be more interesting than she'd thought it would be. This might be something she could get involved in, even if she couldn't make the baby be real to her, as real to her as Zhondra Meyer and the camp.

Lately, nothing seemed very real to her anyway, and her head always seemed to ache. She had always been a very religious woman. The store was full of religious things. She still wore her pin that said *Let Go and Let God.* She still believed that the Bible was the inerrant word of God and that evolution had never happened and that the problem with the children in the schools today was that they didn't pray enough. It was just that, since the storm, everything seemed to be mixed up.

The computer was whirring and pulsing. Rose's head was whirring and pulsing, too. She rubbed her eyes with her hands and reached for the printout that was beginning to pile up next to her printer. Before this was over, she would have pages and pages of words about Gregor Demarkian—and it would be much easier for her to think about that than to think again about all these other things.

2

For the first few days, Stephen Harrow had felt very, very important. He had been up there at the time, up at the camp, and he was known to be nothing more than an intelligent bystander. Newspeople wanted to interview him. He looked good standing in front of a camera, tweedy and academic, like a college professor. His long, thin face and narrow, elegant hands showed well on videotape. His eyes actually looked bluer on television than they were in real life. Stephen found it hard to convince himself that it was him up there, flickering and ghostly in the dark of the bedroom at eleven o'clock. He found himself wondering if this was what actors felt like when they saw themselves for the first time in the movies. Maybe everybody this happened to felt unreal and a little uneasy. Maybe everybody found it hard to distinguish between themselves and the picture on the screen.

Stephen wasn't sure when things had started to change, but he knew why they had changed, and that was enough: He was not a real celebrity, and David Sandler was. Worse than that, of course, was the fact that it was David Sandler who had come stumbling across a blood-spattered Ginny Marsh and gone off with her to find the baby. Stephen had been sitting at the table in the kitchen at the camp at the time, trying not to notice that the women around him wore much fewer clothes than the women he was used to. It wasn't that he was aroused by the show. He couldn't have been. They were ugly women up there at the camp, with the exception of Zhondra Meyer herself. Most of them didn't shave their legs, and none of them wore makeup. Their clothes were funny, too—boxy and made of synthetic fabrics; cheaply made and badly cut. Where Stephen came from, women paid attention to their appearance. Even the women who called themselves feminists had a great deal of interest in matters of style. These women had skin that hung limply away from their bones, that puckered and darkened in unexpected places. Stephen found it painful to look at them. Part of him kept insisting that it must hurt, physically, for women to be so unattractive. They had to have pain like arthritis in all of their joints. It pained him to look at them, and it embarrassed him, too.

Since the media people had stopped camping out on his doorstep, Stephen had begun to think he must know what those women had to live with. He felt blanked out, unreal, nonexistent. He paced back and forth in his study until Lisa came in and demanded that he stop. Pacing back and forth made the floorboards creak. She could hear the creak upstairs and it drove her crazy. Everything was driving Stephen crazy. When he tried to sleep, he got visions of what it had been like, in the middle of the storm. When he tried to make himself breakfast or work on a sermon or read a book, his eyes kept straying to the television set— but there was nothing on it anymore except David Sandler or one of the media people. Stephen had started to wonder if he shouldn't write a book.

There had been a little piece in the local paper that morning about the coming of Gregor Demarkian. Stephen had made himself read it very carefully, twice. Usually he read only the Raleigh paper. It was much more cosmopolitan and—sane—than the one put out here on Main Street. The Bellerton *Times* tended to go in heavily for articles about accepting Jesus. It also favored stories about miracle healings at tent meetings throughout the South. Cripples throwing away their crutches. Paraplegics leaping out of their wheelchairs and racing across the stage. Still, the *Times* had a story about Gregor Demarkian, and the Raleigh paper didn't, and the television news shows didn't, either. Maybe it wasn't true.

Lisa was out on the back porch, sitting in the glider. Stephen could see her, bent over one of those paperback romance books from Maggie Kelleher's store. Her hair was braided down the back of her neck. Her face looked like it belonged on one of those medieval Madonnas, narrow and stern.

Stephen folded the paper up so that it showed the article on Demarkian and nothing else. Then he got up and went to the porch door. The door creaked. Lisa didn't stop reading her book or turn around to look at him.

"Lisa?" Stephen said.

Lisa wagged a foot in the air. "I was wondering how long you were going to sit at that table. You never seem to do anything around here anymore."

"I was reading the paper."

"You've been reading the paper for two hours."

"There was something interesting in it. In the Bellerton paper. Not the *News and Observer*."

"Is it something about you?"

"No, it's not."

"Then I'm surprised you find it interesting."

Lisa was still staring down at her book. Stephen felt a pulse start at the base of his throat, that pulse of anger he got more and more these days, whenever he tried to talk to Lisa. He swallowed against it and walked around the glider until he was facing her. He held out the copy of the Bellerton *Times* and waited. When she still didn't look up, or make any move to take the paper, he shoved it across the top of her book and stepped back.

"Look at that," he said. "Will you please."

Lisa picked up the paper in her left hand and looked at it. "So?"

"That's Gregor Demarkian they're talking about, don't you see? The man who was involved in those murders in the exercise place up in Connecticut."

"I know who Gregor Demarkian is, Stephen. I read the same magazines that you do."

"Lisa, for God's sake. The Bellerton *Times* is saying that he's coming here. To Bellerton. To look into the Ginny Marsh thing."

"He *is* coming here," Lisa said. "Naomi Brent told me all about it. He's a friend of David Sandler's. David asked him to come down and Clayton Hall is ecstatic to have him, so he's supposed to be here any day now. Today, maybe. I can't remember."

"Couldn't you at least have told me about it?"

"Why?"

"Because it's important, for God's sake. It changes everything. I thought this would all blow over in time, you know, the media thing and—"

"You never thought the media thing would blow over," Lisa said flatly. "You thought you'd turned into a movie star."

"—but the way it is," Stephen went on stubbornly, "with Demarkian here, the story is going to get a brand-new lease on life. It's going to be everywhere. It's going to be places it's never been before."

"Stephen, there aren't any places it hasn't been. It's been worse than the Beatles arriving in the United States for the first time, and you know it. It's been a lot worse than the Susan Smith thing down in South Carolina."

Stephen looked away, off the porch and into the yard. The trees were heavy with green, even this late in the air. It was always so warm here. Winter meant what early fall would have back home. Spring meant a change in the atmosphere, not in the weather.

"Do you still think that that's what all this is about?" Stephen asked Lisa. "That it's like that Susan Smith thing? Do you still think Ginny killed the baby?"

"Yes, of course," Lisa said. "Everybody thinks it. Clayton Hall thinks it. He just can't go barging off arresting people before he has his evidence nailed down."

"You think she did all of it? Split the baby's throat and cut it up like that?"

"I think she had to make it look good," Lisa said. "If there's one thing we've all learned from Susan Smith, it's that half-assed stories only get you so far."

Stephen turned around to look at Lisa again. "But why would she do something like that? Why would anybody?"

Lisa pitched her romance novel onto the seat of the glider. "I expect there's a man in it somewhere. There usually is. Some man who's been talking trash to her and telling her he'd marry her if only she didn't have any living children.''

''You don't think Carol Littleton and all those women were up there worshipping the Devil?''

''I think they might have been worshipping the Devil, but I don't think it has anything to do with this. You wait and see. That's what they want Demarkian here for. Just like they got the FBI down in Union so the town cops didn't look too much like heavies, although I've got to say, the town cops down there took a lot more responsibility than Clayton Hall is taking here. But just you wait. They'll arrest Ginny sooner or later, and after that everybody will say that they knew all about it all along.''

''You don't like Ginny Marsh, do you?''

''I don't care about Ginny Marsh one way or the other.''

''Sometimes I think you don't like anybody at all,'' Stephen said. ''Not Ginny Marsh. Not Carol Littleton. Not Naomi Brent. Not me.''

Lisa laid her head back on the glider and stared up at the porch ceiling. ''Actually,'' she said, ''I think I'm having a crisis of faith. I think I've decided that God is dead. I'd talk to you about it, but you think God is dead, too. Do you ever wonder what it is you're doing, being the minister of a church?''

''Religion is more than a lot of fairy tales in an ancient book,'' Stephen said, as gently as he could. ''I thought we'd been over this. Bishop Spong says, in his book about the Resurrection—''

''Bishop Spong doesn't believe in the Resurrection,'' Lisa said. ''And neither do you.''

''Of course Bishop Spong believes in the Resurrection. And so do I. How can you say things like that?''

Lisa got to her feet in one fluid but violent motion. ''You don't believe it really happened, really really, like rain happens. You think it's some kind of symbol. You think *everything's* some kind of symbol. There weren't any wise men. There wasn't any Star of Bethlehem. There wasn't any virgin birth. Symbols, symbols, symbols.''

"Don't say you've started to believe in parthenogenesis at this late date.''

"I think I believe in honesty. I understand David Sandler. I understand Henry Holborn. You and Bishop Spong, I don't understand at all. I'm going to get some lunch.''

"Lisa, for God's sake. Aren't you going to tell me what this is all about?''

"No,'' Lisa said.

Any other woman would have started screaming at him then, but Lisa didn't. She just turned away from him and walked into the house, as if they'd been having a discussion about the refreshments she was going to serve at the Bible study meeting this week. Except that they couldn't have a discussion about that, because he'd canceled the Bible study meeting this week. He was too distracted, with everything that had been going on, and not many people came anymore anyway. In the last six weeks, Stephen had lost two-thirds of his Bible study group to the Bible study group Henry Holborn ran in that big barn of a church of his just outside of town.

Maybe I ought to start telling people I've been kidnapped by UFOs, Stephen thought—but that wouldn't help, that wouldn't get him back what he wanted, that wouldn't turn things around and make them what they had been before. Only one thing would do that, and he didn't know— quite yet—how to arrange for it.

3

From where she sat next to Clayton Hall's desk in the basement of Town Hall—official police headquarters for the Town of Bellerton; official interrogation room when the interrogating was being done by Clayton instead of by one of the men from the state—Ginny Marsh could see the

Carver sisters, two old ladies with fluffy hair, carrying big brown grocery bags full of stuff out of Rose MacNeill's store. The Carver sisters had a niece whose baby was being christened this weekend at the Episcopal Church. Ginny's church didn't believe in infant baptism, but Ginny liked the practice, with its white gown for the baby and its solemn ceremonials. Maybe if Tiffany had been baptized, Ginny wouldn't be feeling so very awful now. And she was feeling awful. She was feeling raw to the bone. The problem was that she couldn't get it out from inside her and make it show on her skin. Even Bobby was beginning to wonder if she hadn't killed the baby. Ginny knew that. They all wanted her to cry and carry on, to weep and wail and go insane. She just couldn't do it. Every time she thought she was about to get started, everything inside her would freeze. There she would be, sitting in front of all those cameras, grinning like she was having a wonderful time. It put her in mind of what the Reverend Holborn was always saying about being possessed by the Devil. Ginny surely thought she was being possessed by something. It had taken over her heart and started to eat her soul.

In the meantime, Tiffany was lying dead somewhere, buried in a funeral Ginny hadn't been allowed to see, and Clayton Hall was finding less and less to say, and those newspeople from New York and Chicago and Atlanta were camped out on Main Street, waiting for what they thought was the inevitable to happen. Because Ginny knew, of course. She knew that everybody thought she had murdered Tiffany and carved those marks on her body and then served her up like a pot roast, proof positive that the Devil was doing his dirty work at Zhondra Meyer's camp. Ginny, however, knew she had done no such thing.

Reverend Holborn was always saying that nobody could go to Heaven if he hadn't been baptized. Babies like Tiffany who died before they could accept Jesus Christ as their personal savior were full of corruption and original sin. They went to Hell like any other unbeliever. What Ginny had been trying to do over the last few weeks, whenever they let her alone long enough to let her think, was to try to talk herself out of believing this. She wanted to think of Tiffany in Heaven with God and the angels. She wanted to think of Tiffany wearing wings.

Mostly, though, she didn't want to think. She wanted to float. Pain was an ocean, warm water holding her up, holding her high over the heads of all these people who had never understood a thing. Pain was a tidal wave, and if they would just let her go, she would gladly drown in it.

Bobby kept talking about what they would do once all of this was over, but Ginny didn't believe this would ever be over. It would go on and on, on and on, on and on. There would never be anything called the future, and she would never be alive again.

four

1

Gregor Demarkian was twenty-five years old the first time he slept in a bed that didn't have a city surrounding it, twenty-five years old and finished with college and his first year of graduate school and newly inducted into the United States Army. Lying awake in the guest bedroom of David Sandler's small but spectacular post-and-beam beach house reminded Gregor very much of that first country bed. That one had been in the South, too, far away from here, in Alabama. The young men who slept around him had been younger than he was and less well educated. Those were the days when there were unspoken assumptions, in the U.S. military and the U.S. government and U.S. society at large, about who you were and who you could be based on what you had been born into and the kind of last name you wrote down on application forms. Most young men who had graduated from an Ivy League college and gone on to get a master's degree at Harvard were shuffled right into officers' training, or advised in the direction of the National Guard. Gregor was dumped right in with the farm boys and the juvenile delinquents from Queens. The first drill sergeant who saw him thought he was Jewish, and told him so, in language Gregor did his best not to remember. The U.S. Army, at the time, was not famous for its efforts against anti-Semitism, and that in spite of the fact that this was after World War II. The camp in Alabama had been flat and hot and clogged with Spanish moss. The campgrounds immediately around the barracks had been barren, but oddly so, as if it had been done deliberately. Up until that point, Gregor had either lived with his mother—his father was dead; his older brother was dead, too, killed at the end of World War II in a battle that probably should never have been fought—or in university dormitories, where there were people whose job it was to make him feel at home. It had never occurred to him that there were places where he would naturally not be at home. He had expected to be comfortable anywhere in the United States, and maybe in Armenia, too, although he had never been in Armenia. People on Cavanaugh Street in those days made a point of showing everyone how thoroughly American they were. Those were the days when Cavanaugh Street was poor. A big tenement had stood where Lida Arkmanian's town house was now. The apartments at the back of it had had no windows. A pawnshop had stood next door to where Ohanian's Middle Eastern Food Store was now—and had been then, for that matter—but in the pawnshop's place there was now a gift store that sold fancy glass balls and vases painted over with purple flower petals.

Gregor turned over in David Sandler's guest bed. There was nothing poor about David Sandler's house, although David had been poor once. He had been a scholarship student in Gregor's class at the University of Pennsylvania. The ceiling above Gregor's head rose into a high peak. The beams that threaded across the air beneath it smelled of cedar. David seemed to have come to some sort of accommodation with the changes life had brought him that was more graceful than anything Gregor had managed for himself. Gregor thought he spent too much time remembering what it had been like when he was twelve, with the bare linoleum on the walls and the window in the back bedroom they couldn't afford a shade for at all and the nights when all that would be on the table was pasta and bread, because that was all they had left. A picture of that pasta and bread had once come back to him, full force and in Technicolor, while he sat over dinner in a Washington restaurant with the then vice president of the United States. He had looked around and seen Henry Kissinger at the next table and Barbara Walters two tables away, and been so disoriented he thought he was going to pass out. Right now he just wished he was female. Women could ask themselves questions like this. How did you learn to forget? What did you do to help yourself start believing in your life? Men thought about things like this and then talked about fishing.

What had reminded Gregor of Alabama—and all the rest of it—in David Sandler's house was the smell just under the smell of the ocean, the flat damp badness of vegetation gone to rot. In Alabama, that smell had been everywhere. In spite of the fact that he had spent only two weeks at that camp, Gregor had carried the smell with him ever since, and it was still part of what he thought of when he heard the words "the South." One thing about being an overeducated ethnic had been very good, even at the time. None of the officers in that Alabama camp had been able to stand him, and none of them wanted to deal with him, and so at the first possible moment, faster than he would have dreamed was possible in the U.S. Army, he had been shipped off to a training facility in Massachusetts, and put on the list for the Officer Training Corps, and that was that. Gregor had all he had ever wanted to have of being a grunt in one of the army's classic proving grounds in the Bible Belt. Just why the army always seemed to want to build their forts on swampland and great plains, Gregor never did learn to understand.

The clock on the night table next to the bed said 5:45. Gregor untangled himself from his light coverlet and got to his feet. Then he went to the door and looked into the big central main room of the house. Everything was quiet. David Sandler's sleeping loft was quiet. Gregor went into the living room and looked around. The sunlight coming in through the windows was very strong. It didn't seem to matter down here that it was late in the month of October.

Gregor looked at the paintings on the walls that he hadn't paid much attention to yesterday, and the books in the bookcases, too. The paintings were all prints from the Renaissance. People expected militant atheists to be modern, but David had always had more than a little of the classical scholar in him. The books were all books for work—books on the history of religion; tracts on various denominations and sects; the really classic literature of atheism, like Bertrand Russell's *Why I Am Not a Christian* and Thomas Paine's *Common Sense.* Gregor made a face. Reading ought to be for pleasure as much as for work, he thought. His apartment back in Philadelphia had almost nothing in it but crime manuals or forensic textbooks, and the entire set of Bantam's paperback editions of the Nero Wolfe novels.

Gregor took another look at David Sandler's door—David was unlikely to wake up soon; he had stayed up late the night before; David was a night person—and went back to the guest room. He shut the door and shucked off his pajamas, navy blue with red piping, a gift last Christmas from old George Tekemanian. Really hip men didn't wear pajamas, according to Bennis. Really hip men wore nothing to bed at all. Gregor reminded himself that he neither was, nor aspired to be, a really hip man, and went in to the guest bath to take a shower.

When he came out of the shower, it was only 6:06 and the house was still quiet. He went to his suitcase, found a pair of good but reasonably relaxed gray flannel slacks and a shirt still in its packaging from the cleaners. He found new underwear and three ties, all shredded, that he decided not to wear. It was going to be too hot to wear a sweater, so he took out a sports jacket instead. Then he laid it all out on the bed and tried to decide if the pieces matched each other. Bennis and Lida and his late wife Elizabeth all seemed to be able to tell just by looking, but Gregor had no idea what they were looking at. Between the time Elizabeth had died and the time he had moved up from Washington to live on Cavanaugh Street, he had played it safe by wearing suits that had been matched by the store he bought them at.

Now that he didn't feel comfortable doing that anymore, he found himself spending too many mornings agonizing about whether he was going to look put together. That, he knew, was Bennis Hannaford's fault. Before Bennis Hannaford, he had never cared whether he looked put together or not, although that might have been because Elizabeth had been there to make it unnecessary for him to care.

Gregor was doing it again. He put on his clothes as quickly as possible. Then he put on his shoes and went back out into the living room. It was still quiet—why wouldn't it be?—and he went out the big sliding glass doors on David's deck to look at the ocean. It seemed impossible that the ocean had gone crazy less than three weeks ago and laid waste to most of the coastline of this state. Right now it looked majestic but calm, like a grand old lioness well past the days when she was able to hunt.

Gregor walked all the way around the deck to the side of the house, where the deck faced the beach instead of the ocean. From there, he could see not only the beach road but the start of town beyond it. Yesterday, that town had been nothing but a blur of crowded images, mostly of television equipment and junior reporters wielding microphones. Now it looked as quiet as David's house was. And why wouldn't it be? The media people were probably as night-oriented as David. The official organs of the town and state wouldn't open until nine. The rest of Bellerton would be, though. If there was one thing Gregor knew about small towns, it was that they woke up early and got down to business with the dawn.

Gregor went back into the house and into the kitchen. It wasn't much of a kitchen, by Gregor's standards. It was open on two sides to the dining area and the living room, and there were hardly enough cabinets to hold a decent set of baking pans. Still, there was a paper and a pencil and a refrigerator nearly coated with little magnets. Gregor wrote David a note—*Gone for a walk; be back soon*—and stuck it on the freezer door. The magnet he used to stick it with was a bunch of letters jumbled together that spelled out:

THE TIME TO BE HAPPY IS NOW. If Gregor remembered correctly, that was a quote from a famous nineteenth-century freethinker named Robert Ingersoll. Freethinker was the nineteenth-century euphemism for atheist.

Gregor went out the front door this time, and then up the slatted wood walk that led over the sand to the sidewalk. Out here he could smell nothing but clean wild ocean. He could hear nothing but birds, cawing frantically above his head as they circled. The house next to David's looked as if it had been badly damaged in the hurricane. Parts of its roof were missing and one of the pilings that held it up was cracked and out of true. Its windows were still boarded up, meaning that its owners, other vacation people like David, didn't intend to occupy it anytime soon.

At the sidewalk, Gregor did the proper city thing and looked both ways to check the traffic on the beach road, saw that there wasn't a car in sight, and crossed. He found himself on a sidewalk corner between two small white houses, both battered-looking but full.

Maybe just because he was finally doing something in particular, Gregor suddenly felt a lot better.

2

In very small towns in the United States, all the real action happens in one of two places: on Main Street, or in the main room of the nearest McDonald's. Gregor thought the nearest McDonald's must be some ways away. Main Street was already humming. The grain-and-feed store was actually open, with big wooden bins placed outside its front door and filled with Gregor couldn't determine what. The other stores he saw—a religious gift shop; a bookstore—weren't open, but they were lit up inside, testimony to the fact that the people who owned them really meant business. Gregor walked down the street. Bellerton gave a very good impression. The sidewalks were well kept. The street was clean and swept. The brick Town Hall had been recently washed. Maybe all that was the result of the cleanup they had all had to do after the hurricane, but in Gregor's experience, keeping a town looking spruce and cheerful took active commitment. When that commitment was lacking, things fell apart in a hurry. Just look at New York.

It took Gregor a couple of blocks before he found what he was looking for, and then it not only met his expectations, it exceeded his hopes. It was called Betsey's House of Hominy, and it was so full of people, they looked as if they were going to start spilling out the windows at any moment. It wasn't a real diner—meaning a restaurant in a retired railroad dining car—but it had been made up to look like one, and there was a sign across two of the front windows in neon script that said: *Get Your Grits*. This being North Carolina, Gregor supposed you really could get grits. The few times he had tried grits, though, he hadn't much liked them. All the men Gregor could see were wearing short-sleeved camp shirts made of various colors in polyester. All the women had big hair. Gregor didn't really believe, in a town that catered to this many tourists, that all the men in it had the kinds of jobs that required going to work in your shirtsleeves—but he did believe that this might be the kind of town where men had to pretend to have that kind of work. In cases like this one, the character of the town or the neighborhood where the crime had happened was vitally important, and it was so hard to work it all out.

Gregor worked up his courage and went in through Betsey's front door. The place was crowded, but not as crowded as it had seemed from outside. Most of the customers seemed to like to sit in the booths that were pressed up against the windows. The booths in the back were all full, too. The counter around the cash register was mostly empty. Gregor sat down on one of the stools and waited for the girl behind the counter to notice him.

Gregor had had Bennis Hannaford working on him for years. He knew better than to call women "girls," but in this case he thought he was justified—and as soon as the girl behind the counter turned around, he knew he was. Gregor didn't think she could be more than fifteen. In spite of the hair and the thick coat of makeup, she looked like she still needed a baby-sitter. She looked not so much innocent as bone ignorant, and not bright enough to do anything about that. Gregor sat patiently on his stool with his hands folded in front of him. The girl contemplated him as if he were a toad who had suddenly decided to order breakfast.

An older woman came through a swinging door from the back, saw Gregor sitting with his hands folded, and bustled up behind the counter. It was only then that Gregor noticed that she was wearing a white uniform just like the girl's. On the older woman it looked natural, instead of like a costume. The older woman brushed the girl away in the direction of the cash register and said, "Sheri Lynn, for Heaven's sake. What can you be thinking of? Have you taken this gentleman's order?"

"Uh," Sheri Lynn said. "Um. No."

The look on the older woman's face spoke volumes. Gregor wondered just how long she had had to put up with Sheri Lynn. The older woman gave him a great big smile and said, "Good morning, sir. I'm Betsey. What can I get for you this morning?"

Back on Cavanaugh Street, Bennis Hannaford was always worrying about Gregor's cholesterol. Bennis Hannaford was not here to worry about it now.

"I'll have two scrambled eggs," Gregor said firmly, "and a side order of sausage and a side order of hash browns. And toast with butter. And some coffee. Oh, yes. And some orange juice."

Betsey wasn't writing this down on anything. "You just give me a minute," she told him. "I'll be right back with your coffee. Sheri Lynn, for Heaven's sake. Donnie Mac wants to pay up."

Donnie Mac must be the young man waiting at the cash register, the one wearing the pin that said: MY BOSS IS A JEWISH CARPENTER. Gregor thought he ought to dispense with Christian charity in this instance and count his change when he got it. A second later, Gregor noticed that he did. Sheri Lynn seemed to be swimming through molasses, physically as well as mentally. She was far too thin, and Gregor thought that might be because she couldn't keep her mind on anything long enough to remember to eat.

There was a man on a stool four places away from Gregor toward the back of the room, sipping coffee and playing with the pens that lined the pocket of his lime green short-sleeved shirt. He swiveled in Gregor's direction and said, "You a tourist down here? Isn't very usual, having tourists down here in October."

"Shh," somebody in the back of the room said. "He's from the city, can't you see that? He must be another one of those reporters."

"He's too old to be a reporter," somebody else said.

Betsey came out of the back room again, picked up a Pyrex pot of coffee from a hot plate behind the counter, picked up a cup and saucer from behind the counter, too, and advanced toward Gregor.

"All of you stop this now," she said. "He isn't a reporter. His name is Gregor Demarkian and he's staying with David Sandler. I know. Minna Lorimer told me."

Gregor had no idea who Minna Lorimer was, but he was instantly grateful to her. It hadn't occurred to him that anyone might mistake him for a reporter. The woman who had called him too old had been absolutely right. Still, this whole town had to be sick to death of reporters.

Gregor held out his hand to Betsey. "Gregor Demarkian."

"Betsey Henner." She shook.

The man four stools down from Gregor said, "You're staying with David Sandler? Does that mean you're one of those atheist people, too?"

"I don't understand how anybody can be an atheist," a young woman in one of the booths declared. "It doesn't make any sense. I mean, where do you people think this big old world out there came from?"

Gregor took a long sip of his coffee. It was too hot, but he didn't care. This was not going the way he had expected it to.

"To tell you the truth," he said, "I've never thought about it. Atheism, I mean."

"Have you accepted Jesus Christ as your personal Lord and Savior?" a young man in yet another of the booths asked.

Betsey Henner blew a raspberry. "Ricky Drake, you just quit that. The man hasn't had a chance to drink his morning coffee."

"We're living in the last days," Ricky Drake said. "You never know when the Lord is going to come. You never know what the Lord is going to do. You have to be prepared."

"Well, he can't be prepared unless he's had a cup of coffee," Betsey said. "For Heaven's sake."

"I believe in Jesus Christ," Sheri Lynn said suddenly. The room hushed, as if it were a major occasion when Sheri Lynn decided to say anything. "I go to the Episcopal Church. My sister's daughter's getting baptized there on Sunday."

It was like somebody had given the place a collective cold bath. Everybody was silent. Everybody looked just faintly depressed, except Sheri Lynn, who looked blank. Betsey Henner sighed the sigh of the perpetually long-suffering and headed toward the back room again. Gregor hoped she was going to get his breakfast, cholesterol overload and all.

In the quiet caused by Sheri Lynn, most of the customers went back to their breakfasts and their own conversations. The man a few stools down was still looking at Gregor, but he didn't seem hostile anymore, just curious. Gregor didn't think there would be anything wrong with satisfying his curiosity. It might even help him get the information he needed. Then a woman of indeterminate age got out of her seat at one of the window booths and sat down on the stool next to him.

"Are you the Gregor Demarkian who is the detective?" Her voice had just a trace of New York flat in it.

"That's right," Gregor told her. "Who are you?"

"My name is Maggie Kelleher. I own the bookstore."

Suddenly, Gregor knew who this woman reminded him of. She didn't look anything like Bennis Hannaford, but she was like her nonetheless. There was something about the way she carried herself, and the calm but challenging look in her eyes—as if she spent her time demanding something of the universe that the universe didn't want to give back.

Ricky Drake stirred in his booth. He was heavier than he looked at first glance, and sullen. "Maggie used to be one of us," he said, "but then she went to New York."

Maggie Kelleher didn't turn around to look at him. "I've read about you," she said to Gregor. "I've read a lot about you. Have you come down here to help the police make it look like Ginny Marsh killed her own child?"

"I take it you don't think Ginny Marsh did kill her own child," Gregor said.

Maggie gave him a long, slow look. Then she hopped off her stool and went back to her booth. Gregor thought she had abandoned him entirely, but in a moment she was back, with a full cup of hot coffee in her hands. She put it down on the counter next to him.

"I was up there on the day of the storm, you know," she said. "Up at the camp."

"And?"

Maggie Kelleher shrugged. She had very elegant, very expressive shoulders. She also had very intelligent eyes. "Half the town was up there, if you want to know the truth. Stephen and Lisa Harrow from the United Church of Christ. He's the minister there."

"He's a bigger atheist than David Sandler these days," the man a few stools down said. "Nobody knows what Stephen's up to being a member of the clergy these days."

"There were a lot of people," Maggie went on.

"Rose MacNeill who owns the religious gift shop. In the big Victorian house. You might have seen it on your way here."

"I did."

"I keep trying to remember everybody who was up there, but I can't. It was the middle of the storm and everything was crazy. And of course, that's the highest ground in town."

"David Sandler said something about the high school."

Maggie Kelleher nodded. "That was the official refuge, of course, but it was safer up at the camp and we all knew it. And Zhondra had made it clear enough that she didn't mind company for the duration as long as the company behaved itself."

"Meaning what?"

"Meaning no acting like Ricky back there would act if he got around someone who was gay. It was all right. The people who felt like that didn't come up anyway. They went to the high school or out to Henry Holborn's place."

Gregor frowned. "Henry Holborn. He's a—what? Minister?"

"Something like that," Maggie replied. "I don't know what you know about places like this, Mr. Demarkian, but there are a lot of guys out here, they didn't go to the seminary or get ordained in a regular religion the way Catholics and Presbyterians do. They went to Bible college—there are hundreds of Bible college all across the South—anyway, they went to Bible college and then they came home and started preaching. And if they got enough people to come listen to them, that got them the money to found and build a church. Henry Holborn is one of those. His place is called the Bellerton Full Gospel Christian Church, and it's enormous."

"Henry Holborn is a good man," Ricky Drake declared. "He's a messenger from God."

"I don't know if Henry Holborn is a messenger from God," Maggie said, "but he is a very successful preacher, the most successful one we've had around here for years, and the complex he built is far enough from the water to be safe from most hurricane problems. So there were a lot of people out there. All the members of his church who could get there, for one. Except Ginny Marsh, who was out at the camp. Bobby was there, though."

"Who's Bobby?"

"Ginny's husband. Tiffany's father. That's the usual thing, isn't it? When a mother is supposed to have killed her children. People usually say it was the husband's idea."

"Actually," Gregor said carefully, "people usually say it was the boyfriend's idea. In the two most famous cases of this kind that I know of, there was a boyfriend in the background, a man they wanted to marry who didn't want to support another man's children. Does Ginny Marsh have a boyfriend?"

"Not that I know of. And this is Bellerton, North Carolina, Mr. Demarkian. If she had a boyfriend, I'd know."

Gregor took another long sip of his coffee. This was not strictly true. In spite of the legendary nosiness of small towns, they were often utterly unaware of the most outrageous things. It might be impossible to find privacy in a place like Bellerton, but it would be easier than Bellerton realized for one of its citizens to keep a secret.

"You say you were up at the camp," Gregor said slowly. "Let me ask you this, then. Did you see anything that might indicate that Ginny Marsh was not lying? Was there some kind of Satanic ritual going on? Was Ginny in your sight all along?"

"Ginny wasn't in my sight all along. But it doesn't matter, Mr. Demarkian. I don't think you've understood me. I said that I didn't think Ginny killed her baby. And I don't."

"I know you don't."

"I didn't say I didn't think Ginny was lying," Maggie Kelleher went on. "I do think she's lying, Mr. Demarkian. I think she's lying through her teeth. About the Satanic rituals. About the way the baby died. About everything."

"But why?" Gregor asked. "If you're trying to tell me she's covering up for her husband—"

"I told you, her husband wasn't there."

"—or for anybody. Miss Kelleher—"

"Ms."

"Ms. Kelleher, collusion in murder is almost as bad as murder. In the eyes of the law, there's not a great deal of difference. In some states, you can get the death penalty for it."

"I don't think Ginny's colluding in murder," Maggie Kelleher said in exasperation. "I don't think she's covering up for anybody, not in the way you mean. You don't understand my point."

"No," Gregor said. "I don't. But I'm trying. What is your point?"

Maggie Kelleher came to some sort of decision. She hopped off her stool and picked up her cup of coffee. She hadn't drunk much of it while she was sitting next to Gregor, but it had cooled off a little. It was no longer steaming.

"Never mind," she said. "I don't know what point I'm trying to make either. I should never have started this conversation. And I've got to go."

"But—" Gregor said.

At that moment, Betsey Henner came out of the back room with Gregor's breakfast. It was on a big, thick, oval white porcelain plate, the kind that Gregor thought must have been invented just to supply diners everywhere. Betsey put the plate down in front of Gregor and stepped back.

"There you go," she said.

"Jesus Christ," Maggie Kelleher said. "What are you trying to do, give yourself a heart attack?"

five

1

In Gregor Demarkian's experience, there were two kinds of small-town police departments: the kind that was all uniforms and noise, and the kind that knew what it was doing. The Bellerton Police Department seemed to be the latter kind. It was only quarter after seven when he got over there, after eating his breakfast and wandering down Main Street for a second time. By then there were children on the sidewalks and young women hurrying onto porches to put mail in their mailboxes. A couple of Main Street stores hung out their American flags. The police department was in the basement of Town Hall. Standing on the Town Hall lawn, Gregor could look into the window well and see the department, or what there was of it, in operation. A big man in a uniform shirt and khaki pants was working at a desk. He wasn't wearing a hat of any kind, and if he was wearing a gun, Gregor couldn't see it. A smaller man, also in a uniform shirt and khaki pants, was typing on an ancient machine at a long counter. Gregor couldn't see a gun on him, either, but he was wearing a holster. There were neither prisoners nor anyone else in the small room. There weren't even any reporters. In fact, Gregor thought, he had managed to get lucky, waking up early the way he had. There were no reporters anywhere in Bellerton, as far as Gregor could see.

The front door to the Town Hall was locked. Gregor

had tried it. He had gone around to the side of the building in search of another door, and found instead a statue in honor of Bellerton's Civil War dead. The statue was of a slouching Confederate soldier with a ragged coat standing on a pedestal. The pedestal had six names engraved into the side of it. Gregor went around to the back and found a small parking lot with three cars in it. He also found a door, although not a door to the basement. You had to go up a rickety set of steps to get to it.

Gregor was just wondering whether to try this door or to go around to the one side of the building he hadn't seen yet when the door opened, and a well-preserved middle-aged woman came out, wearing a flowing flowered dress and very high heels. Gregor worried about women in heels, especially when they were trying to negotiate steep stairs like this set. This woman sailed down them without looking at her feet, and hardly touching the banister. The banister was just a thick metal pipe anyway, tacked on, it looked like, at the last minute, because somebody less surefooted than this had fallen.

The woman was looking him over without pretending not to be. Her gaze seemed to be neutral. Gregor stepped away from the stairs and put his hands behind his back.

"Can I help you?" the woman asked, when she got to the little patch of sidewalk at the bottom of the steps. "Are you looking for something?"

"I'm looking for the police department," Gregor said. "I found it, in a way. I looked straight into one of its windows. It seems to be open. I just can't figure out how to get in."

"The police department's always open," the woman said. "Not that there's a lot of crime out here. But we've got drunks just like every place else."

"I'm sure you do."

The woman cocked her head. "I thought you were another of those reporters, but you aren't, are you? You're that man they wrote about in the paper, the one who's a friend of David Sandler's. Gregory—"

"Gregor Demarkian."

"That's right. The world's most famous detective. So what is it now? You and Dr. Sandler don't think the police department in a place like Bellerton is up to investigating a thing of this kind?"

"I think the police department in Bellerton is doing a wonderful job."

"Then why are you here?"

"Because David Sandler asked me to come. Because I got a letter from a man—Clayton Hall, I think the name was—saying it would be a good idea if I came. In his opinion, that is."

"Clayton knew you were coming? He thought it was all right?"

"He wrote me a letter. He said he thought it was all right."

"We get tired of it, you know," the woman said. "All this hogwash about what a backwards little place we are. Oh, they don't come out and say it. They don't stand up there on the six o'clock news and announce that Bellerton is a hick little hollow full of mental defectives. But they imply it. They go out of their way to imply it."

Gregor cleared his throat. "I'm sorry if they do," he said. "I'm afraid I haven't had much time to watch the news of this on television."

"It's the people they pick to talk to," the woman said. "I learned that when I was up at the university in Chapel Hill. This town has dozens of good people in it. Dozens of intelligent people, too. So who do these television people put in front of a camera as soon as they have a chance? Bobby Marsh and Ricky Drake."

"Isn't Bobby Marsh the child's father?"

The woman ignored this entirely. "None of them understands any of it anyway. They don't understand what it was like down here, just twenty-five or thirty years ago. They don't understand where these people are coming from."

The woman seemed to snap out of it. "Never mind,"

she said, smoothing her hands along the sides of her dress skirt. "It doesn't matter. You want to see Clayton Hall?"

"If he's in. I want to go to the police department."

"You just go around the side of the building there. There's a little set of steps going down, like cellar steps except right out in the open and they're made of concrete. There's a police car parked around that side, too. That's how you can tell."

"I was just going to check that side. Thank you for telling me."

"The first four or five days, there were reporters just spilling out of there, and all over the Town Hall steps, and everywhere else you could see. And equipment with cables, too. You've got to worry about children around cables, you know."

"I'm sure you do."

"Do you think Ginny Marsh killed her daughter?"

"I don't know."

"Clayton Hall thinks she did. Damned idiot. Anybody with a brain in his head could see that Ginny Marsh never did any such thing."

"She could be covering up for somebody who did. For her husband. Or her boyfriend."

"Bobby Marsh was out at Henry Holborn's place when the baby was killed. Everybody knows that. Even Clayton knows that. Do you believe in religion?"

"Believe in it?"

The woman snorted. "Well, I'm not going to ask you if you've accepted Christ as your personal savior, am I? I mean, do you think religion is good for people?"

"Sometimes," Gregor replied. "I don't think I understand what you're getting at—"

"*They* think it's all some kind of mental illness." The woman tossed her head in the direction of Main Street. *They* might not be out there yet, but Gregor knew who *they* were supposed to be. "They think it's all voodoo and fanaticism. You can hear it when they talk. You have to give Dr. Sandler that much. He doesn't talk to people like that."

"Oh," Gregor said.

The woman got a set of keys out of the pocket of her dress. "I'm not a religious person, you know. I don't go to church and I'm not even one hundred percent sure I believe in God and whenever Rose starts in with all that angels business, I go right up the wall. But people have a right to have their beliefs respected. They have a right not to be laughed at by people who don't for one minute intend to even try to understand what's going on. That's part of being an American."

"Right," Gregor said.

"You go find Clayton Hall," the woman said. "I hope you do a little good around here instead of what all the rest of them are doing. I hope you have *some* consideration."

"Right," Gregor said again.

"And just remember this." The woman now had a single one of her keys in her hand, as if she were about to open a door. "Ginny Marsh didn't kill her daughter. Ginny Marsh didn't collude in the killing of her daughter. Ginny Marsh never hurt anybody in her life and won't hurt anybody as long as she lives. But she scares easily."

"What's that supposed to mean?"

"I've got to get moving," the woman said. "I'm supposed to open the library at nine, and I have to get all the way out to my house and back again before then. I have a very busy day."

"I'm sure you do, Miss—"

"Ms. Brent. Ms. Naomi Brent. I run the library. I don't have any more time for this kind of talk, Mr. Demarkian. I have to go now."

She turned away from him then and half ran across the parking lot. Gregor watched her skirt billow out around her. She got to the small green Ford Escort and opened it up and got in. Gregor suddenly remembered that Donna Moradanyan had just bought a Ford Escort. That one was a station wagon, though. And it was blue.

What am I doing? Gregor demanded of himself.

Naomi Brent had started her engine and begun to back

her car out of its space. Gregor started around the last side of Town Hall, still in search of the Bellerton Police Department.

2

Actually, the Bellerton Police Department was not hard to find, once you knew where to look. The steps were exactly where Naomi Brent had said they were going to be, carved into the flat ground on the side of the building. Gregor had the impression that it was not very usual to have basements in this part of North Carolina. In fact, from what he remembered, all the South tended to prefer slab and crawl space foundations. This foundation had been raised a good five feet above grade, however, and the administration of the town at the time it had been built had gone to what must have been a great deal of expense to do it all right. Gregor went down the concrete steps and opened the wooden door at the bottom of them. There was no musty smell of mildew and damp rushing out at him. In spite of the fact that there had been a major hurricane here only a couple of weeks ago, the basement was entirely dry and very fresh-smelling. It was also heavily air-conditioned. Gregor felt the cold hit him like a wall. He was almost sorry he hadn't worn his sweater. He closed the outside door behind him and looked up at the wall next to it, where there was one of those plastic plug-in letter boards with departments written on it.

Tax Department, Gregor read. Water Department. Sewage Department. Police Department.

He had been hoping for directions, but he wasn't going to get any. This was not a town that expected strangers to be wandering around in the basement of its Town Hall. Anybody who lived in Bellerton would know where he was going without having to be told.

From the place where Gregor was standing, the hall went in two directions, right and left. Gregor tried to orient himself, and decided that the front of the building was probably to his left. He went that way, past the Water Department, and got to a corner. He turned the corner and found the office of the tax collector. Obviously, the basement was laid out like a gigantic doughnut, with a concrete block instead of a hole in the middle. Gregor passed a ladies' room and kept on going.

Finally, when he turned the next corner, Gregor heard signs of life. Somebody slammed a door. Somebody called out to somebody else. There was a fire door set up in the middle of the hall—because of worries about fires? because of worries about security?—and Gregor went through it. On the other side of it he found a big sign with the words BELLERTON POLICE DEPARTMENT written on it. He also found an open door with light spilling out of it.

Gregor went to the open door and looked in. The big man he had seen first was now standing at a coffee machine, fiddling with coffee grounds and water. The smaller man was now sitting at a desk and reading. There was a radio in one corner of the room, tuned to the state police band. It was giving out information on traffic conditions on Interstate 95.

Gregor knocked as loudly as he could on the frame of the door and waited. The big man didn't hear him. The small man heard him, and looked up, and jumped to his feet.

"Jesus Christ," he said. "Who are you? Where did you come from?"

The big man turned around now, and looked Gregor over. Then he looked at the small man and said, "You shouldn't swear like that, Jackson. You don't know who you might be talking to."

"Well, I'm not talking to a preacher now, am I?" Jackson demanded. "Look at him. He's one of those reporters."

"I'm Gregor Demarkian," Gregor said.

The big man came across the room and held out his

hand. "I know you are," he said. "I read an article about you in *People* magazine. I'm Clayton Hall."

"How do you do." Gregor shook the man's hand. He never shook hands anymore, except in small towns. People in cities seemed to have given the practice up.

Jackson was looking back and forth between Clayton Hall and Gregor Demarkian. He dropped back down in his chair and said, "My, my. Gregor Demarkian. You finally *got* here."

"Now, now," Clayton Hall said.

"Tell me something," Jackson said. "Are you a religious man, Mr. Demarkian?"

Gregor was beginning to think he ought to become a Buddhist, at least for as long as he was going to stay in Bellerton. He was also wondering if Jackson was this man's first or last name.

"You don't want to get started on all that religious stuff," Clayton Hall said. "Mr. Demarkian just got here. I hope you don't mind too much, Mr. Demarkian. The religion thing has become a sore point down here over the past few weeks. People are beginning to feel—harrassed."

"Harrassed isn't the half of it," Jackson said. "Persecuted is more like it. *Persecuted.*"

"Certain members of the media from up North," Clayton Hall said, "seem to think that belief in a literal interpretation of the Bible is irrefutable proof of mental retardation."

"They think it turns you into an ax murderer," Jackson snarled. "They think it makes you crazy."

"Mr. Demarkian didn't come here to talk about religion," Clayton Hall said. "Or I don't think he did. Why don't you come in and have a seat, Mr. Demarkian. Drink a cup of coffee. David Sandler says you're a very intelligent man."

"David Sandler says *you're* a very intelligent man."

There was a full coffeepot sitting next to the coffee maker, which was just beginning to pour dark brown liquid into an empty one. Clayton Hall picked up the full pot and poured some coffee into a small white Styrofoam cup.

"Have a seat," Clayton Hall said again.

Gregor made his way into the room and found a chair to sit in. All the chairs were wooden and cheap and uniform, the kind of chairs they used to have in schoolrooms when he was a child. The air-conditioning, he realized, was even stronger in here than it had been in the hall. Neither Clayton Hall nor his associate Jackson seemed to notice the cold. Because of it, Gregor took the coffee gratefully when Clayton finally handed it to him, in spite of the fact that he knew what it would taste like. Police department coffee tastes the same everywhere, all over the world. Police departments in Bolivia serve up the same awful brew that sits ready and waiting in police departments in New York. Gregor took a long sip and was instantly warmer. He also felt instantly a little sick.

"I've been walking around town," he said. "Looking at things. I had breakfast in a place called Betsey's House of Hominy. It was interesting."

"I'll bet everybody thought you were a reporter," Jackson said.

"They did at first. There was a woman there named Maggie Kelleher—"

"Oh, Maggie," Clayton Hall said. "Now, Maggie is an interesting woman. Good-looking, too."

"She's got to be *forty*," Jackson said scornfully.

"She knew who I was," Gregor said. "Some other people might have, too, but she was the one who said so. There was also somebody there named Ricky Drake."

Jackson dropped his head into his hands. "Oh, dear sweet Jesus."

Gregor let this pass. "Then when I came over here, I met a woman coming out, who said her name was Naomi Brent. From the library."

"That's right," Clayton said. "She does run the library. Has for years now. She's not exactly your old maid librarian, though."

"She didn't seem so to me, no," Gregor agreed. "But what I'm trying to get to here, what struck me, is that what everybody wanted to tell me was that there was no way they thought Virginia Marsh could have killed her baby. In fact, it seemed to be a general consensus."

Clayton Hall and Jackson looked at each other. "It is a consensus," Clayton said slowly. "In town, at any rate."

"I'd been given the impression by David Sandler that the consensus ran exactly the other way. That one of the reasons he wanted me down here was that he was afraid it was being taken as a foregone conclusion, that Virginia Marsh was guilty, and that he wanted someone here who would look at things differently for a while."

The second coffeepot was now full of coffee. Clayton Hall adjusted it on its metal plate, fussing with it, giving his hands something to do. "Mr. Demarkian, given everything you've ever heard about this case, what is it that you think it's going to turn out to be?"

"I think it's going to turn out to be Virginia Marsh, or Virginia Marsh's husband, or Virginia Marsh's boyfriend, if she has one. That's what it always turns out to be."

"Exactly," Clayton Hall said. "That's the point. And she was there, Ginny was. Up at the camp. And she lied to us and everybody else about why she was up there."

"What do you mean?"

"Ginny told David Sandler, among other people, that she was going up to the camp in the middle of the storm because Zhondra Meyer had refused to let her off the hook for work that day. But it wasn't true. Ginny never called Zhondra Meyer and asked to be excused from work that day. Zhondra would have been more than happy to give her the afternoon off. Not much work was going to get done up there anyway, what with the storm."

"Couldn't that be what Zhondra Meyer is saying now? Maybe Ginny is telling the truth and it's Zhondra Meyer who's lying."

"We've got the phone records, Mr. Demarkian. There

were no incoming calls to the camp that morning. None. Zero. Zilch.''

"Ah," Gregor said.

"And it isn't just the phone call." Clayton Hall was getting worked up now. "There's the blood to account for. When David Sandler found her, Ginny was covered with blood. Some of it was her own blood. Some of it was Tiffany's blood. She was soaked in it."

"All right."

"Yeah," Clayton said. "All right. The point here is wider, though. Because that was all the blood we found. *All* of it. There wasn't a drop of Tiffany Marsh's blood anywhere on the premises of the camp. Not in that grove where Ginny keeps saying she saw the Satan worship. Not anywhere. And we searched that place—Christ, it took days."

"The blood could have been washed away. We are talking about the middle of a hurricane here. A major hurricane."

"The blood couldn't have been washed away from everything," Clayton insisted. "We should have found flecks of it. We should have found something. And then there were these women Ginny says she saw worshipping the Devil. Carol Littleton was the only one she said she recognized. Well, Mr. Demarkian, Ginny Marsh had been working up at the camp for months. And I know Ginny Marsh. I don't believe there were three women up there she wouldn't have been able to recognize, stark naked or not."

Gregor considered this. He had read about the stark naked business. That was one detail the papers never omitted.

"What about this Carol Littleton?" he asked. "What did she say?"

"She says that she and two other women decided to have a celebration of the goddess in a grove at the back of the camp's formal gardens just before the storm really started—"

"The goddess?"

Clayton Hall sighed. "Yeah, the goddess. The Great

Goddess, to be specific. It's the big thing these days with the academic types up in the Research Triangle. Theoretically, millions and millions of years ago, or however long it was, when the human race just got started, everybody worshipped the Great Goddess, instead of a male god, and that meant there was equality between the sexes and everything was better for everybody and women were affirmed and I don't know what all. But I ask you this. If it was all so wonderful, why did anybody ever want to change it?''

"The preachers all think the Great Goddess is Satan," Jackson put in. "Or at least, some of the preachers do. They're always talking about it."

"Let's get back to Carol Littleton," Gregor said gently. "You said she and these two other women decided to go out and worship the Great Goddess. Did they?"

"Yes," Clayton said.

"Have you talked to the other two women?"

"Of course I have. They say the same thing."

"How was this worship carried out?"

Jackson whooped. "Well," he said, in a strongly exaggerated drawl, "for one thing, that business about being stark naked was absolutely right. They did get stark naked."

Clayton Hall was actually blushing. "To tell you the truth, Mr. Demarkian, this embarrasses the hell out of me. It would embarrass the hell out of anybody. They all got naked, you see, and then they knelt in a circle around a pile of rocks, and then they sang this song they say they always sing. It's a special song. One of them wrote it, not Carol Littleton. I don't remember which one it was."

"It's a song to their twats," Jackson said, absolutely deadpan. "That's what they do out there. They get all naked and kneel in a circle and sing to their—"

"Jackson, stop it, for Pete's sake. Now you've got Mr. Demarkian blushing."

"Call me Gregor," Gregor said, trying to will the blush away. It was impossible. He could feel the heat in his face. It was strong enough to scorch.

"It's called 'affirming the goodness of the body,' "
Jackson said. "Did you ever hear of such a thing? And
those asses from New York think the Holy Rollers are
crazy."

Gregor took a deep breath. "Look," he said. "Don't
you realize? This means that Ginny Marsh was telling the
truth about something."

"Maybe it just means she got lucky," Clayton Hall
said. "There's been rumors about the goddess worship for
months. Henry Holborn has been going on and on about it
for months. And Ginny is a member of Henry Holborn's
church."

"They were talking about Henry Holborn in Betsey's
this morning," Gregor said.

"Henry's got the biggest church anywhere around
here," Jackson said. "Big complex out on Hartford Road.
Huge congregation. He must fill three thousand seats every
Sunday."

"Three *thousand?*"

"That's not much," Clayton Hall said. "Some of the
really big evangelists, Oral Roberts, Robert Schuller,
they'll do ten thousand without sweating. But Henry's big
for around here. And getting bigger."

"And he thinks they're worshipping the devil up at
this camp," Gregor said.

"That's right," Clayton Hall said.

The tiny window placed high in the wall looked out on
a window well full of dying leaves and pine needles. Other
than that, all Gregor could see was the sun, and the grating
that protected the well from the lawn. There was a small
bird on the grating, pecking away at the air.

"I think," Gregor said finally, "that what I would like
to do, if you could arrange it, is to go out to this camp and
look around. Would that be possible?"

"More than possible," Clayton Hall said. "Zhondra
Meyer will probably be happy enough to marry you. She's
a very rich society lady from New York, and she isn't used
to this kind of publicity."

"Serves her right," Jackson said.

"What about Ginny Marsh?" Gregor asked. "Where is she? Out on bail?"

Clayton looked uncomfortable. "She's in a jail cell about three yards from here. I know that that's crazy, under the circumstances, but there isn't anybody to go her bail. Bobby won't do it."

"Her husband."

"That's right," Clayton said. "He doesn't have the money. And he isn't so inclined, either."

"Do you mean he's one of the few people in town who thinks she's actually guilty?" Gregor asked.

Clayton threw his arms in the air. "We don't know what to think. He and Ginny were always close. Now he won't talk to us and he won't talk to her and we don't know what's going on. Do you want to talk to Ginny before you go up to Zhondra Meyer's place? She's available. Her lawyer is a personal friend of mine. All it would take is a phone call."

Outside the window, the bird had flown off. There was nothing more to see.

"No," Gregor said. "I don't think I'm ready to talk to Ginny Marsh just yet. Let's go up and see what we can find out about goddess worship."

"Goddess worship," Jackson said, starting to crack up. "Maybe they'll put on a demonstration. Can't you picture it? All those sagging old ladies. All those drooping old—"

"Jackson," Clayton Hall said. Then he looked at Gregor and shrugged. "Sometimes I wish Jackson here would get religion. It would surely improve the tone of this place."

six

1

When the call came in from Clayton Hall, Zhondra Meyer was sitting at her desk in the big study on the main floor of the west wing, reading the papers. She had already read her way through the Bellerton *Times* and the Raleigh *News and Observer*. She had started in on the *New York Times,* too, but had ended up bored in the middle of an editorial about the Middle East. Zhondra's mother was always telling her that she didn't take the State of Israel seriously enough. Zhondra's friends were always telling her that, too, although for reasons her mother would undoubtedly deplore. It didn't matter. Zhondra couldn't think about the Middle East for more than three seconds without feeling her head start to ache. Nothing made any sense over there, and she had the sneaking suspicion that nobody wanted it to. Besides, she had *USA Today* to read, and what was there was a disaster. Being in *USA Today* was like being in *People*. Lots of pictures. Lots of scrupulously reported innuendo. At least, Zhondra thought, they weren't on the front page this time. The crime had occurred far enough back to spare them from that. The story about the camp was on pages two and three of the first section—*all* of pages two and three. There were pictures of the big front gate with its curving crown, like the gate to an old movie studio. There were pictures of Alice and Dinah and Carol in town, all looking dumpy and tired. There were even a few pictures of Zhondra herself, none of them recent. The one that made Zhondra cringe was her coming-out photograph, taken with fifteen other young women, all dressed in white gowns, just before the Christmas Cotillion and New Year's Ball in Manhattan. It seemed impossible to Zhondra that she had ever been that woman: so thin, so stupid, so unaware.

Clayton Hall had wanted to know if he could bring this Demarkian person up to talk to her and the rest of the women about what had happened on the day of the storm. That was how Zhondra thought of it: what had happened on the day of the storm. Thinking about it any other way made her feel sick. She had heard that David Sandler was bringing this Demarkian to North Carolina. She even knew who he was. There had been a profile of him in *Vanity Fair,* which she still read, mostly secretly, in the bathroom. It was one of the few times *Vanity Fair* had ever done a profile without the subject's cooperation, and Zhondra had found it an interesting piece. Zhondra had no idea what kind of mental attitude it took to want to look into crimes and solve them. Even simple acts of stealing bewildered her beyond belief. Trying to think about what had happened on the day of the hurricane blanked her out completely. Zhondra was not a sentimental woman. She wasn't particularly fond of children, and she sometimes loathed infants, who seemed to have been designed to make their mothers' lives impossible. Children were a trap. She had said it often, in the days when she was still speaking and teaching, before she opened the camp. Children are patriarchy's most lethal weapon. She only allowed them at the camp because their mothers insisted on bringing them, and lately it had begun to be considered antifeminist not to allow them. Even so, Zhondra had never wanted a child, and surely not one as small and helpless and pliant as Tiffany had been.

Clayton wanted to bring Gregor Demarkian up here. Zhondra was glad to have them both, and anybody else directly connected to a law enforcement agency, instead of those reporters who had camped out in town. Clayton and Demarkian wanted to question the women who had been taking part in the goddess ritual—well, Zhondra was perfectly happy about that, too. Zhondra knew all the theories behind goddess worship: reclaiming the sacredness of the body; repairing our relationship with nature and the earth; reempowering the spirituality of women. Zhondra thought it was all bunk. If you wanted to give up religion, you should give it up. You should walk right out on it, just like Zhondra had walked out on Judaism. Inventing religions that had never existed and pretending that they came from the beginning of time made no sense to her at all.

Zhondra looked down at the spread-open pages of *USA Today* one more time, decided she had looked hideous in miniskirts, and got up from her chair. She walked to the tall French doors that opened onto the back terrace and pulled back the curtains that covered them. Alice was out there, just where she said she'd be, cleaning out the big stone birdbath. Around her, the shrubs were carved into hearts and spades and diamonds and clubs, just as they had been in Zhondra's grandfather's time. Zhondra had no idea why she had never changed it.

Zhondra went out onto the terrace and waved to Alice, who was hanging almost upside down from the birdbath's center tier. Alice saw her and waved back. Then she circled herself up into a sitting position and began the slow process of getting herself to the ground. The birdbath was still full of water. Alice's jeans were soaked through and her thin cotton peasant blouse was dotted with damp. She had to leap like a gymnast to get clear of the birdbath's bottom tier, and when she landed it looked as if it hurt.

"Hey," Alice said, standing up straight and brushing water and bits of grass off her thighs. "What is it? I practically had that thing straightened out."

"Did you start from the top or from the bottom?" Zhondra asked, honestly curious.

"From the top," Alice replied. "You always lose some muck to the next tier down. Is there something in particular you wanted? This birdbath really needed cleaning out. Our lawn service is worthless."

The lawn service wasn't useless. It just didn't do birdbaths. "Clayton Hall just called," Zhondra said. "He wants to bring Gregor Demarkian up here to see us."

"He does? When?"

"Now."

Alice look nonplussed. "For Christ's sake, Zhondra," she said. "My hair's a mess. My clothes are a mess. I smell like a stagnant pond. Do you mean right *now* now?"

"As soon as they can get up here from town, Alice, yes. Clayton said something about wanting to go over some paperwork with Demarkian and we shouldn't expect them for about forty-five minutes, but that's the upshot of it. I don't think they're going to care about what you look like."

"I care about what I look like. Are you glad he's coming? Gregor Demarkian? When I saw the piece in the Bellerton *Times,* I didn't know what to think."

"I think it would be a good idea if we got all this cleared up. Fast."

"I agree."

Zhondra shook her head. "I don't think you realize. I've been coming here since I was two years old, and I know this place. Half the people in town probably think that Ginny Marsh is telling the God's honest truth, and we're holding Black Masses up here and worshipping the Devil."

"I know that."

"Yes, Alice, you know that, but you don't know what it means. Down there there's somebody—Henry Holborn or somebody else—planning something right this minute. I don't know what, and I don't know when, but it's coming. And when it does, there's going to be real trouble."

"I don't mean to get you pissed off or anything," Alice said, "but I think you underestimate the people in Bellerton. In spite of the newspaper snipes and a few people like Henry Holborn, they've mostly been very nice, at least to me. They don't seem like the kind of people who would, I don't know, dress up in hoods or whatever you're suggesting.''

"Not in hoods."

"What is it, then? There really isn't anything they can do to us, Zhondra. You own this place. They can't revoke the lease or anything. And they can't run us out of town, either. Your lawyers are better than their lawyers."

. "There are a lot of things people can do." Zhondra sounded enigmatic when she didn't want to. "Where are they all, Dinah and Stelle and Carol?"

"Stelle's sleeping. Dinah and Carol were in the dining room, last I heard."

"Get them all together and bring them down here to my study. I want to talk to them before Clayton gets here with Demarkian."

"You mean you want to prime them?"

"No," Zhondra said, "I don't want to prime them. I just want to talk to them. Will you please go and bring them here?"

"Sure."

Zhondra turned away. It was a warm day, but there was the beginning of cold in it, like an undercurrent. Her grandmother probably walked across this terrace the way she was walking across it now, tall and imperious and just a little angry. Lately, Zhondra had been finding all kinds of connections between that ancient matriarch and herself. Sometimes she thought of the jewelry that had been left to her, passed down from one generation of Meyer women to the next, and wondered what it would be like to walk with it covering her, the heavy round dinner rings and diamond tiaras, the diamond chokers and diamond and ruby breast-plates. When nineteenth-century women dressed up to go out, they knew how to dress *up*.

Zhondra left the French doors open and sat down at the desk in the study. The ceiling was so far above her head, the light from the chandelier didn't quite reach into the corners of it. The chandelier was a spreading beehive of crystal and glass. The desk was a polished mahogany tour de force, full of secret doors and spring locks, carved on the sides into curlicues and cherubs.

"You think you're going to just pack up your things and get away from it all," Zhondra's mother had said, when Zhondra had been getting ready to leave home for the last time. "You think you're going to buy your clothes in Kmart and call yourself by a nickname and nobody is going to know who and what you are. But it doesn't work like that, Zhondra. It has never worked like that and it never will."

It was true, of course. The money was on her as tightly and as thoroughly as her skin. What was different was that now, in her forties, she was beginning to like it that way. She had no trouble imagining her own portrait going up beside the others in the gallery on the second floor. Zhondra's mother had made a terrible matriarch. She lacked self-confidence and emotional control. Zhondra knew that she herself lacked neither.

Zhondra picked all the newspapers up and dumped them into the wastebasket. The computer screen was showing a test pattern, meant to keep the machine ready for its next serious use. Zhondra looked at the pictures on the desk instead, all of them in silver Tiffany frames. They were all from long ago. Only one was of her parents, and it had been taken when they were young, before they had had Zhondra in their life. Zhondra found that she liked the way they looked, in their white lawn-party clothes. She liked the big sweep of grass behind them and the rose-garden trellises that made the lawn look decorated.

Christ, Zhondra thought, throwing back her head. *I'd better find a lover soon. I'm reverting to type.*

2

Henry Holborn blamed himself for everything that had happened. He blamed himself for the death of Tiffany

Marsh. He blamed himself for the way Ginny and Bobby were becoming increasingly estranged. Ginny hated Bobby for thinking she might have killed Tiffany. Bobby hated Ginny for not making him absolutely sure she had not. Henry Holborn was absolutely sure. He had known Ginny and Bobby Marsh all their lives. He had known Ginny when she was first in high school and still had so much ambition, before she found out she wasn't really good enough to get any of the things she wanted. That was the way it was with almost all the people who came to his church. The last shall be first, the Lord had said, and Henry had seen it be true. The people who lived in the big Greek revival houses in town, the doctors and the lawyers and the dentists and the accountants, didn't come out to the Full Gospel Christian Church. Neither did the engineers and scientists who had bought the new construction in the housing developments that seemed to be springing up everywhere across the state. The people Henry ministered to were not necessarily down, right this minute, but they had been down. Some of them were well-paid people now, but they had grown up in the shacks and on the dirt farms on the back roads of the state. They had gone to state colleges on loans and scholarships. They had learned the hard way how to get past the handicaps of fathers who drank and mothers who didn't seem to be able to get up the energy to cook a full dinner more than one night a week. The New York newspeople had it all wrong. Henry's parishioners weren't the drunks and the slatterns out looking for some entertainment in the form of holy rolling. They were the children of drunks and slatterns who had worked themselves to distraction and finally made it out.

Henry blamed himself for everything that had happened because he knew he should have seen it coming. God talked to him as much as God talked to anyone. God had privileged him in more ways than Henry was willing to count. Henry had had a vision of the Devil, as clear and strong and real as the presence of a big old tree in the front yard, and he knew the Devil was ready and waiting, moving cautiously but inexorably, coming to get them all. History had been written in advance. This life was a war between the forces of good and the forces of evil. The job of every man, woman, and child alive was to choose up sides. Henry had chosen his side. He had chosen the Lord and all His works. He had chosen to carry the cross with Christ, to suffer mockery and persecution, to preach the Good News to people God really wanted to hear it, all them that were weary and heavy laden. The problem was that Henry had gotten lazy, and complacent, and smug. He had seen the signs and ignored them. He had heard the Devil knocking on the door and pretended he wasn't there. Now the Devil was right in the middle of the house, sucking up all the air, and Henry was having a hard time figuring out what to do about it.

It was just about eight o'clock in the morning, and the Full Gospel Christian Church was already humming. The hurricane had done a lot of damage, more than Henry had admitted to the public. Volunteers were clearing debris out of the fountain in the courtyard and putting new shingles on the steeply sloped roof. The cross on the steeple had survived intact. It was made of tempered steel and inde-structible. The cross in the church's front yard hadn't been so fortunate. It was made of wood, to be as authentic as possible, and it had fallen over and split in two. It was as if God was giving them mixed signals: the church was going to survive or it wasn't. The only thing Henry was abso-lutely sure of was that God would win out in the end, and the Devil and his forces would be vanquished.

Henry's wife Janet came in from the back of the church and waved to him. Henry waved back and came down off the podium. He had to be careful, because his arthritis was bothering him this morning. He ached more and more these days. He was getting old. All around him, volunteers were working hard in the church, cleaning up after what the people who had camped here had done dur-ing the hurricane. When Henry had invited people to come to the church to get in out of the rain, he hadn't realized what it would do to the carpets. He made his way down the central aisle, leaning against the backs of the seats as he went. His chest hurt.

"Are you all right?" Janet asked him when he reached her. "You're white as a ghost."

"I'm fine," Henry said, and oddly enough, it was true. The pain in his chest was gone. The odd feeling that he had suddenly forgotten how to breathe was gone, too. He felt better than he had in weeks. He straightened up, all at once aware of the fact that he had been bending over. "I'm fine," he said again. "How are you? You look agitated."

"I've spent all morning trying to find out about all those things you wanted to know," Janet told him. "It hasn't been easy."

"Has it been fruitful?"

"Yes. It has definitely been fruitful. Or most of it has. Some things don't seem to have any answers, which I think is very, very odd."

Henry looked around the church. There were really far too many people here for them to talk privately, although he didn't think they were going to say anything his congregation shouldn't hear. Still, it was always better to be safe. He opened the door at the back of the church and pushed Janet through it into the hall. The hall was mostly empty. There were long slatted wooden benches against the walls. Henry sat Janet down on one of those and then sat down, too. The walls looked too empty out here, too blank. He was going to have to buy some religious pictures to decorate them with.

"Now, then," he said, "tell me what you found out. About Mr. Demarkian or Zhondra Meyer."

"Mr. Demarkian is the boring one," Janet told him. "You want to hear about him first?"

"Fine."

"Mostly, what I found out about Mr. Demarkian is what I've read in the papers," Janet said. "He used to be with the FBI. He was head of a department there and considered very important. He retired just after his wife died of cancer. Now he acts as a consultant when he's called in on murder cases. He doesn't have a private investigator's license, by the way. I checked."

"That's odd," Henry murmured. "I thought you had to have one. To do the things he does, I mean."

"Maybe it's different if you call yourself a consultant," Janet said. "I've always hated that word. I've never understood for a minute what it was supposed to mean."

"What about Mr. Demarkian's religious affiliations? Does he belong to a church? Has he been born again?"

"I sincerely doubt he's ever been born again, Henry. Don't be silly. To tell you the truth, his religious connections are very fuzzy. He does technically belong to a church, Holy Trinity Armenian Christian Church, in Philadelphia—"

"Well, Janet, if it calls itself a Christian church—"

"It's some kind of Eastern European ethnic thing, Henry. They don't mean by it what we do. They just mean they aren't Roman Catholics."

"Does Mr. Demarkian actually go to this church?"

"I can't tell," Janet admitted. "I found out that his closest friend is a priest, though. The priest of this Holy Trinity—"

"But I thought priests are Catholic."

"Some priests are Episcopal, Henry. And they've got priests in this ethnic church. But the really interesting thing is just how much of a connection Mr. Demarkian does have to the Catholics. You know John Cardinal O'Bannion, the one from Colchester, New York?"

"I know who he is, of course I do. He's in the papers all the time."

"Yes, well. It seems that Mr. Demarkian has accommodated him more than once, in murder cases that the cardinal had an interest in—"

"What kind of an interest?"

"Oh, don't get apocalyptic on me, Henry. It's nothing like that. It's just cases priests or nuns have been involved in, or they've taken place on the grounds of a church somewhere. They've mostly been routine things, except for one or two, and you're not going to get Cardinal O'Bannion on any of them. Anyway, the cardinal seems to pay Mr. Demarkian by contributing to all these Armenian charities, you know, for refugees and things like that. It's a very interesting arrangement."

Henry thought it over. You had to be very careful. The Devil was very clever. Even so, he couldn't see anything really wrong with any of this. There didn't seem to be anything about Mr. Demarkian that was actively evil.

"Tell me about Zhondra Meyer," he said. "Is that the person you said you couldn't get decent answers about?"

"It's very, very hard to get answers about somebody that rich," Janet said. "You wouldn't believe the things you can do to preserve your privacy if you've only got enough money. There are some things, though, that are a matter of public record."

"And?"

"Well," Janet said, "in the first place, Zhondra Meyer has been estranged from both her parents for years."

"Because of the lesbianism?"

"Because of the Communism, in the beginning. She joined the Communist Party of the United States when she was in her junior year at Smith. Then she transferred to the University of California at Berkeley and joined a Communist cell there. Her parents were livid."

"Why did they let her transfer? Why didn't they pull her out of school?"

"They couldn't. Zhondra's got her own money, millions and millions of dollars of it. She came into it when she was eighteen."

"Wouldn't that be nice," Henry said. "Can you imagine having a situation like that?"

"No." Janet was blunt. And uninterested in speculating. Janet liked to think of herself as a strictly pragmatic woman. "The thing is, they have tried to do something about her more than once. To rein her in, so to speak, which means to get control of the money away from her. They haven't been successful. But what's interesting to me, Henry, was what they decided to try.''

"And what was it?''

"They tried to have her declared insane.''

Henry sat up even straighter on the bench. "Do you mean her parents tried to have her declared incompetent,'' he demanded, "or insane?''

"I mean *insane,* Henry. I supposed they would have had her declared incompetent, too, when it was all over, but first they tried to have her declared insane. They had her apartment in San Francisco raided and got her locked up in an insane asylum.''

"Good Lord.''

"You wouldn't believe how hard it is to find this information, Henry. I mean, it's all a matter of public record, but they're very good at making sure they don't get any publicity they don't want to have. There were stories in the newspapers, but they were just little squibs. Even after it all went wrong and Zhondra got released and threatened to sue them.''

"It should have been the movie of the week,'' Henry said. "Are you sure all this happened?''

"Oh, yes, Henry. I'm sure. I checked and double-checked, and I had Deacon Hatcher check, too. He's better than I am at the computer. You can get all this stuff off the Internet, if you know where to look.''

"So what did they use to have her committed? They couldn't have had her locked up just because she joined the Communist Party.''

"I don't know what they used to have her committed. Maybe it was enough that they had all that money.''

"What did she use to get herself out?''

"I don't know that, either,'' Janet said. "I told you the information was sketchy. But I was thinking, you know. . . . I was thinking there might be things we might be able to do with it.''

"Like what?''

"Threaten to make it public, maybe. Just something, you know, something that might make them get out of there. We can't have them up there for years and years, poisoning the air we breathe."

"I know that."

Janet stood up and brushed out her skirt. "I've got to get back over to the house. We're cooking lunch for two dozen people today. All these volunteers. You want me to send the printouts and all that stuff back to you?"

"Yes, Janet. Thank you. Thank you very much."

"There's nothing to thank me for," his wife replied. "I wanted to do it. I want them out of here even more than you do. After all, I'm another woman. They don't make people think odd things about you just because they're there. You're a man."

It took Henry a while to unravel this sentence, and by then Janet was gone. The church's front doors were still hissing closed behind her. The air from outside was still spilling over him like a warm bath. Henry stood up and went back to the door of the big main room of the church. Catholics would call it the church proper, but Henry had no name for it that he felt comfortable using. "Chapel," which was what he had used when he first started preaching, seemed positively ridiculous in the sight of all these seats.

Crazy, Henry thought. Maybe that was the answer he was looking for. Maybe he could blame it all on the insanities of everyone involved.

In the meantime, he had to think it through very thoroughly, and make sure it wasn't the Devil talking to him in his head.

There had been times in his life when Henry had found it very difficult to distinguish between the Devil's voice and God's.

3

In the thick patch of trees at the bottom of the hill on which Zhondra Meyer's huge house stood, Bobby Marsh was sitting in a nest of pine needles, murdering a mouse. He had found the mouse, half asleep and scared to death, nibbling disinterestedly at the bottom of his brown paper lunch bag. He had picked it up without having to chase it at all, and it was so small he had no trouble holding it caught in his hand, squeezing at its neck until he felt the bones break under his fingers. The sensation was unreal, like liquor or marijuana or something worse. When the first bone snapped, Bobby felt something leap with joy inside him. That was what he wanted to happen to all of them, all those women up at the camp and all those other people, too, Hall, Sandler, it didn't matter. They were a roadblock made of flesh standing in his way. They were the worst news he had ever heard. They were taking Ginny away from him. Bobby knew he ought to be thinking about Tiffany. He had been trying and trying to think about Tiffany for days. He just hadn't been able to do it. It was Ginny he thought about, and what a perfect gift she had been to him, what a miracle, turned now to dust.

They have everything and they want everybody else to have nothing, he thought, and then he crushed the mouse in his hands, twisted it and twisted it, until its flesh tore and blood began to spurt out onto his fingers.

The blood was red and hot and warm and almost invisible under the pine trees, and Bobby Marsh suddenly found it all so sad, he started to cry.

seven

1

The first thing Gregor Demarkian noticed about Zhondra Meyer's place was that it had a name, threaded into the wrought iron scrollwork at the top of the gate: Bonaventura. The next thing he noticed was that there was a certain Philadelphia Main Line sensibility going on here. This house was not a camp, or a lodge, or even a mansion. It was some sort of palace. The roof was as spiked as a Viking warrior's helmet. The walls were made of dark gray stone and twisted into peaks and arches more Gothic than anything to be found on an Ivy League campus. The drive curved around a large stone fountain where a curving stone whale spewed water from its spout. Gregor found himself wondering if the man who had built this place had been ignorant of what whales used their spouts for, or if he had had some artistic reason for making this spout do what it did, or if he just hadn't cared, because people with money like this didn't have to care. Clayton Hall drove them through the gate in his little Ford Escort, oblivious.

"They used to open this place to the public when Zhondra's grandmother owned it," Clayton said. "They had it all set up like a museum, like one of those palaces in England, and people came through and looked at the furniture. They had Christmas parties, too, with the place all decorated inside and out and the children's choirs from the school in to sing carols. It was a very nice setup. Brought a lot of tourist money into the town.''

''And Zhondra Meyer changed that?''

''Not exactly. The grandmother died and Zhondra was off in college or something. So the place closed and stayed closed until a couple of years ago, when Zhondra started in with this. First thing she did was give an interview to *Town and Country* magazine that made all the wire services and ended up on *The CBS Evening News.* About lesbians.''

''Mmm,'' Gregor said.

''One thing about Zhondra,'' Clayton said. ''She's no shrinking violet. She likes to stick your face right into it.''

Clatyon pulled his car right up to the curve in front of the front doors and cut his engine. Gregor assumed there must be a back lot somewhere, with a garage. Clayton climbed out onto the gravel drive and stretched. Gregor climbed out and looked around. The big front doors were carved from top to bottom in what looked like curvaceous leaves. On either side of them were tall narrow windows made of stained glass.

''Look at this place,'' Clayton said. ''Man who built it—not the grandfather, I think; the great-grandfather—his wife was dead and his children were grown. He put this place up and came down here to vacation for six weeks every year, mostly by himself. With a dozen servants, but they slept out over the garage. If you see what I mean.''

''Did he have guests?''

''He must have had guests,'' Clayton said. ''I remember in the brochures they used to give out, it talked about the parties he gave. People down from New York. Caviar brought in from I don't know where—and there weren't planes to fly it in, not readily available. I don't think people build places like this anymore even if they can afford it.''

''In Hollywood, maybe,'' Gregor said. ''Or one of those new billionaires, like Donald Trump or Bill Gates.''

''There was this guy Michael Milken once. I thought he'd have a place like this. I don't know how many hundreds of millions of dollars he made every year. Turned out, all he had was an ordinary house, not even very big. I could have owned it myself, if it was built out here instead of in California.''

Clayton climbed the steps to the front door and rang the bell. There was a rope to pull instead of a button to push. The rope was made of something shiny and gold, and it was very well kept.

"Zhondra Meyer can't be letting down the side entirely,'' Gregor said. "Somebody's keeping this place up. Somebody's keeping it up very well. I think you have to rake gravel drives to make them look like that.''

"You surely do. Half the town seems to work up here in one capacity or another. I didn't say Ms. Meyer didn't keep the place up.''

"So what is it that you disapprove of so much?'' Gregor asked. "It's obvious that you disapprove. I can see it in your face.''

"Well,'' Clayton Hall said, "it's like this—''

But he didn't have time to finish. The bellpull wasn't only pretty. It worked. One of the big double doors was drawing open. Gregor stepped back politely to wait. A moment later, he saw the figure of a small, dumpy woman in ragged jeans that bagged out at the knees and thighs. She was peering out at them, worry written all over her face.

"Excuse me?'' she said in a high, tight little voice. "Can I help you?''

"It's Clayton Hall, Alice,'' Clayton said patiently. "I called Zhondra a few minutes ago. She knows we're coming. This is Gregor Demarkian.''

Alice turned her head in Gregor's direction and squinted. She was wearing contact lenses. They were tinted ones, a little off center, so that Gregor could tell. She still seemed to be having trouble seeing him. She looked him up and down and paused for a long moment to stare at his shoes. Then she stepped back even farther and motioned them both in.

"We have to be very careful," she said primly, mostly (Gregor assumed) for Gregor's benefit. "We're always in danger here. We never know what we're going to find when the doorbell rings."

"Now, Alice," Clayton Hall said. "You know that isn't true. You haven't had a single spot of trouble since Ms. Meyer opened this camp."

"We've had rhetoric," Alice retorted self-righteously. "And rhetoric matters. Rhetoric can turn to action at any moment." She shut the door firmly behind them and turned to Gregor. "We send people into the churches, you know, undercover. People they don't think belong to us. We tape them."

"Tape them doing what?" Gregor was startled.

"We tape the sermons," Alice said. "You should hear some of the things we get. Especially down at Henry Holborn's place. They're all crazy, down there. In any truly just society, free from patriarchy, they'd all be locked up."

"Henry Holborn talks the same way about beer as he does about you," Clayton Hall said, "and he isn't rampaging around the countryside, shutting down liquor stores."

"People did," Alice said. "There was a woman named Carrie Nation who went around smashing up bars with an ax. Ideas have consequences. You wait and see."

"If Henry Holborn starts running around with an ax," Clayton Hall said, "I'll know it long before he gets here. We did come to talk to Zhondra, Alice. We even called in advance."

"Zhondra is in her study."

"Yes, well. Would you please go call her for us?"

"I'll go see if she can be disturbed. Sometimes she does her spiritual exercises in her study. If she's doing her spiritual exercises, I won't be able to get her for you."

"If she's doing her spiritual exercises, Alice, we'll sit down right here in the foyer and wait until she's ready."

Alice's face seemed to twist into a corkscrew. "This is private property you're standing on, you know. You don't have a search warrant now. You have no right to be here if we don't say you can be here."

"Zhondra did say we could be here. Alice, for God's sake—"

"It's the hallmark of the patriarchy," Alice told Gregor. "Men under patriarchy always proceed with violence and intimidation. Life under patriarchy is always a brutal competition for position in the hierarchy. It would be different in a gender-reimaged society. That's what we do up here. We reimagine ourselves and the world we live in. We strike a blow for equality."

"By reimagining?" Gregor asked.

Alice turned her back on both of them. "I'll go see if Zhondra can be disturbed," she said. "But don't fool yourselves. We've not stupid up here. We know what happened with that baby. We know Henry Holborn or one of those people murdered it and planted it up here just to make it look like it happened in the middle of worshipping the Goddess. Nothing like that could happen in the middle of worshipping the Goddess. The Goddess is a goddess of life."

"Oh," Gregor said.

Alice seemed to think about turning around to face them again and then decided against it.

"I'll go talk to Zhondra," she told them. Then she started off down the hall to the left, walking with that odd rolling gait some almost-fat people have, the back of her churning like the back of a cement truck.

Gregor turned to Clayton Hall and raised his eyebrows. "What was that all about?" he asked.

Clayton sighed. "I don't know. I've been listening to it for the past three years, and I just don't know. It's like they've got a language of their own, and nobody else can understand it."

"Do you think they really are sending undercover people into these churches they're talking about? Fundamentalist churches?"

"I don't see why not. Anybody can go to church, Mr. Demarkian. All you have to do is show up."

"I don't think that's a situation I'd like very much, if I were in your position. That's a situation that's likely to get dangerous on very short notice."

"I'd be a lot more worried if Henry Holborn was sending people up here," Clayton said. "Alice is one of the calmer people in this place, if you can believe it. The women who come up here are really wound up, and they seem to get more wound up the longer they stay. If you want to know the truth, I wasn't all that surprised when I first heard there had been a murder up here."

"You mean you think there really was some kind of devil worship? That Tiffany Marsh really was killed as a blood sacrifice?"

"Oh, hell, no, Mr. Demarkian. It's not that. It's just that for months now, I've been thinking that—"

There were footsteps in the hall again. Alice chugged back in their direction, looking sourer and angrier than ever. She had her arms folded across her very heavy breasts, making her look out of proportion and unsteady on her feet.

She stopped a few feet from them and dropped her arms. "Zhondra says she's ready to talk to you," she said. "You should come along this way."

"Thank you very much," Clayton Hall said. "I appreciate your help."

"Oh, don't give me *that,*" Alice said furiously. "I'll bet you just love this. Getting some woman you hardly even know to show you around a house like a servant. I'll bet you just live for moments like this."

Alice whirled away from them again and marched off down the hall she had just come to them from, not bothering to look back to see if they were following her. On the other hand, the hall seemed to be a straight shot without curves. Gregor didn't see what they needed a guide for.

"Well?" he asked Clayton Hall.

Clayton was shaking his head. "I know where the

study is," he said. "I don't know about you, Mr. Demar-kian, but I find these women completely bewildering. I mean, why would anybody want to live like this?"

Gregor didn't have an answer for that, either, so he let it go.

2

After Alice, Zhondra Meyer came as something of a surprise. Without realizing it, Gregor had simply assumed that everybody who lived at the camp would stay true to type, and that that type must have been set by Zhondra Meyer herself. Instead, in no time at all, he found himself face-to-face with a tall, willowy woman with abundant dark hair that fell to just above her shoulders, enormous gray eyes, and the kind of cheekbones fashion models have surgery to get. She was dressed in a long, batik-printed skirt and a silk T-shirt that flowed and clung in all the right places. The outfit had been put together at inexpensive places—Gregor had learned enough from Bennis Hanna-ford by now to be able to work that out—but in an odd way it suited both the woman and the room. The room was as spectacular as Zhondra Meyer herself, or maybe more so. The ceilings seemed to go halfway into space. The marble fireplace was big enough to roast a calf in. The ormolu clock on the mantel was old enough and fine enough to fetch five figures at auction at Sotheby's, and probably had come down to Zhondra from some relative or other. Almost nobody went out and bought things like that.

Zhondra Meyer was barefoot. There was a pair of sim-ple thong sandals lying on the fireplace hearth, so simple that Gregor knew they must have cost a great deal of money. Gregor found it interesting to contemplate the things Zhondra Meyer did and did not choose to spend her cash on.

She came forward and held out her hand to Gregor.

"Hello, Clayton. How do you do, Mr. Demarkian, I'm glad you're here."

Alice still hovered in the doorway. Zhondra nodded gently. "It's all right, Alice. I can take it from here. Why don't you go find yourself something to eat?"

"No woman should ever be alone with two male police officers." Alice's face was stony. "You remember we talked about that in meeting last week."

"Yes," Zhondra said. "I know we did. But this is different, Alice. There isn't any need for that kind of precaution here."

"How can you possibly know that? You've never seen that Demarkian person before in your life."

"Alice."

Alice suddenly looked close to tears. "All right," she said. "All right. But you be careful. Keep your whistle on you just in case."

"I've got my whistle on me," Zhondra said.

Alice went out the door, but she didn't shut it. Gregor imagined her lurking in the hallway, listening for the first sounds of violence.

"Is she always like that?" he asked Zhondra Meyer.

Zhondra moved to sit down behind her desk. "Yes," she said, sounding exasperated. "Alice is always like that. You see, she kept trying to divorce her husband. Every time she filed papers, he would show up and break enough of her bones to put her in the hospital, and when she got out he would stalk her until she didn't dare try to go on with the proceedings. It took her six years to get a decree, and then do you know what happened?"

"No," Gregor said.

"He showed up again, broke both her arms and both her legs, gave her a broken jaw, ruptured her spleen so badly she very nearly died, knocked out most of her teeth, and ripped off all of her clothes in the process. I think the police department in Memphis did then deign to arrest this asshole, but you see what I'm getting at here. Alice is always like that because Alice has good reason to be always like that. So do most of the women who come to stay here. That's what this place is for.''

''I didn't say she didn't have good reason,'' Gregor said.

''Of course you didn't.'' Zhondra Meyer put her head in her hands and rubbed her eyes. When she looked up again, she seemed faintly blurred. ''All right, now,'' she said. ''Clayton, Mr. Demarkian. Here we are. What do we do now? I don't want to start sounding like Alice, but things are getting very bad around here. I spend half my time wondering if I'm about to be lynched.''

''Could I clear some things up first?'' Gregor asked. ''I'm just a little confused about what exactly is going on here.''

''Of course,'' Zhondra Meyer said. ''Ask anything you like. Have a brochure.''

Gregor took the four-color glossy foldout from Zhondra's hand. It had a picture of the front gate on the cover and the words: *Bonaventura. A Camp for Gay Women.*

''Well, that answers one thing,'' Gregor said. ''This is a camp for gay women. If you want to call it a camp.''

Zhondra grinned. ''My grandfather called it his hunting cabin, if you can believe it.''

''I live very close to the Philadelphia Main Line, Ms. Meyer. I can believe it. Is Alice a lesbian as well as a battered wife? Or did you make a concession in her case?''

''Actually, sort of both at once. When I opened this place, I thought I was going to have the sort of thing they've got in that town in Mississippi, you know, a place where women could come to come out or to talk about what it was like living in a very antigay culture. And I do have that, sort of. But the more I spoke and the more I listened, the more I ran into battered wives who wanted to give up heterosexuality. I don't know, Mr. Demarkian. I've never been particularly attracted by heterosexuality. I suppose these days I'm just trying to . . . help out.''

''Well, that's not a bad idea,'' Gregor said. ''What about all this talk of goddess worship? Were there women up here worshipping a goddess on the day of the hurricane? Which goddess?"

"The Goddess Sophia, Mr. Demarkian. Don't worry if you've never heard of her. She was constructed, really, by the women's movement. Or specifically, the movement to reclaim women's spirituality. A lot of women seem to need religion very much, even if religion hasn't been very good to them."

"I take it you don't need religion very much," Gregor said.

"Actually, I'm a rank atheist. The very word 'spirituality' makes my eyes glaze over."

"But you don't disapprove of it?"

"I don't really think about it. If a bunch of women want to go out to the pine grove and sing songs to the Great Mother of Us All, I don't see any reason why they shouldn't."

"And that was what they were doing the day of the hurricane? Singing songs to the Great Mother?"

"That's right."

"Naked?"

Zhondra fluttered her hands in the air. "I know it sounds ridiculous," she said, "but it's part of the ritual. Learning to honor your body. Your body is an avatar. The Great Mother lives in every woman. Every woman is therefore beautiful."

"And this requires running around naked in the outdoors during a hurricane?"

"Well, Mr. Demarkian, the hurricane hadn't started when they went out to do it. They should have been done long before they had anything to worry about. It isn't even that long a ceremony."

"But they weren't done."

"No, they weren't," Zhondra agreed. "That's because Carol Littleton was late. She'd gone into town to buy a christening present for her granddaughter, I remember, and she didn't get back until more than half an hour after she was expected. And they didn't want to start without her, so they waited."

"Had the storm started by the time they did?"

"I don't know," Zhondra said. "I wasn't with them then. I'd come inside. We had a lot of people up here, getting out of the weather. A lot of people from town. I invited them. I thought it would be good public relations."

"Was it?"

"God only knows. We were all sitting in here around the fire, with the power off and the candles on, playing out a scene from some ancient movie, I suppose, when David Sandler came in with Ginny Marsh and she had blood all over her. I don't suppose that was good for public relations."

"I don't suppose it was. The women who were supposed to be worshipping the goddess weren't here at the time David Sandler brought back Ginny Marsh?"

"No, they weren't."

"Who was?"

"I really couldn't tell you, Mr. Demarkian. We had a couple of dozen people here. I don't remember noticing anything in particular. Or anyone."

"Would you know just who these couple of dozen people were, if you had to know? Could you write down their names?"

"All of them? No, I couldn't. Some were people I'd never even heard of before. They were here out of curiosity, I guess, or because they lived close. I could give you the names of about half of them, though. There were quite a few people I did know. Like Maggie Kelleher and Rose MacNeill and Naomi Brent. Rose was wearing so much religious jewelry, I thought she was going to rename herself Trinity Christian Church and open up for services."

"All right," Gregor said. "We'll get to that later. For now, let's think about this goddess service the women were holding. How many women were there?"

"Three."

"Were they regular guests at the camp?"

"All three of them have been here longer than a year."

"So you knew them well."

"I knew them."

"Who were they?"

"Well," Zhondra said, "Carol Littleton was one. Dinah Truebrand was one of the other two. She wrote the litany they sang. And then there was Stelle Cary. Stelle is boring. She knew she was a lesbian from the time she was twelve. She's only here because she wanted to spend some time in a place where that wasn't a weird thing to be."

"What kind of litany was this?" Gregor asked, thinking about Jackson and his reference to various parts of the female anatomy.

Zhondra Meyer opened the long center drawer of the desk and pulled out a single piece of typing paper. "I thought somebody was going to ask for that eventually. I've been keeping this for days. I'm afraid Dinah has more zeal than artistic talent."

Gregor looked down at the sheet Zhondra Meyer handed him and blinked.

"Great Mother of Us All, make sacred my body," it read and then:

> *Make sacred all my limbs*
> *Make sacred my throat and tongue*
> *Make sacred my thighs and breasts*
> *Make sacred the folds of my vulva*
> *Make sacred the flower of my clitoris*

Gregor tried to hand the sheet to Clayton Hall, but he wouldn't have it.

"I've already seen it," Clayton said.

Gregor put the sheet down on the desk. "Very interesting," he told Zhondra Meyer. "Does this really help women find their—spirituality?"

"I wouldn't know. It's like I said. I'm an atheist. But you see what I mean, Mr. Demarkian. There's nothing of devil worship about it. There's no violence. There's no sac-rifice. They just sing this thing or something like it, and light candles and close their eyes. They've done it hundreds of times in the last year or so and there's never been any problem with it at all. Why should there suddenly be one now?''

Gregor thought about it. ''You're sure of what went on in these rituals? They couldn't be telling you one thing and doing another?''

''I suppose they could, Mr. Demarkian, but why should they bother? I'm really quite tolerant of other peo-ple's beliefs. I wouldn't have stopped them, even if they had been sacrificing mice or whatever. But they weren't. The whole point about the goddess movement is how non-violent and antihierarchical it is. What they don't like about Christianity is the whole idea of blood sacrifice.''

''Are these three women around here someplace where I could talk to them?''

''Of course. Do you want me to get them now?''

''Not just yet,'' Gregor said. ''What about this pine grove or whatever. Is it close?''

''Just off the terrace and down the hill about fifty feet.''

''Could we go there right away?''

''Of course.''

Zhondra Meyer got off her chair and went to the hearth to put her sandals on. Clayton Hall started to look uncomfortable.

''You know,'' he said, ''we're pretty sure the baby wasn't killed in the grove. It wouldn't be like you were going to view the crime scene or something.''

''I understand that,'' Gregor said. ''I just want to see what this place is like. So many people seemed to be inter-ested in it.''

Zhondra Meyer opened a set of French doors and stepped out onto the terrace. ''Come with me,'' she said. ''It really isn't very far at all. And it's very clean, too. Goddess worshippers don't litter.''

Gregor stepped out onto the terrace and looked around. Even from back here, the house was enormous. It looked like a hotel. He and Clayton Hall followed Zhondra. They went across the flagstones and onto the grass. Then the lawn began to slope gently toward a stand of trees.

"Be careful," she called back to them, "there's a path here and you've got to take it. The lawn is riddled with gopher holes. If you get off the track, you're likely to break your ankle."

Gregor stayed on the track. Clayton Hall wasn't so careful, but nothing awful happened to him. Zhondra Meyer seemed to adhere to the path like a train on a track. It came naturally.

"That's funny," she said, stopping suddenly. "Somebody must have been drunk."

"What do you mean?" Gregor came up behind her.

Zhondra Meyer pointed forward, and Gregor saw it. There was a clearing in the stand of trees, an almost perfect circle of pines. The clearing was covered with dead pine needles. At the center of it was a pile of stones made to look like the lip of a well. Next to the lip was what seemed to be a pile of old clothes.

"They never leave their things out here like this," Zhondra Meyer said, striding forward. "They're always very careful. I wouldn't allow them to do this otherwise."

Gregor put a hand on Zhondra's arm to stop her. "I wouldn't do that," he said. "Not just yet."

"Do what?" Zhondra asked.

Clayton came up behind them both and came to a dead halt. By then, Gregor didn't see how either of them could be missing it. It seemed so clear to him, and so eerie, out here in the pines and the silence and the isolation, out here in the clear morning air.

It wasn't a pile of clothes that was lying next to the stones.

It was a body.

*part
two*

———

one

1

Her name was Carol Littleton. That was one of the few things Gregor could find out, for certain, in all the long two hours that followed the discovery of the body. Most of what went on was what he had become used to over the last few years: the routine of securing the crime scene, and talking to witnesses, and giving the tech men the space they needed to get done what they had to get done. Oddly enough, Gregor had never experienced any of it when he was still with the FBI. Once he became head of the Behavioral Sciences Department, he rarely left his office. When he did, as in the few times in his Bureau career when he had been called in on a murder that occurred on federal lands, he had arrived on the scene long after the initial details had been taken care of. The FBI dealt with the Big Picture, according to J. Edgar Hoover and every director who came after him. Gregor had gotten used to thinking of murders in terms of unified psychological histories and interstate tracking maps and cycles of violence. He didn't think the death of Carol Littleton was going to call for that kind of expertise. She was lying out there in the leaves, tangled in a sheet and a rough brown poncho, looking haggard and heavy and ill. She had two tiny gold earrings threaded through her tiny pierced ears, a single uncertain concession to femininity.

"I'm so glad she turned out to be dressed," Zhondra

Meyer said at one point in the proceedings. She was whispering into Gregor's ear. It had taken the media people in town no time at all to realize that something was going on up here. Locking the front gates of Bonaventura against them did no good at all.

"I was afraid she'd come out here to do a ritual," Zhondra told Gregor, "and then had a heart attack or something. I was afraid she would be lying there with no clothes on, and it would be in all the papers tomorrow. Christ, couldn't you just see it?"

"She didn't have a heart attack, Ms. Meyer, she had her throat cut."

Zhondra Meyer stared at Gregor solemnly. Her already large eyes seemed to get larger. Every visible part of her seemed to turn to glass. Gregor shifted from foot to foot, uncomfortable. It was like being watched by a machine with bad intentions.

"I wonder what she was doing out here all by herself," Zhondra said. "They didn't usually come here on their own. Except to set up for another ritual, maybe, or something like that. I wonder why she was here. . . ."

"You really have no idea?"

"No idea at all."

"Maybe they'll be able to find out by talking to some of the other women. Maybe she was intending to meet somebody here."

Zhondra Meyer looked away across the crowds of police and reporters. There was now a police officer doing nothing but keeping the reporters away from where the police needed to be. There was a little knot of women standing on the sidelines, too, but they weren't causing any trouble. Some of the women seemed to be clones of each other, or members of the same club. They were all stocky, with blunt-cut hair and no makeup, wearing jeans or bib overalls. The rest of the women were birds of plumage, dressed up in red and blue and green. Gregor saw both of the women he had talked to about the case that morning: Maggie Kelleher and Naomi Brent. Then he wondered if it would really be this easy to tell the difference between the women of the town and the women of the camp. Certainly no woman of the town would for a moment dress the way the women of the camp did. Bib overalls and stretched-out blue jeans were not high fashion in Bellerton, North Carolina. Still, Zhondra Meyer did not dress like that. There might be other women in the camp who didn't, either. If you saw a woman in town, a woman you had questions about, how would you be able to tell?

Zhondra Meyer seemed to have made up her mind about something. She straightened up and brushed hair out of her eyes. "I don't think any of the women here are going to do much talking to the police, this time," she said. "We did a lot of talking to the police last time. Obviously, somebody is trying to persecute us. And the police are doing absolutely nothing about it."

"You know," Gregor said, "it might have nothing to do with persecution. It might be a simple case of opportunity. It's very secluded out here."

"It's very secluded in half a dozen places in Bellerton. Murders aren't happening there."

"From what I understand, the first murder didn't happen here."

"Ginny said it did. Not that I have much respect for Ginny, because I don't. But she said it did."

"That doesn't make it so."

"It does make for a lot of trouble, Mr. Demarkian. Police all over the grounds. Everybody's privacy being invaded. I don't think half of this would have happened, half of this poking and prying and fussing, if we had been some more respectable organization, like Henry Holborn's church."

"A murder investigation is a murder investigation, Ms. Meyer. There are procedures that must be followed. There are things that must be done."

"I don't believe the same procedures have to be followed when the suspect is O. J. Simpson instead of some nobody street hood hanging out on Hollywood and Vine."

"I'm not saying there are no inequities in the system," Gregor said. "I'm simply saying that there's a bottom line here. There are certain things that have to be done, no matter who you're dealing with. There are certain questions that have to be asked. There are some things, Ms. Meyer, that just can't be gotten around."

Zhondra Meyer flicked imaginary lint off the bottom of her silk T-shirt. She hadn't been looking at him through most of this conversation. She wasn't looking at him now. She was staring into the clearing at the circle of stones and the men doing their work around it.

"You know," she said, "most people think gay people are marginal. Especially lesbians. They think we have no money, and no clout, and no resources. That's why they think we're easy targets."

"Ms. Meyer, I don't believe a single person in the entire state of North Carolina thinks you have no money or no clout or no resources. Who and what you are have been shouted through every media outlet from *North Carolina* magazine to *60 Minutes*. That was you, I think, that I saw profiled once on *60 Minutes*."

"That was me," Zhondra said. "But I think you're wrong anyway. I think it becomes something worse than a habit. It becomes a conviction in the blood. I think I've put up with it for as long as I have any intention of putting up with it. If Clayton or any of the rest of them are looking for me, you can tell them I've gone back up to the house."

"What are you going to do."

Zhondra Meyer smiled her little cat smile. It made her face look feral. "I'm going to do what I should have done in the beginning, Mr. Demarkian. I'm going to call my lawyers in New York and make sure they get somebody down here to raise holy hell. There are very few things that are more satisfying in this world than being extremely rich when somebody is trying to push you around. I think it's time I took advantage of my advantages."

"Somehow," Gregor said, "this doesn't sound like the Zhondra Meyer of the American Communist Party."

"It's called the Communist Party U.S.A. And you're wrong, Mr. Demarkian. This is very much the Zhondra Meyer of the Communist Party. But that is hardly the point. Tell Clayton that if this place isn't cleaned up when he goes, I'll sue him for what it costs me to get it cleaned. Good afternoon, Mr. Demarkian. I'm in a hurry."

It wasn't afternoon yet. It was barely eleven o'clock in the morning. Gregor didn't mention it. Zhondra was walking away from him, down the path and out through the clearing. A couple of the media people started toward her and then stopped. Even the reporters could sense that she wasn't going to be gracious and forthcoming this morning. The photographers didn't care so much. Gregor counted three separate minicams aimed in Zhondra's direction. He felt every flash that went off in the dark of the trees.

Zhondra Meyer disappeared into the shadows. Gregor looked back at the knot of women and noticed that none of them was talking. They all looked pasty and a little ill, each and every one of them, whether they were wearing makeup or not. Gregor felt cold. The air was nippy. He should have worn his sweater.

He got his mind off his sweater, picked Clayton Hall out of the crush of police officers standing around the stone circle, and headed in that direction.

2

Clayton Hall looked not only tired, but exasperated. The corpse was gone, the tech men were doing their jobs, but everything still seemed to be confusion. Gregor picked up the air of chaos as soon as he got in the middle of the uniforms. Nobody challenged his right to be there. He would have been flattered, but he had a feeling that the explanation was not what he would want it to be. These policemen didn't recognize him. They just knew by looking at him that he was not a reporter—mostly, of course, because he was so obviously too old.

Clayton Hall was standing off to the side a little, talking to a man in blue jeans and a white lab coat. The lab coat was unbuttoned down the front, showing a plain white shirt and a fancy Western vest, leather with carvings and studs. Gregor seemed to remember having been introduced to this man when he'd first arrived. This was the one private doctor in town, the one who worked as a medical examiner in the few cases that required it.

"It's not that we've got a lot of murders in Bellerton," Clayton had explained at the time. "We don't. What we have is a lot of drunks splattered across the highways on Saturday nights."

Gregor thought that that was probably an exaggeration. How many drunk driving deaths could a small town have in a single year? Then he remembered all the tourists who came to Bellerton in the summers and changed his mind.

Clayton Hall was shifting from one foot to the other. Gregor walked up beside him and waited.

"Let me try to get this straight," Clayton was saying. "She wasn't killed here. And you're sure of it."

The man in the white lab coat looked exasperated himself. "What I'm trying to say," he said, in the first truly pronounced drawl Gregor had heard since coming to North Carolina, "is that her throat wasn't cut here. Her throat was cut before she was dead—"

"You're sure of that."

"Yes, Clayton, I'm sure of it. It doesn't take a state police tech lab to figure that out. What it takes a state police tech lab to figure out is whether she died from having her throat cut or whether there was some other reason."

"Why in hell would there be any other reason?" Clayton demanded. "There looks like there's a gouge four inches deep in that woman's neck—"

"More like one and a half—"

"Whatever. Enough. Getting her throat cut like that would have been enough to kill her."

"Yes, it would have, but that still doesn't mean that's

what she died from. We can't know what she died from until we get the lab to check what has to be checked. What I'm trying to get across here, though, is that you've got this problem for the second time. The baby wasn't killed here. This woman wasn't killed here. You've got to figure out what it is about *here* that makes it so damn popular for—I don't know what. Misdirection, maybe.''

"But the baby never was here," Clayton said. "Ginny said she was here."

"Yeah, well, there's one more thing you better think about. Far as I know, Ginny's been locked up in the town jail for weeks now. She wasn't out here killing this woman. And if this woman died of having her throat cut, Ginny couldn't have done it under any circumstances. She isn't big enough."

"The woman could have been drugged first," Gregor said.

The man in the white lab coat turned to him and looked him up and down.

"Oh, Gregor," Clayton said. "I was wondering where you were. This here is John Chester. He serves as—"

"Coroner when you need one," Gregor said. "I remember."

John Chester nodded his head. "I know who you are, too. The Great Demarkian. The Armenian-American Hercule Poirot. Do you think you can explain to Clayton here the difference between knowing she didn't have her throat cut here and knowing she was killed here?"

"I think I've got it, John. Really. I think I've got it."

"Maybe." John Chester didn't sound convinced.

"Where have you been?" Clayton asked Gregor. "I was looking all over for you a little while ago."

"I was talking to Zhondra Meyer," Gregor said. "And trying to stay out of the way, too, of course."

"You don't have to stay out of the way." Clayton looked distracted. "I tried to talk to Zhondra a little while ago. I didn't feel like I was getting through. If you know what I mean."

"I know what you mean. I think Ms. Meyer is on the warpath."

"Really?" Now Clayton looked pained. "Well, it was coming, wasn't it? I suppose we got off lucky to keep her calmed down up to now. She threatening to call her lawyers?"

"I think she's already calling them."

Clayton threw his head back and looked up into the pines. "Well, that just about tears it, doesn't it?" he said. "All of this and Zhondra Meyer's New York lawyers. And in the end, she'll turn out to be right and here we'll all be, looking like hicks with egg on our faces."

John Chester looked like he had heard this lament before. "Listen, Clayton," he said. "I've got work to do. Why don't you drop over to my house this afternoon and we can go over what I've got?"

"Sure," Clayton Hall said.

Gregor put out his hand and touched John Chester on the arm. "Just a minute, do you mind? Could I ask you one or two more things?"

"If you're going to ask how I know her throat wasn't cut here, I don't want to answer. You shouldn't need me to tell you."

Gregor didn't need John Chester to tell him. He could see, even now and at a distance, that there was no significant amount of blood anywhere near the circle of stones.

"I just want some intelligent guesses to go on with," he said. "Do you think it will turn out that she was killed by having her throat cut?"

John Chester nodded. "Oh, yeah. You get a good look at it, you can see she was good and alive when that cut happened. She lost a lot of blood. Her skin is absolutely white. What I'm not so sure of is, whether that was what her murderer intended her to die of, if you see what I mean."

"No," Gregor said.

John Chester gestured to the circle of stones. "It bothers me," he said, "all this concentration on the stones, all this hokey-looking evidence to say that there was some ritual involved.''

''So you don't think Ginny Marsh was telling the truth when she said she saw devil worshippers kill her baby at a Black Mass?''

''I know she wasn't telling the truth when she said the baby was killed here,'' John Chester said. ''It couldn't have been.''

''Do you think Ginny Marsh killed her baby?''

John Chester shrugged. ''I think it's most likely she did or Bobby did. Her husband, Bobby Marsh, the baby's father—''

''I know,'' Gregor said.

''The common thing is for it to be one or the other, or both of them together. Or a boyfriend, of course, but I don't know of any boyfriend in this case. You go around and around it, don't you? All the usual explanations.''

''But Ginny Marsh couldn't have killed Carol Littleton,'' Gregor said. ''You just told us that yourself.''

''I know. But Bobby could have. He's big and strong and dumb enough. Not that I've got anything against Bobby Marsh, you understand, he's just not too bright.''

''The other thing, of course, is that you haven't answered me,'' Gregor said. ''You didn't tell me if you thought they did it, either one of them or the two of them together.''

John Chester sighed. ''I don't exactly have an answer for you, Mr. Demarkian. I guess I thought it would all be cleared up by now. Ginny would just—bend under the strain and tell us what happened.''

''Which she hasn't,'' Gregor said.

''She definitely hasn't,'' Clayton Hall said. ''If anything, she's getting quieter and quieter by the minute.''

''What about Bobby Marsh?'' Gregor asked.

''Mostly he drinks,'' John Chester said. ''He's in the bars every night, and out on the road by two in the morning, too. One of these days I'm going to have to scrape him off the highway.''

"Do you think that indicates guilt or innocence?"

"I think it indicates that Bobby and the Reverend Holborn are having their problems again," John Chester replied. "Bobby is a deacon in Henry Holborn's church. Whenever they're on the outs, Bobby goes to hell. I think he may be trying to get there literally."

"Do you think they've fallen out over the murder of the baby?"

"No way to tell," John Chester said.

"Do you think this murder and the murder of the baby are connected?"

"I couldn't really say. They'd have to be connected at least superficially, though, wouldn't they? Even if it was just a copycat kind of thing, somebody trying to make us think the murders were connected." John Chester sighed. "I'm sorry I couldn't be more help than this," he said. "It's just that there isn't much to go on with all this. And there are a lot of people involved I don't know. The women who live up here, for instance."

"And that makes a difference?"

"When you know people, you have a fair idea of what they're likely to do," John Chester said. "Not always and not completely. It's easy to get fooled. Even so, you've got some parameters. But with strangers—" He shrugged again.

"Do you think this murder was committed by a stranger? Do you think the murder of the baby was?"

"I think none of this makes any damn sense at all," John Chester said. "I think—oh, Jesus."

"What is it?" Gregor said.

"God damn it to hell," Clayton Hall said. "How did they get in here? I'm going to bust somebody's ass just for letting them in here."

"What is it?" Gregor asked again.

There were too many people milling around in the clearing, that was the problem. Gregor had a hard time seeing past the cops and the women. Then he realized he was looking in the wrong direction. It wasn't the path where the commotion was. The disturbance was arriving from the other direction, from the far side of the clearing, through the thick stand of trees.

The disturbance was being led by a six-foot cross painted gold and mounted on a long stick. The cross was held high in the air, and it came with chanting.

Dear sweet Jesus Christ, Gregor thought. Now what have I gotten myself into?

3

It wasn't just a cross and chanting. It was dozens and dozens of people. It took only moments for that to become clear. It took only moments more for the implications of that to be felt. The clearing was really very, very small. Gregor was pushed back into the knot of women and separated entirely from the uniformed police. The uniformed police were pushed in the other direction. They should have responded, but they seemed to be stunned. The cross advanced inexorably. People fell away from in front of it, like vampires in a Bela Lugosi movie. Then Gregor realized that what he had first thought of as chanting wasn't chanting at all, but singing, done badly. They were trying to do "Give Me That Old Time Religion," but too many of them were tone-deaf.

He turned around and saw Maggie Kelleher standing beside him, her arms wrapped around her chest, her forehead furrowed into deep lines.

"What is this?" he asked her. "Who are these people?"

"It's Henry Holborn and the Full Gospel Christian Church," Maggie said. "It looks like the whole Full Gospel Christian Church. Henry is the older man next to the cross."

It was a young man who was actually holding the cross. Gregor turned his attention to the man beside that one and decided there was nothing much to see. Henry

Holborn seemed to be an ordinary, well-kept man in late middle age, not somebody you would notice twice on the street.

"Somehow, with everything I've heard about him, I thought he'd be more—charismatic," Gregor said.

"He's charismatic enough," Maggie told him. "Just you watch. I can't believe he's doing this."

"Doing what?" Gregor asked.

In the center of the clearing, the cross had been raised high into the air. It was stuck up among the pine boughs now, partially out of sight. Henry Holborn had his eyes closed and his head thrown back.

"Lord God Almighty, Lord Jesus Christ, hear our prayer," Henry Holborn cried.

The rest of the crowd who had come with Henry Holborn, and some of the people who had not, said something fuzzy that Gregor took to be "Amen."

"Lord God Almighty, evil has been done in this place," Henry Holborn said. "Satan has been worshipped in this place. The powers of Hell have been called into being in this place."

Where were the police? Gregor wondered. Where was Clayton Hall? If Henry Holborn and his people were doing nothing else, they were destroying a vital evidence scene. At least the state police ought to be doing something, even if Clayton didn't have the resources.

"Lord Jesus Christ," Henry Holborn said. "Cleanse this place. Take the evil out of it."

"Amen," the crowd said.

"Soften the hearts of these evildoers and bring them to Your righteousness."

"Amen."

"Cast the Devil and all his minions into the outer darkness."

"Amen."

"Cleanse this place."

"Henry Holborn ought to be locked up," Maggie Kelleher said furiously. "I can't believe Clayton is letting him get away with this."

"I can't even see Clayton," Gregor said. "Are there people here who belong to Holborn's church but aren't in the core group?"

"Half the town belongs to Holborn's church. Excuse me, Mr. Demarkian. I've got to get out of here before I commit a murder of my own."

Gregor had no idea how Maggie was going to get out of this crowd. He could barely move himself. Henry Holborn and his entire congregation seemed to be swaying, like tall grass in a high wind. The young man who was holding the big cross on the stick had put the stick down in the middle of the circle of stones, as if he were claiming the circle and all it influenced for his sovereign Lord.

"Lord God Almighty, in the name of Christ Jesus, cast the Devil out and preserve Your good and faithful servants from the evil and destruction he brings whenever he is called."

"That's *enough,*" Clayton Hall said, appearing suddenly out of nowhere. It took Gregor a full second to realize who he was. Standing in the middle of Henry Holborn and his followers, Clayton looked a little ridiculous—and smaller than Gregor had remembered him.

"That's enough," Clayton said again, louder this time, so that everybody heard him and the noise in the clearing began to ebb. "When I say it's enough, I mean it's *enough.*"

Then Clayton took his gun out of the holster, aimed it into the air, and fired.

two

1

The reporters were all up at the camp, milling around the edges of the clearing, trying to get one of Henry Holborn's people to talk to them. Naomi knew, because she had just come down from the camp herself. Gregor Demarkian had been there, and Clayton Hall, and all the police and state police from this part of the state. Naomi had watched them work with a sick feeling in the pit of her stomach, a kind of heat that made her think of what a hot flash might be like. She still didn't know what it was she had gone up there for. It had seemed natural at the time. When she left the library and started to walk toward Zhondra Meyer's place, she found herself in a whole drift of people headed the same way. Maggie Kelleher had been there, and Rose MacNeill, and even Charlie Hare. Later, she had seen people up there she never would have expected, like David Sandler, and Stephen Harrow from the Methodist Church. They couldn't all have been listening to the police band. Naomi had a CB radio in her office at the library, and a few other pieces of equipment, too, computers and fax machines. She kept ordering equipment and the Town Council kept giving it to her, reflexively, as if they didn't even bother to read the requisition forms she filled out. Maybe they didn't. Maybe, like her, they were all much too busy chasing ambulances in their heads and wondering what kind of trouble it was their friends and neighbors had gotten into this time. Naomi had seen more than one member of the Town Council up at the camp this morning. They had eager looks on their faces and hair slicked back with the sweat of excitement, just like everybody else.

Coming back down into town again, Naomi began to wish that she had never gone up. She was wearing very high heels with open toes and skinny straps. It hurt to walk in them, and one of the straps had torn away and fallen off in her travels, she didn't know when. Besides, she was feeling more than a little ashamed of herself. What was it she had expected to see? What was it any of them had expected to see? Naomi seemed to remember thinking that there would be a corpse up there, out in the open—but she was smart enough and old enough to know that was impossible. She remembered Carol Littleton, vaguely: a stout, stolid, plain woman who did nothing at all to take care of herself. Sometimes Naomi wanted to take the women from the camp and shake them by the shoulders. It wasn't necessary to cut your own hair with kitchen scissors or let your body run to fat or dress in thick denim sacks with no shape to them. Even if you didn't want to wear makeup—Naomi couldn't imagine a woman not wanting to wear makeup— there were things you could do to your face to make it look more alive, more human, more *important*. Carol Littleton had been one of those women who look perpetually on the verge of tears. When those women were from the South they drank, secretly, and sat on the broad platforms of their columned front porches, looking dazed. Carol Littleton had always looked dazed. Who on earth would want to cut her throat? There was no reason to murder a woman like that. It was so much more effective just to ignore her.

Main Street was deserted, although Naomi could tell she wasn't the first one back. She could see Charlie Hare through the plate glass window of the feed store. The OPEN sign was hanging on Maggie Kelleher's bookshop door, in spite of the fact that this was the one day a week she didn't have any help. Naomi looked at the library and bit her lip.

She didn't really want to go back there just yet. She really could be fairly sure that it would be deserted. It was the reporters she had to deal with most these days. They all wanted to use the microfilm machine and read old copies of the Bellerton *Times*. They filed stories about racial incidents that took place in 1899 and religious revivals that went bad in 1902 as if it had all happened the day before yesterday. Naomi wanted to plant something for them to find: stories of space aliens; stories of pastors talking to little green men from Mars right in the middle of the Hartford Road. These people from New York were so stupid, and so prejudiced, they would probably believe them.

Naomi stopped on the sidewalk and saw she was standing next to Rose MacNeill's big Victorian house. In the window of the curving tower that faced the street was a stained glass sun-catcher, spelling out the message JESUS IS LORD. Naomi saw Rose MacNeill, too, through a window closer to the front door. She was fussing with a display of something, talking to someone who was out of sight.

I don't have to stand here in the middle of Main Street, Naomi thought. I can go into Rose's shop just like anybody else. Then she looked guiltily down the street, at the library again. They paid her to work, for God's sake, not to visit at Rose's, not to run all over town trying to get a look at a body. She had been away from her desk for hours.

Naomi turned off the sidewalk onto Rose MacNeill's brick front walk, went up the steps to the front porch, and started to knock on the door. Then she remembered that this was not a house any longer, but a store, and went right in. The big front hall inside was very cool, almost frigid. It was funny, Naomi thought, the things you *didn't* think to notice about your neighbor's business. You wanted to know who was sleeping with whose husband and which wife had a fit about the drinking and threw which husband out—but a simple thing like this, that Rose must have had this big old house retrofitted for central air, didn't catch your attention at all.

"Naomi?" Rose stepped out from behind a pile of books. The books were all paperbacks by Hal Lindsey—*The Late Great Planet Earth; The Liberation of Planet Earth; Satan Is Alive and Well on Planet Earth*—and Naomi felt a rush of contemptuous impatience. It wasn't that Hal Lindsey was more than a little bit harebrained in his theories of life, death, and resurrection. A lot of people were a little harebrained. The problem with Hal Lindsey was that he wrote badly, and for that Naomi could never forgive him.

Rose was brushing dust off her hands onto her apron. "I saw you up at the camp," she said. "I think I came down before you did. Can you believe it? It's turning into a charnel house up there. Bodies with their throats cut. At least this time it wasn't a baby."

"She used to come into the library sometimes," Naomi said. "She seemed harmless enough. There was nothing unusual about her."

"She came in here once, too." Rose was nodding. "It was the day of the hurricane, the day little Tiffany was killed. I was just telling that man Gregor Demarkian about it. I got sort of stuffed into a corner with him while they were clearing out Henry Holborn and his people. My, my. Can you imagine Henry acting like that? I still think of him as being back in high school, raising hell and being good-for-nothing."

"I think he's still good-for-nothing," Naomi said. "What did Carol Littleton want in the store on the day of the hurricane?"

Rose had started fussing with another display. This one was of angels: angel dolls in robes and chiffon net gowns; angels on pins and angels on desk calendars. There were even angel bookmarks printed with the words *The Angel of the Lord Declared unto Mary.* Underneath the display there was another pile of books. These were a single title in hardcover, called *Angels: How to Tell the Good Ones from the Bad Ones and Bring the Power of God into*

Your Life. Rose straightened a couple of these, although they didn't look like they needed it.

"She was looking for a christening gift," Rose said, "for her granddaughter, I think it was, but really, it was pitiful. She didn't even know the right word for it."

"For what?"

"For a christening," Rose said. "Can you imagine someone being brought up so ignorant of religion that she doesn't even know what to call a christening? In the United States, for Heaven's sake. In this day and age."

"Some people belong to churches that don't have infant baptism," Naomi said. "When they baptize adults, they don't call it a christening. And Jews don't have christenings at all."

"I didn't say everybody had christenings. I said most people knew what they were. Knew the word for them, at any rate. She bought a present for her granddaughter anyway."

"She did? What was it?"

"One of those Madonna pictures you hang on the wall. One of the midsize ones, in a frame. She didn't know what to call that, either. She kept asking for a picture of a mother and a baby. I felt sorry for her after a while, and it was funny, because when I first knew she was in the store, I was scared stiff."

"You were?" Naomi was bewildered. "Why?"

Rose made a face. "Well, you never know, do you? And the things I heard. I didn't know anybody up at the camp then. From the things Henry Holborn was saying, I thought they had horns and tails up there."

"And you've changed your mind?"

Rose turned her face away. "I think the way Henry Holborn talks sometimes is very dangerous. I don't think he should be allowed to do it."

"But he is allowed to do it," Naomi said. "That's what the First Amendment is all about."

"Well, I don't know about the First Amendment. I just know that you shouldn't talk trash like that. And he lies about things, you know. I don't mean he tells outright lies, but he leaves things out and that makes what he's saying a lie. Do you know what I mean?"

"No."

"Well, for Heaven's sake, Naomi. Think about it. Henry's always going on and on and on about how Zhondra Meyer's camp brought all this evil here and flooded the town with homosexuals, but that isn't true, is it? Remember Miss Thornton and Miss Bates?"

"Oh," Naomi said, the memory pushing a little puff of laughter out of her throat. "Oh, yes. I haven't thought of them in years. Miss Bates had hats, and Miss Thornton bought army surplus boots and smoked a cigar."

"There was Mr. Catervay, too," Rose said, "who used to disappear for weeks at a time on buying trips to New York City, but we all knew what was going on. It isn't a new thing to have homosexuals here. We've always had them. We just never paid them any mind."

"They never pushed our noses in it, either," Naomi said.

Rose sniffed. "Well, maybe. But maybe they're pushing it in our faces because Henry Holborn is always pushing his stuff in theirs. That's something new these days, too. Tent preachers didn't used to get rich like that when I was growing up. And they didn't—attack people directly. They attacked sin, but they didn't attack people."

"Yes," Naomi said slowly. "I do know what you mean. With Henry it's sometimes like he targets individuals, like he has personal vendettas against real-life people."

Rose went to a display of Jesus statues. The statues were tall and carefully painted ("hand painted," the sign at the base of the display said) and sitting on a revolving pyramid. Naomi had never understood what people did with statues like these.

"There's another thing," Rose said. "I've been thinking and thinking about it, and I don't care what the Bible says. The Bible isn't always one-hundred-percent right about its scientific facts. Look at all that business about creation and evolution, and about the Earth being flat.''

''I thought you were a creationist,'' Naomi said. ''I thought you wrote a letter to the Bellerton *Times* in favor of teaching creationism in the public schools.''

''I've changed my mind since then. I've been *thinking* about it, Naomi. I don't think homosexuality is an abomination and an offense against God. I think it just is.''

''What?''

''I think it just is,'' Rose insisted. ''I think people are just born that way. And if you're born that way there's nothing you can do about it and nothing you ought to do about it. Just like being born black or white. Do you see what I mean?''

''No,'' Naomi said desperately, ''I don't know what you mean. Do you mean you're in favor of gay rights laws now? Or what?''

Rose went behind the counter and stood next to the cash register, a mulish look on her face. ''I mean I think the way Henry Holborn has been talking around here is just wrong. That's what I mean. I mean I think he caused these things somehow, Tiffany and that Carol Littleton, too—''

''You think Henry Holborn murdered both Tiffany Marsh and Carol Littleton?''

''I didn't say I thought he murdered them. I said I thought he caused what happened to them. It's not the same thing. It's not—it's not an action, it's an—an atmosphere—'' Rose was floundering.

''Well,'' Naomi said. ''I think I see what you mean. I've never been a big fan of Henry Holborn's myself.''

''I know you haven't. But a lot of people are. Big fans of his, I mean. It makes me sick.''

''I think I'd better get back to the library,'' Naomi said. ''I've been away all day, practically. Are you sure you're going to be all right now, all alone here the way you are?''

''I'm not alone,'' Rose said. ''I've got Kathi opening

boxes in the back room. There are a lot of boxes. It's going to take hours."

"All right," Naomi said. "Well. I'll see you later."

"You think about the things I said to you. You'll see I'm making sense. Something ought to be done about Henry Holborn."

In Naomi's opinion, something ought to be done about Rose MacNeill—what in God's name had gotten into her? The most conservatively Christian woman on the North Carolina coast, and now she was turning into—what? A liberal?

Naomi propelled herself back out onto Main Street and looked around. The town still looked deserted. It made her almost misty-eyed for the days before Tiffany Marsh had been murdered, the days when the town was almost always deserted during the seasons when tourists were not in residence in force.

Naomi started walking down Main Street, limping badly in her high, uncertain heels. She was thinking so hard about Rose, the obvious didn't occur to her until she was almost at the library door. But the obvious was obvious, and it was going to occur to everybody sooner or later, if she wanted to let them know.

Rose was more right than she realized. Henry Holborn could have killed both Tiffany Marsh and Carol Littleton. And Naomi was the only person in town who knew how it could have been done, because she had seen him.

2

When Stephen Harrow walked through the front door of the bookstore, Maggie Kelleher was sitting in the loft, looking through a hardbound leather copy of the complete works of Aristotle. Maggie had no idea why she had this particular edition of this particular book in the store. Its retail price was something over fifty dollars. God only knew, nobody was going to buy it. The tourists who came in here only wanted trash—or, at best, very very very good genre work, like P. D. James. The few people in town who did like to read classics bought their books at the Barnes & Noble superstore up in Cary, and didn't buy leather-bound editions, either. Maggie thought of the Aristotle, and the few similar volumes she kept up there—*Les Miserables* in French in hand-tooled red Moroccan leather; *The Brothers Karamazov* in deep brown calf—as talismanic. Other people had Henry Holborn or the Episcopal Church or old Father Kennedy at St. Mary's. Maggie had these tokens of another life in another place, a life that had once been all she thought she would ever want. A life with a man in it, she put it to herself now—and almost giggled, out loud, in spite of how awful she felt about Carol Littleton and everything that was going on up at the camp. It was something worse than a shame, what was happening to Zhondra Meyer's dream project. Zhondra claimed that she was being persecuted, and there were times when Maggie could almost believe it. *Something* seemed to be directing itself against the establishment up there. Maggie didn't believe in the devil, but in this case he would suit, and in this case she would use him. He might be the devil in the disguise of Henry Holborn or some other fundamentalist nut from one of the neon churches on the roads outside town, but until she could put a face to him, she would go on thinking of him as the devil. She just wished it would all come to a stop, right now, before it got any worse. The whole town was winding itself up tight.

When the bell on the door tinkled, Maggie thought it must be David Sandler. He had been her only steady customer since the tourist season ended. Reporters came in, off and on, now that so many of them were stuck here covering the murder. They made a lot of noise and bought magazines. Maggie looked over the loft rail and saw Stephen Harrow standing in the middle of the big main room, looking at Linda Lael Miller's latest. He looked both strained and confused, a man lost in an alien landscape. Maggie wondered where he had bought all those theology books that lined the shelves next to the fireplace in his living room.

Stephen put Linda Lael Miller's book back on its shelf. Maggie got to her feet and went to the loft rail to lean over.

"Stephen?" she called down. "Just a minute. I'll be right with you."

Stephen stepped back and squinted. "Oh, Maggie," he said, "it's you. I thought I was going to find what's-his-name."

"Joshua has the day off," Maggie said. "Did you need him for something? I've got his home number on my desk someplace."

"No, no," Stephen said. "It's all right, really. I just didn't expect to find you here. I saw you up at the camp."

"Everybody was up at the camp. Was that pitiful, or what? We're all turning into a bunch of small-town ambulance chasers."

"I am a small-town ambulance chaser, Maggie. I've been small-town one way or another all my life."

"Well, I haven't been. It embarrasses me sometimes, the way I behave lately. Give me a minute and I'll be right down."

Maggie put the Aristotle back in its slipcase and back on its shelf. She didn't want to leave a volume like that lying around. She had even taken the three leather volumes with her on the day of the hurricane, so that no matter how hard the store got hit, they wouldn't get damaged. Of course, she could have fallen and dropped them and landed them all in the mud, but she hadn't thought of that at the time. It was like mothers taking babies with them into a storm. You took them because you wanted to be sure. You took them because you didn't trust anyone to protect them as well as you.

Maggie went back to the loft stairs and then down. Stephen was sitting in the big armchair next to the front window, one of four Maggie had scattered around for the convenience of her customers. This was the kind of thing they were always recommending at seminars at the Independent Booksellers' Association convention. The idea was that small bookstores had to make up in service for what they couldn't provide in the way of discounts. Maggie didn't know if it actually worked. She could remember herself when she first got to New York, dirt poor and always scrambling for money. If there hadn't been discounts she wouldn't have been able to buy books.

"Here I am," Maggie said when she got to the ground floor. "Do you actually want a book today, Stephen? Sometimes it seems like nobody in the world wants books between October and March, except David Sandler, and I don't think he counts. He isn't usually here this time of year."

"Does David Sandler come in here a lot?" Stephen sounded politely interested. "I don't think of him as really being here, if you know what I mean. As being part of town."

"Well, usually he isn't."

"That's true. He isn't." Stephen shifted in his chair. He was much too thin, almost skeletal. The hard surfaces of the chair seemed to hurt him.

"I wonder what it's like sometimes," he said, "being an atheist. I can't really imagine it. I had a professor once who said you could never make yourself not think something, and it's true. I can't make myself not think of God as real."

"I can't make myself not think of God as fake," Maggie said. "It all depends on where you're starting, Stephen. I don't think it's that big an issue."

Stephen shifted in his chair again. "No, no, I don't suppose you do. I don't suppose anybody does unless they're in my position. Lisa thinks I might as well be an atheist. Did you know about that?"

"No."

"She says that I don't believe in any of the things that were supposed to be Christian when she was growing up, and she's right, in a way, or she would have been. I went to a very rationalist seminary."

"What's a rationalist seminary?"

"Oh, it's a kind of theological orientation. I can't believe I'm talking to you about this. You must find it so boring. The men who taught me—and it was all men at the time; that wouldn't be true now—the men who taught me believed that Christ was a man like any other man, that he wasn't divine, that he didn't rise from the dead. In fact, they believed that nobody would ever rise from the dead, at least not bodily. All that sort of thing in the Bible—the story of the resurrection, the parts in Revelation that tell of the Second Coming and the return of souls to their bodies—all that is just symbol, metaphor. A way of explaining what religion does for us psychologically if we use it rightly and without fanaticism."

"Good God," Maggie said. "Is that what Methodists believe these days?"

"Some Methodists do. Some Presbyterians do, too. The most famous American theologian of that kind is an Episcopalian bishop named Spong. I have all of his books."

"I suppose I don't understand why you would have gone into the seminary at all if that was what you thought was going on," Maggie said. "Why bother to be a minister? What did you think you were going to be ministering to?"

"But I didn't believe in all that when I entered the seminary." Stephen's voice was suddenly intense. "I believed in—well, all the things you believed in. What Henry Holborn believes in, mostly, except that I had an exegesis that let me accept Genesis and Darwin at the same time, which was a good thing because as far as I could tell, the evidence for evolution was conclusive."

"I think it's conclusive," Maggie said. "Most sane people think it's conclusive."

"Henry Holborn says that evolution is the thin edge of the wedge. Once they get you believing that the Bible is wrong about how the world was created, then they can go after everything else the Bible says, too. I used to think Henry was nuts. I'm beginning to think he was right."

Maggie backed away a little. This was not good. This was not good at all. It wasn't only Stephen's voice that was too intense. His whole face looked flushed and feverish. His eyes looked twice their normal size. It made Maggie suddenly afraid to be alone in this shut-off room with him.

"Let me get you a cup of coffee," she said hastily. "I have some on the hot plate in the back."

"I was up at the camp this morning," Stephen said. "Did you know that? I saw you there."

"I saw you, too. You weren't close enough for me to say hello to."

"I was thinking the whole time I was up there that the Devil is very real," Stephen said. "I used to think the Devil was all red and fiery and frightening. But he isn't, you know. He isn't frightening at all, not when you're talking to him. He's just a voice inside your head."

"You've been hearing the Devil as a voice inside your head?"

"What? Oh. No. That wasn't what I meant, exactly. I'm sorry, Maggie. I'm making you nervous."

"A little," Maggie said.

"It's just been on my mind so much lately," Stephen said. "Tiffany. The camp. Holborn. The things I was taught in seminary. It all comes together somehow. Do you see what I mean?"

"No."

"No, no, of course not. I'm sorry, Maggie. It's just that I'm very tired. And wrung out, of course, from everything that's been happening. It's going to be a real circus now, don't you think? That poor woman dying like that, and the reporters all around, right there when it happened."

"Do you want that coffee? You really don't look very well, Stephen. I could put a lot of sugar and milk in the coffee. Maybe it would perk you up."

Stephen was struggling out of his chair. "That's all

right, Maggie. I don't need anything. I ought to go home, really. I was just feeling—''

"Yes," Maggie said. "I think I know what you were feeling. I think we're all feeling it."

"Are we? Well, maybe we are. Maybe it was just me who didn't know what it felt like, before now."

Stephen opened the shop door and stepped halfway out onto the sidewalk on Main Street. Then he turned back and gave her a little smile and a wave. Maggie felt a sudden urge to grab him, shake him, twist him around—but in the next moment, he was gone and the door was shut and she was by herself.

I ought to close up early and go right home, Maggie told herself, sitting down in the chair Stephen had vacated. She felt weak in the knees. She had the distinct feeling of just having survived a close call, but she didn't know a close call with what.

Something better break in this murder case soon, Maggie thought, because if it doesn't, I think the whole town is going to end up certifiable.

3

Down at the other end of Main Street, David Sandler came out of Louise's Card and Candy Shop, carrying a small paper bag full of licorice bears. He started up the street in the direction of the library just as Stephen Harrow emerged from Maggie Kelleher's store. David had made it to the first corner before he realized what was wrong with what he was seeing. Stephen Harrow was reeling, sailing side to side as he moved, as if he'd just downed an entire bottle of 151-proof rum. When he got to the lamppost between Maggie's store and Charlie Hare's, he grabbed it in both hands and sagged forward.

David Sandler sped up, instinctively. He thought Stephen Harrow was going to fall over. Instead, Stephen righted himself and seemed to come to his senses. By the time David caught up to him, Stephen Harrow was walking normally, but very slowly, in the direction of the Methodist Church.

"Stephen?" David said. "Are you all right? I just saw you nearly collapse."

"I'm fine," Stephen said. His voice was strong enough, but distant. Its cheerfulness sounded forced. "I was just a little dizzy there for a moment. I've gotten over it now."

"You don't know you've gotten over it," David said. "It could be some kind of illness coming on. It could be anything. Let me walk you home."

"No, no. You don't have to do that. Thank you very much and everything, but I don't need it. I'm fine."

"You don't look fine. You're white as a sheet."

"I'm just a little depressed, that's all. Because of that poor woman up at the camp. Because of everything. Aren't you depressed?"

"Yes, I am. But I'm not nearly passing out on Main Street."

"I'm not, either, David, not anymore. I really will be all right. You ought to go on with whatever it was you were doing."

"I was going to go into Maggie's and buy a book."

"Well, good. You go do that. Maggie could use the company. The store is absolutely dead."

"I'm sure it is." David hesitated. Part of him did not want to leave Stephen on his own. Stephen *had* been reeling. Stephen *had* been close to passing out. Another part of him didn't want to hang on to Stephen when Stephen didn't want to be hung on to. One of the cardinal principles of David Sandler's life was that people ought to be left alone when they wanted to be left alone. People had the right to make stupid decisions as well as wise and good ones.

"Are you sure now?" David said. "You can make it back to the church on your own?"

"I won't have any problems at all."

"I'd go see a doctor pretty soon if I were you, though. It never hurts to check."

"I'll take your advice under consideration. Really, David. I'm all right. You don't have to worry about what's going to happen to me."

Stephen shook his arm free and moved on. David stood on the sidewalk watching him go. The farther away Stephen got, the faster he seemed to go and the straighter he seemed to get. It really was all right, David told himself—but it still didn't feel right, and he wished he could think of something to do about it.

Instead, he turned back the way he had come. It was an oddly beautiful day, bright and clear—but empty, much too empty, and much too quiet, too. Maybe it was just that he still had the sound of Henry Holborn and his people singing "That Old Time Religion" in his head, but he kept thinking that he ought to hear something besides tree leaves rustling and sand scraping along in the gutters.

On the way back down the sidewalk, he passed in front of the Town Hall on the side where the jail window was, but on the other side of the street. He thought for a moment that he saw Ginny Marsh in there, looking out, counting his footsteps on the pavement.

three

1

After a while it got to the point where there was nothing left to do. The crowd was dispersed, as Clayton Hall insisted on describing it. He meant that after he had fired a few shots in the air, most of the people who had been watching from the sidelines decided they had things they would rather do. That was the case even with some of the reporters, who had all begun to look nervous and jumpy. After all, none of them had volunteered for combat duty. This was not supposed to be a dangerous assignment in the same sense as spending a few weeks in Sarajevo or Beirut. What Gregor noticed was that the people from town were faintly irritated and the strangers were more than a little alarmed. The people from town knew Clayton too well not to know what he was doing with a weapon. The strangers didn't want to take anything for granted. After all, you never knew what people would do, especially these people, especially down here. These were the people who joined the National Rifle Association and claimed to keep at least two guns in their houses at all times. In the end, however, it was Henry Holborn who set the tone for everybody else. When the shot was fired, it seemed to change something in him, something deep. Gregor saw the metamorphosis in the older man's face, working itself out like the plot of a bad soap opera. As soon as it was done, Henry Holborn's face collapsed. His shoulders slumped. His body seemed to half melt into putty. He turned around to the people behind him and waved his arms.

"Wait, wait," he called out. His voice had none of the boom to it that it had had when he was praying. Gregor could barely hear him. Few of his followers could hear him, either. The crowd on the edges of the clearing had begun to thin. Gregor saw Maggie Kelleher slip away, and Naomi Brent, and David Sandler. He recognized a few other people, too, like Betsey from the diner. Ricky Drake was in among Henry Holborn's people, looking both belligerent and scared. Gregor started to fade back, toward the trees.

"Wait," Henry Holborn called out again—and then a vast murmuring went up, a thousand tinny voices talking at once. Up until then, Henry Holborn's people had been absolutely quiet. Now they were all talking at once, and it was like listening to bees humming along the telephone wires. In the sudden normality of this scene, they had become normal, too—not zealots and monsters, but ordinary men and women, old and middle-aged and young, small-town people who had come to witness another death they didn't believe they had anything to do with.

It took a while to get the clearing free of civilians, and a while more for the tech men to do what they needed to do and pack up their equipment. Gregor spent all that time sitting on a rock just into the trees, thinking. This was not an easy operation. There was no wide path up here that an ambulance could take. The ambulance was parked down in Bonaventura's back drive, along with the police cars and the mobile crime unit that belonged to the state police. Gregor watched Clayton Hall writing down things in a small steno pad, but he didn't ask what those things were. He knew a look of bewilderment when he saw it, and he was bewildered enough himself. He was also enormously tired. He hadn't paid much attention to the time he had gotten out of bed this morning, but it had been early, and he had been moving ever since. He wanted to lie down and take a nap, but there was no place to do it among the trees. He wouldn't have lain down in the clearing even if it hadn't been full of people. Over the course of the afternoon, the clearing had taken on a personality for him. Ghosts floated above it, and bodiless voices whispered in the trees. He stared and stared at the stones, but there was nothing in them that could tell him what it was about this place that was so important to somebody, so central, that it had become the stage of choice whenever a body was supposed to be found. There was just something *about* this place.

Now it was hours later—almost three, Gregor thought, wishing he could be sure of the reading on his watch in all these shadows—and the whole of Bonaventura seemed to be deserted. There were birds in the trees and rustlings in the pine needles under his feet. Gregor didn't even want to think of what kind of little animals might live in a stand of trees like this one. Rats. Chipmunks. Snakes. He strained to hear what was to be heard and decided nothing could be. He had heard the last of the official cars drive away a good five minutes ago. He thought that even Clayton Hall must have gone back to town. The first forty-eight hours after the commission of a crime were supposed to be the important ones, but in Gregor's experience they were also times of relative paralysis. Maybe it was different for big-city police officers who dealt with homicides every day, but for small-town cops like Clayton Hall, and detached federal professionals like Gregor himself, there was always a period when the most important thing was to assimilate everything that had happened and everything that they had had to see. Human beings had been murdering each other for millions of years. It had to be perfectly natural. It didn't look natural when you came face-to-face with it, though, and the feeling of strangeness and wrongness and alienation persisted. It might be perfectly natural for human beings to murder each other, but it went against something deeper than nature. It was this something-deeper-than-nature that made up Gregor Demarkian's religion, as far as he had ever had one. He wondered what Father Tibor would think if he came out and told him that.

When there was absolute quiet all around him, when

even the birds had stopped calling to each other in the air, Gregor began making his way down the hill toward the house. The trees were such thickly needled pines that they made it impossible for him to see much of anything until he came to the very edge of them. Then he saw the narrow path leading to the terrace and the back of the house. The terrace was empty, although at least three of the French doors were standing open. Gregor's slick leather shoes kept slipping against the pine needles. Bennis was right. One of these days, he was going to have to give in and buy the kind of thing most people wore on their feet, like sneakers or moccasins. If he kept on exploring forest clearings in wing tips, he was going to end up breaking his neck.

Gregor got to the terrace and began to look through each of the open French doors in turn. The first two, although fairly far apart, opened onto the same room, a big tall-ceilinged reception room, full of Louis XVI furniture, the walls painted with Italian Madonnas, fat-cheeked, vacant-eyed women holding fat-cheeked, squirming infants. Gregor tried to imagine doing, in this room, the things people ordinarily did in living rooms: playing cards, watching television, reading books, gossiping about the neighbors. It was impossible. This was a room for a king and queen to receive their court in. At the very least, it should have a butler stationed at its main door, ready to announce the name of anyone who wanted to come in. Gregor drifted down the terrace to the last of the open French doors. It was the terrace door to Zhondra Meyer's big study, and Zhondra was there, sitting at the desk, tapping away at a computer. Some people might have found something incongruous in this, but Gregor didn't. The computer seemed to him to be the only thing about the study that made the room even faintly livable. Obviously, he was not cut out to be a very rich man.

Zhondra Meyer looked up from what she was doing, saw Gregor standing at the terrace door, and blinked.

"For God's sake," she said. "What are you doing here? I thought you'd all gone."

"Everybody else has." Gregor stepped through the door into the study. "I've been sitting on a rock up there, thinking. I just came to, so to speak."

"Well, you can just go, too, right this minute," Zhondra Meyer said tartly. "I told you up there, hours ago. I've had it with all this. I'm not answering any more questions, and I'm not cooperating with any more police officers."

"I'm not a police officer. I'm not even a private detective. Did Clayton ever get to talk to those two women we came up here to talk to this morning? Dinah and—"

"Stelle," Zhondra Meyer said. "He talked to them, sort of. He grilled them or whatever you call it. You know what I mean. He asked them a lot of questions about whether or not they killed Carol, and he reduced poor Dinah to tears."

"I take it he decided that they hadn't killed Carol Littleton."

Zhondra waved this all away. "I don't know what he decided. He went away, that's all, and I was glad to see him go. Everybody around here is in a state of panic. I don't know what I'm going to do."

"Did you call your lawyers?"

"Oh, yes."

"And?"

"They're going to send somebody down here in the morning. It's wonderful what having a couple of hundred million dollars can do. People just fall all over you to be nice to you."

"I'm sure they do."

Zhondra Meyer tapped the desk at the side of her keyboard. "I really do think you ought to go now, Mr. Demarkian. There's nothing you can do here at the moment. There's nothing I'm really willing to let you do. Rack it up and call it the end of a bad day."

"Do you really want to find out who murdered Tiffany Marsh?"

"Of course I do," Zhondra said.

"Do you really want to know why somebody is using your place as a dumping ground for dead bodies?"

"I think these are ridiculous questions, Mr. Demarkian. I don't understand what it is they have to do with you."

Gregor came all the way into the room, found a tall yellow wing chair, and sat down in it. "I would like to talk to Dinah and Stelle, if I could. Right this minute. After I talk to them, I'll be more than willing to go back to town on my own two feet, without having to be propelled in that direction by you."

"What if I don't want you to talk to Dinah and Stelle?"

"I don't think that circumstance is likely to come up, Ms. Meyer. In spite of your tone of anger and exasperation, it's my very good guess that you're scared to death. I promise you I won't grill either of your guests. I just want to ask them a few questions."

"If you were Clayton Hall, I'd throw you out on your ear."

"But I'm not Clayton Hall."

Zhondra Meyer seemed to consider this seriously, watching Gregor's face all the time. Then she reached out and grabbed the phone that had been pushed to the side of the desk by the computer equipment.

"Alice?" she said, after she had punched a few buttons and waited a while. "Is that you? Are Stelle and Dinah there?" She listened. Then she nodded. "All right. Send her to me in the study, will you? I'll talk to Dinah when she gets back. And Alice—pay attention to me. I don't want parsnips again tonight, do you understand? I don't care how wonderfully healthy they're supposed to be."

Zhondra hung up the phone and looked at Gregor. "Well," she said, "there you are. Stelle is on her way. Dinah went into town about half an hour ago and isn't expected back until evening. If you think I'm going to leave you alone in here with Stelle, you're out of your mind."

"You don't have to leave me alone in here, Ms.

Meyer. I'm not going to say anything I don't want you to hear."

"It's not what you're going to say that worries me, Mr. Demarkian. It's what you're going to do. You'd better behave yourself."

Gregor was going to tell her that he always behaved himself—but he didn't. The room was oppressive. The air was thick with humidity. He was tired. He was staying focused by an act of will. Whenever he began to relax, his mind started to drift. It drifted right out of the room and back up to the clearing, where it made light conversation with the wind.

2

The appearance of Stelle Cary should not have been a shock, but it was—and in that shock Gregor Demarkian realized just how odd this whole trip had been. Stelle Cary was a black woman, tall and middle-aged and bony, with a little potbelly that strained against the fabric of the smock she wore over her jeans. Her face was free of makeup, but her ears were hung with beaded strands in bright colors and silver disks that seemed too heavy. If it hadn't been for the earrings, Stelle would have provided the perfect picture of a woman you wouldn't look at twice on the street. Her clothes were worn and nondescript. Her face was worn and nondescript. Her carriage was halfway between youth and defeat.

What had shocked Gregor when Stelle first walked into the room was her color. He had become so used to seeing white people, and only white people, in Bellerton, that race had become a nonissue, unimportant because the conditions for it did not exist. He had, he realized, especially not expected to find a black woman at the camp, at least not as a guest. In his experience, institutions like the one Zhondra Meyer was trying to set up appealed almost universally to middle- and upper-middle-class white women with axes to grind. Other women, poor or black or whatever else they might be, didn't have time for retreats into the North Carolina pines. Here Stelle was, however, and she didn't look ready to go away. She stood at the side of Zhondra Meyer's desk like a sentinel with bad posture.

Gregor got out of his chair and held out his hand. "Excuse me," he said. "At my age, I have a hard time leaping to my feet. I'm Gregor Demarkian."

Stelle Cary took Gregor's hand and shook it, looking amused. "You don't have to leap to your feet. It doesn't look like you could leap much of anywhere."

Gregor let this pass. "At the moment, I can hardly stand up. Do you mind if I sit while we talk?"

"Not unless you mind if I sit."

"Go right ahead."

Stelle perched on a corner of the big polished desk. Zhondra Meyer frowned at her back and then said, "Mr. Demarkian is a private detective of sorts—"

"I'm not a private detective at all," Gregor interrupted.

"I know who Gregor Demarkian is," Stelle Cary said. "He's all over *People* all the time. I heard they were going to make a TV movie out of his life, but I didn't see anything come of it."

"They couldn't get my permission," Gregor said grimly, "and they never will. You look—calmer than I expected you to look. After what happened this morning, I mean."

"You mean Carol," Stelle Cary said. She hopped off the corner of the desk and went to the open the French doors. "I don't see any reason not to be calm," she said after a while. "A couple of the women are getting hysterical, but it doesn't make sense to me. Carol and that poor little baby. Do you think there's some psychopathic killer stalking the camp, intent on wiping out any lesbian he can get his hands on?"

"No," Gregor said.

"I don't either," Stelle told him. "So you see, there's

no reason not to be calm. That doesn't mean that I'm not sorry that what happened to Carol happened to Carol.''

"So Carol Littleton was a friend of yours.''

"Of mine and Dinah's, yeah. That is, as far as people make friendships here. This is an odd sort of place, Mr. Demarkian. In some ways, it isn't a real place at all. Zhondra is the only one who is committed to it. The rest of us are all on our way from someplace to someplace else.''

"I know. Would you mind telling me what you're on your way away from?''

Stelle smiled faintly. "Well, for one thing, Mr. Demarkian, I'm on my way from jail. I just did three years in Illinois for possession with intent to sell. Not, by the way, that they ever actually caught me selling anything. There are these federal sentencing guidelines set up by how much is found in your possession, and I had quite a bit in my possession. It was one of the few times in my life I ever felt like I had enough.''

"I take it there weren't any complications to this charge? No weapons violations? No violence?''

"I've had a man or two who was interested in having guns around, but I could never see the point. You have a gun around, you're likely to get mad and use it and then wish you hadn't.''

"There are other weapons besides guns.''

"I don't deal in weapons, Mr. Demarkian. I just deal in dope, and I don't sell it to other people. I take it when I can get it.''

"I thought we'd decided that was all over,'' Zhondra Meyer said.

Stelle shot Zhondra a cynical little smile. "Zhondra thinks it's like giving up chocolate,'' she told Gregor. "She thinks you do it and that's it. I keep trying to tell her, it's all a matter of time.''

"I don't see how you can want to do that to yourself anymore,'' Zhondra said. "You were destroying your body. You were destroying your mind. You were in jail. You were as helpless as the patriarchy wants us to be. What good was that doing you?''

''Zhondra doesn't understand how good it feels to be high. I love to be high.''

''But you're not high now. You're not using drugs now.''

''I'm not using drugs in the ordinary sense now, no,'' Stelle told him, ''but I don't have to be. I've got religion at the moment.''

''What?''

Stelle came back from the French doors and sat down on the corner of the desk again, grinning. ''I've got religion,'' she repeated. ''I've had religion before, other times and other places and other ways. You know anything about drug rehab?''

''No,'' Gregor said.

''Well, the dirty little secret about drug rehab is that the religious-based programs are about twice as effective as the psychologically based ones. Not that either of them are very effective, you understand. The figure I heard was a ninety-eight-percent failure rate. But the religions do better than the shrinks, and you know why?''

''Why?''

''Because religion is another kind of drug,'' Stelle said, ''especially those Holy Roller religions, where you dance around and speak in tongues and get baptized in the spirit. You can get higher doing that than I've ever been able to get on crack. I can remember one time getting so out of it at a meeting that I walked on the top of a space heater in my bare feet and didn't feel a thing. The next morning I woke up and found out I couldn't walk. The soles of my feet were blistered raw. I had to go to the hospital and get fixed up. But I never felt a thing at the time, and when I think back on it, the only thing that comes to mind is that it was all great, I was the happiest I've ever been. I'd do it again in a second.''

''And have you done it again?'' Gregor asked. ''Are

you still part of a—what did you call it?—Holy Roller religion?"

"Nope." Stelle shook her head. "I liked the way it felt, you understand, but when I was down I'd start thinking, and the more I thought the more ridiculous it all got. People rising from the dead. Pie in the sky when you die. Do you believe any of that stuff?"

"I don't think about it, most of the time," Gregor said. "What about you? If you're not taking drugs, and you're not involved in Holy Roller religion, what are you involved in?"

"Oh, these days I worship the Goddess." Stelle sounded more cynical than ever. "The Goddess of wisdom and nature, the Great Mother of us all. It's the hip thing, especially here. Religion without patriarchy."

"It's much better than all those things you were doing before," Zhondra said. "It gives you an arena to express your spirituality and it gives you a political analysis of your condition at the same time. That way you don't start turning it all on yourself, telling yourself it was your fault. That's what the patriarchy is hoping you will do."

"Actually," Stelle said drily, "I was partial to the idea of original sin myself. We're all born wanting things we can't have and craving things that aren't good for us. Too many white people want to feel superior to somebody, and black people are handy. I'd really rather get high than do anything about my life, and the stuff I need to get high with is handy, too."

"I hope you don't think we go around here looking for somebody to be superior to," Zhondra Meyer said. "We understand that racism is systemic. Every woman in this house struggles with her own racism every day."

"Right," Stelle said. "Is this what you wanted to talk to me about, Mr. Demarkian? I thought you were looking into the death of that baby."

"I am," Gregor said. "Would you mind my asking you a few things about the day of the hurricane?"

"Ask away."

"Let's start with the ceremony the three of you were going to do," Gregor said. "Carol Littleton was late."

"That's right." Stelle nodded. "She'd gone into town to buy a christening present for her granddaughter. She bought it in that silly store that sells all the religious things, angel statues, stuff like that. The one in the Victorian house. Although, to tell you the truth, I couldn't understand why she was doing it. It wasn't like she was going to be invited to the christening. She hadn't even seen the baby."

"Carol Littleton didn't get along with her children?"

"She got along with her son all right," Stelle said. "It was her daughter that was the problem. Shelley, I think her name was, but I'm not really sure. Anyway, Shelley really hated the idea of Carol being up here. She *really* hated it. And then, of course, there was Carol's ex-husband."

"What about him?"

"He took this whole business of Carol's becoming a lesbian as a personal insult. Men take it that way sometimes. Sometimes I think men are all born a little cracked."

Gregor considered Carol Littleton's daughter and her ex-husband. Then he said, "So, when Carol finally showed up it was—what? In the middle of the storm? Close to the start of it?"

Stelle hooted. "If any one of us had known anything about hurricanes, we would have gotten ourselves inside and stayed there. Instead of that, we were standing around in that clearing, Dinah and me, and it was drizzling on our heads. And then Carol came running out from the house."

"You couldn't see her from the clearing, could you? The trees would have prevented that."

"I'd gone down to the end of the path to see if I could find out where she was. She came running out of the house just as I got there. She was all worked up, nearly crying."

"About what? Did you ask?"

"I asked. She said something about Shelley, and about how you could never trust anyone, not really, you could never really know them, people were entirely unpredictable.

It was quite a hash. Carol got that way when she talked about her daughter."

"Was she coming out of this room here?"

Stelle shook her head. "I don't think so. I wasn't really paying much attention, but it's my impression that she was coming out of one of the center sets of doors, the ones that open on to the living room."

"Does that make sense to you, now that you think about it? Was that a likely way for her to come?"

"It depends on where she was coming from," Stelle said reasonably. "I guess I just assumed that she'd come down from upstairs and was taking the shortest way out. The big front staircase is just outside the living room door."

Gregor hauled himself to the edge of his chair and put his elbows on his knees. "So," he said, "Carol came out of the house, and the two of you got together, and then you went to the clearing. Am I right so far?"

"Right."

"And this woman Dinah was there when you got there."

"She was sitting on a rock. Dinah's the one who is really into all this stuff. Carol and I just did it because— well, I like to get high, and Carol needed something to take her mind off the new baby and how she wasn't getting to see it. But Dinah's a believer. She won't even stand inside the circle of stones. She says it's blasphemy."

"All right," Gregor said. "So then you were all together. What came next?"

"Well." Stelle shot Zhondra a look. Zhondra gave an elaborate shrug.

"It's all right, Stelle," Zhondra said. "He knows all about it."

Stelle sighed. "I suppose by now the entire state of North Carolina knows about it. Maybe the entire world. What came next, Mr. Demarkian, is that we got out of our clothes."

"All of them?"

"All of them."

"What did you do with them?"

"We put them in a pile under one of the trees. It didn't matter what happened to them as long as they were out of the way while the ceremony was going on."

"Fine," Gregor said. "What did you do next?"

"We took up positions around the circle of stones and knelt down."

"And?"

"And we started praying. We were singing this chant thing, this song that Dinah wrote. About how wonderful women are and how beautiful all their parts are. It was weird, really. I mean, there was all this thunder and lightning, and it worked somehow. I mean, it all seemed part of the ceremony. Crash. Bang. Boom. Chant. When the rain really started coming down, I was surprised as hell."

"Did you run for the house when that happened?"

Stelle Cary burst out laughing. "Mr. Demarkian, we couldn't run anywhere. We were stuck. The trees were whipping around like jump ropes. The rain was coming down in buckets. There was hail. All we could do was take cover under one of those trees, hold our clothes over our heads, and hope we didn't get hit by something serious. We were there all night."

"All night?"

"Well, all day and most of the evening, anyway. We didn't get out until the storm was all over and Zhondra came looking for us and told us the baby was dead. And told us that Ginny was saying we killed it. I thought I was going to bust a blood vessel, and Carol started to cry and couldn't stop."

"Ginny Marsh was never in the clearing that day?"

"Not that any of us saw."

"The baby wasn't either?"

"Again," Stelle insisted, "not that any of us saw. I suppose they could have been hiding in the trees. Especially if the baby was, well, you know, already dead. So that it wouldn't cry."

"Is that what you think happened? That somebody killed it and then hid in the trees near the clearing?"

"I don't think anything, Mr. Demarkian. Except I think Ginny probably killed the child. I never did like Ginny much. She's too—intense."

"That's interesting," Gregor said. "Everybody else I've talked to seems to like her a great deal. They keep trying to convince me that she couldn't possibly have killed her own baby."

"Mothers kill their children every day," Stelle said. "And I think if that girl didn't kill the baby, she's fronting for the man who did. And it would have to be a man, wouldn't you think?"

"It usually is," Gregor admitted.

Stelle Cary leaned back and stretched her arms and back, arching. "Do you know what I think?" she asked Gregor. "I think it's all very simple, and the only reason Carol was killed was to make it look like it wasn't. I think Ginny and that husband of hers are in it together, and I think the good Reverend Henry Holborn is masterminding the whole thing. I think I'm sick and tired of the South and I'm sick and tired of religion and I'm sick and tired of being a lesbian feminist, too. I think I'm going back to my old neighborhood in Chicago and see who's still around that I know."

"I think," Gregor said carefully, "that that would be both unfortunate and unwise."

Stelle hopped off the desk, grinning brilliantly. "I think you can take that advice and stuff it where the sun don't shine," she told him. "And now, if you two will excuse me, I think I'm going off to get something to eat."

Stelle Cary headed for the study door and disappeared into the hall. Zhondra Meyer watched her go, then blew a raspberry and collapsed into the chair behind the desk.

"Honestly," she said. "Some people."

four

1

The next morning, Gregor Demarkian woke to find that David Sandler had written dozens of notes to him on sticky paper and stuck them all over the house. The one on the refrigerator said:

Where have you been? Make some time to talk.

This, Gregor thought, was not entirely fair. He'd had plenty of time to talk the night before, which he had spent sitting by himself on David's deck, looking out over the ocean. Last night had been David Sandler's night to go up to Chapel Hill, where he taught a once-a-week seminar in the philosophy of free thought at the University of North Carolina. Gregor remembered wondering whether anybody ever used the words ''free thought'' anymore, or even knew what they meant. At any rate, Gregor had been alone, with the first glass of wine he'd had in months. The waves had pounded against the thick wooden pilings that held up David's house. The full moon had floated in the blackness above the water, looking fat and smug. In the long run, Gregor didn't think it had been such a good idea, being on his own like that. He had spent too much time on his own in the first six months after Elizabeth died. He had sold the apartment they had lived in together for so many years, and rented a smaller one, and spent night after night sitting on its little balcony, watching the traffic on the Beltway. After a while the cars had begun to look like gigantic beetles,

chasing each other and snapping their jaws. Like most
other men of his generation, Gregor had never learned to
take care of himself emotionally. He had had Elizabeth for
that, and before Elizabeth his mother. Every once in a
while, there had been gaps, like during the time he had
spent in the army, but he had taken care of those by bulling
through them, and making sure they didn't last too long.
After Elizabeth died, the gap seemed to last forever. He
wondered sometimes if he had gone back to Cavanaugh
Street in the hope of finding a place to rest, like a shark
looking for a place to die. God only knew, he hadn't been
able to think of anything to do with himself, or any reason
to go on getting up in the morning, when he had been left
to himself. Even the work that he had done for twenty years
had failed to move him. He thought of the country filling
up with rapists and murderers and drug dealers and kidnap-
pers, and he just didn't care.

He didn't know what it was—the moon, maybe, or the
uncustomary wine—but after a while he couldn't sit in the
silence and not hear another human voice. He went back
into the house and turned on the television in the study. He
found three religious stations and the networks. Two of the
networks were showing sitcoms. The third, CBS, had one
of those tabloid news shows, with a story about a man in
Tennessee who had first been suspected of being a serial
murderer because of the way he treated his cats. He locked
his cats up in his garage for days at a time, without food or
water, and made it impossible for them to get out. The
religious stations all seemed to be showing preachers of
one kind or another, appalled at the state of the country and
the state of the world. Gregor stopped and listened to the
nun for a few minutes, because she was the only one of the
three who didn't sound hysterical. She was talking about a
movie called *Priest,* which she didn't like. All the priests in
it were either terrible people, or untrue to their vows of
celibacy. Then the program went to a break, and the station
logo came on. Gregor found that he was watching something called the Eternal Word Television Network. He

wasn't ready for eternal words. He turned the television off and got up and went into the living room.

It was, by then, exactly ten o'clock. Gregor didn't know if David Sandler was going to walk through the door at any moment, or if he customarily went out for dinner or drinks after his class and wouldn't be in for hours. There was a black, old-fashioned-looking telephone on the end table next to the couch. It took a while for Gregor to realize that what bothered him about it was that it had a rotary dial instead of a touch-tone pad. Gregor sat down next to it and put it into his lap. He wasn't sure how to go about this with a rotary phone. He wasn't even sure if he could. It was incredible how dependent people got on technology, even people like him, who didn't like technology. He had grown up with rotary telephones. He picked up the receiver and did what he would have done then. He dialed the operator.

It took a little while—the operator was young; she wasn't used to dealing with rotary phones, either—but he finally got the call charged to his credit card and the phone ringing in Bennis's apartment. It rang and rang. Gregor almost decided that Bennis must have gone out: up to Donna Moradanyan's apartment, or across the street to Tibor's. He tried to imagine what it was like, now, on Cavanaugh Street. Had Donna Moradanyan decorated for some holiday? She liked to decorate in style, wrapping whole town houses up in ribbons and bows. They were christening somebody's baby at Holy Trinity Armenian Christian Church this Sunday. Maybe Donna had decorated for that. Maybe he ought to put down the phone and give it up. The operator was going to break in at any moment, to tell him this wasn't working.

Far away in Philadelphia, the phone was picked up, and a muffled voice said muffled words that Gregor couldn't make sense of.

"Bennis?" he tried, wondering if he had a bad connection or just a wrong number.

There was more muffled noise again and then, "Gregor? Where are you? I just got out of the shower."

Bennis had been smoking again. Gregor could hear it in her voice. Bennis's voice always got raspy and raw when she had been smoking, especially now, when she spent most of her time trying to quit.

"I'm in North Carolina," Gregor said. "I'm at David Sandler's house. He's out giving a seminar."

"On atheism? In North Carolina?"

"On free thought, in Chapel Hill. In case you didn't know, free thought was a movement in the eighteenth and nineteenth centuries—"

"Deism and the French Revolution," Bennis broke in. "Yes, Gregor, I know. I had a very expensive education. Are you all right? I haven't been seeing you in the news."

"I think that you'd take that as a good sign. I do."

"Has anything been going on down there?"

"Well," Gregor said, "there was another murder today."

"Oh, God." Bennis exhaled a stream of smoke. The sound was so distinctive, Gregor could almost see her do it. "I'm sorry," she said. "I didn't watch the news today. I've got a copyedited manuscript to go over. I've been frantic. Was it another child?"

"It was a middle-aged woman with a grown daughter and a new grandchild. She lived up at this camp that Zhondra Meyer runs, the one for lesbians. Did I ever ask you if you knew Zhondra Meyer?"

"Yes, you did, Gregor. I don't know Zhondra Meyer. I know *of* her. Even I couldn't have met every debutante in the industrial northeast. Not that Zhondra and I would have run into each other on the deb circuit in our day, anyway."

"Why not? Because you came out in Philadelphia and she came out in New York?"

"No, idiot. Because she's Jewish and I'm not." Bennis laughed. "I mean, for God's sake, Gregor, what do you think debutante parties are for?"

"I've never had the faintest idea."

"Well, I don't have the faintest idea what they're for now, but in my day the idea was to get the girl married before she had to graduate from college. All the girls I knew had dropped out of Smith by their senior year and had big weddings.''

''You didn't drop out to get married.''

''No, I didn't, and from what I remember Zhondra Meyer didn't, either. I don't think she's ever been married. Which makes two of us. Nobody gets married anymore, Gregor.''

''Of course they do. Donna Moradanyan got married.''

''That's not what I meant. So what about this middle-aged woman who died? Was her death connected to the death of the baby?''

''I think so.''

''Why?''

''Because the methods appear to be similar. Because some effort was made in each case to make it appear that the murders had taken place in a stand of trees behind Zhondra Meyer's house. Listen to me call it a house. Do you know what that place is like? Bonaventura?''

''I've seen pictures of it. It's infamous in a way, Gregor. The old man went down there and built this enormous thing, and in those days nobody he'd ever heard of lived anywhere around. People couldn't figure out what he was doing.''

''I'll bet they still don't know. Do you know anything about Zhondra Meyer? Does she have a reputation?''

''What kind of reputation?'' Bennis asked. ''I mean, for God's sake, Gregor, the woman's sex life has been in every tabloid and magazine for decades. It's not as if she were making herself out to be a virgin.''

''That wasn't the kind of reputation I mean. I don't know if I can explain it. She seems very imperious. In spite of all the rhetoric about patriarchy and revolution, if I had to describe her to somebody, I'd say she was very much like one of those robber baron matriarchs. A will of iron. The unshakeable conviction that any way she does anything is the right way to do it.''

"I don't think the robber baron matriarchs had that much self-confidence," Bennis said. "I seem to remember they were always social climbing, until it finally occurred to them that they had more money than anybody else and they could do what they wanted to do. But I know what you mean. I've met women like that."

"But not Zhondra Meyer. You haven't heard anything like that about her on the grapevine?"

"Gregor, for God's sake. I've been off that particular grapevine for years. I don't hang around with debutantes anymore. I live on Cavanaugh Street and write fantasy novels."

"I wish I had someone on some grapevine somewhere," Gregor said. "I hate these things where I'm trying to figure out people I don't know and can't get a handle on. It's like bouncing around in the dark, playing ghost."

There was a pause on the line while Bennis lit another cigarette. Gregor heard the flare of the match.

"I thought you had this all sewn up before you left," she said. "I thought you said the mother had killed the baby, or her husband or her boyfriend had, and it was just a matter of waiting until somebody confessed to it."

"I still think that sometimes."

"So what's the matter? Did you meet her and decide that she was just too wonderful to be guilty?"

"I haven't met her."

"What?" Bennis was astonished. "How can you not have met her? Won't her lawyer let you talk to her?"

"I haven't asked to talk to her."

"But why not? For God's sake, Gregor, under the circumstances, I'd think that was the first thing you would do. I mean, she's the one they've arrested."

"Actually," Gregor said, "they haven't arrested her. They have her in protective custody. It's a little fuzzy, just what's going on around here with that. And it isn't as if I've never seen her. She was on that talk show. You taped it for me."

"She was on that talk show by satellite hookup from

jail." Bennis sounded something worse than exasperated. "Gregor, are you all right? What are you doing down there?"

Gregor Demarkian sighed. "At the moment, I'm sitting in the middle of David Sandler's living room, running up my AT&T calling-card bill. How's everything up there? Is Tibor coming out of his slump?"

"Tibor's fine. Tibor's always been fine. It's you I'm worried about. You haven't been yourself lately, to be original about it."

"I've never been anybody but myself," Gregor said. "Really. I've been fine. I am fine. I'm just a little tired. I miss Cavanaugh Street."

"Well, that's healthy enough."

"Maybe I'm past this sort of thing, Bennis. Maybe I ought to give up murders and write my memoirs."

"Maybe you ought to see a doctor as soon as you get home. Gregor, what's going on with you these days?"

"I've got to go now," Gregor said. "That's David's car pulling into the garage. I've been a terrible guest ever since I got here. I'd better make some time to talk to him."

"You're trying to get out of having to talk to me," Bennis said.

"I've got to go now," Gregor insisted. "Right away. Really. I'll call you in a couple of days."

"I'll make that appointment with the doctor for you myself."

"I'll talk to you in a couple of days," Gregor said again. "Say hello to Tibor for me. And Donna. And Lida, too, if she's gotten home by now. Say hello to everybody."

"Gregor—"

Gregor put the receiver back into the cradle. It wasn't true that David's car had just pulled into the garage—and even if it had, Gregor couldn't have heard it from the living room. David Sandler's garage wasn't attached to the house, because state environmental regulations said that you couldn't park a car directly on the beach. David kept his car in the lot near the boardwalk. Gregor put the phone back on the end table. His head hurt.

No matter what Bennis thought, it wasn't true that there was something wrong with him. He was a little tired, but that was perfectly natural. Then again, he had been thinking about Elizabeth a lot, too much maybe, more than he had for years. If that was a symptom of something, Gregor didn't know of what. He got up and poured himself another glass of wine from the bottle he had left on the coffee table. It was some sort of red something that David had told him was supposed to be served at room temperature. After the glass was full, Gregor took a sip off the top of it—necessary, to keep it from spilling; why had he poured it so high?—and then went back out on the deck to look at the moon again.

When he and Elizabeth had first been married, when they had both been very young, they had talked often about owning a house near the sea, a place where they could go and simply be together. That was before they had realized that Elizabeth would never be able to have children. They had imagined themselves with a family, toddlers filling buckets with thick wet sand, ten-year-olds running through the kitchen to pick up a glass of milk on their way to do important goofing off in the upstairs bedrooms. Gregor sometimes wondered how different he would have been, how different Elizabeth would have been, if there had been children in their lives. He tried not to think about the possibility that she might not have died when she did if she had given birth at least once. The kind of cancer Elizabeth died of was far more prevalent in women who had never had children.

The moon kept drifting behind clouds that made it look as if it were twisting and writhing. In the first year after Elizabeth died, there had been times when Gregor had thought that he could hear Elizabeth's voice, calling to him from other rooms. Now her voice sang to him from out across the water. He could see her as clearly as if she were standing beside him. "Elizabeth," he said to her, out loud, and she answered him with music. Then the breeze got chilly and his body went all over cold, and he knew that he was alone.

After a few more minutes, he went back into the house and then into the guest room where he was supposed to sleep. He closed the door without turning on the light.

Since there was nothing he wanted to see, he didn't need the light to see it by.

2

Now it was morning, and Gregor was standing in the kitchen, turning David Sandler's refrigerator note over and over in his hands. David was home, and asleep. Gregor knew that because David slept in an open loft on the house's minimal second floor, and he snored. Gregor got orange juice out of the refrigerator and poured himself a glass. In the bright sunshine of this morning, it didn't seem possible to Gregor that he had been hearing Elizabeth's voice on the water in the dark. He never heard Elizabeth's voice anymore. It had left him when he moved back to Cavanaugh Street and started to live his life again. Gregor put his glass of juice down on the counter and fumbled around among the equipment there, looking for the means to make coffee. David had a formidable aluminum coffee machine, but as far as Gregor could tell, he had never used it. It was as shiny and clean inside as the day it had been brought from the store. Gregor poked around in the cabinets and came up with a large jar of instant, fortunately not Taster's Choice. If there was one thing Gregor truly couldn't stand, it was those silly commercials with the British woman and the American man. He put the kettle on to boil and dumped instant coffee into the bottom of a large white mug. When the water boiled, he poured it over the coffee and stirred more vigorously than he needed to. He had too much energy this morning. He was restless and jittery, eager for someplace to go. He thought about calling

Clayton Hall, and decided against it. He wasn't ready for Clayton Hall yet. He finished his orange juice, rinsed the glass out in the sink, and left the glass to dry in the white plastic drainer. David was still snoring away upstairs. Gregor thought it was a good thing that David had never married. With a snore like that, he would have been kicked out of the marriage bed and down the hall to the study in a week.

Gregor got his coffee half finished, and made up his mind. The loft was reached by a spiral staircase. Gregor had never understood the attraction of spiral staircases. They showed up everywhere people had the money to pay for them, but they were damned hard to climb. Gregor climbed this one very carefully, holding on to the rail with one hand and his coffee with the other. When he got to the top, he made himself walk a full foot onto the platform before he looked back and down. Looking down didn't make him feel as sick as he thought it would, which he found somehow reassuring. There was a big bookcase that served as the headboard of David's bed on one side and as a shield from the living room on the other. Gregor went around it and found David sleeping in a T-shirt, wound into the sheets as if he had tried to braid himself into the bed. Gregor pulled up the small armchair that was resting against the bureau and sat down. Then he cleared his throat as loudly as he could. It didn't make a dent in the noise. It would have taken a freight train to make a dent in the noise.

So Gregor leaned forward and grabbed David by the shoulder. "David," he said. "David, wake up."

David Sandler shuddered, and turned, and snored more loudly. Gregor pushed him again.

"David, for heaven's sake. I want to talk to you."

David opened his eyes and squinted, his eyelids full of early morning grit.

"Gregor? What is it? Has something happened?"

"I wanted to have a chance to talk to you before I went out."

"What . . . time is it?"

Gregor looked down at his wrists and found them bare. He had been forgetting his watch more and more lately. "I don't know," he told David. "I think it's about six-thirty or seven. I woke up at six."

"Six-thirty or seven . . . and you woke up at six. Do you do that all the time?"

"Pretty much."

"Right." David Sandler sat up in bed. His T-shirt had UNC TARHEELS printed across the front, and what looked like a college seal. His hair was a mass of tangles. He settled the sheet down around his waist and yawned. "So what is it? Is there something going on? What's your hurry this morning?"

"I want to go into town and talk to Clayton Hall, but I don't want to do it without asking you a few questions. I've got to have a long talk with Clayton Hall. And I suppose it's time I faced the inevitable."

"What's the inevitable?"

"At least attempting to talk to Ginny Marsh. I've been avoiding it. I've been avoiding it very conscientiously. It wasn't until I talked to Bennis last night that I realized it."

"You talked to Bennis last night? I hope she's well. I hope you gave her my regards."

"I didn't give her anybody's regards. It wasn't that kind of conversation. Don't you want to get up and get dressed or something?"

"I don't want to get up at all," David said. "If I get dressed, I'll never get back to sleep. I was out until two this morning."

"All that time in Chapel Hill?"

"Actually," David said, "I stopped at Maggie Kelleher's house on the way back and had a couple of glasses of wine."

"Ah."

"Don't say 'ah' to me, Gregor. I'm a grown man and she's a grown woman. It's not like we were a couple of teenagers sneaking out when her parents weren't looking."

"It's just that I didn't realize you were involved with somebody down here."

"I'm not," David said. "Not yet. I'm just—working on it."

Gregor decided to let this part of the conversation go. He didn't want David to ask if he was involved with anyone himself. It would be a question that would be impossible to answer. Yes—if it meant that there was somebody he cared about. No—if it meant that he was sleeping with her. He took a long sip of coffee and put all thoughts of sleeping with Bennis Hannaford out of his head. He didn't even want to think about thinking about it. It disturbed him.

"Go back to the first murder," he said instead. "When you found the mother coming at you covered with blood, as you put it. She was alone?"

"Absolutely alone," David agreed.

"Fine. Did she actually tell you that the baby was in that clearing at the back of the house? Did she say that specifically?"

David thought about it. "No," he said. "She just said the baby was dead and the body was behind the house. She didn't say where behind the house."

"Did you follow her immediately and look?"

"No, I didn't. I went into the house itself, into the study, where all these people were sitting around. There were people in the living room, too, but the people I knew were mostly in the study."

"People like who?"

David got into a cross-legged position and scratched his head. "Maggie," he said finally, "and Zhondra Meyer herself, of course. And Rose MacNeill. I remember because she kept praying all the time. And Naomi Brent. I think Stephen Harrow might have been in there, too."

"Might have been?"

"It was dark, Gregor. The electricity was out. There was a fire going in that enormous fireplace—have you seen the fireplaces up there yet?—and there were some candles, but you know what it's like trying to make anything out in light like that. Stephen was around later, I know, because I talked to him. After we'd all gone up the hill and found the baby.''

"And the baby was there, in the clearing, already dead.''

"Oh, yes.''

"What about Carol Littleton, the woman who died? Did you know who she was at the time?''

"Oh, yes. I knew her, and I know Dinah and Stelle. At least I recognize them. They might have been in the living room. They weren't in the study.''

"You're sure?''

"Positive.''

"But they also weren't in the clearing when you got to it.''

"Nobody was in the clearing. The place was a mess. I don't know how I can explain it to you when you didn't see it. This was a major hurricane we were dealing with here.''

"I know that. But Stelle Cary told me yesterday that they were in the clearing for the whole of the storm. That they were trapped there by the storm.''

"Well, they weren't there when we got there, that's all I know. But maybe it's not as much of a contradiction as it seems.''

"How not?''

"Well, by the time we actually made our way up there, the storm had started to die down. Maybe Dinah and Stelle and Carol left just as we were making our way up.''

"Wouldn't they have had to come down by the same path?''

"It would have been simpler,'' David admitted, ''but they might not have been able to find the path. It would have been hard to find anything in all that chaos.''

"That still leaves the problem of the baby,'' Gregor pointed out. ''If Stelle and Carol and Dinah did what Ginny Marsh is accusing them of doing, then fine. They were there. They killed the baby. The body of the baby was there. But if they didn't kill the baby, then you have to ask how and when the body was put in the clearing, and by whom.''

"I thought you had already decided by whom. I thought you were one of the people who believed it was Ginny who did it."

"Ginny may have done it, but if the sequence of events is the way we've just worked it out, she didn't put the baby's body in the clearing. She didn't have the baby with her when you found her."

"No," David said. "No, she didn't."

"Was she out of your sight for any significant period after that?"

"She wasn't out of my sight at all," David answered. "I was hanging on to her with both hands. I didn't know what was going on. I was scared to death."

"I don't blame you," Gregor said. "But you see my point here. There's a little glitch in the evidence. Looked at this way, it seems much more likely that Stelle and Dinah and Carol did just what Ginny Marsh says they did, at least insofar as they are supposed to have killed the baby. I think we can rule the devil worship nonsense out. Just a nice Baptist girl misinterpreting the bizarre."

"I don't think Dinah and Stelle and Carol killed that baby," David said. "Especially not Carol. You have no idea how besotted she was by babies."

"A lot of child murderers are besotted by babies, but I'll give you a plausible scenario. Dinah and Stelle and Carol decided to worship the goddess with a good old human sacrifice, the way she's been worshipped through most of history. So they got hold of the baby, and they killed it, and then Carol Littleton couldn't handle the guilt. And now Carol Littleton is dead."

"Do you really believe that, Gregor? That they're practicing blood sacrifice up at the camp?"

"No. I just said the scenario was plausible, more plausible right now than anything else."

"You ought to tell the whole thing to Ginny's defense

lawyer. Maybe it would get her out of—protective custody.''

Gregor stood up and drained the last of his coffee. "I've got to go into town," he said. "I'm not very interested in talking to Ginny Marsh's defense lawyer, but I am interested in talking to Clayton Hall. Are you going to be around later this afternoon?''

"I'm going to be right in my office, typing away."

"Good. Maybe I'll come back for lunch and tell you what I've found. You ought to get up earlier in the morning. It's better for your health.''

"You're the one with the paunch, Gregor. Don't forget to lock the door on your way out.''

Gregor made his way down the spiral staircase again, moving slowly to make sure he wouldn't fall. It had always seemed shameful to him that he had so little sense of balance. Someone who had been in the positions he had been in ought to be more sure on his feet.

five

1

It took Rose MacNeill almost all day to get herself to go up the hill to the camp—on her own this time, not in a crowd, not because of an emergency. Actually, Rose used to go up there all the time when she was a little girl. That was in the days when the camp was not a camp but Bonaventura House, and open to the public like a museum. In high school, Rose and her girlfriends like to go look at the furniture and the wallpaper. It was much better there than in the pictures in the decorating magazines, richer and more magnificent. Rose could just imagine herself sweeping down the big central staircase in a floor-length ball gown with a tiara of diamonds on her head. Waiting at the bottom would be hundreds of people, in ball gowns, too, walking carefully under heavy loads of jewelry, and the men in tuxedos. Rose knew girls who dreamed only of growing up to be the kind of housewife who was married to a doctor. They imagined themselves giving barbecue parties on broad back patios on lawns that brushed the territory of the eighteenth hole. They pictured themselves in smart little suits from Neiman-Marcus and Lord & Taylor. Rose was more ambitious than that. She wanted to sweep through galleries of mirrors in Balenciaga and Cartier pearls.

Of course, Rose thought now, looking up from the box of pen and pencil gift sets she was unpacking, she had only wanted those things in her dream life. In her real life, she had been eminently practical, and more than happy to live in Bellerton and be part of what Bellerton was all about. She could, she told herself, have gone on like that forever, if everybody else hadn't kept changing all the time. It was other people changing that made her so mixed up. She looked down at the pen and pencil sets and grimaced. They were nice little sets, in gold and silver tone, with inscriptions on each piece. DO THE WORK OF GOD AND YOU WILL PROSPER, one said. It didn't cite chapter and verse, so Rose assumed it wasn't from the Bible. That was strange. Why would anyone want a pen and pencil set with something inscribed on it that wasn't from the Bible? Why would anyone want a pen and pencil set with anything inscribed on it at all? Rose could feel the irritation rising in her. She had been nuts all day—*all day*—and it was getting worse. She could hardly sit still for a minute before she wanted to leap to her feet and run around the room, smashing things. One of the reasons she was in the back room doing the unpacking was that she didn't want to be in the store where the unpacking had already been done, looking at things. The false cheerfulness of it all appalled her. She had never thought of it before, but what she was selling was an almost pathological desire to be cheerful at any price. She had little plastic wand doohickeys with haloed angel heads bouncing around on small springs off the tops of them. They cost $5.95 and had CHRIST IS LORD written up the side of them. She had bookmarks with pictures of Christ coming in glory through the clouds and the words JESUS CHRIST IS LORD written under His feet. They cost $4.69 and were encased in sharp-edged plastic shields. Rose had walked around amid it all, first thing she got in, before she even opened up. She kept wanting to ball her hands into fists and hit at it, punch at it, until she had it strewn all over the carpet, in shards. As soon as Kathi came in for the day, Rose went into the back and the unpacking. She usually arranged it so that it was the other way around, but she couldn't stand the idea of talking to the little old ladies who came in to buy thank-you notes with pictures of the cross on them in gold and white. If she had to discuss white leather gift Bibles or the latest book by Beverley LaHaye about why it was better to be a stay-at-home wife, she was going to murder someone.

Now she stood and looked around. It had to be almost noon. The sun was that way in the sky. Rose had once been very good at judging the position of the sun. That had been in high school, when she hadn't been able to stand the thought of sitting through one more minute of English or math. Now she couldn't stand the thought of being sur-rounded by—these things—one more minute, either. She kept imagining herself standing on the terrace of Bonaven-tura, holding a wineglass in her hand, listening to the sound her high heels made on the flagstones. She hadn't had a glass of wine in years. It wasn't Christian, at least not in the way Christianity was practiced around here. She wished she was imagining herself at Bonaventura in a ball gown instead of in her ordinary clothes. She wished she was imagining herself with someone, instead of all alone. It all went around and around. It made her dizzy, but she couldn't make it stop. Everything seemed to be out of con-trol. She knew she ought to be thinking about baby Tiffany, or that poor stumpy woman Carol Littleton, but they didn't exist for her. She watched Maggie Kelleher on the six o'clock news, saying how awful it all was, and the senti-ment seemed inconceivably overwrought. It had all hap-pened to other people. It had nothing to do with her.

The door to the storeroom popped open and Kathi looked in, curious and just faintly annoyed.

"What are you doing back here?" she demanded. "You have a headache or something? You've been back here all morning."

"I've been back here because there's been work to do," Rose snapped. The pen and pencils sets were strewn all over the floor, not stacked neatly on a shelf the way they were supposed to be. If Kathi had ever done something like this, Rose knew perfectly well that she would have brained the girl. Kathi knew it, too. She kept looking from the mess on the floor to Rose and then back again.

"Are you sure you're all right?" Kathi said.

"I'm fine. I'm better than fine. If you're back here, you're not out there watching the store."

"There's nobody in the store," Kathi said reasonably. "And if somebody comes in, we'll hear the bell."

"Somebody could come in and keep the bell from ringing. Somebody could show up just wanting to steal something."

"How could somebody keep the bell from ringing? It rings if you just lean against that door."

"I think you're very naive, Kathi, I really do. You don't realize the kind of people there are out there. Clever people. And we've got all these strangers down from New York."

"I think you must be sick," Kathi said. "You're not making any sense at all today. Do you want to go upstairs and lie down and leave it all to me for the rest of the day?"

"I want to go for a walk," Rose said, wondering where that had come from. Did she want to go for a walk? Where would she walk to? "I want to get out in the air."

Kathi was as solid and boring and unfazed as always. "Fine," she said. "You go take a walk."

"I could be the whole afternoon."

"I've been here for the whole afternoon by myself before."

"The painters might come," Rose said, thinking that she knew exactly where she wanted to walk to. "The ones who are going to fix the front room and the kitchen because of the storm damage. You'd have to give them directions."

"You wrote out the directions. Don't you remember? You put them on lined paper next to the cash register so you could hang them on the door in case you had to be out and the painters were coming. I've been looking at them all day."

"Oh," Rose said.

Kathi blew her bangs out of her eyes with a long

stream of air. The gesture made her almost repulsively unattractive, and Rose winced.

"I'm going to go back out front in case somebody comes in," Kathi told her. "If you want to go for a walk you should go for a walk. You aren't doing any good around here. And I can lock up by myself, Rose, I've done it before and you know it."

It would be a terrible thing, Rose thought, if Kathi knew how stupid Rose thought she was. Everything about Kathi was graceless and disjointed, almost as if she were an embryonic form of what those women up at the camp had come to maturity at, whatever that was.

"Go for a walk," Kathi said again, stopping in the storeroom's door. Then she disappeared into the hall, and Rose held her breath, waiting for her to be truly gone.

After that, it didn't take very long. Rose had been wearing a frilly little apron to unpack the pen and pencil sets. She took it off and dumped it into one of the open cardboard boxes on the floor. Her feet hurt, but she didn't want to exchange her elegant high-heeled shoes for serviceable flats. All in all, she thought she looked pretty good. Her hair had been colored only a few days ago. Her skirt was wide and full of flowers. Her blouse was made of silk so fine, you could almost see through it.

Rose went out in the hall, looked up and down it to make sure that Kathi wasn't lurking anywhere, and then headed for the back and the door to the driveway. She let herself out into a day that seemed hotter than it should have been. Usually by this time of year the worst of the heat was gone. She went around the little paved walk to the front of the house and Main Street. She saw Charlie Hare on a chair outside his store, reading the newspaper. Ever since she had had that blowup with Charlie about religion the other day, he'd been telling people that she was possessed by the Devil.

Well, Rose thought, maybe I am.

She kept carefully to the side of the street away from Maggie Kelleher's and Charlie Hare's. On this side of the street, there were mainly souvenir stores that catered to the tourists. She was finding it very hard not to run. She was also finding it very hard to breathe. The headline on the Bellerton *Times* was all about this new murder. There was a black-and-white picture of Carol Littleton on the front page, looking even more blurry and out of focus than Carol had in real life.

At the end of the long center block of Main Street—the block with Charlie Hare's and Maggie Kelleher's stores on it—Rose made herself stop and draw in air. Then she walked another whole block, crossed the road, and turned down Barton Street. Town Hall was on her right, a mass of blank-faced brick. She started breathing a little more easily as soon as she knew she was past the point where anybody could see her. Most of the houses on Barton Street belonged to summer people and were shut up for the winter.

Barton Street, like all the streets on this side of Main, petered out after less than three blocks. There were still roads out here, but they weren't town roads. The houses were slutty-looking, too, shacky and listless. They reminded Rose of what happened to people who didn't take care of themselves.

She made her way left along the last sidewalked stretch, making a little loop so that she came out right in front of the short road that led up to the camp. She had been afraid that she would find somebody walking on it, one of those women coming in to town to shop or have lunch, but there wasn't anybody there. She looked right and left to see if anybody was watching her and then felt foolish doing it. In places like Bellerton, if somebody wanted to see you, they saw you. There could be dozens of old women sitting behind the drawn living room curtains of all the houses she could see. There was just no way that she would ever be able to tell.

She started up the camp's road, limping a little on her heels, propelled forward half by determination and half by fear. Almost as soon as she started to make the climb, she felt that everything was different. The air was charged out here. It even smelled unusual. The flowers on the bushes at the roadside looked heavier and brighter than the same kind of thing Rose had seen in town. Maybe something happened to people when they came up here on their own. Maybe they got drunk on the air, and did things they didn't know they were doing.

Rose must have been drunk on the air herself. She was already at the gate to Bonaventura and she didn't remember getting there. She had expected it to be closed, locked tight to keep out the media and the curious, but it wasn't. Rose stepped through it onto the gravel drive and felt her ankle twist. It was impossible to walk on gravel in very high heels. It was impossible to do anything when you couldn't get any air. Rose pulled her foot up and her heel out of the soft ground under the stones and leaned over to examine the damage. She was still half gasping for breath when she saw a shadow fall across hers and heard Zhondra Meyer say, "Well, what is it? Are you hurt? Do you need something? You're not here to stay. You're the woman who runs that religious gift store in the Victorian house in town."

Rose straightened up, very carefully. She had always found looking at Zhondra Meyer painful. Zhondra was so beautiful, and so strong a presence. Being very close to her was like being enveloped in light. Rose felt that Zhondra was sending out rays, like heat, but stronger than heat.

"I—" she began, and then, "My name is Rose MacNeill. We've been introduced before."

Zhondra cocked her head. "But you *are* the woman who owns the religious gift shop. I've seen you a million times."

"Yes," Rose said. "Yes, I am. Christening presents. Gift Bibles. Note card sets with pictures of Christ Our Lord and Savior on every sheet. That kind of thing."

"I know the kind of thing," Zhondra said. "I've been in your store. But what do you want up here?"

Rose's lips felt suddenly dry. Every part of her felt suddenly dry. And hot. And afraid. She wanted to step back a little, out of Zhondra Meyer's orbit, but she was afraid she would stumble again.

"She came into the store, you know, on the day of the hurricane," Rose said. "Carol Littleton, I mean. She wanted to buy a christening present for her granddaughter."

"I know she did. Is that what you came up here about?"

"No, no. I was just thinking about it. About how strange it was. I wasn't very nice to her."

"Most people weren't."

"I've known people like that," Rose said. "People who seem to—to almost attract abuse."

"You mean people who cause their own abuse? You mean the abuse is their fault?"

"No, not exactly," Rose said. "It's just that it seems as if there are some people, if you froze them solid and put them in a room with twenty-five other people, and then you got some real psychopath to go in and pick the one he wanted most, they'd be the ones who got picked. Bad luck, maybe, or—what did we use to say a few years ago? Bad karma."

"I didn't think Christians believed in karma."

"They don't. Goodness, you should hear Pat Robertson talk about Eastern religions. I don't know if you know who Pat Robertson is. He's on this thing called the Christian Broadcasting Network. He—"

"I know who Pat Robertson is."

Rose turned to look at the house, the massive blocks of it, the peaks and towers. It was just like the worst kind of fairy tale castle, the one the wicked stepmother always lived in. Rose rubbed her arms with the palms of her hands. She felt hot. She felt cold. She felt as if she were about to faint.

Rose looked back to Zhondra Meyer and saw that her eyes were deep and still and perfect.

"I think," Rose said carefully. "I think that I have come to stay. As a guest. If you know what I mean."

"You want to stay here," Zhondra Meyer said, just as carefully.

"Yes," Rose said. "I do. I want to stay here."

"Do you know what we're all about, what this place is set up to be?"

"Of course I do. Everybody knows. Henry Holborn preaches about you every Sunday."

"It might not be what Henry Holborn thinks it is."

"It's what I think it is. I know it."

"It wouldn't do you much good with that store of yours."

"Maybe I'll change the store."

"You couldn't stay in your church, either. Not if you go to Henry Holborn's."

"I don't go to Henry Holborn's church," Rose said. "But I wouldn't want to stay in my church, either. I don't even know if I want to stay in town. I get so—so crazy sometimes. Do you know what I mean?"

"I know that I don't trust you," Zhondra Meyer said. "You want to give up much too much of your life for sex."

It was an awful moment, one of the worst Rose could remember in her life. She was sure that Zhondra Meyer was going to make her go away. She could already see what it would be like, stumbling her way back down that hill, open and exposed to any old lady who might happen to be watching, turned down. Why had she always been so sure that rejection was something that showed in her face?

Then Zhondra Meyer seemed to soften. Rose's stomach twisted and leapt.

"Come inside for a minute," Zhondra said. "Come and talk to me. I think there are a few things you ought to know."

As far as Rose MacNeill was concerned, she had been waiting for a chance like this for years, and now it was here, where she could almost hold it. She wondered if it would be the way she had imagined it to be, or even better.

2

Henry Holborn had seen the Bellerton *Times* with the picture of Carol Littleton on it, and bought a copy. He had seen several out-of-town papers, too, including the Raleigh *News and Observer,* but he hadn't bought any of those, not even the ones with his own picture on them. In the early days of his career, he had always bought a copy of any periodical that mentioned him, even if the mention was meretricious and awful. Lately he didn't bother to read his publicity. They all said the same things, these people, especially the ones from the very big cities in New York and California. They all seemed to think that giving your life to God turned you into the equivalent of Bigfoot—a hairy mythical monster who was likely to bite.

Henry Holborn was standing in the middle of the big room in the basement of Town Hall that served as the office of the Bellerton Police Department, next to the desk Clayton Hall was using to do his paperwork. It was exactly one minute before noon, and Jackson had already gone down to lunch. He was probably down at Betsey's, talking it all over with anybody who would listen, including any stray reporters who might happen to be around. Henry wished he had Janet with him for this, but she was gone, too, to the mall, to do some shopping.

"We can't let the world stop just because you got arrested," she told him, when he asked her to come with him this morning. "Even if you did get arrested in a just cause. I've got three Girl Scout meetings this week and I'm not ready for any one of them."

Henry Holborn wasn't ready for Clayton Hall, not really, but he waited as patiently as he could. This was what was known as carrying your cross with Christ, although Henry thought that might be more of a Catholic thing than a Protestant one. He thought he would preach on it one Sunday, when the congregation had had enough of thinking positive thoughts.

Clayton was hammering away at a computer keyboard

with one hand and trying to wrestle legal-sized papers into submission with the other. Henry drew a chair up from one of the other desks and sat down.

"For the Lord's sake, Clayton, what all are you doing? We've been at this for half an hour."

"You're the one who had to go marching on up to Bonaventura carrying a cross and singing 'That Old Time Religion.' By the way, Henry, if that's what your choir sounds like on Sundays, I think I'll just skip it."

"You'll skip it no matter what the choir sounds like. And of course they don't sound like that. The congregation sounds like that. That's why we have a choir."

"Maybe you ought to get yourself some heavenly intervention. I've heard of tone deaf, Henry, but that was pitiful."

"Why don't we just process this stuff and let me get out of here? I'm not doing myself any good down here and I'm not doing you any good down here, either."

"Just following the rules, Henry, just following the rules."

"Well, you may be following the rules, Clayton, but you know darn well you're not going to get me prosecuted for anything on this count. You don't want to and nobody in town wants you to."

"Zhondra Meyer wants me to."

"Ms. Meyer has a lot of money, but she's still just summer people."

"Ms. Meyer has a very fancy law firm in New York," Clayton said patiently, "and I've got Gregor Demarkian to worry about, too. We at least have to look like we're trying to play it straight."

"But we are playing it straight, Clayton. This whole thing is ridiculous. What are you going to charge me with?"

"Trespassing."

"There's a public right-of-way right through the back of that property and there has been since 1866."

"Interfering with a police investigation," Clayton said. "Obstructing justice."

"I didn't obstruct justice. Not for a minute."

"I'm going to have to charge you with something, Henry. That's just the way things are these days. The time is long gone when we could just patch things up among ourselves."

"Do you think that makes the world a better place, Clayton? Because I don't."

"What I think about it doesn't matter a damn, Henry. The world is the way it is. There's nothing either you or I can do about it."

"There's something God can do about it."

Clayton Hall dropped his papers into a messy little pile on the desk. "Don't preach God to me, Henry," he said. "I've known you too damn long. I was there the first time you ever went wild, and I've got vivid memories of four or five times since then."

"I've quit since then, Clayton."

"I know, and more power to you, but I meant what I said. Don't preach God to me. Someday I may meet an angel from Heaven with a message to me from the Almighty, and him I'll listen to, but you I won't, and that's final."

Henry got off his chair and went over to the window to look out on the window well and the feet of the people passing along this side of the building. Everything seemed so normal out there, and yet he knew it wasn't. Everything seemed so calm, and yet it was about to explode. Clayton might not want to listen to any more talk about God, but it was God who wanted to be heard, and Henry's job was to make Him heard.

"Clayton?" he asked. "Do you like this man, this Demarkian?"

"Yes, I do," Clayton said. "He has a few things in common with people around here. He can look pretty slow on the surface. He isn't slow at all."

"No, I didn't think he was slow. But I wonder what

he's really doing down here. Why would a famous man like that want to come to Bellerton?''

"That's what he does, Henry. He goes places where there are murder investigators who need an expert to consult with. He's an expert."

"And you think he's here because the murder of Ginny's baby got so much publicity."

"Because of that and because he's a friend of David Sandler's. You know, Henry, we've been over all this before. Is there some point you're trying to make here?"

"I don't know."

And that was the truth, Henry thought. He really didn't know. He was just tired and cranky and worried, and everything seemed to be going wrong. Having somebody like Gregor Demarkian around, a complete stranger who wasn't tied to them in any way, just seemed wrong.

"Sit down again now and sign these papers," Clayton Hall said. "Then we'll be done and you can go."

"All right."

"And you tell your people that I expect each and every one of them who was involved in that nonsense yesterday to come in and see me. And tell them not to think I didn't see them, because I did. I saw every one of them. And if you talk to Ricky Drake—"

"I'll talk to Ricky," Henry said. "Don't worry about it."

Clayton handed Henry a pen. "You attract loose cannons, Henry. Ricky Drake is one of them. Bobby Marsh is the prince lunatic of all time. You've got to understand that if you attract them, you have to control them."

"I do control them. God controls them."

"If God controls them, He's doing a sloppy job. Get a move on with the signing, Henry. I want to go to lunch, myself."

Usually, when Henry Holborn was in town, he had lunch at Betsey's just like everybody else. He didn't think he would do that, today. Loose cannons, Clayton called them. Henry knew boys like Ricky Drake and Bobby

Marsh. He had been one himself. It was the other people he was worried about, the quiet ones, the ones who never made any trouble until, wham, one day they snapped, and there you were.

People seemed to be snapping right and left around Henry Holborn these days, and if the Devil wasn't responsible for it, he didn't know who else it could possibly be.

six

1

It wasn't as easy to get in to see Ginny Marsh as Gregor had hoped it would be. Clayton Hall called for him from one of the desks in the police department and then put him on the phone to talk to the young lawyer in Charlotte who had agreed to take the case. He had expected hostility, or at least aloofness. No matter what the papers said Gregor Demarkian was going to do in Bellerton, what he was doing was working with the police. Instead, he got a polite voice with the second district drawl of the trip, sounding curious. It also sounded tired. The lawyer's name was Susan Dunne, and Gregor thought she must work too hard and sleep too little. Everything she said had that dazed quality to it, as if she found it difficult to concentrate even on emergencies.

"I looked you up when I found out you were in Bellerton, working with the police," she told Gregor, yawning into the phone. "You've had a very interesting life."

"Have I?"

"Reading about you is like watching that old *Perry Mason* television show. The real murderer is never the murderer the police already arrested. Real life is almost never like that, you know."

"Real life is the only life I've got, Ms. Dunne. Do you believe Ginny Marsh killed her baby?"

It wasn't the kind of question a lawyer had any right

answering about a client. Susan Dunne said, "What interests me about this case is that the police have far less to go on than they think they have. I mean, it isn't an incriminating factor against Ginny Marsh as an individual that in other cases of this kind it has happened, maybe even frequently, that the mother killed the child."

"No," Gregor agreed, "it isn't."

"Sometimes the police seem to have made up their minds, Mr. Demarkian. Sometimes they seem to be already seeking the death penalty."

"I'm surprised Ginny Marsh is still in jail."

"So am I," Susan Dunne said. "You wouldn't believe what the court system is like where you are, talking about cro—"

"Cronyism?"

"I didn't say any of this."

"I wouldn't repeat it."

"Even so."

"Would you mind telling me where you're from, Ms. Dunne?"

"I'm from New Orleans."

"Ah. And where did you go to law school?"

"I went to Yale. I went to Yale College, too, if you have to know. What is all this about? Are you worried that Ginny doesn't have adequate representation?"

"No. I wanted to confirm my impression that you were not a small-town woman."

"Oh, for Pete's sake. I've heard that one. Small towns run differently from other places. Well, they shouldn't. And my client, who has not been formally charged with the murder, should not be sitting in the town jail just because the judge knew the town attorney in high school."

"I didn't say she should."

"It's hard to tell just what you're saying, isn't it, Mr. Demarkian? All right. Let's do it this way. I'm due to come down to Bellerton tomorrow morning. Let's meet in the main foyer of Town Hall at nine o'clock."

"I'll be there."

"Assuming you've got the permission of the police, I'll bring you down to talk to Ginny."

"Thank you. And I do have the permission of the police."

"I'll stay with you the whole time you do talk to her."

"All right," Gregor said.

"No matter who it is you are or who you think you are, this time you're working with the police, and I can't have my client talk to you without an attorney present. I'm the attorney. I intend to be present."

"I understand that, Miss Dunne. I find it entirely commendable."

"All right, then. As long as you do. And you must also understand that I may cut off some of your lines of questioning. Just because you think they're interesting doesn't mean I'm going to think they're in the best interests of my client."

"Of course."

"I wish I trusted this more, Mr. Demarkian. I wish I trusted you more. But I don't."

"Do me a favor," Gregor said. "Over the time between then and now, think about something for me."

"What?"

"Well, I'll tell you. A number of people I've talked to here have come up with the same thesis. They don't think Ginny Marsh murdered her child, and they don't think she helped anyone else kill it or that she's covering up for her husband or a boyfriend. When she says she had nothing to do with it, they believe her."

"That's good."

"What they don't believe," Gregor continued, "is that she's telling the truth about the Black Mass or whatever it was. And they don't think she's mistaken, either. They think she's lying through her teeth."

There was a lot of quiet breathing and coffee drinking down in Charlotte. Finally Susan Dunne said, "I find that interesting, Mr. Demarkian. In fact, I find that very interesting. Maybe you're more right than I want to realize.

Maybe she does need a small-town lawyer, a Bellerton lawyer even, just to keep track of all the . . . permutations.''

"Nobody can keep track of all the permutations.''

"Yes. Well. We can go through all this again tomorrow.''

"Of course. I'll be looking forward to seeing you.''

"Oh, I'll be looking forward to seeing you, too, Mr. Demarkian. I'll be very glad to get my eyes on you at last. I've got to go.''

"I want to thank you again for the time you're giving me. You must be a very busy woman.''

"I don't think 'busy' is the word for it. I look forward to meeting you, Mr. Demarkian, and to discussing Bellerton's other recent murder. That place is getting to be like Detroit.''

"I doubt it.''

"I don't know what I doubt anymore. Good afternoon, Mr. Demarkian. I'll see you tomorrow.''

This time the phone went to a dial tone. Gregor looked at the receiver for a moment, then put it down. Clayton Hall was sitting on the corner of a desk a few feet away, kicking one heel in the air. Gregor finally realized what it was about the police station that kept striking him as so strange: There were no religious symbols in it. Like many small towns in the South, Bellerton interpreted the Supreme Court's decisions limiting religious expression in public places very narrowly. If the Supreme Court said you couldn't have a nativity scene in the middle of the town green for Christmas, then Bellerton wouldn't have a nativity scene on the town green for Christmas, but that didn't mean it wouldn't have a perfectly nice crèche in the lobby of the Town Hall. If the Supreme Court said that public schools couldn't hang copies of the Ten Commandments on public school classroom walls, then Bellerton wouldn't hang copies of the Ten Commandments on public school classroom walls—but more than two thirds of the students in every class would be wearing crosses on chains around their necks, and some of them would show up on the schools' front walks in the morning, praying in loud voices and holding hands. What Gregor had particularly noticed was the way in which verses from the Bible seemed to be inscribed on plaques and hung everywhere. There was one in the lobby upstairs, and one just inside the front door of the library, too, which Gregor had seen on one of his restless excursions around town. The police department, though, was bare. There wasn't as much as a single cross around Clayton's or Jackson's neck. There wasn't a single Bible on a single desk. There weren't even any quotes from the Declaration of Independence or the Constitution—familiar tactics, Gregor knew, because the quotes so often had God in them. Clayton Hall was watching him look, kicking his free foot higher and higher in the air.

"So what is it?" Clayton said. "You didn't expect her to just let you go in and sit down with Ginny on your own, did you?"

"No," Gregor admitted. "That's all right. I was thinking about something else."

"If you were thinking this place is a dump, I agree with you. Everybody agrees with you. It isn't going to change anytime soon."

"I was thinking this was the only place in town, public property or private, where I haven't seen a single religious symbol of any kind."

"Why should we have religious symbols in the police department? The perpetrators can bring their own religious symbols. They do, too."

"I didn't say I thought you ought to have religious symbols," Gregor said patiently, "it's just that, well, to be frank, Clayton, relative to where I come from, this is a very religious town."

"Baptist territory," Clayton said solemnly.

"Baptist and Assemblies of God and denominations even smaller than that. I was talking about the pervasiveness of it. It really is everywhere."

"Excuse me if I don't get your point, Mr. Demarkian, but no matter how significant all that kind of thing may seem to you, it's no big deal to me. I grew up in Bellerton. We used to be a lot more religious than we are now. The Supreme Court used to let us get away with it."

"I'm sure they did, Clayton, but the point is—" Gregor drummed his fingers on the desk next to the phone. "Look," he started up again, "do you think Ginny Marsh saw a bunch of women worshipping the devil in that clearing up at the camp?"

"I think Ginny Marsh saw a bunch of women worshipping the goddess," Clayton said.

"You think she saw them on the day of the hurricane?"

"I haven't got the faintest idea. She saw them. If she killed that baby, it could have been weeks before, because all she needed was the excuse, and once she'd seen them the excuse was handy. Even if there hadn't been anybody out there worshipping the goddess at the time."

"What about Carol Littleton?" Gregor asked. "Who do you think killed her?"

"I don't know."

"Do you think she was killed by the same person who killed Ginny Marsh's baby?"

"I don't know. Not if Ginny Marsh killed her own baby, though. Ginny is still safely in jail."

"Do you think Carol Littleton was killed because of religion?"

Clayton hopped down off the desk he had been sitting on. "If you mean do I think that Henry Holborn or one of his people decided to go off half-cocked and start exorcising devils for himself, the answer is no. Henry can be pretty damned irritating at times, but he's not violent."

"There are people around him who could be violent," Gregor said.

"Oh, I agree with you." Clayton Hall nodded vigorously. "I was telling Henry the same thing myself just a couple of hours ago. And it worries me a little, probably more than you realize. But the fact is that we haven't had any violence from any of them at any time for any reason. We haven't even had any pro-life violence, and there's an operating clinic not three miles from Henry Holborn's church, one of the few first-rate clinics in North Carolina. You can't lump people together, you know. You can't say that just because there are crazy fundamentalists in Halford, Mississippi, that everybody who believes in the fundamentals is crazy.''

Actually, Gregor thought, that wasn't the point. He wished he could get it clear in his own mind. He wasn't one of those people who automatically thought all religions and all religious believers were dangerous, or insane, or worse. He even showed up at Father Tibor's church every once in a while, out of politeness, and enjoyed himself there. It wasn't that there was something wrong about religion. It was that there was something wrong about religion *in this case*.

''You got something on your mind?'' Clayton Hall demanded. ''You want to tell the rest of us about it?''

''You're the only 'rest of us' there is at the moment, Clayton. And there's nothing to tell, not in the way you mean it. I was thinking there was somebody I would like to talk to.''

''Well, if it isn't somebody in jail or under suspicion of murder or living up in Massachusetts, I might be able to arrange that for you.''

''I've talked to her before, but I didn't know her. The lady from the library. Ruth something.''

''Naomi,'' Clayton said drily. ''Naomi Brent. Now I can tell Henry Holborn that at least once upon a time, you read the Bible.''

''I heard Bible stories in my Sunday school classes,'' Gregor said. ''In Armenian. Can we go talk to this Naomi Brent?''

''Sure, if she's in. Why don't you let me call over to the library and find out? Then it's just across the street.''

''I know where the library is, Clayton.''

Clayton picked up the phone. "That's the trouble with small towns like this," he said. "They're too easy to get to know."

2

The walk between the police department and the library felt endless, because for the first time in Gregor's experience, Main Street wasn't mostly deserted. There were the reporters on the front steps on Town Hall, but they didn't count. There weren't as many of them there as when Gregor had first seen them, either. Maybe the story was going stale, and some of them were being recalled to San Francisco and Tulsa. Maybe, and much more likely, all the waiting was boring beyond belief, and they took off as often as they dared to drink coffee in Betsey's or buy magazines at Maggie Kelleher's bookstore. What made this short walk really awful was that the people of Bellerton were out in force. Gregor saw Maggie Kelleher standing in front of her store's plate glass window, talking to a man in a wooden rocker who seemed to own the store next to hers. He saw Ricky Drake on the steps of Betsey's diner, stopped dead in his tracks to stare at them. A short, sharp movement caught his eye, and Gregor looked up to catch sight of an old woman retreating hastily behind a second-story curtain. He had a thick sheen of sweat across the back of his neck.

"Jesus," he said to Clayton Hall.

The library's big front doors were right in front of them. The doors were shut, so they wouldn't let out any of the air-conditioning. Clayton opened one and ushered Gregor inside. Gregor landed in the lobby right in front of the plaque he had been thinking about, the one with the words WISDOM IS THE JEWEL OF GOD AND THE CROWN OF THE JUST MAN written on it. Gregor didn't know much about the Bible, but he did know this was a quotation from Ecclesiasticus, one of the books of the Bible that Catholics accepted and Protestants did not. The Bellerton Public Library seemed to be more ecumenical than many of the church groups Gregor had heard of.

There were inner doors as well as outer ones. Everyone believed in air locks these days. The inner doors were made of glass. Through them, Gregor could see the few people who were in the library. They were mostly old people, reading newspapers at long wooden tables. There was a young woman at a little computer desk that served as the card catalogue these days, tapping things onto the keyboard with one hand and wrestling with a baby with the other. The baby was bright and cheerful and determined and strong. He kept getting away and having to be chased after.

Clayton pushed open one of the inner doors and said, "You coming? Or are you asleep on your feet?"

"Both," Gregor told him. "It's a good-sized library for a small town."

"Have you been in here before?"

"Just as far as this vestibule. I poked my head in one of those mornings when I was wandering around, exploring."

"It *is* a good library for a small town," Clayton said. "The town council did a good job. They raised some money from taxes and some from fund-raisers and then they got a chunk from the state, and they used it wisely, if you ask me. No paying somebody's second cousin to make a mess of the foundations."

The young woman behind the checkout desk was not the one Gregor was looking for. For one thing, she was too young. For another, her hair was a bizarre shade of yellow that he had never seen before on anyone, anywhere. She was wearing a big silver cross around her neck on a delicate gold chain. So were at least three of the old ladies who were reading newspapers at the long table in the middle of the room. Clayton passed by them all, waving at the young woman behind the desk, whose name appeared to be Tisha. Then he headed for the staircase at the back and started climbing.

"Naomi's office is on the second floor," he explained. "That's because she's a really big noise with a doctorate in library science and everything. She's also local, by the way. Doctorate or no doctorate, I don't think the council would have hired her if she wasn't local."

"I knew she was local," Gregor said.

Clayton looked as if he wanted to ask Gregor how he knew, but they were at the top of the steps now. There were more stacks up here, and more wooden tables and wooden chairs—but small ones this time, just big enough for one or two people. Gregor followed Clayton to the back of the big room and found himself facing three brown metal doors. One of them was marked MEN. One of them was marked WOMEN. The third was blank.

"Here we are," Clayton said, knocking on the blank door. He didn't wait to hear an answering summons. He just opened the door and stuck his head in. "Naomi?"

Naomi was sitting at her desk near the windows. She had her back to the door when Clayton opened it, as if she had been watching the birds in the trees as she waited for their arrival. As soon as she heard the door swing open, she turned. Gregor thought she looked paler and more strained than the first time he had seen her.

Naomi Brent had been holding a pencil in one hand when the door opened. Now she dropped it on the desk and said, "There you are. What kept you? You were just across the street."

Gregor didn't think anything had kept them. Clayton said, "Naomi, I'd like you to meet—"

"Mr. Demarkian and I have met," Naomi cut in. "I'm sorry about my—demeanor yesterday morning, Mr. Demarkian. I wasn't at my best."

"You seemed fine to me."

Naomi turned to Clayton. "I yelled at him," she explained. "I accused him of trying to make everybody who believed in God look like a rube and a dimwit. And he didn't deserve it, of course. He wasn't doing anything like that."

Clayton grabbed one of Naomi's visitor's chairs and sat down at it. It was made of some kind of shiny metal and a vinyl meant to look like black leather, with no arms. Gregor got the impression that Clayton wished he could straddle it.

"I'm surprised to hear you were defending religion," the police chief said. "That isn't what we usually get from you. Remember all that nonsense about *The Catcher in the Rye*?"

"Henry Holborn wanted *The Catcher in the Rye* taken out of the library, or at least put behind the desk and only loaned to adults or something. I never did get it completely straightened out. And of course, there was a whole slew of things he just wanted out of here completely. All the novels by Stephen King."

"I've read Stephen King novels," Gregor said, feeling confused. "What's wrong with Stephen King novels? There wasn't any sex to speak of in any of the ones I read."

Naomi Brent burst out laughing. "Oh, dear, Mr. Demarkian. You're terribly out-of-date. Nobody worries about sex in books anymore."

"They don't?"

"Oh, well, they do, a little, of course," Naomi said. "Especially if it's unconventional sex, and to Henry Holborn conventional means sex with the person you're married to, no one else, period."

"Also sex in the missionary position," Gregor said, "and—"

But Naomi Brent was shaking her head vigorously. "No, no, Mr. Demarkian. You really are behind the times. Tim and Beverly LaHaye, these enormously big evangelists, wrote a guide to lovemaking a few years back, and trust me, it wasn't restricted to the missionary position. You'd be amazed what a husband and wife can do together in bed these days and still be holy in the sight of the Lord."

"I think I'll decide not to think about it," Gregor said.

"Anyway," Naomi said, "the big thing these days is

occultism. They see occultism everywhere. And I do mean everywhere. If you ask me, Stephen King is one of the most traditionally Christian writers I've ever read. His whole philosophy of life comes straight out of St. Augustine—although I don't know if he knows it. All they see is that people in these books talk to ghosts and sometimes the hero or the heroine has magical powers, like the little girl in *Firestarter* who could start fires just by thinking about it. And you know what magical powers mean to them. Somebody must be worshipping the devil."

"The other day," Gregor said, "you were warning me about having just this attitude you're displaying now."

"I go back and forth, Mr. Demarkian. I don't think I meant to say that you shouldn't—dislike—this end-times philosophy Henry Holborn and his people have. Did you know that Henry Holborn thinks we're about to see the end of the world?"

"At the start of the new millennium, I suppose."

"That's right, Mr. Demarkian. Millennial fever. But down here, where so many people believe in very simple, very direct forms of Christianity, it gets into the air. It becomes part of things. If you see what I mean."

"Not exactly."

Naomi Brent looked down at her hands. "Sometimes, when Henry Holborn gets to talking, you can almost see the Devil right there at your shoulder, grinning like hell, ready to snatch your soul. I had a girl who used to come in here, both her parents were practical agnostics, she was never taken to church, and two months after she started her freshman year at Brown, she nearly had a nervous breakdown. She was totally isolated up there. It was crazy."

"So what was it about Henry Holborn and his people you were defending to me the other day behind the Town Hall?" Gregor asked.

"Oh," Naomi said, "it was just, I didn't want you to be like other people and think they were stupid. Or naive. Or ignorant. Brain-dead backwoods hicks, that's what most of those reporters think of them. But they aren't stupid and they aren't hicks and they surely don't live in the back-woods anymore. I just wish they'd get past all this stuff about the Devil. It's making me nervous. Even the Catholics are doing it and they used to have more sense."

"The millennium will come and go," Gregor said gently, "this time just as it did last time. And when the world hasn't ended and Christ hasn't come again in glory, people will calm down."

"That's longer than I want to wait, Mr. Demarkian."

"That's longer than I want to wait, too," Gregor said, "but that's the time we've got, and I don't think anything will really change until it's over. Do you mind very much if I ask you a few questions about the night that Ginny Marsh's baby died? I realize that it was a while ago, and that with the new murder you've probably been distracted, but—"

"It was the night of the hurricane, Mr. Demarkian. I'll remember it all my life."

"Good. I take it you ended up in the study at Bona-ventura during the storm. You were there when David Sandler came in with Ginny Marsh and said that the baby was dead."

"He didn't say that the baby was dead," Naomi corrected. "He hadn't seen the baby yet. He said we had to find the baby."

"All right. So he said you had to find the baby, and he had Ginny with him, and she was—"

"All wet and covered with red. Her clothes were soaked through with red. Some of it was dye that had run from her shirt, but some of it was blood, and there was blood all over her hands and her arms. The paper came out and said it, later."

"Who else was in the study at the time that David Sandler got there?"

"Oh, lots of people. Zhondra Meyer herself, of course. She spent the whole storm sitting behind that big desk of hers, behaving like a queen bee. It was something to see. And Maggie Kelleher was there, sitting on the rug in front of the fire. And Rose MacNeill. Oh, and that woman Alice, you know, Zhondra Meyer's assistant.''

''And that was all?''

''Oh, no, Mr. Demarkian. There were dozens of people there. All of the women from the camp. The women were mostly in the living room next door, where we couldn't see them, but they were there. I meant, those were the people from town that I was talking to. You know, the people I know.''

''You didn't see Carol Littleton?''

''No, Mr. Demarkian, I didn't.''

''Would you have known who she was?''

''Sure. She came into town all the time. Some of them up there almost never come in, but Carol did. She came into the library every Tuesday and Thursday, right at eleven o'clock. And she was in the library on the morning of the storm, too. That's how I knew that Zhondra Meyer was taking people in up at the camp. Carol told me. And I thought, you know, that Bonaventura was a hell of a lot more interesting than the Bellerton Public High School, so why not?''

''Is that how most of the people from town who went up to the camp found out it was okay to go there? Because Carol Littleton told them?''

''I don't know, Mr. Demarkian. But she surely was telling lots of people. It was one of the only two topics of conversation she had that morning.''

''What was the other one?''

''Her granddaughter. Her daughter's daughter. The one that was going to have the christening she wasn't going to be allowed to go to. Not that that matters much anymore.''

''Mmm,'' Gregor said.

The phone on Naomi Brent's desk rang and she picked it up. She said hello and then listened in silence, frowning more deeply every second the tinny little voice came at her over the line. Finally she said, ''All right, just a minute, let me put him on,'' and handed the phone across the desk to Clayton.

"It's Jackson," she told him. "I think he's saying that something else has gone wrong up at that house."

Clayton Hall and Gregor Demarkian looked at each other. Then Clayton put the receiver to his ear and said, "Jackson? What the hell is up?"

There was more tinny noise coming over the line, and then a small click: Jackson hanging up. Clayton handed the phone back across the desk to Naomi and turned to Gregor Demarkian.

"We better go," he said. "If Jackson has his ass on straight, Zhondra Meyer just committed suicide."

part
three

———

one

1

They were all up there on the terrace when Clayton and Gregor arrived, all the women who lived at the camp. Later, Gregor knew, the rest would arrive: the reporters, the people from town. That only went to prove that it wasn't a question of being a hick or not being one. The reporters would tell each other that they were only up here because they were doing their jobs. The truth was that they craved even more blood lust excitement than the rest of the world. Gregor was surprised to see how many women there were. Every time he thought he had the group all together, there seemed to be more of them than before. He recognized the woman called Alice, and Stelle Cary, standing in two separate knots of women on opposite sides of the terrace. He recognized one or two others he didn't have names for. There was a wind high in the trees, bending the tops of the pines back and forth above his head. The air was warm and thick with water. Bonaventura, Gregor thought, didn't belong here. It was a cold weather house, built by a cold weather man. It ought to be somewhere that snow could fall on it, and the fires lit in its fireplaces.

Gregor and Clayton had expected all the women to be staring toward the stand of trees and the circle of stones. In fact, they had expected them to be in the stand of trees and trampling through the circle of stones. Instead, they were all standing on the terrace, looking at each other, watching

Clayton and Gregor come around the side of the house on the narrow gravel path.

Clayton went up to the woman named Alice and took off his hat. Alice looked ready to explode. It was obvious that she had already been crying. Some women could produce tears with no wear and tear on their faces, no bloating, no redness, no streaks of strain. Alice was not one of them.

"Now, Alice," Clayton said. "What have you done with her? Is she still in the clearing?"

"Of course she isn't in the clearing," Alice said. "She's never been in the clearing. She's upstairs in her own room."

"Did you move her, Alice? I know it's natural, with a suicide—"

"She didn't die in the clearing," a woman said, a small woman with a black braid down her back and a flowered dress. "She died upstairs in her room. We didn't move her."

"We didn't want anybody to be able to say we'd messed everything up," Alice said. "We didn't want to read in the papers that the reason you were never able to catch Zhondra's murderer was that we destroyed all the evidence."

"She's up there hanging," the small woman with the black braid said. "She has the rope swung over the chandelier hook. We would have taken her down if we could. None of us could figure out how."

"It's just as well that you didn't," Clayton said. "Alice was right. It would destroy evidence."

The woman with the braid blushed deep scarlet. "There's one other thing," she said, looking from Gregor to Clayton and back again. "She left a note."

"She left it upstairs?" Gregor asked. "Near where you found the body?"

The small woman nodded.

"Is it still there?" Gregor said.

The small woman looked at Alice and blushed again. "Well, it made sense to read it, didn't it?" Alice demanded defiantly. "It was right there out in the open where anybody could see."

"It had 'to the police' written on the envelope," one of the other women said, a middle-aged one with lines of disapproval on either side of her mouth. "I thought it was like opening somebody else's mail."

"It wasn't mail," Alice said. "It was a note. It was probably a forged note. We had to see what it said."

"I think we should have left it where it was," the small woman with the braid said stubbornly. "I know how you feel about it, Alice, but it just makes sense. There was no hurry for us to read it. We could have let the police handle it and read it later when it was released."

"If it ever was released," Alice said. "And how would we have known that the same letter was released as the one they got? Once they had it and none of us had read it, they could have said anything. They could have made up whatever they wanted."

"Do you have the letter?" Clayton asked, holding out his hand. "Come on now, Alice. No matter what's happened to Zhondra and what hasn't happened to her, there have already been two murders on or near this property. Let's go at this with a little common sense."

Alice hesitated, looking more mulish by the second. Then she plunged her hand into the pocket of her jeans and came up with a crumpled envelope. Even in the battered state it was in, Gregor could see that it was made of very good, very expensive paper, the kind people ordered from jewelry stores with their initials engraved on it. It was almost as thick as cardboard and made of cream linen, but Zhondra Meyer's initials were nowhere to be seen.

Clayton took four small sheets of paper out of the envelope and began to read them over. Gregor could see that the words on them had been typed, and that there were no initials on these pages, either. He tried to remember if he had ever seen notepaper with Zhondra's initials on it anywhere at Bonaventura, but it wasn't the kind of thing he noticed if he had no reason to, and up until now he had no reason to. Still, Gregor thought it was odd, the first solid piece of evidence he had seen that Alice and his own instincts might be right, that it made no sense at all for Zhondra Meyer to have committed suicide. Zhondra Meyer was the kind of person who *should* have had good notepaper with her initials engraved on it. Clayton handed the little typewritten note to him, and Gregor took it.

"To Whom It May Concern," it said, and then:

I have tried as long as I could to go on with this, but it really isn't any good, and it isn't going to get any better. For the past few weeks, ever since Tiffany died, I have been in agony. Many of us here have been. I'm not going to name any names. As impossible as it might be for the police and others of that kind, we never intended to kill anyone. We never expected that to happen. We thought we were just going out to the woods to worship the Goddess, to be part of nature and to glory in it. We should have realized. The Goddess has always been worshipped with blood. When the Jesuits dug through the pits of the Incan ziggurats they found piles of skulls of infants, piled up at the bottom where the fire had been. Maybe Henry Holborn is right. The Goddess calls to you, and what she wants is something more dramatic than allegiance. We gave her what she wanted, Carol Littleton and I.

Just to make sure that everybody understands what has to be understood: Carol and I were the only ones involved when Tiffany died. Carol found her in her carrier seat, set up on the long table in the hall. Ginny wasn't there at the time; I don't know where she'd gone. It was my idea to dedicate her to the Goddess, to baptize her in blood. Carol and I were both going to cut little notches in our wrists, and sprinkle the blood on Tiffany's head, and make her ours instead of

Henry Holborn's God's. We took her out to the side terrace near the dining room. Nobody ever goes near there anymore, except to eat when we have formal dinners, and there is an altar there that Dinah and Stelle set up a couple of months ago. After that, I'm not entirely sure what happened. We have a chant we sing that Carol found in an old book in my grandfather's library. You can find it in there if you look, laid out on the desk near the fire, with a brown leather cover. I forget what the name of it is. We had the chant to sing and we sang it, and then everything seemed to get out of control. I'm not sure I could tell you what happened after that, except that after it was over, Tiffany was dead.

There is nothing on earth that can sober you up like holding the corpse of an infant in your hands. We were standing there on the terrace with a dead baby, and for a while we didn't know what to do. That was when we decided to put it up in the clearing, near the circle of stones. That was a place that belonged to the Goddess. That was a place where we thought the baby would be at peace. We wrapped Tiffany up in a blanket and started up the hill toward the clearing, going around the back way. There were dozens of people in the study by then and in the living room, too, and we didn't want to be seen.

Nobody in their right mind would have been out in that weather, but Ginny was, in the woods, just popping out at us where we didn't expect it. Carol screamed when Ginny ran into us. She was holding the baby and she dropped it. When the baby fell she twisted in the air. The blanket fell off. When Ginny saw the baby hit the ground, she jumped on her, and that was when I first realized we had cut her up. There was blood everywhere, I don't know where it came from, we all seemed to have too much of it on ourselves. Ginny was just nuts, and I was frantic. I pushed her out of the way and grabbed the body and ran. I went up into the woods as far as I could go, but it wasn't as far as I wanted to go. I kept thinking that if I could only make it to the circle of stones, everything would be all right. God only knows why I thought that. In the end, though, I could hear Ginny coming back, and David and the others. I couldn't see much of anything in the wind and the rain. My clothes were soaked through and there was hail coming down. I dropped the baby and started running back to the house. I wanted to be away before they could find me, even though I didn't think then that they would suspect me of anything.

After that, there isn't much to tell, except, of course, that I killed Carol, because she was so nervous and because she wanted so much to confess. Yesterday, I still thought that mattered. I still thought I could go on with my life as if nothing at all had happened. Now I realize that I don't even want to go on with my life. Sometimes I lie in bed and listen to the voice of the Goddess speaking to me, but it is a wicked voice, and I don't want to talk to it anymore.

You have to be careful, I think, about what you let into your soul, more careful than I have been. Henry Holborn would say that, the way things have been with me, I will spend the rest of eternity hearing the voice of the Goddess, but even at this late date and with everything that has happened, I don't think he's right. God or Goddess, Christ or Satan, it all works out the same for me. After this there is nothing but blackness and the rest that is the obliteration, finally, of even the will to move. That's what I want to be part of now, and that's what I will be going to, and no matter how anybody reading this may feel about it, I am very glad.

Ginny Marsh had nothing to do with any of this. Her only real crime was to panic so badly that she didn't know who she was seeing and what she was doing, and under the circumstances, that seems entirely natural to me.

—Zhondra

Gregor put the little stack of papers into a neat pile and stuffed them back into their small square envelope. Clayton Hall was staring at him. So were the women on the terrace. In the background, he could hear the shrill wailing of sirens. Any minute now, the house would be full of people. Gregor knew they had to get to work before then.

"Well?" Clayton Hall demanded. "What do you think?"

"I think it's a very interesting letter," Gregor said carefully. "I think it's one of the few sincerely genuine confessions I've ever read. Don't you?"

"You think it's genuine?" Clayton Hall said.

Alice exploded. "I knew it was going to be like this! I knew it. Zhondra never killed anyone in her life. And she didn't kill herself. It's just what you want to think. It gets you off the hook. It makes it so that you don't have to go after some man."

"I can't believe you think it's genuine," Clayton Hall insisted. "It's typed, for God's sake. Whoever heard of a suicide who typed her farewell note?"

"I'm sure there are some who have," Gregor replied, "but it doesn't matter in this case, because a suicide didn't write it. Can we look at the body now?"

The small woman with the black braid scurried forward. "I'll take you up there," she said. "You ought to get a look at it. She shouldn't just be left there, as if she weren't anybody, and nobody cared for her."

"What's your name?" Gregor asked her.

"Grace," she said.

"Well, Grace," Gregor said, "maybe you ought to lead the way up, and Clayton and I will follow."

2

Zhondra Meyer's bedroom was like Zhondra Meyer's study. There were other bedrooms in the house, and other studies, but Zhondra had chosen the best and most important ones. It was an instinct Gregor had noticed in her from the first. Magnificence was Zhondra Meyer's birthright. She had been born into a world where the van Goghs on the dining room walls were real.

She was, as Grace had said downstairs, hanging from a rope that had been swung over the chandelier hook in the middle of the fifteen-foot ceiling. Gregor looked around and saw that the other end of it had been weighted to the sash of the window that overlooked the front drive. That had been very smart. Furniture, no matter how heavy, could move. If you weighted a suicide rope to a piece of furniture, you might jump off your chair and find that you dragged it all with you, so that you landed on the ground with nothing awful happening to you at all. There was a chair, too, a high-backed, heavily carved wooden thing with a thick green seat cushion made of velvet. It looked a lot like the ones Gregor had seen downstairs. Maybe one of the matriarchs who had come to Bonaventura before Zhondra had been the kind of women who liked "sets." Maybe, if Gregor went carefully through the house, he would find the infamous "twelve of monogrammed everything" it had once been thought necessary for every bride to bring to her first marriage house.

Gregor looked up at the body. Zhondra Meyer was hanging fairly high in the air, making it difficult to get a good look at her face. Everything in the room conspired to make it difficult to get a good look at anything. What was it the Victorians had loved so much about the dark? The big white marble fireplace surround was the only touch of lightness in this sea of dark. The bedspread and the bed curtains were both made of heavily embroidered, wine-dark damask. The bed itself was made of thick dark wood, ornately carved. The curtains were deep green damask. The carpet was a muddy, jumbled mess of dark red and dark green, in a paisley. Even the painting over the fireplace was dark. It was, Gregor saw, an authentic Caravaggio, and Caravaggio in one of his least optimistic moods.

The ambulance was now at the front of the house, right under the windows of the room. Gregor went to the center window and looked out. The reporters were here, too, but not as many townspeople as he had expected. Maybe they had begun to get tired of it all, it was happening so frequently.

"Gregor?" Clayton Hall said.

"The ambulance just arrived," Gregor said. "That's good. I'll be happier still when the state police get here."

"So will I. What do you think of all this?" Clayton gestured to take in the whole room, almost making the corpse seem a matter of decoration. "Does it make sense to you?"

"Some things make sense to me," Gregor said. "Have you seen her face?"

"I've been trying to."

"It's hard, I know, but if you tilt back you can just make it. Get a good look. Get a good look at her tongue."

"I can't see her tongue."

"Exactly. Neither can I. You ever see a hanging victim before?"

Clayton Hall stroked the side of his face thoughtfully. "Yeah," he said slowly. "I have. A couple of times."

"And?"

Clayton Hall walked around the body, to see if he could get a better look from the other side. "You think that woman Alice had it right," he said. "You think Zhondra Meyer was actually murdered."

"I think she didn't die by hanging," Gregor said. "And I think she didn't get up there on her own."

"But I thought you said that you thought the confession was genuine."

"I did. I do."

"But what's all this about then? Was she killed like the others? Was her throat cut?"

Gregor tried walking all the way around the body in a big circle. Usually it was terrible to look at the corpses of people who had been hanged. Their tongues stuck out. Their eyes protruded. Zhondra Meyer's face was almost as smooth and undamaged now as it had been in life.

"You can't tell," Gregor said finally. "The rope gets in the way, and she's just too far up. But I don't see any blood on the rope, and that's probably significant. My guess is that she's had her neck broken. Either she broke it herself or it was broken for her."

"Do people commit suicide by breaking their own necks? Except by hanging, I mean."

"It didn't have to be suicide. It didn't have to be murder. It might just have been an accident."

"That woman didn't end up swinging from a chandelier hook by accident."

"I didn't say she did. I said she might have broken her neck by accident. A very lucky accident for somebody. The chandelier hook would have come later."

"You can't tell me you really believe that," Clayton Hall said. "You sound like one of those murder mysteries from the twenties, with a million and a half coincidences and then one big blowout of a revelation scene at the end."

Gregor Demarkian looked up at the body one more time and sighed. "No, I don't really believe that. I just don't understand—I wish we had some gloves. We should have brought them with us. I want to start looking for things."

"What things?"

"I don't know."

The door to the bedroom opened and the first of the

ambulance men came in, a very young man in a white uniform with a cocky manner. He took one look at Zhondra's body hanging on the hook and went white.

"Ah," he said. "Oh."

"Jesus Christ," another ambulance man said, coming in behind the first.

The second man was older, though, and better at controlling his emotions than the first. He brushed by the younger man and put the chair at Zhondra's feet upright.

"You two need me not to touch anything so you can keep your crime scene?" he asked.

"You shouldn't touch anything you don't have to," Clayton told him, "but you can get her down. Do you have gloves so you don't—"

"—mess up the fingerprints on the chandelier or the hook. Yeah, I know. I've got gloves and we're not going to have to touch the hook anyhow. Hey, Sheldon. Get ahold of yourself."

Sheldon was the younger man. He didn't look as if he was going to get ahold of himself anytime soon, but he did break out of his trance and start fumbling at his uniform, looking for the requisite gloves.

Gregor stepped away from the body, giving the ambulance men room to move and himself room to wait.

3

It took nearly half an hour of waiting, but eventually the time came. What had to be done had been done. The tech men had their hair samples and fingerprint possibilities and little pieces of dust that could only be picked up in special, miniature vacuum cleaners. This was the kind of evidence the FBI almost never had anything to do with—or at least not in the cases Gregor had been asked to handle. Over the last few years, Gregor had found that he liked this routine. There was something steadying about it, the way funerals were steadying. It took the apocalyptic and whittled it into shards, making it manageable.

The tech men had just gone over the dresser and the big wardrobe for fingerprints. There seemed to be little piles of dust everywhere. Gregor put on the gloves Clayton brought him, and tugged at the fingers, trying to make them stretch. The gloves were made of cotton and wouldn't budge.

"All right," Clayton said. "What do we do now? I suppose you've got a mind to make a search."

"Yes, I have."

"Somebody will search this place even if we don't. The Staties will search it."

"I'm looking for something in particular."

"What?"

"I don't know."

"You can't just go on saying you don't know like that, Gregor. It doesn't make any sense."

"I know," Gregor said. "Let's go look in the dresser."

"For you don't know what."

"Right."

It was, Gregor thought then, very good for him that he was now a famous man. This was the kind of behavior the police did not put up with from people who were nobody in particular. Gregor went over to the dresser and opened the top drawer. It felt clumsy in his hands. His fingers didn't seem to work right in the cotton gloves. He pulled the drawer out as far as it would go without falling on his feet and then felt along the bottom of it, but there was nothing. Then he drew the drawer all the way out and put it on the floor. It was filled with good silk underwear, trimmed in lace, in five muted but distinctive colors. Gregor knew nothing at all about women's underwear, but he knew expensive when he saw it, and this stuff was definitely expensive. It was outrageously expensive. It was so expensive, even Bennis didn't own anything like it, and Bennis truly loved to spend money.

"Underwear," Clayton Hall said. "Really great underwear. But that's all there is."

Gregor ignored him and slid out the second drawer. He checked its underside, as he had with the first, and then he pulled it all the way out, too. This one was filled with sweaters, all cashmere, all impossibly thick. Gregor checked each and every one of them, carefully running his hands up the sleeves and down under the necks. There was nothing.

"I wonder what something like this costs." Clayton Hall picked up a long black turtleneck tunic.

Gregor might know nothing about women's underwear, but he knew a great deal about women's sweaters. Bennis practically lived for sweaters. "About six or seven hundred dollars," he told Clayton Hall as he went back to the dresser for the third drawer.

Clayton let the sweater fall back onto the pile from which it had come. "Six or seven hundred dollars? For one sweater?"

Gregor checked under the third drawer and then pulled it out. This one had more sweaters, but cotton ones, and what seemed like hundreds of silk scarves. Gregor stepped back and looked around the room. This was ridiculous. He was going about it entirely the wrong way. If he was Zhondra Meyer, where would he have hidden it? He had no doubt that she would have hidden it. She wouldn't have kept it in her desk. It would have been too easily found there. She wouldn't have put it in her safe. She wouldn't have had easy access to it there and besides, someone might suspect. Where would she have put it? Or, Gregor amended in his head, more likely, *them.*

Zhondra Meyer's bedroom had enough furniture in it to stock a warehouse. Besides the dresser and the wardrobe and the bed, and the chair that had been used to make it look like Zhondra had killed herself, there were two more dressers and another wardrobe. In front of the fireplace there were two green velvet-covered wing chairs and a long oval coffee table. The coffee table was covered with photographs in silver frames. Both the photographs and the frames were old. Gregor saw a picture of a man and woman in twenties hairstyles and full riding habits, leaning against each other and laughing.

"That's it," he said.

"What's it?" Clayton asked.

Gregor picked up one of the frames. "That's where she hid them," he said. "Or some of them. There could be dozens and dozens around this house. But maybe not. Maybe they're all here."

"What are here?"

"Zhondra Meyer's personal insurance policy against untoward publicity." Gregor opened the back of the frame and peeled away the stiff cardboard backing. He took out the three small snapshots that had been stuffed back there and looked at them. They were not photographs of anyone he knew, just pictures of women, naked, making love to other women.

"Jesus," Clayton Hall said. "What was she doing? Peddling pornography on the side?"

"Zhondra Meyer didn't have to peddle pornography," Gregor told him. "She just wanted to keep her name out of the papers. I should have realized there would be something like these around. She's been remarkably lucky about her publicity for this place. Not a single disgruntled recanter. Not a single confused, lonely, psychologically disturbed woman going to the press with—well, God knows what."

"Goddess worship," Clayton Hall said.

Gregor was opening photograph frame after photograph frame, but coming up with nothing but more women and more women. He came upon a picture of Alice in a very embarrassing position and passed it by immediately. He had no wish to shame or embarrass anyone. Maybe there were other places in the house where pictures were hidden. Maybe he would look and look, and never find what he was looking for.

"You got something in particular you're trying to go after?" Clayton Hall asked him.

Gregor picked up a long frame with a photograph of dozens of people gathered together for a formal dinner and opened the back of it. There were at least eight snapshots nestled behind the photograph. He took them out and started to go through them. Women and more women. Women looking happy. Women looking sad. Women looking like they didn't know what was happening to them and never would.

The picture he was looking for was second from the last. He came upon it so unexpectedly, he almost missed it. Then the shape of the body alerted him and he stopped: a man this time, instead of a woman. He held the picture closer to his face.

"Now what?" Clayton demanded, when Gregor handed it over. Then he looked down at the picture and blanched. "Holy Christ. It's Stephen Harrow. From the Methodist Church."

"It had to be him," Gregor explained, "because he was the only one who wasn't here. On the night of the storm. I'd ask people who had been in the study on the night of the storm who they had seen there, and he was never one of the ones. But he was here afterward. Plenty of people saw him then."

"He could have been in another room."

"He could have been, but it won't work out that way, Clayton, trust me. There's only one way all of this makes sense, and it starts with Stephen Harrow. But I don't think it's going to end with him."

Clayton studied the photograph. "I wish I knew who that woman was," he said. "She looks vaguely familiar, but I can't even guess. But I damn well know who she isn't. She isn't Stephen Harrow's world-class bitch of a southern wife."

two

1

The news about what had happened to Zhondra Meyer, or what Zhondra Meyer had done to herself, was on all the news shows at six o'clock, and around town long before that, for anybody who happened to be listening. Henry Holborn should have heard about it long before he walked into Betsey's House of Hominy to get something to eat at six. Henry was the most well-connected man in town. More of the people in Bellerton went to his church than went to any other. Then, too, there was Janet, who had her hooks into half a dozen networks in half a dozen places. Janet always knew who had just had a miscarriage or who was getting a divorce or who was picked up for drinking in Raleigh or Chapel Hill. The problem was that Henry Holborn was not at home listening to Janet, or to anyone else. He had not been home all day. He had kissed Janet goodbye that morning, and come into town, and had his little daily talk with Clayton Hall—and then he had just stayed in town, walking around, doing nothing, until the bells in the Methodist Church told him that it was six. He knew something had happened up at the camp. The reporters had gone racing up there at one point, and come racing back later, to make phone calls in their cars and write things on notepads. An ambulance had gone up there, too, with siren blasting. Henry had been way on the other side of town when that had happened, near the sea and up past Dennisson's Point, and he had thought that there was something silly about the fuss the ambulance was making. People always made so much noise about life and death, emergencies and calamities. Turn on the television these days and you were as likely to get a doctor running up the hospital stairs to respond to a Code Blue as you were to get sex and violence. It was as if everybody on earth had decided that there was no reason anymore to hide their need to celebrate disasters. They even made them just to watch them, as far as Henry could tell. Was there any other reason for what was happening in Rwanda and Bosnia? In the end, of course, there was only one reason. There was God in His Heaven and His plan for the people of this world. Even the Devil was part of God's plan. Henry very firmly believed this. No matter how bad things were beginning to look, it was all a sham and a delusion. These were the last days. Any minute now, the Antichrist would rise up and ask all the people of the earth to wear the mark of the Beast. Any minute now, Christ would come in glory on His throne, surrounded by an army of angels, singing hosannah in the highest. All day today, Henry had been able to hear the angels singing, as if they were just out of sight behind a curtain of clouds. The earth was full of dark things, now, with tentacles that lashed like whips and tongues that stuck like needles. Henry saw it in the way the dark waves of the ocean rolled against the white sand of the shore. He saw it in the faces of the men who sat in wooden chairs outside Charlie Hare's store. He even saw it in the display cases that lined Rose MacNeill's front windows. Bright perky little girl angels with off-kilter halos and desperate smiles, meant to be pinned onto the collars of women's everyday blouses. Pictures of Christ with His eyes rolling back in His head and His arms stretched out, as if He were about to be tortured, as if He were about to faint. There was a sign on the board in front of the Methodist Church announcing a christening for this coming Sunday. When Sunday came, they would baptize an infant who didn't know what they were doing and think they had done something holy in the sight of God. Henry's heart ached so badly that he thought, on and off, that he was having an ordinary heart attack. Maybe this was what the Rapture would be for him: dead on Main Street in an instant, with God before Clayton Hall got to ask another bothersome question.

When the bells of the Methodist Church rang, Henry Holborn was on Main Street, not half a block from Maggie Kelleher's shop. The bells rang and he stopped in the middle of the street, looking up. He had been this way before in this long day of walking. He knew that Maggie Kelleher had a copy of Darwin's *Origin of Species* in her front window and a sign that said: SEE WHAT ALL THE TROUBLE IS ABOUT. He knew that Rose MacNeill had come home not half an hour ago, upset and looking disheveled. He knew that Stephen Harrow was working in his study, poring over books and listening to the small television he kept on a bookshelf between his books on theology and his books on the history of science. Henry only wanted to walk and walk and walk, until his legs fell off or until something happened, whichever came first.

Instead, when the bells rang, Henry Holborn decided he was hungry. As he hadn't eaten since breakfast, this was not surprising, but it surprised him. It surprised him, too, that Main Street was so deserted. He didn't know when Charlie Hare had closed up shop and disappeared, along with all the old men he'd been sitting with, but Charlie was gone and the sidewalk in front of his store was empty. He didn't know when Maggie Kelleher had hung the Closed sign in her window in front of all those copies of Darwin's book, but the Closed sign was there and the bookstore was dark. Town itself was getting dark. It was that odd time of year, when night came neither early nor late. The sun was setting behind the spires of Zhondra Meyer's lesbian camp, making the old house look like Dracula's castle, covered in blood.

Henry found himself just outside Betsey's House of Hominy and stopped. The place was packed, mostly with reporters. There wasn't much of anywhere else to eat in the town of Bellerton, unless you counted the sandwich place attached to the health food store, which most people didn't. The reporters didn't want to drive out to the mall to have dinner at McDonald's or farther out still, where there were good restaurants that served steak and lobster and French food, all at exorbitant prices. It struck Henry Holborn suddenly that he had been fourteen years old before he had ever eaten in a restaurant of any kind. Before that, he hadn't even stayed to have his lunches in the cafeteria at school. That first restaurant had been very much like this one, not much more than a diner. Henry had thought it was magic anyway.

He went up to the door and opened it to look inside. Betsey had her air-conditioning turned up high, in spite of the fact that it was a cool night. The television was on behind the counter. Everybody seemed to be watching it.

Henry came all the way inside, letting the door close behind him. There was only one stool left at the counter, with Naomi Brent on one side of it and a stranger on the other. The stranger was probably a reporter, but there was no help for it. Henry sat down on the stool and looked up at Betsey's enormous wide-screen TV. A perky blonde with a ribbon in her hair was sitting behind a curved desk, trying to look solemn. For Henry, this was exactly what was wrong with the entire concept of feminism. If you put red and orange together, the colors clashed. If you put a woman in a suit and tried to make her look solemn, she looked hopeful instead, spoiling the effect.

"Police at this time are not revealing just what was in the note Zhondra Meyer left when she took her own life," the anchorwoman said, "but speculation has been rife that it was a confession to the two murders that have taken place in Bellerton over the last month. Sources close to Bellerton Police Chief Clayton Hall say that enough evidence was found in Zhondra Meyer's bedroom to answer most of the questions that have become important in these cases. If a Satanic cult really has been operating out of Bonaventura

House, state officials now say they have enough to go on to get it closed down."

"Oh, for Christ's sake," somebody in the back of the room said. "They can't close down a Satanic cult. It's a *religion.*"

"Shhh," somebody else said.

The television went to a commercial. Millions of children seemed to have descended on a McDonald's restaurant at once. Henry Holborn turned to Naomi Brent.

"Naomi? Did I hear that right? Zhondra Meyer committed suicide?"

"That's what everybody's been saying," Naomi said. "Weren't you around this afternoon? They had the ambulance up there and everything."

Betsey came down from the other end of the counter, her apron out of true, her expression harried. "Good evening, Henry. Can I get you something?"

"You could get me a cup of coffee and a tuna fish sandwich," Henry told her. "Betsey, am I hearing this right? Zhondra Meyer committed suicide? And confessed to what? Killing Ginny Marsh's baby?"

Betsey brushed hair out of her face with the flat of her hand. "That's what everybody's saying, and that's the official word, too, but I've heard other things. You just sit here for a while and you'll hear other things, too."

"One of *them* says that Zhondra Meyer was murdered," Naomi Brent said, tossing her head backward, meaning to take in all the reporters in the room. "But nobody's buying it. It's just what *they* want to think. They don't want to imagine for a minute that one of their precious New Yorkers could come down here and cause a lot of mayhem and blame it on us."

Betsey had gone away to get some coffee. Now she came back again, cup in hand. "It's true, what Naomi says. They want to make us look like a bunch of murdering cretins. They think we go to church on Wednesday nights and have fits."

"I, for one, think it makes perfect sense that Zhondra

Meyer killed them," Naomi Brent said. "Not that I think that she was worshipping the Devil or anything like that. I don't believe that people really worship the Devil. No offense meant, Reverend."

"No offense taken," Henry Holborn said automatically.

"They think we're all violent and dangerous down here," Betsey said, "and ignorant, too. You should hear the way they talk to me sometimes. It makes me sick."

"And they lie, too," Naomi said. "They lie to make their stories come out better. They only interview people the rest of us would consider a little odd. They only listen to what they want to hear. But it's true, you know. It makes much more sense that Zhondra Meyer killed them."

The man on the stool on Henry's other side stirred. He was a young man, with hair that hung a little too far over his ears, and eyes that looked ready to fall out of his head. He had a bacon, lettuce, and tomato sandwich in front of him and a big plate of fries, but he didn't seem to have touched either.

"Wait a minute now," he said. "What about Susan Smith? She was a southerner from a small town. She was religious. She killed her children."

"Susan Smith was a mentally disturbed girl with a history of depression," Naomi Brent said, "and she wasn't religious. She didn't belong to any church that I ever heard of."

"She talked about God all the time," the reporter said. "She talked about her faith. What do you call religious?"

Betsey had disappeared again. Now she was back, with Henry's tuna fish sandwich on a plate.

"I call religious giving your life to Jesus Christ as your Lord and Savior," she said. "I call it making a commitment to the Lord, not just mouthing off about how God is up there somewhere and you're sure He loves you because you can just feel it."

"Oh, Lord," Naomi Brent groaned.

"It wasn't Zhondra Meyer who started all that talk about worshipping the devil," the reporter said. "It was some preacher. And you've got to admit. Religious people aren't very tolerant."

"Oh, tolerant," Naomi said. "We're tolerant enough if people just behave themselves."

"But that's the point," somebody else said now, another reporter from another part of the room, a woman. "People have a right to live their lives as they see fit. They shouldn't have to deal with people who are trying to impose their religion on everybody else."

Naomi raised her eyes to heaven. "Why is it," she demanded, "that when religious people try to tell other people what they feel is right and wrong, that's imposing their religion, but when secular people do it, it's free speech?"

"And what about the high school?" Betsey said. "According to the Supreme Court, it's just A-okay for the high school to have an Atheists' Club, but it can't have any religious club, because that's establishing religion."

"But it would be establishing religion," the first reporter said. "The religious clubs wouldn't be just clubs. They'd be recruiting organizations. The point would be to coerce more people into believing in Christianity."

"The Atheists' Club is a recruiting organization," Naomi said. "They're always putting up signs announcing how they're going to have a presentation that might change your mind about God if you only heard it. And besides, this isn't about God at all, I don't think. This is about homosexuals."

"I don't think homophobia is a very attractive trait," the young reporter said stiffly.

"I don't think anyone here is homophobic," Henry put in. "I don't think anybody here is *afraid* of homosexuality. I think a good many of us abominate it, but that's a different thing."

You could feel it in the room then, the sea change, the shift. Up until the time that Henry had said his little piece about homophobia, everything had still been basically all right. People were listening to Naomi and Betsey talk, but not taking them very seriously. People were nibbling away at sandwiches and sipping at coffee and thinking about home. Henry's voice seemed to boom out over all of them. It sounded too loud even to him. The words seemed to hang in the air after they had been said, drops of water threatening to become rain.

"Shit," the reporter sitting at Henry's side said. "I can't stand this anymore. This is total crap."

Henry had no idea what the young man was talking about: Bellerton? the murders? this diner? God? It wasn't logic but emotion that swung Henry around on his stool. He had spent the day without feeling much of anything at all. Now it was all coming up in him, like bile rising in his throat, and he was furious.

"I do not understand," he said, feeling the blood pounding under his skull, "what it is about being the resident of some big city that makes it impossible to respect other people and their beliefs instead of—"

"I know who that is," somebody else in the room said. "That's the preacher. The one who had the cross up at the camp when that woman's body was found. The one who's always talking about the devil."

"How can you talk about respecting people?" the woman who had spoken before said. "You don't respect women. You'd rather see them dead than let them be independent of men."

"I've never wanted to see a woman dead in my life," Henry Holborn said, confused.

"Wait a minute," Betsey said, suddenly visibly scared. "Wait a minute, now. We should all calm down."

"Oh, I'm sick of calming down." The woman was sitting in the big semicircular booth in the far back corner with three other people. The three other people sat there while she stood up and strode across the diner to where Henry Holborn was sitting. She was an attractive-looking woman, in her thirties, in a suit. In any other situation, Henry Holborn would barely have noticed her.

She got to Henry Holborn's stool, grabbed him by the shoulders, and spun him around. "Listen to me," she demanded. "You think you're all sick of us? Well, I'm sick of all of you. I'm sick of having my radio alarm go off every morning and some loudmouthed jerk come on telling me to accept Christ as my personal savior. I'm sick of sitting at traffic lights behind cars with bumper stickers that say 'Abortion Stops a Beating Heart.' I'm sick of listening to you all go on endlessly about how wonderful you all are. You're a bunch of tenth-rate backwoods hicks, and if you don't know it yet, you'd better learn."

Betsey drew herself up to her full height and puffed out her chest. "Get out of here," she demanded. "Get out of here right this minute. And don't come back."

"Oh, I'll get out all right," the woman said. "I'll be happy to. But before I get out of town, I think I'm going to leave all of you something to remember me by. Maybe I'll give a lot of money to that camp up there so that they can open an abortion clinic. This is the twentieth century. It's practically the twenty-first. Get *real.*"

"Get *out,*" Betsey said.

Henry Holborn still had a cup two-thirds full of coffee sitting in front of him. The woman leaned past him and picked it up. For an instant, there was some doubt about what was going to happen next. The young man sitting next to Henry looked faintly alarmed. Naomi was struggling to her feet, getting ready to defend Henry if she could. Even so, the room was incredibly hostile. Henry had preached to rooms like this when he was first starting out, and calling them nests of vipers was not indulging in exaggeration. Blood lust was as old as the human race. Look at Adam and Eve. Look at Cain and Abel. The urge to kill came out of hiding whenever it got a chance.

The woman had Henry's coffee cup in her hand. Henry knew what she was going to do, but he couldn't make himself move out of the way of it. It was like waiting for the Apocalypse.

"Wait a minute," the young man on the other side of Henry said, but it was too late.

The coffee cup was high in the air over Henry Holborn's head. The woman turned it upside down and let a cascade of brown liquid fall into his hair. Then she waved the cup even higher, and the saucer too, and sent them both crashing to the floor.

"To hell with all of you," she said.

Then she put her arm flat against the counter and swept it as far as it would go, sending plates and cups crashing to the floor, Naomi's coffee, Henry's tuna fish sandwich, the young reporter's BLT. There was suddenly glass everywhere, bouncing up from the linoleum, skittering along the floor.

"I'll call the police," Betsey screeched. "I'll call the police right this minute."

"Call anyone you want to," the woman said. "I'm over at the Super Eight Motel on the Hartford Road. Room 233. I'll be there for the rest of the night."

Then she strode to the diner's front door, yanked it open, and walked out.

Henry felt the tension in the room like a thin film of mayonnaise. He thought somebody else was going to blow, more damage was going to be done. Instead, way behind his back where he couldn't hope to see, a faint giggling started. It got louder and louder and stronger and stronger and suddenly they were all doing it, all the reporters. Henry and Naomi and Betsey were struck dumb. Some of the reporters were laughing so hard, they were choking. The young man sitting next to Henry had his head down on the counter and his eyes were streaming with tears.

To Henry, of course, it was his worst nightmare become real, it was everything he had ever been afraid of happening at once.

He was in a public place, and everybody was laughing at him.

2

Out at the beach, David Sandler sat in a canvas chair on his deck, nursing a glass of wine and watching Maggie Kelleher watch the moon. It had just come up, and now its pale light was a stream across the water, like a streak in a woman's dark hair. David had called Maggie up as soon as he realized that Gregor would not be back for dinner, again. He had had no idea, when he asked Gregor down here, that investigating a murder would mean he never saw his houseguest at all. Or hardly ever. The wine was a good Vin Santo David had brought down from New York. He had a pile of almond biscotti on a plate on the deck floor, in case Maggie should want to dunk cookies while she drank. It would have been a good evening, except that Maggie was depressed, and that made David depressed, too. He had known Maggie on and off now for at least five years, but only recently had he begun to know her well.

"So," he said, "do you think it's all true? Do you think Zhondra Meyer killed Tiffany and Carol and then killed herself out of remorse?"

"No," Maggie said.

"I don't either," David admitted. "It's too easy, isn't it? I can't imagine Zhondra Meyer actually committing suicide."

"I've been hearing things ever since it happened that it might be a murder after all," Maggie said. "Did your friend say anything? I heard somebody say that the police wanted to talk to Stephen Harrow."

"Stephen Harrow? Why?"

"I don't know. Maybe they think he did it. Maybe he was Zhondra Meyer's lover."

"Zhondra Meyer was a lesbian."

"Well, David, that doesn't always do it, does it? People do all kinds of crazy things, especially with sex. And Zhondra always appeared to me to be the kind of person who did what she wanted to do when she wanted to do it, and the hell with everybody else."

David shifted slightly in his chair. "Gregor doesn't tell me anything. It's no better than reading the morning papers, having him here. Except that Gregor is Gregor, and I like having him here. I like having you here, too, Maggie."

"I know you do. I like being here."

"You ought to give a little more consideration to my proposition," David said. "I know it sounds radical at the moment, moving back to New York, but believe me, we could work it out."

"I never said we couldn't."

"You just don't want to. Maybe it's just that you don't want to with me."

Maggie swung her foot around and nudged him in the knee. "It's not you that's the problem, David. It's New York. I've already lived in New York."

"And you didn't like it."

"I liked it fine. It didn't like me. There are people who are natural New Yorkers, David, and I'm not one of them."

"It would be different this time, Maggie. I have a perfectly good apartment on Riverside Drive. You wouldn't have to shack up in some godforsaken hole you're paying fifteen hundred dollars a month for."

"I know that."

"And you wouldn't be—trying all the time, if you know what I mean. It wouldn't be a test. I think that's what goes wrong with New York for too many people. They only go there to make their fortunes. They don't go there to live."

"I didn't make my fortune, David."

"Most people don't."

"I felt more like a hick after I'd been there for five years than I had when I came. Maybe it was just that I knew so much more, it was so much easier to see my inadequacies."

"You don't have any inadequacies."

"Oh, yes, I do, David, yes, I do. I'm much too gullible, for one thing. I believe too much of what people want me to believe."

"If you did, you would never have gotten to New York in the first place. From what I hear on Main Street, for most people in this town, New York is a cross between Sodom and Gomorrah and hell itself."

"Maybe I was just interested in getting myself to Sodom and Gomorrah."

"I think that's usually a boy thing."

"Have you ever really been fooled by somebody?" Maggie asked. "Have you ever really—believed in somebody—and had it not be true?"

"Of course," David said. "It happens all the time. Did you have a bad experience with a boyfriend? Is that it?"

"What? Oh, no. No. It doesn't have anything to do with boyfriends. It was just that—"

"What?"

Maggie got out of her chair and went to the deck railing, to look out over the ocean.

"I wish I could find out things for real," she said. "I wish I could know what was true about people and just know, the way you know that gravity is real, or that evolution happened."

"I don't think life works that way, Maggie. There are people right here in this town who don't even think evolution happened."

"I know. I was thinking about that, too."

"I wish you would think about coming with me to New York."

"Sometimes," Maggie said, "I think the world is full of secrets, and none of them is mine to give away."

There was a breeze coming in off the water now, warm and mild. David wished they had something else to talk about, that they were somewhere else, away from Ginny Marsh and Carol Littleton and Zhondra Meyer, in New York where if Maggie felt sad he could take her to the opera or out for Tibetan food. He had spent half his life telling himself that he would come down here one day to live permanently, and now he knew that it wasn't true. He wouldn't be able to stand it here on the water for months at a time, with no access to the lights and the noise and the music and the people. It made him feel claustrophobic just to think of staying here for the rest of the year.

"Come back and sit down again," he said to Maggie. "I'm getting lonely without your company."

"Is that what you would be like in New York?" she asked, laughing. "Demanding and possessive?"

"In New York," David said solemnly, "I would be like myself."

three

1

Gregor Demarkian had spent his life dealing with recalcitrant bureaucracies. He had not expected to find one in Bellerton, which was a small town and which, by definition, should have been easier to handle. Instead, in the crunch, he found that he was dealing not with a town, but with a county. It was the county prosecutor he would have to convince of his "brilliant theory," the term "brilliant theory" having been coined by Clayton Hall when they were all still up at Bonaventura and then held on to the way a leech holds on to fresh skin. They had been in Zhondra Meyer's room at the time, with the investigation swirling around them, and Gregor had sat down on the floor to show Clayton Hall how it would work. He had been aware at once that he had put himself in a very undignified position. His pants were being stretched in odd angles. His shirt was coming out from under his belt. Clayton's big beer belly hung in the air above him like a hot air balloon. Gregor wondered if he had one himself and what it looked like to other people. Then he turned his attention back to the pages of the suicide note/confession, spread out across the Persian carpet. The picture was there, too, the one of Stephen tangled naked with a woman nobody could identify, except that everybody knew it could be neither Lisa, Stephen's wife, nor Zhondra Meyer. The hair in the photograph was just too light.

Do it later, Gregor had thought at the time, pushing reflexively at the pages of the suicide note in order to make them straight.

"Look," he'd said to Clayton Hall. "There are a couple of things in this note that mitigate against the possibility that it could have been written by Zhondra Meyer. Let's start with that."

"Because Zhondra Meyer was a Jew."

"Because she was Jewish, yes, that's one thing. Look, the writer refers at one point to giving the baby a 'baptism in blood,' and that—"

"But Jewish people know about baptisms," Clayton interrupted. "My daughter Jenny's roommate from Sweet Briar was Jewish. When Jenny's baby had her christening, Rachel was right there with a silver spoon for a present."

"I'm not saying that Jewish people don't know about baptisms," Gregor said. "I'm saying that the phrase in this note is almost tossed off. The writer isn't making some complicated theological argument. The letter just says, 'It was my idea to dedicate her to the Goddess, to baptize her in blood.' Just like that. As if it were the most natural thing in the world."

"And you think that means the letter couldn't have been written by a Jew."

"No," Gregor said. "I think that means the letter couldn't have been written by Zhondra Meyer. It's not just that Zhondra was brought up Jewish, it's that she was something worse than an agnostic. She was impatient talking about religion no matter what religion it was, and that included the goddess worship that several of her guests were engaged in at the time of Tiffany's murder. You would have expected her to pay some attention to that after all the mess it seems to have caused."

"That could have been a ruse," Clayton said. "That could have been a deliberate attempt to put us off."

"I agree," Gregor said. "But it's more than just that Zhondra Meyer didn't seem to be much interested in religion—it's that she didn't think in terms of religion, if you see what I mean.''

''Vaguely.''

''It's also a question of the way the goddess religion was practiced up here. Have you ever heard anybody up here talking about a baptism in blood in any context whatsoever?''

''No, I haven't,'' Clayton said, ''but if they really have gotten into human sacrifice up here, they aren't likely to just go telling us about it. They're going to do their best to keep it secret.''

''Of course they're going to do their best, Clayton, but make sense for a minute. These aren't professionals you're dealing with. They're not psychopaths, either. I know. I've met them. Do you really believe that if there had been something going on up here that was commonly described as a baptism in blood—that nobody up here would have made any mention of it in any way, even obliquely?''

Clayton opened his mouth and shut it again. He looked depressed. ''No,'' he said finally.

''Good,'' Gregor told him. ''But there's something else you've got to take into consideration here. 'Baptism in blood' isn't just a cute little catchphrase that somebody thought up to throw into the letter. It is something.''

''What do you mean, it is something?''

''I mean it's a real phrase in real theology—Roman Catholic theology, to be exact, not some pseudoreligion like goddess worship that was made up from whole cloth the day before yesterday.''

''I sometimes wonder how anybody distinguishes between pseudoreligions and the real thing,'' Clayton said drily. ''It all seems like a lot of religious hocus-pocus to me.''

''Point taken,'' Gregor said, thinking that he now knew for certain why there was no religious paraphernalia flung around the police department's big basement room. ''But now back to business. Do you know what a baptism in blood is?''

"No."

"It's what's said to happen to unbaptized people who die in defense of the faith. It's the baptism of the early Christian martyrs, to be exact. It's also an attempt to get around the Bible and the tradition, both of which are very sticky on one particular point."

"What point is that?"

"The point that no one can enter the kingdom of heaven without having been baptized in water and the spirit. There wasn't any New Testament as we know it at the time of the great Roman persecutions. The Catholic Bible didn't get put together until after the Emperor Constantine made Christianity a state religion in 300-something. When it did get put together, there was that inescapable little problem of baptism, and the equally inescapable little problem of the fact that, historically, so many of the early Catholic saints hadn't been baptized at the time they were martyred. And we're talking about horrible martyrdoms here, people who suffered gross atrocities and refused to recant from the faith."

"Fanatics," Clayton said.

"Fanatics," Gregor agreed, "but you can see what the problem is here. The Church didn't want to say that these people must be damned. How could God possibly be just if he would condemn a man to hell who had just let his eyes be burned out of their sockets rather than declare that Christ had not risen and that the Christian religion was not true?"

"I sometimes wonder about the justice of God on a day-to-day basis. Did people really do things like that? Good Christ."

"The historical record is difficult to verify," Gregor said. "Remember, the winners write history, and Christians wrote what we now know about the early Church and the way the Roman Empire responded to it. By the time we get around to the age of the Church fathers, however, it doesn't matter, because everybody believed it had happened that way, and that left the theological problem to be solved.

That's how we got the baptism of blood. Dying in defense of the faith confers baptism on the martyr whether he thought he wanted baptism or not. It doesn't matter if he's a believer or an unbeliever. It doesn't matter if—''

''—if she's a child,'' Clayton said.

''Actually,'' Gregor sighed, ''it does matter. In cases of children below the age of reason, it's really very complicated. We're getting past what little I know about the subject.''

''I'm amazed at how much you know about the subject.''

''Yes, well, I have a friend who's a priest. An Armenian priest, not a Catholic priest, although I know a few Catholic priests, too. Anyway, my friend the Armenian priest—lectures me sometimes. On the things he's working on. He writes theology quite often.''

''And he's lectured you on the baptism in blood.''

''It was years ago,'' Gregor said, ''but it stuck in my mind. Anyway, we're talking about a fairly sophisticated concept here, and it occurs to me, just in passing, that when you go by the board in front of the Methodist Church, under the hours for services there's a line that reads 'Stephen Harrow, A.B., A.M., Th.D.' ''

''You're right,'' Clayton Hall said. ''It does.''

''I think it's fairly common these days in a number of the mainline denominations. Getting a doctorate in theology, I mean.''

''But you can't say that it had to be Stephen Harrow who wrote this letter,'' Clayton said, ''not just because he's had a lot of schooling in theology. Henry Holborn has had a lot of schooling in theology. I may not like him, but he did go off and go to Bible college.''

''It's not the same thing. As far as I know, baptism in blood is not a concept accepted in fundamentalist Protestantism. From what I've been able to see, Bible colleges of the type you're talking about mostly teach biblical interpretation.''

''Yes, yes, they do.''

"And from what I hear," Gregor said, "listening to the radio and the television programs, the fundamentalist churches aren't much interested in finding excuses for why people can be saved without being baptized."

"I think they make an exception for infants these days," Clayton said, "but not all of them do."

"Whatever. So far, Stephen Harrow is the only person in town connected to Bonaventura who would have known of the concept and who would have been able or likely to use it casually. And there's one other thing to take Henry Holborn out of the picture."

"What?"

"He was sitting in his own church at the time that Tiffany Marsh died. He was there all day. Dozens of people saw him. Unless you're going to tell me that Henry Holborn has learned to fly through the air like Peter Pan, I think we're both going to have to concede that he was sitting in that church on the Hartford Road the whole time the first murder was going on."

Clayton picked up the photograph of Stephen Harrow and turned it around and around in his hands. "Christ preserve me from ever showing up in a picture like this," he said. "Everybody on earth looks ridiculous in pictures like this."

"Look at the background," Gregor told him. "It's fuzzy, but you can make it out if you try. Trees and leaves and pine needles."

"The trees behind Bonaventura House?"

"I think so, yes."

"They did their screwing up by the circle of stones?"

"Probably a little way off. They look like they're actually lying under some branches, instead of directly in a clearing. I hate pictures taken with telephoto lenses, unless the lenses are the really expensive kind, and nobody goes in for those except a couple of private eyes I know and the government. Zhondra must have bought this one at her local camera shop and decided it would do."

"It did do," Clayton said. "It did very well. If you're right, it managed to get her killed."

"Oh, I don't think it was this photograph that got her killed. I don't think Stephen Harrow knows we have it. I don't think he knows it even exists. No, my guess is that Zhondra got fed up with everything that was happening to her plan, and decided to try to put two and two together."

"Right," Clayton Hall said.

Gregor picked up the pages of the letter. They should have been more careful with it. It was sometimes possible to get fingerprints off letters. It used to be possible to match typefaces, too, but that was getting harder and harder. Everybody had daisy wheels these days. Daisy wheels were easy to destroy.

"Gregor?" Clayton Hall said.

Gregor stuffed the letter back in the envelope, and that was the end of the crime scene for him. He hung around for at least two more hours, but his mind was elsewhere, and he didn't even listen to the questions Clayton asked the women waiting on the terrace.

2

Now it was well past dinnertime, and they were still stuck, sitting in the police department's basement office, waiting for the county prosecutor to show up and let them get on with it. Jackson had gone out to get them some food. Gregor had been hoping for a timely delivery from Betsey's diner, but Jackson had driven all the way out to the Interstate instead, and come back with bags and bags of McDonald's. Big Macs. Supersize fries. Quarter Pounders with cheese. Vanilla milkshakes. Gregor thought of Cavanaugh Street, where the Ararat restaurant could be counted on to have big bowls of meatballs in a bulgur crust and stuffed cabbage and big flatbreads and things to dip the flatbreads into, made of chick-peas and eggplant and codfish roe. Sometimes he came home to find a bowl of *yaprak sarma* in his refrigerator, courtesy of Lida Arkmanian or Hannah Krekorian or one of the other women in the street who thought he was entirely incapable of taking care of himself. Somehow, he thought Jackson would not be intrigued by any of this. Still, Tibor was intrigued by all of it, and he loved McDonald's. At least once a week, Tibor got Bennis to drive him down to the biggest McDonald's in Philadelphia, and they sat together in a booth, with Bennis nursing a coffee and trying not to mind that she couldn't smoke, while Tibor ate his way through several examples of the burger of the month and three Super Size boxes of fries.

Bennis.

Gregor looked around the big room. Jackson was squirreled away in one corner, eating Big Macs with a concentration most men couldn't manage to bring to sex. Clayton Hall was sitting with his feet up on one of the desks and his eyes closed. Outside, it had finally started to get dark. Through the window well, Gregor could see the first twinkling lights of street lamps reflected on the sidewalks and the grass. Up on Cavanaugh Street, so much farther north, it would be darker.

Gregor went across the room and nudged Clayton Hall in the shoulder. "Clayton?" he said. "Are you asleep?"

Clayton Hall opened his eyes. "No, I'm not asleep. Has something happened? Have the county boys gotten here yet?"

When the county boys got there, they could wake Clayton Hall for themselves. "I'm looking for a pay phone, Clayton. Is there one anywhere in this building?"

"You don't have to use a pay phone. You can use any of the phones in here."

"It's going to be a long-distance call. A very long-distance call. And it's going to take some time in the making."

"Then you definitely ought to use the phones in here. What do you want to pay for something like that for?"

"It's a personal call."

"I don't care what it is. Long distance can put you out

of pocket for weeks. I know. I've got a daughter who went away to college.''

Gregor thought about making the call here, in the middle of this room, with Clayton and Jackson just feet away. He thought of Bennis, hiding in her bedroom closet when she was alone in her apartment, just because she was calling her brother Christopher.

''Clayton,'' Gregor said. ''It's a personal call. A *personal* call.''

''Oh,'' Clayton said. ''You mean you want to call a woman.''

''Something like that, yes.''

''I hope you're going to call that woman they always show you with in *People* magazine,'' Clayton said. ''That's some good-looking woman.''

''Yes,'' Gregor said. ''Yes, she is. Where can I find—''

''You go out the door, turn right, and go up the stairs. The telephone booths are right up there through the fire door. It's the back of the lobby. Old-fashioned booths, too. Made of wood.''

''Wonderful,'' Gregor said.

''I wish I had a woman like that that I could make a phone call to.'' Clayton sighed. ''All I've got is a wife, and the woman is committed to cotton flannel and old blue jeans.''

''Bennis is committed to old blue jeans, too,'' Gregor said, and then escaped before Clayton could say what men always said to a line like that: that Bennis filled hers differently. Somehow, Gregor never really thought of Bennis clearly from the neck down. She was a beautiful head with great clouds of hair and impossible eyes floating around, discorporeally, in space.

The hall was dark. When Gregor got to the end of the part of it he had been walking down, he stopped and felt for a light switch that wasn't there. Then his eyes adjusted to the darkness and he saw a pair of fire doors with a stairwell behind them. He opened these and searched around for a light switch again. This time he was luckier. There was a whole bank of switches along one wall. He turned them all on at once, and a second later the fluorescent panels in the ceiling over the stairway began to flicker. Suddenly, Gregor knew what this building reminded him of. It was the elementary school he had gone to in Philadelphia, just a few blocks off Cavanaugh Street, all the years he had been growing up. That had been a brick building, too, with very high ceilings and the smell of disinfectant and wood polish in the air. They had torn that school down years ago and built one that wasn't much better. The new one was old itself and half destroyed. Nobody sent their children there if they didn't have to.

I'm doing it again, Gregor told himself as he climbed the stairs. It's as if I got caught in a time warp, and I'm finding it harder and harder to climb out. But it had been better now for a while—Gregor couldn't quite pinpoint how long a while. It had been much better.

At the top of the stairs, he went through another set of fire doors and found himself, as Clayton had said he would, at the back of the lobby. The booths were right there, made of heavy blond wood that had been polished so often they looked slick. Gregor went into the first of these and sat down on the little cushioned seat. The booth might be old fashioned, but the phone wasn't. The phone company had replaced the rotary instrument that must have occupied the booth in the beginning with a brand new touch-tone model. Gregor fed a quarter into it and dialed first AT&T and then his calling card number. It was incredible how many numbers you had to hold in your head these days, and how little time you spent talking to actual people. Bennis sometimes complained to him about what she called the "virtual universe."

The phone was ringing on Cavanaugh Street. Gregor wondered suddenly if Bennis would be out, off at the Ararat, up in Donna Moradanyan's apartment, taking care of

Donna's son Tommy while Donna and Russ found some time for themselves. Sometimes, when Bennis was working, she just didn't answer the phone.

Bennis answered the phone. "Hello?" she said, sounding distracted. Then she turned away from the receiver and coughed. Gregor knew she had turned away, because the cough sounded like a hiccup instead of an explosion. "Hello?"

"I'm surprised to find you home," Gregor said. "I thought you'd be down at the Ararat, at least."

"That's what you said the last time you called. I am going to the Ararat in a few minutes. I'm meeting Tibor there. You sound better."

"I feel better."

"Is it because of all this stuff with Zhondra Meyer? I saw it on the news, you know, it's been all over everything. They said she left a note and confessed to all the murders."

"Well," Gregor said, "there's a note confessing to the murders of Tiffany Marsh and Carol Littleton, that's true enough."

"I take it it wasn't Zhondra Meyer's note."

"It's a complicated situation. I don't think I've ever seen anything like this before. I've read about things like this, but I haven't seen them."

"But is the case over?" Bennis asked. "Will you be able to catch whoever did it? What's going on down there?"

"I know who did it," Gregor said, "in every possible sense in which I can use that phrase. I'm sorry if I'm obscure, Bennis. It really is a very complicated situation. I can't explain it in the terms I usually use to explain these things in."

"You're not saying anything about being able to catch the murderer," Bennis said. "That's the problem, isn't it? It's like that thing with the Hazzards: You know who but you're not sure if you can do anything about it."

"It's not that simple, Bennis. It really isn't. And it's

not what I called to talk to you about. I called to talk to you about you.''

''Me?''

Gregor had forgotten how uncomfortable these old phone booths were. Everybody complained about the new little stalls where there was no place to sit. They forgot how confining the old phone booths were and how hard the seats were that you had to sit on—even the seats like this, that had cushions. Gregor readjusted himself in the booth, putting one foot on the wall under the phone to keep himself propped up, and felt ridiculous. Teenagers sat like this, when they were trying to get up the courage to do something they were afraid of.

''I've been thinking about that musician or whatever he was,'' Gregor said, ''the one in California.''

''That was months ago,'' Bennis said quickly.

''It lasted a matter of days. Do you know you do that a lot?''

On the other end of the line, there was the sound of Bennis striking a match, then the sound of Bennis exhaling. ''Gregor, if you want to give me some kind of lecture on the way I run my social life, you don't have to because Tibor already—''

''Do you know that the only long-term commitment you've ever made to a man was before I knew you?''

''You must have been drinking.''

''You were living with that man Michael What's-his-name, the Greek, in Boston, before your father died and you moved back to Philadelphia. That was the year we met. Do you remember?''

''I remember how we met, Gregor. I'm never likely to forget it.''

''Between that time and this, you haven't had a single long-term relationship. Not one.''

''I haven't met anybody I wanted to have a long-term relationship with.''

''You haven't met anybody you wanted to go on seeing for longer than two weeks.''

"Two weeks is as long as it makes sense to give most of the men I've known in my life," Bennis said, "and that includes the Michael I was living with in Boston, who turned out to be a world-class Greek-American son of a bitch. Gregor, what the hell is this all about?"

"I think you do it on purpose."

"What?"

"I think you go out with these—nuts—that you find, these—crazy people—because it's your way of making sure that you don't end up committed to something or somebody because you don't really want to be committed to something or somebody."

"Wonderful," Bennis said. "When did you take up pop psychology, Gregor? What comes next? An exploration of the ramification of the position of Saturn in my astrological sign?"

"What I do," Gregor continued, "is keep myself married to Elizabeth. It's been—I don't know how many years anymore, it's been so long—but I'm still married to Elizabeth."

There was quiet now on the other end of the line, and smoking, the deliberate inhaling and exhaling of breath. Gregor was surprised to realize that he was having a hard time breathing himself. He felt like Sherlock Holmes at the Reichenbach Falls, ready to go over a cliff.

Bennis inhaled again. Then she exhaled again. Then she said, "You know, Gregor, this is all very interesting, but do you really think you know what you're doing?"

"Yes," Gregor answered. "I really think I do."

"*I* think it would be a very bad idea to get started in this direction and then screw it up."

"I agree. I'll try not to screw it up. You should try not to screw it up, either."

"What are you going to do now?"

Gregor wedged the door of the telephone booth open so that he had some air. The foyer around him was dark. He wondered if Clayton and Jackson were still alone downstairs, or if the county boys had finally shown up, ready to roll.

"There are some things I still have to do down here," he said. "It's like I told you. This is a very complicated situation. It's going to be difficult to work out."

"How difficult?"

"I don't think I'll be able to get back to Philadelphia until the day after tomorrow. And that's the best I can do. At the very least, I'm going to have to give a deposition. At the worst, I'm going to have to give six. It's that kind of thing."

"What happens after you give all these depositions?"

"I'll come home."

"And then what?"

"Then," Gregor said, "I think you and I ought to go out to dinner somewhere, not the Ararat. Somewhere we can talk."

"Will you tell me about the case?"

"If you want to hear about it."

"I always want to hear about it."

"I've got to go back downstairs," Gregor said. "There's some administrative system here I don't exactly understand, all about counties and God knows what. We're waiting for the county prosecutor. I'll get back as soon as I can."

"You do that. In the meantime, I think I'm going to sit down and drink some serious liquor."

"You ought to quit smoking," Gregor said. "You're going to kill yourself before we have a chance to work all this out."

Bennis might have said good-bye, or she might not have, Gregor didn't know. It could have been nothing but another outflow of smoke. What he did know was that the line was cut, and there was the buzz of a dial tone in his ear.

He hung up the receiver on his end and climbed out of the booth. The foyer was still dark. The building was still quiet. Stephen Harrow was probably still sitting in the rectory of the Methodist Church, thinking he had actually gotten away with it.

It was amazing, Gregor thought, how hard it was for people to change the way they did their thinking.

four

1

One of the county boys turned out to be a county
girl—the county prosecutor, in fact, who was a short, shelf-
breasted woman in her forties, pit bullish and extreme.
Gregor didn't think he was going to like her much, in the
beginning. She wasn't there when he first got back from his
phone call to Bennis. Only Clayton and Jackson were. It
wasn't long, though, before headlights could be seen
through the window well and cars pulled to a stop in the
parking lot in back. Car doors opened and closed. High
country voices talked about the weather. There was a separate entrance to the police department at the back. The
county boys and the county girl came through there, their
shoes clattering on the metal-tipped stairs.

Minna Dorfman didn't like to waste time on triviali-
ties. Whatever gene it was that other southern women had
that made them want to talk for hours about the state of
their gardens and their neighbors' morals, Minna didn't
have it. As soon as she came in, she opened her briefcase
and spread out its contents on the one decently large and
uncluttered desk in the room. Then she pulled a wooden
chair into the middle of the room, sat down in it, and
crossed her legs at the knee. Minna had sharp blue eyes that
were much too small for her face. They looked like bullet
holes that had been drilled into a large white pillow.

Minna Dorfman also folded her hands in her lap. It

was this gesture that Gregor found so foreboding. She looked like a psychopathological schoolteacher, getting ready to do her class in.

''Well?'' she said.

Clayton Hall handed over the ''suicide note'' they had been meant to believe had been written by Zhondra. The prosecutor read through it more quickly than Gregor would have believed anyone could read through anything, then repeated: ''Well?''

''We feel,'' Clayton told her, ''that that note is basically accurate, but that the names have been changed to put us off the scent.''

''Why?'' Minna demanded.

''It wasn't really meant to be a confession,'' Gregor explained. ''He—I'm fairly sure it was Stephen Harrow— needed to confess psychologically, I think, but didn't want to in practical reality.''

Minna Dorfman drummed her fingers against the nearest desktop.

''Let's start from the beginning,'' she said. ''The first murder was the murder of the child, am I right?''

''That's right.''

''And,'' Minna went on, gesturing at the note, ''that murder is confessed to in here. In a way. It's not entirely clear how the child was killed. Is he confessing to that killing or not?''

''My guess is that he doesn't know if he committed it or not,'' Gregor answered. ''He says in the note that the situation was confused, and I think that's probably just what it was. There was a hurricane. There was the goddess worship with a live baby. I think it was a little like being drunk.''

''So I think that's what the murder of the baby was,'' Minna said slowly, ''a matter of fooling around with something that got out of hand. Goddess worship.''

''I don't think I would have believed it before I came down here,'' Gregor said, ''but it seems perfectly plausible to me now. Millennial fever, somebody called it. This place seems to be almost infested with religion.''

''I believe it,'' Minna Dorfman said. ''I grew up less than five miles from this room. But you know, Mr. Demarkian—it is Mr. Demarkian, isn't it?''

Gregor nodded.

''You know,'' Minna went on, ''no matter how hysterical people from up North get, Holy Rolling is really not the last refuge of nut cases and homicidal maniacs. When there's a murder or some child abuse on television, it seems like it's always the Holy Roller that did it, but it isn't like that in real life. When we pick a man up for murder and mayhem, he's more likely *not* to belong to a church than to belong to one. This Stephen Harrow,'' she continued, ''didn't you tell me he was a member of the clergy?''

''It's the Methodist Church,'' Clayton Hall put in, ''and Mr. Harrow isn't from around here. He's from up North. He's got a lot of fancy degrees in theology from fancy universities up there.''

''He's not exactly a fundamentalist,'' Gregor conceded. ''But I don't think that was the point of all this, either.''

''So what was?'' Minna asked.

Gregor picked up the manila envelope where Clayton was keeping the things they had found at the scene of Zhondra Meyer's death. He looked through the papers until he found the photograph and then handed it to Minna. She stared at it for a full minute, unblinking, and then handed it back.

''The man is Stephen Harrow?''

''That's right.''

''Who's the woman?''

''We don't know yet,'' Gregor said. ''We are meant to infer, of course, that the woman is Carol Littleton.''

''You mean Mr. Harrow knows somebody has this picture? Who? Where did you get it?''

''In Zhondra Meyer's bedroom.''

''You mean she was blackmailing him?''

"No," Gregor said, wishing that Minna had stuck to her original plan. "I have no idea if Stephen Harrow has ever seen this photograph. In the note, though, which he was trying to make look like a suicide note from Zhondra, he uses Carol Littleton as the other woman. And there *was* a woman. I think the report of what went on on the terrace is completely accurate. They did take the baby out there to worship the goddess. Stephen Harrow, at least, had no intention of doing anything—untoward. Something untoward happened, nevertheless. And Stephen Harrow, at least, panicked."

"You keep saying 'Stephen Harrow, at least.' Do you think the woman kept her head? Do you think her motives were different?"

"I don't know," Gregor said. "I don't know who she is. I'm not sure, at this point, that she's important."

"She's important if she was part of the murdering of that baby," Minna pointed out.

"But there was nothing to say that the baby was murdered. Ginny Marsh came out of the rain claiming to have seen her child sacrificed by worshippers of the goddess—which she might have done, depending on where she was when she witnessed what she said she witnessed—and we've all been running with that interpretation ever since. But the child might not have been deliberately killed."

"The child had her throat cut from ear to ear," Minna Dorfman said. "She was an infant."

"I know. I know, I know, I know. But they were out there on that terrace and there was a lot of confusion and I'm not sure they really knew what they were doing. I'm not telling you that this is the way you would have to argue it in court, if you brought a case against Stephen Harrow. I'm trying to set this out so that it makes sense."

"I'd like to bring a case against that woman, too," Minna Dorfman said. "Are you sure you don't know who she is?"

Clayton Hall shrugged. "She's some woman from up

at the camp, that's all. Or some woman who spends a lot of time there. They all worship the goddess in that place."

"It was Stephen who killed the other two," Gregor said firmly. "Carol Littleton and Zhondra Meyer. They might not have been infants, but they should count, too."

"And they do count, Mr. Demarkian," Minna said. "I never said they didn't. Are you sure it was Stephen Harrow and not his—friend—who killed Carol Littleton and Zhondra Meyer?"

"I think so, yes," Gregor told her. "Assuming the woman he is involved with *is* somebody from town or from the camp, it's difficult to see how she could possibly have killed either of them. We've been watching all those people. And as soon as anything happened, we took statements from each of them to determine where they had been and when. I don't think we found any gaps anywhere."

"If we had found gaps," Clayton Hall said, "I would have called you people a long time before now."

"Unless you're going to believe that there are two people wandering around here murdering people," Gregor went on, "which I, in this case, don't, then you're stuck with the fact that nobody else but Stephen Harrow seems to have had the opportunity to commit all three of these crimes. The one I'm most interested in, of course, is the first, because we've got better than usual testimony on that one. Believe it or not, the hurricane helped. It put everybody together in one room."

"It put all the people in town together in one room," Clayton corrected. "Most of the women from the camp were in the living room next door."

"The women from the camp vouched for each other," Gregor said firmly. "The only people missing who should have been in the living room were Stelle Cary, Carol Littleton, and Dinah What's-her-name. The three who went out to the circle of stones and had a ceremony to the goddess. They got caught in the storm."

"But if that was the case," Minna Dorfman asked,

"why couldn't they be the ones who killed the baby, just the way Ginny Marsh swears they did?"

"For all the same reasons that the police didn't arrest them in the first place," Gregor said. "Because they didn't have any blood on them anywhere. Not even a trace. Because they weren't in the right places at the right times. Because they were always together."

"And Harrow?"

"Harrow," Gregor said, "keeps disappearing from places. As far as I can tell, nobody remembers him being in the study at all before the hurricane, but he was surely there afterward, and his wife was there the whole time. If we talk to her, I'll bet anything she'll say they came up to the camp together."

"Unless she lies for him," Minna Dorfman said.

"No chance," Clayton Hall told her.

"The most important thing here," Gregor insisted, "is that Harrow was present when the baby died—however she died—and everything he has done since then has been to hide his involvement in that death. Everything. Including the deaths of Carol Littleton and Zhondra Meyer."

"Why did he kill Carol Littleton? I thought you said she was off with these other women during the storm. She couldn't have seen him with the baby if that were the case."

"I don't think she did see him with the baby," Gregor said. "I think she might have seen him with his girl, or, even more likely, with some of the paraphernalia of goddess worship. One of the other women who went up to the circle of stones during the hurricane, Stelle Cary, told me that Carol showed up for the ceremony very late and that she came running out of the house all upset just before they left for the clearing."

"And think that's when she saw Stephen and his girlfriend?"

"I think that's when she saw Stephen and something."

"I think that's a little vague to be going on with," Minna insisted. "You need more details than you've got before you can do what you want to do here, Mr. Demarkian. And what about Zhondra Meyer? Did she see him with his girlfriend, too?"

"Zhondra Meyer knew all about Stephen's girlfriend," Gregor said. "That's obvious from the picture. And I think she may have known all about his flirtation with goddess worship. If you want details, Ms. Dorfman, what we ought to do is go over there, to the rectory, and ask him."

"Without a lawyer," Minna said. "Without giving him a warning."

"There's no need for warnings yet," Clayton Hall said. "We don't want to arrest him. We only want to talk to him."

"He doesn't have to talk to us without a lawyer present." Minna shook her head. "He doesn't have to give us the time of day."

Gregor got up from the desk he'd been sitting on. "But he will," he said. "He will. He's desperate to talk. That's why he wrote that note."

Minna got up, too, and walked across the room to the window. She clasped her hands behind her back and said, "All right, let's say we go over there. We knock on the door or we ring the bell. Then what?"

"Then I can do the talking," Gregor said.

Minna Dorfman nodded. She still had her back to them. The flat brown thinness of her hair was plastered against her skull like wet rubber. Her hands were mottled with liver spots before their time.

"Yes," she said finally. "Mr. Demarkian, I expect you could do the talking. Have you been formally deputized?"

"No," Clayton Hall said.

"Then formally deputize him," Minna Dorfman said. "I don't want to hear after all this is over that we had some kind of unauthorized personnel on the scene, and that taints all the evidence we got. God help us, if we're going to go over there and do this, we're going to do this right.''

2

If there was one thing Gregor Demarkian would always remember about North Carolina, it was the night. Night here was beautiful when he was sitting on David Sandler's deck, looking out at the big moon and the black ocean. It was beautiful here, in town, with trees and small gracious buildings all around him, with the heavy scent of night flowers and the solemn chill of coming winter blowing in his face. The Town Hall and the library were dark. Betsey's diner and many of the Greek revival houses on the side streets were lit up. Sometime while Gregor wasn't paying attention, twilight had ended.

The rectory of the Methodist Church was lit up like Times Square. There were lights on in all the downstairs rooms that Gregor could see, and some of the upstairs ones. There was a light on on the porch as well. Next door, the church itself was dark, its windows shuttered over to protect it from vandalism and teenagers. Gregor thought the doors were probably locked. He preferred the old tradition in the Catholic Church, maintained so seldom now, because the world had changed so much, of keeping the doors of the church open at all times. So many souls wanted to be saved in the middle of the night. That, Gregor thought, would be an attractive way to believe in God—if he could have believed in God, which he didn't. He was even attracted, sometimes, to Henry Holborn's version of Christianity, with its passions and its enthusiasms. He didn't know what went on in the locked and shuttered Methodist Church from week to week, but he didn't think anybody's soul got saved at Sunday services.

The bulb in the porch light spilled light down the steps and onto the walk. Gregor could see through the tall front windows into the living room, which was empty. There was a fire in the fireplace and a portrait of Einstein over the mantel. Gregor, Clayton Hall, and Minna Dorfman had discussed it among themselves back at the police department—talking to Jackson and the men Minna had brought with her, too—and decided that descending on Stephen Harrow like an army wasn't going to do anybody any good. The idea was not to frighten him. The idea was to give him a chance to be listened to.

Gregor climbed the porch steps and knocked on the front door. Nothing happened. He looked around for a doorbell and couldn't find one. He knocked again. This time he heard noise from inside the house, as if someone were stumbling against the furniture, walking too fast. A moment later, he looked through the front windows and saw a dark-haired woman hurrying down the strip of hardwood floor next to the broad green carpet that the living sofa sat on. An instant later, she was opening the door and peering out to see his face.

"Yes?" she said, hesitant.

Clayton Hall stepped forward. "It's me, Lisa. This is Gregor Demarkian, you've read about him. And this lady here is Minna Dorfman from the county prosecutor's office."

"The county prosecutor's office?"

"We're investigating a murder," Clayton Hall said firmly. "We've got a few things we'd like to talk to Stephen about. Could we come in?"

Gregor thought Lisa Harrow was going to turn them down, or tell them her husband was not here. He could see her closing the door in their faces right now. Then there was more sound from the back of the house, and over her shoulder Gregor saw Stephen Harrow come in.

"Lisa?" he said. "What's going on here?"

"It's Clayton," Lisa said. "He's got some people with him." Gregor didn't think he'd ever seen anyone so nervous in all his life.

Unlike his wife, Stephen Harrow didn't seem nervous.

If there was an opposite of nervousness, he was it. He drew Lisa gently away from the door and motioned them all to come inside.

"Come in, come in," he said cheerfully. "Clayton. It's been a long time since we've sat down for a talk. And Mr. Demarkian. I've read about you, of course, millions of times, and we talked up at the camp a couple of days ago. But I'm afraid I don't know—"

"Minna Dorfman," Minna Dorfman said. "I'm from the county prosecutor's office."

"I don't understand why we need someone from the county prosecutor's office," Lisa said.

Stephen ushered them all into the living room proper, shooing them ahead of him like geese to the couch. He went back into the foyer and shut the front door, hard, so that the sound of the latch catching echoed through the house. Then he came back to the living room and sat down in one of the two big chairs that flanked the fire.

"I don't understand why we need someone from the county prosecutor's office," Lisa said again. She wasn't sitting down at all, but pacing back and forth in front of the fire. She looked ready to jump out of her skin.

Stephen leaned forward and caught her by the arm. "Sit down," he said, guiding her to the other chair flanking the fire. "Relax. We're all going to have a little talk."

"About what?" Lisa demanded. "You've been talking all night and I haven't understood a word of it."

"I've been telling her about how I killed Zhondra Meyer," Stephen said pleasantly. "That's what you all came here for, isn't it? To find out how I killed Zhondra Meyer?"

"I think we'd like to hear about Carol Littleton as well," Gregor said. "We understand why you killed Zhondra Meyer. With Carol Littleton, it isn't so clear."

"Jesus," Clayton Hall murmured.

Minna Dorfman wasn't saying a word.

Lisa Harrow looked ready to cry. "He's been talking

like this all night," she said. "I don't understand it. He couldn't have killed anybody."

"But I did," Stephen said, and that's when Gregor realized that the man's eyes were shining. There was a light in them, literally; Gregor thought he must have taken some kind of speed, like diet pills.

"I did kill them," Stephen said again. "I killed them both. I wanted them dead. In the beginning I thought it was all hogwash, you know, all that stuff Henry Holborn talks about all the time. The Devil. But the Devil is here. The Devil lives inside my head."

"Oh, Jesus," Clayton said. "He's going to an insanity plea."

"I don't think 'the devil made me do it' is going to go over very well in North Carolina, Mr. Harrow," Minna Dorfman said crisply.

"Carol wasn't there when the baby died," Gregor said, calmly, softly, gently, insistently, willing all the rest of them to shut up. "Who was there when the baby died?"

"Carol saw me with the candles," Stephen told him. "Before the hurricane. She saw both of us. She thought we were committing an act of desecration. She thought we were blaspheming against the Goddess."

"And later she changed her mind?" Gregor prompted. "Later she put two and two together?"

"Later she wanted to know why I hadn't told you about the candles," Stephen answered. "Carol was never any good at putting two and two together. I told her it was private. I asked her to come and meet me behind the rectory. Lisa had to go into Raleigh for something. I don't remember what."

"You killed Carol Littleton here? At the rectory?"

"I killed her in my car," Stephen said. "I had to get her around, you see. I had to get her body up to the clearing. I had a big rubber sheet that I used for camping and I put that in the backseat before she came, and then when I got her in there I just—"

"Cut her throat?"

"Broke her neck," Stephen said. "I cut her throat later. I think she was still alive then, but I'm not sure. I didn't think anybody could still be alive after they'd had their neck broken, but I think she was."

"It happens every day."

"You can't cut the throat of a grown person the way you can with a baby," Stephen said. "They won't stand still for it. I drove the car around to the back of Zhondra's property. There's a dirt road up there and not much else. There's not even a real fence. Nobody ever thinks of going in that way."

"And you put the body in the clearing," Gregor said.

"That's right. I threw it on the ground and dumped a bunch of things on top of it. It was very early in the morning. Lisa had just left, right before I called Carol to come over, and Lisa always likes to leave early when she's going to Raleigh. And it was hours and hours before the body was found, too, although it was earlier than I thought it would be."

"Earlier? Why earlier?"

"I thought I'd have a couple of days," Stephen replied. "I knew they weren't going up there to worship the Goddess anymore. Zhondra put a stop to it after Tiffany died. I thought she would just lie up there for a couple of days and . . . decompose."

"And all this because she saw the candles."

"They were very special candles," Stephen said. "They were for worshipping the Goddess and only for worshipping the Goddess. I had them right before the storm, and I was bringing them out the side of the house, through the kitchen. She saw me, you see. Clayton didn't do a very good job with the searching. I don't think he ever got to that terrace. There was blood all over that terrace when it was finished."

"When what was finished?" Gregor asked evenly. "Do you mean after the baby was dead?"

"The baby cried and cried and then it stopped. That's all I remember about that. There was the rain and the lightning and the thunder and the baby was wailing on and on and on and then it was dead, lying right there in my hands pumping blood all over me, all over us both."

"Dear sweet Jesus," Minna whispered. "If it was pumping blood, it was *alive*."

"You remember killing Carol," Gregor said. "Do you remember killing Zhondra?"

"I broke her neck, too," Stephen said. "That was a woman who could put two and two together. She had everything all figured out. I was only coming up to get the candles. I would have left her alone after that. I didn't want to go wandering around her camp. What did she take me for?"

"You typed the suicide note?" Gregor asked. "You got her hanging with the rope over the chandelier hook?"

"I used the chandelier hook as a pulley. It wasn't hard. It was easier than killing her."

"We would have figured it out in the end, you know," Gregor told him. "There are ways to tell, during an autopsy, whether a person died from hanging or not. There are ways to tell even before an autopsy."

"But you didn't have to figure it out," Stephen said. "I told you all of it. I told you all of it myself."

Tears were streaming down Lisa Harrow's face, a great waterfall of them. "You can't believe a word he says," she told them woodenly. "You can't. He must be crazy."

"I'm not crazy," her husband said. "I'm possessed. Don't you know that by now? I invited the Devil into my soul, and he set up house. I think he's set up house for good."

"He's been talking like that all night," Lisa said. "He's been telling me I'd be better off dead."

"We'd all be better off dead," Stephen said, and that was when Gregor saw it, coming out of the pocket of Stephen's academic tweed jacket, a little Colt gun with a silver handle. It was a lady's gun, the kind made to look stylish in a purse, next to a silver lipstick and compact set. It couldn't belong to Stephen Harrow unless he'd bought it blind on the street somewhere, caring nothing at all but that he had something to shoot with.

Clayton Hall saw the gun, too, and started to rise. "Jesus Christ. Stephen. What do you think you're doing?"

Stephen pointed the gun at Clayton and smiled. "Sit down for a while, Clayton. I'm just making sure I get my full say in before you all decide to jump me. I've still got a lot to say."

"Nobody's going to jump you until you've said everything you want to say," Gregor told him. "There's nothing you have to say that we don't want to hear."

"There's nothing I have to say that you do want to hear," Stephen corrected happily—and he was happy, Gregor thought, deliriously happy. He was the happiest man Gregor had ever seen in his life. "I know all about it now, from beginning to end. I know more about it than I ever thought I was going to know. I'm a genius in the spiritual life. But it's time, you know."

"Time for what?" Minna Dorfman asked.

"Time to do what they're always telling you to do, all those people who think they know better," Stephen told them. "Time to let go and let God."

"What?"

Stephen held the gun high over his head, so that light hit the silver metal and bounced off, making rainbows. "It belonged to her, you know," he said. "It belonged to Zhondra. I never had much use for guns. I thought they were barbaric."

"Maybe you ought to let me have that now," Clayton said, getting up again. "You're going to hurt somebody with it if you go on waving it around."

"Oh, well, Clayton. You know how it is. You never hurt anybody as much as you hurt yourself."

"Crap," Clayton said, making a desperate dive in Stephen Harrow's direction.

It happened too fast. Clayton's body was still in the air, mid-jump, when Stephen pressed the barrel of the gun to his own throat and blew a hole in his windpipe.

five

1

The news about Stephen Harrow came over the radio while Maggie Kelleher was closing up shop. The shop had actually been closed to business for hours, but Joshua had been doing inventory and Maggie had been drinking wine at David Sandler's house and now all the mundane things were left to be done that should have been done before, like cashing out the register and putting the money in the bank. Now, drifting through the rooms of the little bookstore, Maggie wished she had stayed at the beach and made love to David until dawn. As it was, they had only managed one single hurried coupling on the sand. It was so hard to figure out what was going on sometimes, when you were trying to sort out messes like sex and love. Maggie tried to imagine herself in David's apartment in the city, and saw herself only as she had been on her own and alone in New York. Maggie the invincible, she thought now. She had a half-full glass of wine in her hand. The bottle of Vin Santo, the new one, was sitting on the desk in the front room. She thought of herself walking down Sixth Avenue in the dark, dressed in a long skirt and high-heeled boots and a short heavy coat, carrying an enormous tote bag. Maggie the invincible. Maggie the almost bag lady. Maggie who had never really been good enough to do what she wanted to do with her life, and who was now old enough to know it. That was why all this business about going to New York with David was so hard for her. The "with David" part was easy. That had been coming. It was something of a relief that it was finally here. Maggie thought she could live with David forever, nestled among the books. It was New York she wasn't sure she wanted. Maybe, for David, she would be like that girl in *Lost Horizon*—beautiful and desirable as long as she stayed in Shangri-La, nothing but a skeleton and hanks of hair the moment she stepped outside it. Maggie the invincible, she thought again, and laughed out loud. In Bellerton she was something special, exotic, set apart. In New York, she was nothing better than another girl who had almost had a career but then hadn't, in the end, because it hadn't worked out, because she hadn't wanted it enough, because in that race there were so many other runners.

She was standing in the loft when the news about Stephen Harrow came over the radio, thinking of all the good things about New York—including the fact that she would not be the only one she knew who loved books like these, with their bindings and their leather. When she heard Stephen Harrow's name, she took a small sip of wine and put the glass down on a shelf. When she had heard the news story through, she picked up the wine again and went to the railing of the loft. Beneath her, the big main room of the bookstore looked dark and shadowy and sinister. The only light on down there was the little one behind the desk, where Joshua was filing the last of the inventory into an IBM PC. If she married David, she would have to buy a whole new set of winter clothes. She would have to learn which subways went where again. She would have to get her books from other people's bookstores.

She leaned over the railing and called down. "Josh? Did you have the radio on? Did you hear that?"

"Of course I heard that," Josh said. "Jesus Christ."

Maggie took another sip of wine and started down the curving metal stairs. Through the big plate glass window, she could see her little patch of Main Street, looking like something out of a Stephen King novel in the puddled light from the arc lamps. In Maggie's mind, everything was like some novel or the other or some movie or the other. That was the way her brain worked. The problem was, when she tried to think of what she and David were like, she couldn't.

She got to the bottom of the steps and took another sip of wine. Josh looked at her steadily in the darkness, until she almost thought she could see his eyes glow.

"I wonder if it's true," she said. "Do you think it's true?"

"It has to be true," Josh said. "Stephen Harrow. For Christ's sake."

"For someone who doesn't believe in God, you call on the name of the Lord a lot."

"Don't go all religious on me. I've had enough of religion. Stephen Harrow. Can you imagine him killing that little baby?"

"No."

"Well, you'd better imagine it," Josh said triumphantly, "because there it was, all over the news. I can't wait to get out of here, Maggie, I'm telling you. I can't wait to get out to some civilized place like California or Chicago. Towns like this are snake pits."

Maggie sat down on the bottom of the metal steps. "Are you intending to leave anytime soon?" she asked him.

"Soon as I can get some money together. I've been thinking about applying to a graduate program out there. At Berkeley or San Francisco State. At least it would get me out there and give me some people to talk to. I can figure out what to do after that when I'm settled in."

"But what about the money," Maggie persisted. "Do you have it? Are you going to be able to get it in the next year or so?"

"Is there a reason for all this questioning, Maggie? Are you anxious to get rid of me? I thought I was doing a pretty good job for you here. If you don't think I am, you don't have to wait for me to go to California. All you have to do is fire my ass."

"I don't want to fire your ass." Maggie finished off the wine. "I want to hire it on a much higher level."

"I don't think you ought to drink any more of that," Josh said. "This is beginning to sound like sexual harassment."

Maggie got off the stair and went over to the desk, where the bottle of wine was. She wasn't drunk, just floaty—and she thought that was nice, for once. Main Street looked almost as sinister from where she was standing at the desk as it had from where she had been sitting on the step. Out there, the whole town seemed to be alive, and hostile, and angry with her. It wanted to chuck her out, the way—the way what?

"Are you all right?" Josh asked her.

Maggie took her now-refilled glass of wine and went back to sit on the step again. "I've been thinking that maybe just after Christmas, I might put you in charge of everything. Make you the manager here. Let you hire somebody to help you."

"Put me in charge how?"

"Put you in charge period. Without any interference from me. Or without much, anyway. David and I are thinking of getting married."

"Married?"

"It isn't like thinking of going to Mars, Joshua. People do get married. They get married every day."

Joshua stopped even pretending to work on the inventory. "I know they get married every day. What has that got to do with putting me in charge of the store? Does David want you to quit work so he can support you?"

"David wants to go back to New York. He was going to write this book he's working on down here, but it hasn't been working out. He'd go back to New York and I'd go back with him."

"Smart move."

"In the meantime, I'd have to have somebody here who could look after the store, because I don't think I want to give it up, not yet."

"For insurance," Joshua said wisely. "Just in case this thing between you and David doesn't work out."

"Anyway, I thought that you could take over and I could pay you a higher salary and that would work for a while until I knew what I wanted to do. But if you're going out to California right away—"

"I don't have the money to go out to California right away."

"Well, then."

"I wish you seemed happier about it. That's what I hate most about small towns like this. They make everybody ambivalent."

Maggie took another sip of wine and closed her eyes and rested her head against the staircase railing. I am happy, she thought. I'm not ambivalent about anything.

The odd thing was, really, that it was true. She wasn't ambivalent about anything. She knew just what she wanted to do about David. She had known now for a couple of years, ever since they had started to be together. She wondered why all those other things mattered so much—pride and career and status and whose money was whose—but she didn't have an answer to that and she didn't have the strength to find one. She just wanted to go out to her place, and in the morning she wanted to get up and pack—even though she knew perfectly well that they wouldn't be leaving that soon.

"Maggie?" Josh said.

"Shh," Maggie said.

"I'm about to go home now," Josh said. "Maybe you ought to get up and go home now, too."

Maggie Kelleher took another long sip of her wine, and laughed.

2

Ever since Zhondra Meyer had been murdered, Rose MacNeill had been afraid—so afraid she found it hard to breathe, so afraid she found it hard to walk, so afraid she thought she was going to die right on Main Street. The fear was complicated by her anger, which was still white-hot and strong, even after she knew that Zhondra would never be able to feel it anymore. Hell was the first thing Rose MacNeill had thought of, when she heard that Zhondra Meyer was dead—Hell the way she had been taught to think of it in her childhood, when hellfire-and-brimstone preachers had been hellfire-and-brimstone preachers instead of gung-ho positive-thinking pep club leaders who only wanted to let you know that God's love was there for you. It wasn't God's love Rose wanted, but God's hate, that white-hot fire of retribution that was supposed to visit all the wicked on the last day and before. Henry Holborn was right, she thought. The camp was like a village of the damned. The women there were a pestilence and an abomination, and they would bring the curse of God down on all their neighbors.

"I don't think you understand," Zhondra had told her, in that clipped New York voice with its faint trace of society caw. Behind her, the fire had been raging and leaping, a figure of Hell for Rose to contemplate while the interview went on, much too slowly, turning her out.

"I don't take lovers from among the women who stay in this house," Zhondra had said. "I don't admit as guests women who want to be my lovers. Especially if I don't want to be theirs. It's much too complicated."

Complicated, Rose had thought at the time. Complicated, complicated, complicated. The fire was leaping and dancing and she was so cold, so cold. She wanted to leap across Zhondra Meyer's big desk and put her hands around the woman's throat. It was bad enough to be turned away by a man. It was worse to be turned away by a woman and worse yet, worse yet—what? She had thought she was going to go up the hill to the camp and never come down again. Now she not only had to come down, but to do it slowly, and in humiliation. The pictures on the walls of Zhondra's study were all portraits, big and brooding. Rose had thought they were all staring at her, getting ready to laugh. She was laughable, really. She was worse than laughable. She was a sagging middle-aged woman with delusions of grandeur. She had honestly thought that just because she was attracted to Zhondra Meyer, Zhondra Meyer would have to be attracted to her. She had honestly thought that just because she was dying of love for Zhondra Meyer—what? Rose had been with enough men in her life to know that this was not the way love worked. Why did she think love with women would be different?

The next thing she knew, she was stumbling down the hill, her eyes blurred with the start of tears she wouldn't let come. She had broken the heel on one of her shoes and the toes of both feet had blisters. She was in so much pain when she moved she thought she was going to pass out. She was in so much pain even when she didn't move. The hill seemed to be endless, and much steeper than she remembered it. The streets between the hill and the center of town seemed to be more numerous and more full of people. Everyone must have seen her go up to talk to Zhondra Meyer. Everybody must have realized what she was going up to do. Everyone must have seen her come down again, rejected, turned down, shut off. Everyone, everyone, everyone.

When she got to her big Victorian house, she took the back way in and went up the stairs to the rooms on the second floor where she lived. Kathi was in the store taking care of business. Rose turned on the tap in the bathroom sink full blast on cold. She put her head under the water and let the chill go through her. She wanted to be cold, as cold as she had ever been, as cold as a corpse.

After she heard that Zhondra was dead, it was different. Then she had thought it was only a matter of time. Clayton Hall would get to her. The whole town would get to her. Everybody would know everything about her and then—

She was still in the bathroom upstairs when she heard the news about Stephen Harrow, and after the report was finished she had turned the dials on her little portable radio, searching for some other station that had the news. She had come so close, she thought. She had almost given up everything she had ever known and everything she had ever loved and everything that had ever been any good for her, and for what? For a perversion she had no idea if she would actually like once she tried it? She thought now of Zhondra's long-fingered white hands, with their blunt-cut nails. She had once lain in bed and imagined those hands trailing along her body, the tips of the fingers brushing against the tips of her nipples, the flats of the palms lying in the hollow curve made by her waist. She had imagined herself drunk on emotion, defenseless and free, able to do nothing else but feel.

Now she stood up, and brushed the carpet lint off her skirt, and went to the bathroom door. It was late, but Kathi was still here, making pudding in the kitchen to take over to the church in the morning. There was something going on with the Sunday school classes later in the afternoon, and Janet Holborn said they all needed food. Rose didn't use to go out to Henry Holborn's church to worship, but now, after all that terrible stuff had happened with Zhondra, she knew she needed to get back to basics, back to the Lord. The Lord was the only person she had ever known who had been able to make her feel safe.

Rose went down the little hall to her kitchen, and found Kathi filling custard cups with rice pudding. The little television was on, showing a sitcom Rose didn't recognize, instead of one of the religious stations, which was what she and Kathi usually watched. Kathi saw her glance at the program on the television and changed the channel, blushing.

"I heard all that stuff about Stephen Harrow coming from your radio," she said. "I thought one of the local stations would have news."

"Did it?"

"CBS had a bulletin sort of thing," Kathi said. "It didn't say much. You know what I think?"

"What?"

"You know those sirens we heard about an hour and a half ago? All that fuss in the street? I bet that was this."

"Oh," Rose said. "I bet you're right."

"I told you we should have gone to see what was going on. I know you think it looks trashy, Rose, but sometimes you have to sacrifice your dignity for your education. I wonder how many people went to see."

"Not as many as you think," Rose said. "We don't usually chase ambulances in this town. Just police cars."

"I'll bet those reporters were there," Kathi said. "Oh, I wish we could have seen. Isn't it exciting? Now it's all over with, and we're going to find out everything on the news shows or people will know it around town. I hate mysteries. I can't even read the fake kind. I like to know what's going on."

"Yes," Rose said. "I do, too."

"And they'll have to let Ginny Marsh out of jail now, too. I never did think she'd done any of those awful things they said she'd done, and I don't think a lot of people in town thought it, either. It'll be good to see her back in church."

"Yes," Rose said. "Yes, it will."

"Is there something wrong with you?" Kathi asked. "I thought you'd be excited. I'm excited. I can't believe the way all this worked out. That damned Yankee phony with all his fancy books about God, as if nobody could understand God if they hadn't gone to Yale and studied—whatever."

The custard cups were lined up in rows on the kitchen table. Kathi was wearing a big white pin with red letters that said IT'S A CHILD, NOT A CHOICE. Rose sat down in one of the kitchen chairs and put her chin in her hands.

"I've been thinking," she said.

"About what?" Kathi asked her.

"About the camp, really. Now that Zhondra Meyer's gone, it probably won't last long."

"Now that Zhondra Meyer's gone, it won't last at

all,'' Kathi said with satisfaction. "What I heard is that that fancy family of hers from up in New York is on their way down here already, or their lawyers are, and that's going to be the end of the lesbians in Bellerton. I just hope I get a chance to go up there and see it when they throw them out."

"The problem," Rose said, "is that they'll be back."

"But how?" Kathi looked confused. "They wouldn't have anyplace to go."

"I'm not saying that these particular women will be back," Rose said. "I'm saying that once it starts, it never finishes. You have to be vigilant all the time."

"Vigilant how?"

"Well, I was thinking about forming a group. A churchwomen's group, with women from all the different Christian churches, you know the ones I mean, not only Henry Holborn's. We could get together and sort of monitor things, keep our eye on what's going on in town, so that something like this couldn't get set up within our borders ever again."

"But how could we do that? The camp was on private property."

"We could picket," Rose said, beginning to see her way to the end of this. "We could go out there and make noise. They do it all the time, the lesbians and the secular humanists and all the rest of them. Why shouldn't we?"

"We do do it, don't we?" Kathi asked. "With pro-life."

"Pro-life is different. Pro-life is a special case. I'm talking about our everyday lives here. I'm talking about the air we breathe and the atmosphere we bring our children up in."

"It sounds like a lot of work."

"It is a lot of work," Rose said. "But it's a good idea, believe me. And if we work hard enough, we'll never be saddled with another lesbian camp again, or anything like it. We'll never have to watch the homes we live in be eaten up by the filth that comes spewing out of a place of that kind.''

Kathi looked worse than confused. ''Well,'' she said. ''Actually, that was one of the few things I liked about them up there. They were so clean all the time.''

Rose got up out of the chair and went to the stove to make coffee. There was no use talking to Kathi, of course. She didn't have the brains God gave a flea. But Rose was sure she was right, even without Kathi to confirm it. Rose was sure that this was the best idea she had ever had in her life.

They would form an army of women, that was what they would do, and once they were armed and ready, nobody would ever dare to go against them.

3

As soon as he'd heard, Bobby Marsh had gone over to the jail to tell Ginny about what had happened with Stephen Harrow, and for the first time in weeks he had been feeling almost good. It was late, long past visiting hours, but he knew that Jackson would let him in. Jackson and Clayton were pretty loose about Ginny's visiting hours anyway. Now, with Stephen Harrow having confessed, they would have to let Ginny out into the world as soon as possible. In the old days, that would have been right away, as soon as Clayton was able to find his key to the cell, but these days Bobby understood that Clayton had to follow procedures. It was the Supreme Court that had done that, and the federal government, which just went to show how the government in Washington was always interfering in people's lives and making things worse. Bobby wanted to grab Ginny up in a bundle and take her home to her own bed. By all rights, he should be able to. Even without that in the offing, though, Bobby thought Bellerton was really beautiful, one of the finest towns on earth. In the dark like this, with the streetlights on, it seemed to glitter and glow.

Bobby took in Rose MacNeill's big Victorian house, and Charlie Hare's feed store, and Maggie Kelleher's bookshop. Town Hall loomed up in front of him like a big brick temple. There were people who wanted to go away to big cities, like Los Angeles and Miami. There were people who wanted to go away to Europe. Bobby wanted to stay right here.

He went in the police department entrance on Town Hall's side, and waved to Jackson as he came down the hall. The police department was otherwise empty. They must all be out at the hospital or the morgue or someplace, or maybe State Police headquarters. Bobby didn't know where they were, and he didn't care. Stephen Harrow was dead. Stephen Harrow had confessed. The world was all right again. Jackson came out into the hall with a big ring of keys in his hand.

"I told her you were coming as soon as you called," Jackson said. "She already knows what's been going on. She's been listening to the radio."

"Is she happy?"

"I wouldn't say she was happy, Bobby. Ginny hasn't been happy since the baby died."

"I know," Bobby said. "I know."

"You can't expect her to be happy, Bobby. Not with Tiffany dead. It wouldn't be right for her to be happy."

"No," Bobby said. "Of course it wouldn't."

They were already halfway across to the little double jail cell. It wasn't much of a jail, at least, this place where Ginny had been. It wasn't like being on the work farm or in the state penitentiary. Bobby reminded himself that that probably didn't make much difference to Ginny. He reminded himself of a lot of other things, too, like Ginny's favorite color (cornflower blue) and the fact that she loved to have him send her flowers. He would have to do that on the day he brought her home. He would have to have the house full of cornflower blue flowers.

Ginny was sitting on the chair in her cell with the reading light on, reading her Bible. She looked up at them and put the Bible down on the bed. Bobby expected her to smile at him, but she didn't. Jackson used the key to open the cell and drew back the barred door.

"You two could talk in the conference room," Jackson said. "You'd have more privacy there."

"That's a good idea," Bobby told him.

Jackson turned away and walked back down the hall, pushing open the conference room door as he went. Bobby felt elated. Jackson wouldn't be behaving like this if there was any chance at all that Ginny wouldn't be released. He would stick around and make sure she didn't get away instead. Ginny was standing in the middle of the cell with her arms wrapped around her body, not looking at him. Bobby was amazed that her hair looked so good, so shiny and curly and long. It had to have been hell trying to take care of it in a dinky little small-town jail cell.

"Ginny," Bobby said.

"Yes," Ginny said. "I hear you."

"Let's go down to that conference room Jackson was talking about," Bobby said. "It's got to be more cheerful there. Anything's got to be more cheerful than here."

Ginny looked around. "I suppose it does."

"Come on, then," Bobby said.

Ginny looked around. "I don't think so," she told him. "I think I'll just stay right here."

"Jackson told me that you'd been listening to the radio," Bobby said. "He told me you knew all about it. About Harrow."

"Oh, I know about Harrow, Bobby. Stephen Harrow is dead."

"Stephen Harrow confessed to the murders," Bobby said. "Didn't you know that?"

"I knew that, Bobby."

"But you're free to go, don't you see that? I mean, not tonight. They've got their paperwork to do and all that crap. But you're off the hook now. Stephen Harrow confessed. Everybody will know you didn't kill Tiffany."

Ginny cocked her head. "Really, Bobby? Will everybody know?"

"Of course," Bobby said.

"Even you?"

Bobby felt a chill go up his spine, a vise of ice close around his testicles. "I knew you didn't kill Tiffany. I always knew that."

"No," Ginny told him. "I don't think you did."

"I was just—confused, that's all," Bobby said. "I couldn't get around the things you were saying. The goddess worship and all that. It didn't make any sense. But I didn't think you killed Tiffany."

"You thought I killed her just like everybody else thought I killed her," Ginny said. "All those people who were supposed to be my friends, and my family, and my husband."

"I am your husband," Bobby said. "We were married in the sight of the Lord."

"I don't seem to have much time for the Lord these days, Bobby. I'm too busy figuring out what I'm going to do with myself next."

"You're going to come home to me."

"I don't think so."

"It will get better." Bobby willed himself not to feel the panic that was rushing up into his head like a geyser of bile. "You'll see. We'll feel better after a while, both of us will, and then, I know you hate to hear it now, then we'll have another child."

"I don't want another child."

"You don't want one now, but you will. You will. Reverend Holborn told me. And once we have another child, the wound will heal, it will heal, it won't be gone but it won't hurt so very much and then we can—"

"I think you'd better get out of here," Ginny said.

"Ginny, please, all right? Please don't do this to me. I'm trying as hard as I can."

"You always try as hard as you can," Ginny said, and suddenly Bobby could see it, deep in her eyes, everything she thought of him, and it was not good. Loser, whiner, weakling, mouse. Loser, loser, loser. Loser most of all. You never got away from the place you started at. You were always the person you were born to be.

"I think you'd better get out of here," Ginny said again.

This time Bobby left, half running, not looking in through the open conference room door. He should have called for Jackson. He should have told someone that he was leaving. But he just ran and ran, ran and ran, until he was out in the air and couldn't remember how he'd gotten there. There was a cool breeze in the tops of the trees and a chill on the ground. Or maybe it was hot. He couldn't decide. He couldn't tell. He didn't know what he was going to do.

Ginny had always been his anchor, and now his anchor was setting him loose.

six

1

It was two days later before Gregor was able to get out of Bellerton. The paperwork and odds and ends took much longer than he had expected them to. The waiting took forever. There wasn't much to do except buy books at Maggie Kelleher's bookshop and sit on David's deck, reading them, while David tapped away on his computer in the study, working on his definitive history of American atheism—or whatever it was. When he was very, very restless, Gregor went into town and shopped for presents for people at home. Donna Moradanyan got a four-foot-tall ceramic statue of a guardian angel from Rose MacNeill's shop. Her little son Tommy got a cap gun and caps, which were illegal in Pennsylvania but very legal here, where Gregor had seen dozens of little boys smashing cap strips with their shoe heels in the street. Walking around Bellerton wasn't very comfortable. Now that the reporters were mostly gone, Gregor was the most visible stranger in town. David Sandler didn't count, because he wasn't a stranger here anymore. Gregor wasn't sure he liked having people watch him the way they did here. It was so intense, he sometimes wondered if he were imagining it. Curtains seemed to flick in windows as he passed. Eyes seemed to move as he walked in front of them, doing nothing more important than buying an apple from the bin in front of Charlie Hare's store. He wanted to buy a present for Bennis, but he wasn't sure what. He wanted to call Bennis, too, but that seemed like the wrong idea. She hadn't called him. In the end, he bought Tibor a T-shirt with University of North Carolina symbols on the front and back. He bought Lida Arkmanian a beautiful polished conch shell mounted on a frame. It was too hard to buy things for Bennis, he decided. She was too rich. She had too much already. She had eccentric tastes. Besides, when he thought about Bennis he got restless, and the restlessness was almost unbearable. He didn't know what he was going to do if he had to stay in North Carolina much longer.

When the day came, he laid his suitcase out on the bed in David's guest room and did his best to pack it "right," although he knew that neither Bennis (who would notice) nor Lida Arkmanian (if she were home) would think he had made anything else but a mess of it. He packed shirts and shoes on top of each other, neatly folded. He packed socks rolled into balls in the corners. He packed ties that he tried not to look at, because they were almost always a mess. He had no idea why he did what he did to ties, but they always ended up ruined. Maybe this was some trauma left over from his childhood—some unexamined grief work, as the therapists liked to say—some resistance to leaving the immigrant ghetto of Cavanaugh Street as it had been to become part of the great American middle class. Examined or not, though, he was just going to have to get over it. The Cavanaugh Street that existed now was nothing like the Cavanaugh Street that had existed then. He was going back to town houses, not tenements, and women who bought their clothes at Lord & Taylor.

The morning he was due to leave was as bright and warm as summer. Sun streamed in through the tall windows and skylights of David's house, brighter than klieg lights. Gregor folded cotton sweaters and thought about David's sleeping loft, which was the only room in the house that could be completely closed off from the sun. David's guests, obviously, were expected to get up early. David sat in a corner of the room on a chair he had brought out from the kitchen. He had his legs stretched out and a cup of coffee in his hands. Gregor and David were the same age, but Gregor knew that David looked much younger. He was thinner, for one thing. He'd had less sadness and much, much less worry. Gregor didn't know if he would have wanted that kind of life for himself or not. In one way, it was good. There was nothing noble about suffering, no matter how apocalyptic, or how trivial. In another way it wasn't, because it left you cut off from reality. Gregor Demarkian had always liked reality.

"So," David was saying, "I think you ought to come, because you ought to meet her, at least once. I mean, that's why I got you down here. Because I was worried it was going to be a witch hunt. Because I was worried they were going to send Ginny all the way to the gas chamber without knowing whether or not she did it."

"I don't think they have the gas chamber in this state," Gregor said. "I think they execute by legal injection."

"Whatever. You don't have to stay forever. Just come and watch her blow out the candles or whatever she's going to do—"

"Like a birthday party?"

"Well, it is like a birthday, isn't it? Her new birth out of jail. It was Rose who set it up, and Naomi from the library. It's going to be a nice little party. And besides, like I said, you should see her at least once before you go."

"You don't give Clayton Hall enough credit. He may sound like a rube to you, but he knows what he's doing."

"I never said he didn't know what he was doing. Come."

"I have a train to catch. I'm tired and I want some serious Armenian food. I want to go home."

"You can do it before you go to catch your train. Come."

"There's somebody at your front door, David. You ought to go answer it."

There was somebody at the front door, too. The doorbell was ringing. Gregor could see the tall man on the front step from the guest room window—Henry Holborn, he thought, the reverend who had made all that fuss up at the camp. Gregor had talked to Holborn once or twice during his stay in Bellerton. The talks had not been long and they had not been very deep. Gregor's impressions had been favorable, but not for any particular reason: Henry Holborn had seemed to him like a decent man, in spite of all the fire and brimstone and ingrained fear of the devil. David opened the front door and stood back to let Henry Holborn in. Gregor folded a cotton knit polo shirt he hadn't worn once and put it next to his favorite gray wool sweater. He had worn his gray wool sweater so many times, it was unraveling from the hem and the sleeves and coming apart everyplace else.

"He's over in the guest room, packing," he heard David Sandler say. "You come along this way and I'll get you a cup of coffee."

"I don't need a cup of coffee, David," Henry Holborn said. "I just want to talk to Mr. Demarkian."

Gregor put a little snow globe with a model of the state capitol in it into the suitcase. He had nothing more to pack. David Sandler and Henry Holborn were coming across the hardwood floor of the living room together, clattering. Gregor took his best tweed sport jacket from where it was lying across the desk and put it on.

"There he is," David said, coming through the guest room door. "All finished packing and everything. I've been trying to talk him into coming to Ginny's coming-out party."

"Everybody in town is going to be at that party, almost," Henry Holborn said politely. "So are those reporters that are still in town, even if there aren't too many of them anymore. You might have a good time, Mr. Demarkian. You'd certainly be welcome."

"Besides," David said. "He saved Ginny's life, and he's never even met her."

Henry Holborn came into the guest room and looked

around. "Well," he said. "I can see you're busy. I'm very sorry to bother you. And I know this is just silly as anything—"

"That's all right," Gregor said. "If there's something I can do for you?"

Henry Holborn was looking at the big abstract painting on the wall. "It's just that it doesn't matter anymore. Now that what's happened with Stephen has happened, I mean. It's just—"

"What?"

"Well, when I first heard about Zhondra Meyer committing suicide, I knew she hadn't, you see. I *knew* she hadn't. But then, everything happened with Stephen, you see, and . . ." Henry Holborn shrugged.

Gregor was intrigued. "How did you *know* Zhondra Meyer didn't commit suicide? Were you there?"

"No, no," Henry Holborn said. "She was with me. The night before she died, I mean. She came to see me."

"About what?"

"About buying me out."

"Buying you out?" David Sandler said. "Jesus Christ, Henry."

There was a flicker of annoyance about the profanity in Henry Holborn's face, but just a flicker, nothing more. Henry Holborn believed the things he believed, but he also lived in the world he lived in, and he was used to it.

"I don't know if you realize," he said to Gregor, "but I—meaning the church, of course, the Full Gospel Christian Church—have rather extensive holdings just outside of town."

"He's got a hundred and thirty-three acres and fifteen buildings," David said. "And they aren't small buildings."

"She didn't just want that," Henry Holborn said. "She wanted the housing development. She wanted everything. I don't know if anybody's told you, Mr. Demarkian, but the church has a big tract of land out at the end of the Hartford Road, right on the county line, and we've built houses on it. For our members, mostly. The church handles the credit, you know, because most of them can't go to the banks.''

"Two hundred twelve houses up there last time I checked,'' David said.

"She offered me twenty-five million dollars for it,'' Henry Holborn said. "In cash. Just like that. And I thought, you know, when I heard she was supposed to have committed suicide, that she couldn't have. Because people don't make offers like that and then go off and kill themselves, not unless they're taking drugs or doing something else to make their minds not work right, and one thing I have to give Zhondra. Her mind always worked just fine.''

Gregor considered this. "It could have been an act of desperation,'' he suggested. "Maybe she had had all she could take of hostility from the town, and she felt driven to make a really crazy offer.''

"I think she had had as much as she could take of hostility from me and my people,'' Henry Holborn said, "but I don't think she was acting in desperation. I've seen people in desperation. I see it every day. I saw Stephen Harrow the day before he confessed to the murders.''

"So did I,'' David said. "He was crazy.''

"I believe in the Devil,'' Henry Holborn said. "I believe that Satan is a real and existent presence in this world. But Stephen Harrow was wandering around town, seeing the Devil in the flesh right in front of his face. Zhondra was not like that when she came to talk to me. She was perfectly calm and perfectly lucid. She acted as if she was trying to buy a good winter coat and knew she was going to have to pay more than she wanted to to get it.''

"He said he could see the devil in the palm of his hand,'' David said. "I asked him if he wanted me to help him home, but he didn't. I thought—I don't know what I thought. But I look back on it now, and I don't think he was in his right mind.''

Henry Holborn moved away from the abstract art. Gregor didn't think he had ever really seen it. "Oh, well,'' Henry said. "It's like I said. It doesn't matter anymore, now that all that happened with Stephen. But it was on my mind, so I decided to come to you and get it off."

"I don't mind," Gregor said. "It's an interesting piece of information."

"She actually had twenty-five million dollars in accessible cash," Henry said. "After she made the offer, I had her checked out. It was impossible to get all the information, of course, with people who run on that track, so much of it's hidden. But she could get twenty-five million dollars in cash if she wanted to, and she could probably get more."

"I wonder what it's like to live with something like that," David said. "Not having to worry about money is one thing, but on that scale—" He shrugged.

Gregor patted the top of his suitcase and looked out the window. It really was a bright and sunny day, the kind of day silly rock-and-roll songs are always talking about. He wondered what Stephen's wife Lisa was going to do, and what Bobby Marsh was going to do, too, since the news was all over town that Ginny no longer wanted to have anything to do with him. In the detective novels Bennis gave him, the story was always over when the murder was solved. Everything was put back in order. Everyone went back to living happily, undisturbed by the sudden eruptions of blood. In real life, there never seemed to be an end to it. The repercussions went on and on and on, like ripples on the ocean, destined to never reach another shore.

"You know," Gregor said, "I think I've changed my mind. I think I will drop in on that party."

"Oh," David said, surprised. "Well, good. Good. Let's go over."

"You really will be very welcome, Mr. Demarkian," Henry Holborn told him. "After everything you've done, I'm sure Ginny would be thrilled to have you there."

Gregor didn't know if Ginny would be thrilled to have him there or not, but he did know he needed some kind of closure.

He was also very hungry, and he knew more about David Sandler's cooking than he wanted to.

2

It was impossible to make Betsey's House of Hominy look festive. It was a solid little diner with metal frames on the windows and vinyl on the floor, and no matter how many balloons got tacked to its ceiling, it would never be anything else. The ceiling this morning was covered with balloons, in five or six different colors. There were even a few of the shiny silver Mylar kind, filled with helium and bouncing on the currents of air that came through the open windows. There were little bouquets of balloons in every booth and at intervals along the counters. There were ribbons and bows on every coatrack. People seemed to be stuffed into the corners and plastered to the walls, there were so many of them. What there wasn't was a banner, of the kind Gregor had gotten used to from the parties Donna Moradanyan threw at home. There was nothing saying "Congratulations Ginny!" or "Welcome Home Ginny!" or "Happy Jailbreak Ginny!" Maybe there was nothing that could be put on a banner that the organizers of this thing thought would be appropriate. There was a cake, however, sitting on a cake stand on the counter with the two seats in front of it left empty, so that nobody would elbow it onto the floor and ruin the whole thing. The cake had almost as many tiers as a wedding cake, and was iced in white and pink. All that was written on top of it was "Ginny."

There wasn't anyplace to sit. Gregor wedged himself into the crowd behind David Sandler and Henry Holborn and finally took up a place against the wall near the front door. Nobody was paying attention to him. Ginny was seated on the counter next to the cake—literally on the counter, with her legs folded under her, like a Girl Scout at a tent meeting at camp. Her hair cascaded down her back in loops and curls. The collar of her shirt was open to reveal a gold cross on a gold chain around her neck. Oddly, she was heavier than Gregor remembered thinking she would be, when he had seen her on television. For most people, the camera added pounds instead of taking them off. Maybe she had gained weight in jail, sitting alone in that single cell with nothing to do but eat. In a situation like that, Gregor himself would have found something to read, but Ginny Marsh didn't look like the sort of young woman who liked books.

Betsey herself had put a round of candles on the cake, and now everybody in the room started singing something, Gregor couldn't tell what. The tune was "Happy Birthday," but it was obvious that the two blond women Gregor remembered as Rose MacNeill and Naomi Brent had written new words to the music. Whatever it was they were saying got a laugh from the people closest to them. Then Ginny leaned over and blew out the candles on the cake. It was right to call her Ginny and not Virginia, Gregor thought. She lacked the elegance to carry the more formal name. Ginny was, in fact, the perfect picture of a small-town nice girl, the kind of girl who would be respectful of older people and kind to younger ones, happy to canvass for the March of Dimes and diligent about donating food to the Christmas basket drive at her church. When the news had first broken about the death of the child, some of the news programs had done their best to demonize her. Nobody wanted to be taken in again, not after what had happened with Susan Smith. In the end, it had been impossible to demonize Ginny Marsh. There were no demons there. She was what she appeared to be, every minute of every day. She didn't change into a werewolf after dark.

Somebody started to pass around the cake, and somebody else got up to leave. Gregor grabbed the empty chair and sat down. He didn't want any cake, not at this hour of the morning, but he did want to stay awhile and watch. Rose MacNeill and Naomi Brent both looked feverish, probably because they had too much to do and weren't used to this kind of party. Gregor saw Ricky Drake saying grace over his food—but Henry Holborn just ate his, picking it up in his hands instead of using the little plastic fork that he'd been handed. Now that the cake had been cut, people were starting to drift out. It was an ordinary workday for most of them. They had places to go and people to see.

It was after the crowd had really started to thin out that Ginny Marsh came over to him, bouncing and weaving through the few people who were left as if she had little springs attached to the bottoms of her shoes. Maggie Kelleher had pointed him out to her. Gregor saw it happen. Ginny paused every few feet on her way across the floor to say something to somebody, to smile and nod and make small talk.

By the time she got to him, the only people close to him were David and Henry Holborn, and they were talking to each other about the difficulties of running a small publishing house. David had run one for a decade, specializing in books that argued against the propositions of Christianity. Holborn wanted to start one to specialize in books that would argue in favor of those same propositions. Since it all came down to paper and ink and printers' deadlines and the First Amendment, they had a lot to say to each other.

Ginny pulled up one of the loose chairs now littering the floor and sat astride it, with her arms across the chair back and her chin on her arms. She looked like she was in the process of posing for a Norman Rockwell painting.

"Hello," she said. "You're Gregor Demarkian. You're the great detective. Maggie Kelleher pointed you out."

"I saw her," Gregor said. "I don't know what kind of great detective I am. These days I seem mostly to be retired."

"You haven't been retired down here," Ginny said. "You shouldn't be so modest. I know what you've done since you came to visit David. You've been wonderful. I wouldn't be here if you hadn't helped me out."

"Here?"

"At this party." Ginny's right arm made a sweeping arc in the air. "I'd still be back where I was, in jail, or in the county jail. I know that. I know what all of them were thinking. Did you know that I'd separated from my husband?''

"Oh, yes," Gregor said. "I heard that."

"He didn't believe in me, either," Ginny said. "None of them did, not really. Some of them say they did, but it isn't true. It's strange what you find out about people, when you've been through something like this."

"You find out a great deal," Gregor agreed. "But most people never find themselves in a situation like this."

"Well, it's a good thing, isn't it? It's a good thing. It's too horrible to think about, even now, after all this time. I'm glad you came down to help me, Mr. Demarkian. You did help me. You helped me more than you'll ever know."

"Oh, I think I know," Gregor said. "I think I know exactly. You know what's puzzling me, at the moment?"

"What?"

"I keep wondering how long you expect to get away with this. Because you must know you can't get away with this forever. You have to know that that just isn't possible."

Gregor Demarkian had never believed in shapechangers, but now Ginny Marsh seemed to be one. She changed right in front of his eyes. Her eyes went sharp and small. Her nostrils pinched. She lost all her small-town quasiprettiness in a flash. All that was left of it was her hair, cascading blond and bright over her shirt collar and down her back.

"I don't know what you mean," she said, her voice very low, very low, impossible for anyone around them to hear.

"Of course you know what I mean," Gregor said. "You killed your child."

"Stephen killed my child," Ginny said. "You proved it."

"I proved no such thing. Stephen killed Carol Littleton and Zhondra Meyer, yes, that he did, but he didn't kill the child. You killed the child. You were the only one who could have."

"How can you say that? Stephen went out on the

kitchen terrace with Carol Littleton and took Tiffany with him. It was in his confession. It was in all the papers—"

"It wasn't part of his confession," Gregor said, "it was in the fake suicide note he wrote for Zhondra Meyer. And he had to have a name, of course, because he couldn't remember killing the child. Because he hadn't killed the child. And he had to have a reason, too, for killing Carol Littleton later. He couldn't tell us why he really killed her. That would have destroyed everything he had been working for."

Ginny turned her face away. "I still don't understand what you mean. I think you're being cruel, that's all. I think you like to—to torment people."

"When you cut Tiffany's throat, she was alive, Ginny. She was alive. The blood pumped out of her. That's what Stephen said."

"I didn't cut Tiffany's throat. I'd never do anything like that. I loved my baby."

"Oh, Ginny," Gregor said. "You've never loved anybody but Ginny and you know that. I know that. I've watched you operate, on television before I came down, here today at this party. You're a remarkable young woman, in a way. You killed the child with your own hands, but then you got better. You sat in that jail cell day after day and killed Carol Littleton and Zhondra Meyer and Stephen Harrow, too, all without raising a finger."

"Stephen killed Carol and Zhondra," Ginny said. "You told me so. And Stephen killed himself. Clayton Hall was there. He saw him. You saw him. Even Lisa saw him."

"I know who saw him, Ginny. I know you were sitting all alone in that cell they gave you, reading your Bible and biding your time. But you killed them anyway. All the way along, all Stephen was trying to do was stay sane and protect you. He did the second part reasonably well, but he didn't manage the first. By the time Stephen Harrow put that bullet through himself, he was something worse than out of his mind. He was staring into the pit of hell and hearing it call to him."

"He was crazy all along," Ginny said. "He must have been, to do what he did."

"No, Ginny. He wasn't crazy all along. He was troubled, but you made him crazy. He would have confessed to killing the child if he had killed it, Ginny. He needed to confess. He wanted to."

"He blanked it out," Ginny said. "You hear about people doing that all the time. When something's too horrible for them to remember, they blank it out."

"You were the only person who was gone, Ginny. The only person besides Stephen Harrow who wasn't anywhere to be found in those two rooms, except for Carol and Stelle and Dinah, and they were together."

"They say they were together. They could be lying for each other. They do a lot of lying up there at that camp. They're all lesbians."

"There isn't anybody else, Ginny. There's only you."

"You can't prove any of this," Ginny said, straightening up. "It's all—it's all just a fantasy in your head."

"Oh, I don't know," Gregor said. "People say I'm so wonderful at solving crimes, but that isn't really what I do best. What I do best is to find the evidence that's needed to arrest and convict after the crime has been solved. That's a much more useful talent."

"It doesn't have anything to do with me."

"North Carolina has the death penalty, Ginny."

"That doesn't have anything to do with me, either."

"I think it does. I've never believed in the death penalty. I've always thought there were too many chances to make a mistake, to convict the wrong person, to execute the wrong person. But in your case, Ginny, those scruples would not apply. So I'll tell you what."

"I don't want to hear any more," Ginny said. "You have nothing to say to me."

Gregor leaned forward and put his hands on the sides of Ginny's chair. "Listen to me, Ginny. I am going to come back to North Carolina, and when I do, it's going to be for one reason and one reason only. I am going to come back and watch you die.''

Ginny stood up, quickly, abruptly, almost making the chair topple and Gregor topple with it. ''I've got some people I've got to talk to. I can't say it's been nice talking to you.''

Then she turned around and hurried off, pushing through knots of people with barely a nod of her head, half running, as if she had to get to the bathroom right this second or suffer something dire. Gregor watched her until she disappeared into a crowd of people. Then he went up to where David Sandler and Henry Holborn were still talking about cover copy and publicity releases and said, ''I've got to go now, David. If I don't hurry, I'll miss my train.''

''I've got to drive you,'' David said, standing up. ''Henry, why don't you come out to the house for dinner some night next week? We can go over all this. I'm sorry to have to rush off on you like this—''

''No, no,'' Henry Holborn said. ''You go right ahead. Mr. Demarkian is probably eager to get home.''

''I'm sure he's glad he came,'' David said. ''Aren't you, Gregor? Gregor loves to work on cases like this. It's his life.''

Gregor shook Henry Holborn's hand, said good-bye, and then stepped outside. David's pickup truck was parked at the curb, with Gregor's suitcase already in the back. Gregor started to walk around it to the passenger side door, and then he stopped.

Back on the tailgate, where David had once had a fish with feet and the word ''Darwin'' written inside, there was now no fish with feet. There was, however, a fish without feet, and what was written inside it was ''Jesus.''

Gregor wondered how long it would take David Sandler, the most famous atheist in America, to notice.

epilogue

———

1

Donna Moradanyan's decorations were still up from the christening. The first thing Gregor Demarkian saw when he came back to Cavanaugh Street was his own brownstone building, wrapped up in white satin from stoop to roof, with a bow and a cross on top. He looked up and down the street, then shook his head. In his absence, Donna had gone off her nut. The front of Holy Trinity Armenian Christian Church was wrapped up in white satin, too, and Tibor hated it when Donna decorated the church. He thought it looked less than dignified. Gregor wished there were more people around, outside, where he could see them. It was late in the afternoon. The sun was hanging very low in the sky. The street lamps had already begun to glow. The windows in Lida Arkmanian's living room were open and the big chandelier was lit. Lida must be back from California. Gregor told the driver where to stop and got out his wallet to pay him. It seemed odd that he had lived here so long now that it had begun to seem natural to think of this as home. When he had first come back to Philadelphia, he had still been living, mentally, in Washington, D.C. He woke up in the morning and reached out for the small square alarm clock that had been on his bedside table in the apartment in Foggy Bottom. He and Elizabeth had had a town house once, but they had sold it when they realized just how sick Elizabeth was. Elizabeth always said they sold it so that they could be more sure about the money. Gregor had always agreed with her, but he didn't agree with her now. If there was one thing working for the federal government could get you, it was excellent health insurance that covered everything. Gregor had started to hate the house, that was all. He had begun to see it as a monument to Elizabeth that he would be expected to live in, rattling through the rooms alone when she was gone, using their silverware and their china like some badly incarnated ghost. They had bought that house years before, when they had still expected to have children. Gregor could never get over the feeling that if Elizabeth had had children, she would not have had the cancer that ultimately killed her.

In the town house on Cavanaugh Street, Gregor checked the hall table for his mail and noted in passing that there was no light under George Tekemanian's door. There was no mail for him on the hall table, either. Gregor went up the stairs and stopped on the landing in front of Bennis's apartment. There was a light on in there and the sound of a CD player pumping out "You Can Call Me Al" by Paul Simon, but Gregor didn't knock. He went up to the third floor and let himself into his own apartment. He left his suitcase in the foyer and waked through the living room and down the hall to his bedroom. Then he took off his clothes and threw himself in the shower. His mail was lying on his bed—put there by Bennis or Tibor or Donna Moradanyan. If he went into his kitchen, he would find food in his refrigerator—put there by Lida or Hannah or even Sheila Kashinian. Cavanaugh Street was a predictable, well-ordered place, the kind of place everyone said was so good for children. Gregor got out of the shower and wrapped himself in the big terry cloth robe Bennis had given him one Christmas. His apartment was full of things Bennis had given him, the way her apartment was full of things he had given her. They must both have been out of their minds, or willfully stupid. They had probably been a little of both.

Gregor went back down the hall and through the living room to the kitchen. There was food in his refrigerator, along with notes. The note on the meatballs with the bulgur crusts said: *"Krekor, call me when you get in. There is a crisis about the birthday party for Sheila.—L."* Gregor took the bowl out and put it on the kitchen table. Then he got a smaller bowl out of the cabinet next to the sink and put five big bulgur-covered meatballs inside it. Then he covered the smaller bowl with plastic wrap and put it in the microwave. Sheila Kashinian's birthday party could wait. In fact, Gregor thought, it could wait forever. The thought of Sheila's husband Howard dancing on tables and talking to lamp shades, which he often did when he was drunk, which he often got when he was at parties, did not make Gregor's heart leap for joy. Gregor put water on to boil for instant coffee and picked up the phone. "You Can Call Me Al" had become "Kodachrome." He could hear it through his kitchen window, meaning that Bennis's kitchen window downstairs must be open, too. Gregor had been around Bennis long enough to know that these two songs were not on the same album, and that it didn't matter, because Bennis's CD player could handle more than one disc at a time, and play songs off both of them in any order you wanted it to. It was not as good as the CD player old George Tekemanian's grandson Martin had given him, which held nine discs at once and could be programmed to do everything but give the State of the Union address while wearing a tuxedo. Gregor punched Bennis's number into the phone and sat down on a kitchen chair to wait for her to pick up. The music coming through his kitchen window got instantly softer.

"Hello?" Bennis said when she picked up.

"I'm home," Gregor told her.

"I thought I heard you wandering around up there," she said. "I've been watching you on television. You ought to come downstairs and tell me how the good Methodist minister ended up killing a little baby."

"He didn't," Gregor said. "The mother did."

"That's not what Dan Rather said. And I believe Dan Rather."

"You can go on believing Dan Rather. It's a complicated situation. I'll explain it to you, if you want me to."

"I want you to."

"Not now," Gregor said. "I'm sitting in my kitchen in a robe. Is everything all right here, Bennis? Has Tibor been well? I was worried when I left."

"Everything's been fine. Tibor is spending the day with some people from the UN or something. He's supposed to be giving a seminar in New York on the religious implications of war next month. He was never as obsessed as you thought he was, Gregor. That was mostly in your head."

"I know."

"He was just upset," Bennis said. "And I think that's entirely natural. Did Lida leave you a bowl of those big meatball things?"

"Yes, she did."

"She left me some, too. I was out shopping and when I came home there they were, sitting in my refrigerator. She's planning a big surprise party for Sheila Kashinian's birthday."

"I figured that out," Gregor said. "Are you ready to go to dinner with me?"

"Right this minute?"

"Don't be ludicrous. How about this evening, around seven?"

"Fine," Bennis said.

The microwave beeped. Gregor opened the door and took the bowl of meatballs out, very carefully, using only the tips of his fingers. "I'll make reservations for that place with the candles that you took me to. The one where the tables had those big pots of flowers."

"Fleur de Lis."

"Right."

"Gregor?"

The water was boiling for the coffee. Gregor took the kettle off the burner and reached for a white mug and the bottle of Folger's. "What?" he asked.

"I think you ought to come down earlier than that," Bennis said. "To tell me all about the mother and the Methodist minister. Or whatever."

"I'm nervous, too, Bennis," he said.

"Good."

"I'll be down as soon as I can."

"That's good, too."

"Play something a little less hiccuppy. If you've got anything less hiccuppy."

"I don't think I'm ready for Joni Mitchell yet, Gregor. Come on down."

"I will."

Bennis hung up. Gregor poured hot water over his Folger's and then picked up both the mug and the bowl to take them back to the bedroom. The music from downstairs seemed to have been shut off altogether. Once he was beyond the kitchen, he wouldn't have been able to hear it anyway. This building was too well built for sounds to travel between floors. He put his mug and his bowl down on the bedside table and picked up the phone book to find the number for Fleur de Lis. He was pacing back and forth in front of his mirror, wondering how long he would have to wait for the coffee to cool enough for him to drink it and how many rings he would have to listen to before somebody at Fleur de Lis picked up, when he saw the three pictures of Elizabeth lined up like soldiers across the center shelf of the built-in bookcase next to his bed. He wondered suddenly when he had put them there, almost out of sight, instead of next to his phone where he would see them all the time. She was beautiful, Elizabeth was. When he had first met her, he had thought she was the most beautiful woman he had ever seen. There was still something magical about her, captured in these old photographs. Maybe there would never be a day in his life when he would not turn over in a bed he was sleeping in alone and half expect to find her there. Maybe there would never be a night in his life when he didn't think he half heard her calling him, just out of sight in the next room. That was what it meant to be married and in love with somebody for thirty years. It did not mean that that was all you'd ever have or all you'd ever want or all you'd ever think about.

The phone was picked up on the other end of the line and a very harried woman said, "Fleur de Lis."

"Yes," Gregor said, walking over to the bookshelf as he talked. "My name is Gregor Demarkian. I would like to make a reservation for quarter to eight."

"Oh, Mr. De*mark*ian," the woman said. "Oh, of course. A reservation. For quarter to eight."

"For two. For one of those booths in the back, if you've got one available."

"Of course we've got one available. Of course we do."

"Good," Gregor said.

The woman was still fussing, Gregor couldn't figure out about what. He looked at the pictures one more time and smiled slightly at the one of Elizabeth dressed as a clown, holding her nieces on her lap. Then he took all three down, one by one, until he was holding them in a stack in his free hand.

"There!" the woman at Fleur de Lis said. "All done. We'll be expecting you at quarter to eight."

"Thank you," Gregor said.

He hung up. Then he took the pictures of Elizabeth over to his bureau and put them in the bottom drawer, in among the expensive presents people gave him that he never used. Silk handkerchiefs. Monogrammed socks. He shut the drawer.

Elizabeth would have appreciated the idea of monogrammed socks. She would have appreciated all of Cavanaugh Street, but she was not here to see it, and he was, and he had to get on with his life.

2

A little over an hour later, Gregor was lying on the big black leather couch in Bennis Hannaford's living room, his jacket thrown over the back of a chair on the other side of the room, his shoes in a little pile on the floor, his tie already a total mess. Bennis was moving back and forth between her bedroom and her bathroom, talking as she went. The whole apartment smelled of sachet and roses. The CD player was putting out Bach in a very low-key, unaggressive way. Gregor reminded himself every once in a while to be grateful for small favors, or for Bennis's Philadelphia Main Line debutante upbringing, which in this case probably amounted to the same thing. Under the circumstances, he wouldn't have been able to blame her if she had subjected him to the Hallelujah Chorus from Handel's *Messiah*.

"So," Bennis said now. "What I don't understand is, why did Ginny Marsh want to kill her baby?"

"For the same reason most of these women kill their babies," Gregor said. "I don't know if you realize it, but child murder of this kind is not entirely unheard of."

"I watched the news about Susan Smith, Gregor. I thought she had a boyfriend and that was the point, to get rid of the children so that she could marry the boyfriend."

"Actually, that's up in the air in the Smith case," Gregor said. "There was a case exactly like that out on the West Coast a while back. But that's not the point, Bennis. It doesn't matter if they have a boyfriend or if they don't. They're bored. They feel trapped. What's trapping them is the child."

"You wonder why they don't just leave the child off at social services or something. Or put it in a basket and take it to a church. Tibor was telling me that that happened at Father Ryan's church a couple of years ago. They took care of everything."

"I don't understand why people do half of what they do, Bennis. I just know that they do it. I thought it was going to be Ginny Marsh from the beginning. I told David that."

"I know. Did she have a boyfriend somewhere that I haven't heard about?"

"She was having an affair of a sort with Stephen Harrow, the Methodist minister. It mattered to him. It mattered to him a great deal. That's what kept messing us up. The murders, the other murders besides the murder of the child, didn't really make any sense. I didn't realize until much later that they had been done by two different people for two different reasons. Stephen Harrow wanted to protect Ginny Marsh. And Ginny Marsh—"

"—wanted to be free? But Gregor, for God's sake. What did Harrow think after he saw her kill her own child? How could he possibly go on protecting her after that?"

"I think he thought it was his own fault," Gregor said. "I think he thought of her as this innocent little child, who was very easily led, and he had let her get involved in all this goddess worship nonsense. He had even helped her with it. And then, you see, it got out of hand, and she did something he was sure she didn't want to do—later, I think, he thought she didn't even remember doing it. So while she sat in jail, he made damned certain that nobody could expose her."

"But she had done it on purpose," Bennis said.

"Oh, yes. Very definitely. Ginny wanted a second chance. She wanted to be free of Bobby Marsh and free of Tiffany and free of Bellerton, North Carolina, and she took what she thought was the most direct route to get her there. And she's no Susan Smith. This wasn't an act of desperation committed under stress. She isn't going to make a tearful last-minute confession. She isn't going to stand in front of an army of television cameras and tell the world how she feels remorse. She doesn't feel remorse, and she thinks she's going to get away with it, now that Stephen Harrow is dead."

"He was really in love with her, then," Bennis said.

"He was married to a cold woman who had come to feel nothing but contempt for him," Gregor told her. "He was living in a place as foreign to him as Qatar or Morocco would be to you or me. *He* was living under a great deal of stress, and she came along like a promise of deliverance. Under ordinary circumstances—back home on his own ground, with a marriage that was going reasonably well—I don't think he would have looked at her twice."

"Even so," Bennis said. "It seems like a small enough reason for killing a child. I don't know why I think so, but I think there ought to be some really big reason for killing a child. Something catastrophic or apocalyptic or—something."

"But there isn't," Gregor said gently.

Bennis came down the hall and into the living room, wearing a navy blue silk kimono wrapped tightly around her. She was so small, barely five foot four, barely a hundred pounds. Wrapped in navy blue silk she looked smaller still. She sat down on the arm of her big club chair and swung her feet.

"You know what Lida would say, and Hannah and the rest of them. It isn't natural. It goes against the maternal instinct."

"There isn't any maternal instinct," Gregor said firmly. "Mothers kill their children all the time. They sell them for the money to buy crack. They leave them in garbage cans. They abuse them terribly. And men do it, too, of course. But nobody ever said men had a paternal instinct."

"What's going to happen to her?" Bennis asked. "Is she going to get away with it?"

"I don't know."

"Aren't you at least going to try to make sure she doesn't?"

"Of course I'm going to try. I'm already trying. And I'm fairly sure—and Clayton Hall and the North Carolina state police are fairly sure—that we can put enough together to arrest her. The problem is in convicting her. She's going to say that Stephen Harrow killed the child, and she's going to be able to point to the two murders he did commit to make that look plausible. The law says beyond a reasonable doubt, Bennis. It's a good rule, most of the time."

"I know. But you hate to think of it not being such a good rule this time. I think it was the same in the Susan Smith case. You wanted horrible things to happen to her, really terrible things. You wanted Old Testament justice just this once."

"If we arrest her, there will at least be the publicity," Gregor pointed out. "There will be a lot of publicity for a long time, and that will put a crimp in the great escape she's attempting to make. That might be a small consolation, but at least it's some."

"Not enough."

"I didn't say it was enough, Bennis. I was just trying to live in the real world without going nuts."

There was a pack of cigarettes and a lighter on the long coffee table in front of the couch Gregor was sitting on. Bennis leaned forward and got a cigarette out and lit up.

"So," she said. "On to the subject we've both been avoiding. Do you really want to wait until we get all the way out to dinner to tell me what's on your mind?"

"I thought you already knew what was on my mind."

"I know in general. I meant in detail."

"It's not really all that hard to explain. I can give it to you in a single word. Spain."

"Spain."

"I think we should go to Spain, you and me, alone. For about a month."

"A month."

"I would have suggested longer, but you always seem to have so much to do. I didn't want to get in the way of one of your book deadlines or whatever."

"I don't have a book deadline anytime soon. It's not that. It's just—Gregor, what are you and I going to do alone in Spain for a month?"

"You must be joking."

Bennis blew a stream of smoke into the air. "Fine," she said. "Just fine. But nobody could do that and nothing else for one solid month."

"I was talking about sight-seeing," Gregor said blandly.

"Like hell you were."

"Maybe we could talk, Bennis. Maybe we could just sort of not be on Cavanaugh Street, not be around the people we know all the time, not have so much to take into consideration. Maybe we could go to Spain and just concentrate on one thing and one thing only for a while, and see just how far that takes us."

"Is there a reason for Spain in particular? Why not California? Or Greece? Or the North Pole?"

"I went to California with Elizabeth once. We had a good time."

"Not California, then."

"I don't have any associations with Spain, Bennis, and as far as I know, you don't either. And I've been retired for years now, and I haven't done anything but take busman's holidays. I just want to get away someplace and sit on a beach and read silly books. *Not* murder mysteries."

"Are you sure you want to do that with me?"

"Of course I am."

Bennis's cigarette was smoked almost down to the stub. There was an ashtray on the other end of the coffee table from the cigarette pack and the lighter. Bennis got up and put her stub out in it.

"I'd better get dressed," she said. "It's getting late. Are you going to be all right in here?"

"I'm always all right in here. If I get hungry, I can raid your refrigerator."

"Help yourself. Gregor?"

"What?"

"I bought a new dress."

"Don't tell me what it cost," Gregor said. "If there's one thing I have to thank God about in this relationship, it's that you make your own money."

3

In Bennis's living room, there were no pictures except the original paintings for the covers of her first three books.

She kept the only two photographs she had—one of her mother in full riding habit standing next to a horse; one of her brother Christopher and her sister Emma standing together in the wind on one of the balconies of the Eiffel Tower—on that same built-in bookshelf in her bedroom where Gregor had kept the pictures of Elizabeth in his. The difference was that Bennis had many more people in her family, living and dead, but didn't feel the need to build shrines to any one of them. Bennis was good at leaving and staying gone, in a way that Gregor didn't think he ever could be. Upstairs, his apartment was spare and clean and stripped, as if he had only moved into it the day before yesterday. For most of the time he had lived on Cavanaugh Street, his real life had been somewhere else—back in Washington, D.C. Bennis's real life had been here, with forays into unknown venues only for adventure. Her rooms were crowded with bits and pieces of the things that really mattered to her: a bookcase with nothing in it but copies of the books she had written, in every conceivable edition, in every conceivable language; big papier-mâché models of the landscapes of her fantasy series, painted in bright greens and deep golds and aggressive Day-Glo orange; a pink plastic unicorn little Tommy Moradanyan had brought her back from a trip to Florida. It wasn't that there had been no pain in Bennis's life—if anything, Gregor reminded himself, there had been too much—but that she seemed to be able to get past it. Or maybe she didn't. That would be an interesting thing to find out during a month alone in Spain—just how much of Bennis's life he hadn't been paying attention to all these years.

He heard the bedroom door click open and the sound of high heels on the hardwood floor of the hall.

"Are you ready?" he asked her. "It's getting to the point where we ought to get out of here if we're going to be on time."

"I'm just putting on an earring."

Bennis always put on her earrings blind, instead of in front of a mirror. She had pierced ears, and she would poke at them with the sharp end of the post, making Gregor wince. He looked up just as she entered the room. Then he sat up and stared. She was wearing a black, calf-length dress with a wide skirt made out of lace and a tightly fitted bodice made out of satin, but that sort of thing didn't begin to describe it. It was what it didn't have that was important. It didn't have anything over the shoulders. It didn't have any back at all.

"How does that thing stay up?" Gregor asked her.

"Maybe it doesn't," she told him.

"How do you stay up in it?"

Bennis gave him a look meant to shut him up. Her earring had finally decided to go into its hole. She snapped the clasp shut and then picked up a black lace shawl from the table near the window. Gregor had noticed it before, but hadn't thought of it as anything important. Bennis always had clothes lying around on furniture.

Gregor got to his feet. "I think you're wrong," he told her. "I think it would be perfectly possible to spend an entire month in Spain doing nothing but, uh—"

"I wouldn't try joking around like that, Gregor," Bennis said. "Someday, somebody might decide to take you up on it."

Then she walked away from him into the foyer, opened her front door, and went out.

If you loved Jane Haddam's BAPTISM IN BLOOD, you will want to read the next Gregor Demarkian mystery, DEADLY BELOVED.

Look for DEADLY BELOVED in hardcover from Bantam Books at your favorite bookstore in June 1997.

Turn the page for a special advance look at Gregor's latest adventure.

*DEADLY
BELOVED
A Wedding Mystery*

*by
Jane
Haddam*

There was a fog in Fox Run Hill that morning, a thick roll of gray and black floating just an inch above the ground, like the mad scientist's dream mist in some ancient horror movie. Patsy MacLaren Willis moved through it much too quickly. There were stones on the driveway that she couldn't see. There were ruts in the gutters where she didn't expect them. It was just on the edge of dawn and still very cold, in spite of its being almost summer. Patsy felt foolish and uncomfortable in her short-sleeved, thin silk blouse. Foolish and uncomfortable, she thought, dumping a load of clothes on hangers into the rear of the dull black Volvo station wagon she had parked halfway down the drive. That was the way Patsy had always felt in Fox Run Hill all the time she had lived there, more than twenty years. It was as if God had touched His finger to her forehead one morning and said, "No matter what you do with your life, you will always be out of step, out of touch, out of place."

The clothes on hangers were her own: navy-blue linen dresses from Ann Taylor with round necklines and no collars; Liz Claiborne dress pants with pleats across the front panels under the waists; Donna Karan wrap skirts with matching cropped jackets. The clothes went with the Volvo in some odd way Patsy couldn't define. The clothes and the Volvo went with the house too—a mock-Tudor seven thousand square feet big, set on a lot of exactly one and three-quarter acres. Fox Run Hill, Patsy thought irritably, looking up at all the other houses facing her winding street. An elegant Victorian reproduction. A massive French provincial with a curlicue roof and stone quoins. A redbrick Federalist with too many windows. The only thing she couldn't see from there was the fence that surrounded it all, that made Fox Run Hill what it really was. The fence was made of wrought iron and topped with electrified barbed wire. It was supposed to keep them safe. It was also supposed to remain invisible. Years ago—when the fence had just been put up, and the first foundations for the first houses had just been dug on the little circle of lots near the front gate—someone had planted a thick stand of evergreen trees along the line the fence made against the outside world. Now those trees were thick with needles and very tall, blocking out all concrete evidence of real life.

Patsy checked through the clothes again—dresses, slacks, blouses, skirts, underwear in pink satin lightly scented bags—and then walked back up the drive and into the garage. She poked against the pins in her salt-and-pepper hair and felt fat wet strands fall against her neck. She shifted the waistband of her skirt against her skin and ended up feeling lumpy and grotesque. Three days before, she had celebrated her forty-eighth birthday with a small dinner party at the Fox Run Hill Country Club. Her husband, Stephen Willis, had reserved the window corner for her. She had been able to look out over the waterfall while she cut her cake. She had been able to look out over the candles at the people she had been closest to in this place. It should have been the perfect moment, the culmination of something important and valuable, the recognition of an achievement and a promise. Instead, the night had been ugly and flat and full of tension, like every other night Patsy could remember—but it was a tension only she had recognized. If she had tried to tell the others about it, they wouldn't have known what she meant.

Nobody here has ever known what I meant, Patsy thought as she came up out of the garage into the mudroom. She kicked off her sandals and left them lying, tumbled together, under the built-in bench along the south wall. She padded across the fieldstone floor in her bare feet and went up the wooden stairs into the kitchen. The house was cavernous. It should have had a dozen children in it, and a dozen servants too. Instead, there was just Stephen and herself, having their dinners on trays in front of the masonry fireplace in the thirty-by-thirty-foot family room, making love in a tangle of sheets in a master bedroom so outsized, the bed in it had had to be custom-made, and all the linens had to be special-ordered from Bloomingdale's. Patsy stopped at one of the four kitchen sinks and got herself a glass of water. Her throat felt scratchy and hard, as if she had just eaten razor blades. I hate this house, she thought. Anybody would hate this house. It was not only too large. It was fake. Even the portraits of ancestors that lined the paneled wall in the gallery were fake. Stephen had bought them at auction at Sotheby's, the leftover pieces of somebody else's unremembered life.

"I paid only a thousand for the lot," he'd told Patsy when he'd brought them home from New York. "They're just what we've always needed in this place."

Patsy put her used glass into the sink. That was the difference between them, of course. Stephen *did* like the house. He liked everything about it, just the way he liked everything about Fox Run Hill, and the country club, and his job at Delacord & Tweed in Philadelphia. Last month he had bought himself a bright red Ferrari Testarosa. This month he had been talking about taking a vacation in the Caribbean, of renting an entire villa on Montego Bay and keeping it for the three long months of the summer.

"The problem with us is that we've never really learned to enjoy our money," he'd said. "We've never understood that there was more that we could do with it than use it to invest in bonds."

Patsy had fished the lemon slice out of the bottom of the glass of Scotch on the rocks she'd just drunk and made an encouraging noise. The family room had a cathedral ceiling and thick, useless beams that had been machine-cut to look as if they had been hand-hewn, then dyed a dark brown to make them look old. Stephen's voice bounced against all the wood and stone and empty spaces.

"Now that I won't be traveling anymore, it'll be better," he had told her, "you'll see. I know that you've been terribly lonely, dumped in this house with nobody to talk to for weeks at a time. I know that you haven't been happy here."

Now the water-spotted glass sat in the sink, looking all wrong. Everything else in the kitchen was clean to the point of being antiseptic. The sinks were all stainless steel and highly polished, as if porcelain had too much of the roadside diner attached to it, too much of the socially marginal and the economically low rent.

"Damn," Patsy said out loud. She walked through glass doors that separated the kitchen and the family room from the foyer and stared up the front stairs. The stairs made a circular sweep up a curved bulge in the wall that was lined with curved leaded windows looking out on the drive and the front walk. Outside, the Volvo looked dowdy and frumpy and square—just like Patsy imagined she looked dowdy and dumpy and square everywhere in Fox Run Hill, next to all those women who worked so hard on treadmills and Nautilus machines, who came to parties and ate only crudités and drank only Perrier water. The clock at the top of the stairs said that it was 6:26. Patsy stopped next to it, at the linen closet, and rummaged through the stacks of Porthault sheets until she found the gun.

Patsy turned the gun over in her hands. It was a Smith & Wesson Model 657 41 Magnum with an 8-3/4-inch stainless steel barrel, muzzled by a professional silencer that looked like a blackened can of insect repellant. She had bought it quite openly at a gun shop in central Philadelphia, with no questions asked, in spite of the fact that it was a heavy gun that most women would not want to use.

Most women probably couldn't even lift it, Patsy thought, walking down the carpeted hall. The only real sounds in the house were Stephen's snoring, and the whir of the central air-conditioning, pumping away even in the cold of the morning, set so low that crystals of ice some-times formed on the edges of the grates.

In the bedroom, Stephen was lying on his back under a pile of quilts and blankets, his mostly bald head lolling off the side of a thick goose-down pillow, a single naked shoulder exposed to the air. When Patsy had first met him, he'd had thick hair all over his body. In the years of their marriage, he seemed to have shed.

Patsy spread her legs apart and raised the gun in both hands. She had fired it only twice before, but she knew how difficult it was. When the bullet exploded in the chamber, the gun kicked back and made her shoulder hurt. She wished she'd thought to wear a set of ear protectors like the ones they'd given her when she went out to practice at the range. Then she remembered the silencer and felt im-mensely and irredeemably stupid. Could anyone as naive and ignorant as she really do something like this? Why didn't she just turn around and go downstairs and get into the car? Why didn't she just drive through the front gates and keep on going, driving and driving until she came to a place where she could smell the sea?

Stephen's body moved on the bed. He coughed in his sleep, his throat thick with mucus. He was nothing and nobody, Patsy thought, a cog in the machine, an instru-ment. He was the one who had wanted to live locked up like this, so that he could pretend they were safe. If I don't do something soon, he'll wake up, Patsy thought.

She tried to remember the color of his eyes and couldn't do it. She tried to remember the shape of his hands and couldn't do that either. She had been married to this man for twenty-two years and he had made no impression on her at all.

"I know how unhappy you've been," he had told her—but of course he didn't know, he couldn't know, he would never have the faintest idea.

Stephen shifted in the bed again. A little more of him disappeared under the covers. Patsy aimed a little to the left of the shoulder she could see and took a deep breath and fired. Stephen made a sound like wind and jerked against the quilts. Blankets fell away from him. Patsy changed her aim and fired again. He seemed to be dead, as dead as anyone could get, but she couldn't really tell. There were three black holes in the skin near his left nipple but no blood. Then she saw the red, spreading in a thick wash on the sheet underneath the body. The longer she looked at it, the more it seemed to darken, first into maroon, then into black. She let the gun drop and brought her legs together. She suddenly thought that it was so odd—even in this, even in the act of murdering her husband, the first thing a woman had to do was spread her legs.

Patsy walked over to the night table on Stephen's side of the bed and put the gun down on it. The air was full of the smell of cordite and something worse, something foul and rotted and hot. Patsy made herself kneel down at the side of the bed and look Stephen in the face. His eyes were open, deep brown eyes with no intelligence left in them. She grabbed him by the hair and turned his head back and forth. It moved where she wanted it to, flaccid and heavy, unresisting. She let his head drop. His eyes are brown, she told herself, as if that really mattered. Then she walked out of the suite and into the hall, closing the single open bedroom door behind her.

The house was still too large, too empty, too hollow, too dead. Now it felt as if it no longer belonged to her. Patsy walked down the hall to the front stairs and down the front stairs to the foyer. She went through the foyer to the kitchen and through the kitchen to the mudroom. She walked into the garage and then carefully locked the mudroom door behind her. The Volvo was still packed and waiting on the gravel. The fog was still rolling in puffs just above the ground. No one would come looking for Stephen at all today. Anyone who came looking for her would assume that she had gone into the city to shop.

Patsy got into the Volvo and started the engine. Molly Bracken, who lived in the elegant Victorian, came out onto her front porch, looking for the morning paper. Patsy tooted her horn lightly and waved, making just enough fuss for Molly to look her way. Molly waved too, and Patsy began to drive around the gravel circle and head for the road.

The sun was coming up now, forcing its way through the clouds, eating at the fog. It was going to be a perfect bright day, hot and liquid. There were going to be dozens of people down at the Fox Run Hill Country Club, hanging around the pool. The city was going to be full of teenagers in halter tops and shorts cut high up on their thighs.

I am going to disappear, Patsy told herself, smiling a little, humming the ragged melody of something by Bob Dylan under her breath. I am going to disappear into thin air, and it's going to be as if I'd never been.

2

Evelyn Adder hid her food all over the house, in the attic and the basement as well as on the two main floors, in underwear drawers and empty boxes of Tide detergent and behind the paperback romance novels on the bottom shelf in the alcove off the library, in all the places her husband, Henry, would never think to look for it. It was Henry who had bought the refrigerator with the lock on it that now took up the west corner of the enormous main floor kitchen that had once been the thing Evelyn liked best about the brick Federalist. The locked refrigerator had all the real food in it—the meat and the butter, the bagels and the cream cheese, the Italian bread and the pieces of leftover lasagna and the slices of Miss Grimble's Chocolate Cheesecake Henry liked to eat with his coffee after dinner. The other refrigerator, big as it was, held only those things Henry thought Evelyn should eat, and only in those amounts he thought suitable for a single day. Every morning Henry would get up and decorate Evelyn's refrigerator with grapefruits sliced in half and lettuce and cucumber salads tossed with balsamic vinegar. Then he would sit down at the kitchen table and explain, patiently, why it was they were doing things this way. Henry had been a college professor when Evelyn first met him. He had, in fact, been

Evelyn's own college professor, at Bryn Mawr, in medieval literature. It was only after they were married that he had written the book called *How to Take It Off, Keep It Off, and Never Make Excuses Again*. It was the book that had made him rich enough to buy this house in Fox Run Hill.

"How do you think it looks," he would ask her as he arranged grapefruit halves on plates. "What do you think people think it means, that the most successful diet book author in America has a fat wife?"

In the beginning, of course, it had been Evelyn who was thin and Henry who was fat—although Evelyn's thinness had never been entirely natural. Like most of the other girls she was close to at Bryn Mawr, she tended to binge and purge, except they hadn't called it that then. That was in the days before anybody knew about "eating disorders." Evelyn and her friends would get up in the middle of the night and eat five or six gallons of ice cream apiece. They would shove down whole large pepperoni pizzas and three or four pounds of potato chips and thick chocolate cookies from Hazel's in Philadelphia by the bag. Then they would rush into the girl's bathrooms, stick their fingers down their throats, and throw it all up. Evelyn got so good at it, she didn't even have to stick her finger down her throat anymore. She could throw up just by thinking about it. She didn't think of herself as "disordered" either. If anything, she imagined she was being "classical," like those Romans her Introduction to Western Civilization professor was always telling them about, the ones who ate and ate at banquets until they were sick, then went out into the courtyard and vomited so that they could start all over again. Evelyn would sit in Main Line restaurants and order only salad, no dressing. She would sit upright over the salad and pick at lettuce leaves and sprigs of parsley. Sometimes on outings like this she was so hungry her stomach felt full of ground glass. She would sit across the damask tablecloths and the matched china, watching Henry eating piece after piece of batter-fried shrimp loaded with tartar sauce, and want to rip his throat out with her teeth.

"You're a real inspiration to me," Henry had said at

the time. "I never knew anybody who had so much self-control before."

The food Evelyn kept around the house these days was no more real food than the grapefruit halves and lettuce salads. It was mostly what she could shoplift when she and Henry went to the grocery store together. Henry wouldn't let her go to the grocery store on her own anymore. He had even taken away her car so that she couldn't get there when he wasn't looking. Evelyn had to sneak things into the voluminous pockets of her linen tent dresses or shove them into the hollow between her breasts made by her well-constructed bra. Sometimes she picked up a twelve-pack of Hostess cupcakes in the dessert aisle, took it into the ladies' room at the back of the store, and ate the whole thing, right there. Sometimes, when it was cold enough to wear her good long coat, she could push pastry and candy bars through the slit she had made in the lining and come home with a major haul. One way or the other, she got what she wanted. The brick Federalist was full of food. There were Devil Dogs and Ring Dings under the winter quilts in the linen closet. There were big bags of Cheez Doodles and smaller ones of pizza-flavored Combos in the decorative curved wood Shaker baskets that made a display in the study. There were Slim Jims and packages of Chips Ahoy cookies in the hollow base of the Indian brass lamp in the formal living room. Evelyn Adder weighed three hundred and eighty-five pounds at five foot five—and there was still not a moment in her life when she was not hungry, hungry hungry hungry, so hungry she felt as if she were being sucked inside out.

"I don't understand how you got this way," Evelyn's mother would say, visiting from Altoona. "Nobody in our family ever got this way."

Evelyn kept chocolate-covered marshmallow pinwheels and long thick sticks of pepperoni and big hunks of blue cheese under the winter jackets in the window seat on the half-landing at the front of the house. Sitting there, she could hear Henry as soon as he started to move around in the master bedroom at the top of the stairs. She could also see out onto Winding Brook Road. She saw Patsy Mac-Laren Willis pack her Volvo full of clothes and get into it and leave. She saw Molly Bracken come off her porch and go down her walk and get the morning paper from the end of her drive. Evelyn sat there for hours, thinking about all the other women on this street, thinking about herself. Between six o'clock and quarter to eight she finished six and half pounds of pepperoni, three and a half pounds of blue cheese, and thirty-four chocolate-covered marshmallow pinwheels. She also came to this conclusion: Nice little working-class girls from Altoona should not go to Bryn Mawr, or marry their medieval literature professors, or move into places like Fox Run Hill. They would only end up afraid of their own houses, and so hungry they would never get enough, and so frantic they would never be able to think straight. Like her, they would sit around wondering how long it would be before their husbands decided to hire good lawyers and get themselves divorced.

It was now five minutes to eight. Evelyn had stopped eating ten minutes earlier, when she had heard Henry get out of bed and go to the shower. She had put away all the packages and dusted crumbs off the polished oak of the window seat. Now she heard Henry get out of the shower and pad across the wall-to-wall carpeting to the dressing room. She got up and started to make her way downstairs, slowly and painfully. All movement was painful for her these days. Her feet hurt so much when she stood up on them, she wanted to cry. They had become big too, so large and wide she had trouble finding shoes to fit them. She had started buying expensive men's athletic shoes made of black leather and decorated with brightly dyed stripes meant to look like lightning.

"Your feet will get smaller when you lose the weight," Henry would tell her. "They won't hurt so much either. Believe me. I know."

When Evelyn had first met Henry, he had been massive, impressive, beautiful. Now, thinner, he seemed diminished to her. His mouth was always pinched tight. His flesh hung slackly against his bones no matter how much he exercised. When she saw him with the other men on the stone terrace of the country club, drinking gin and tonic, hefting tennis rackets, Henry was always the one who looked fake, phony, totally out of place.

"Marriage is a crap shoot," Evelyn's mother always said, and: "You have to take men the way you find them."

I would be happy to take Henry the way I found him, Evelyn told herself. I just don't want him the way he is now.

There was a professional doctor's scale in one corner of the breakfast nook. Henry had put it there to check Evelyn's progress every morning. He had also locked up the coffee and the tea and the Perrier water, so that she couldn't drink them before he got up and blame any weight gain on fluid in her system. He made her take off her shoes and stockings and dress and stand in the nook in her underwear, her big breasts spilling down over the rounded swell of her belly, her thighs lumpy and veined and mottled blue and red with fat and age.

"Look at you," he would say as she stood there, a breeze coming through one of the open skylights, feeling cold, feeling stupid, feeling as ugly as she had always known she was inside. "Look at you."

Upstairs in the bedroom there were mirrors now, all along one wall, so that she couldn't escape looking at herself. If she tried to close her eyes, she fell. If she fell, she had a hard time getting up. Henry would have to get up himself and help her. Then the questions would start. What are you doing up and dressed this early in the morning? Where are you going? Where are you hiding the food?

"Look at you," he would say, spinning her around so that she was forced to face the mirrors. He would grab at the front of her dress and tear. The dress would pull away from her body and hang off her shoulders in tatters. In the mirror a grotesque fat woman with bulging eyes and pussed red pimples along the line of her jaw would stare back at her, hateful and angry, as hateful and angry as Henry had gotten to be.

"Look at you," he would say, and one day, provoked

beyond endurance, finding a trail of crumbs wound along one of her massive breasts, he had torn at her bra too. He had torn it right off, snapping the elastic painfully on her back, dragging the spike of one bra hook into her flesh until she bled. Her breasts bounced up and down and side to side, and that hurt too. Her nipples and the area around them were as thick and dark and dry as leather. There was a mountain of crumbs in her bra, between her breasts. It popped into fragments as soon as her breasts came free and scattered over the white wall-to-wall carpeting like ashes blown into town from a distant forest fire.

"Look at you," Henry had screamed loud enough so that Evelyn was suddenly glad of all that central air-conditioning, all those sound buffers placed on all the properties, all those illusions of space and grace. Her breasts were shaking, hurting, bouncing. They were so big now that she even wore a bra to bed. Henry's face was so red, she thought he was having a heart attack. His eyes seemed to be coming out of his head. The knuckles on both of his hands were white. Suddenly he reached out and snatched at her underwear. He grabbed the elastic waistband in his fists and pulled with all his might. The elastic tore and the nylon tore after it. A second later Henry had shreds of underwear in his hands and Evelyn was standing naked. The only thing Evelyn remembered after that was that her pubic hair seemed to have disappeared. It was hidden by the curtains of flesh that had draped themselves around her, hanging like an apron from her waist.

Look at you, Evelyn thought now, listening to the sound of Henry's footsteps on the staircase. A second later he was in the kitchen, dressed in white chinos and a bright red polo shirt and deck shoes, his hands in his pockets, his hair combed to make maximum use of the fact that it was every bit as thick now as it had been when he was twenty. I really hate this man's face, Evelyn thought as she waited for him. I hate it so much, I would like to boil it off with acid. Then she was just glad that she hadn't been sitting down when he came into the room. More and more lately, she didn't quite fit on a single chair. More and more, Henry tended to notice it.

"Well, Evelyn," he said, sitting down in one of the breakfast nook chairs. "Are we going to find any surprises on the scale today?"

Evelyn suddenly thought of Patsy MacLaren Willis, out in her driveway with all those clothes. There had never been a divorce in Fox Run Hill as far as Evelyn knew. It was the kind of place men moved with their second wives. Still, she thought, there was a first time for everything.

ABOUT THE AUTHOR

JANE HADDAM is the author of fourteen Gregor Demarkian holiday mysteries. *Not a Creature Was Stirring,* the first in the series, was nominated for both an Anthony and the Mystery Writers of America's Edgar awards. Other titles in the bestselling series include *A Stillness in Bethlehem, Bleeding Hearts,* and *And One to Die On.* She lives with her husband and two sons in Litchfield County, Connecticut.

"Charmingly original."
—*Publishers Weekly*

"Haddam's usual deft writing, skillful plotting, and gentle humor . . . refreshing and entertaining."
—*Booklist*

Not a Creature Was Stirring

"Vintage Christie [turned] inside out . . . *Not a Creature Was Stirring* will puzzle, perplex, and please the most discriminating readers."
—*Murder Ad Lib*

Precious Blood

"A fascinating read."
—*Romantic Times*

Act of Darkness

"Juicy gossip abounds, tension builds and all present are suitably suspect as Demarkian expertly wraps up loose ends in this entertaining, satisfying mystery."
—*Publishers Weekly*

THE HIGHEST PRAISE FOR JANE HADDAM'S HOLIDAY MYSTERIES

And One to Die On

"Sharp, stylistic prose, unique characters, wacked humor, and a skillfully interwoven plot all contribute to an excellent read from the author of *Bleeding Hearts*."
—*Library Journal*

"Ms. Haddam is synonymous with unique mystery novels."
—*Rendezvous*

"Has all the sparkle and complexity her fans have come to expect."
—*Kirkus Reviews*

Bleeding Hearts

"A rattling good puzzle, a varied and appealing cast, and a detective whose work carries a rare stamp of authority . . . This one is a treat."
—*Kirkus Reviews* (starred review)

"Absolutely delightful."
—*Romantic Times*

"An absorbing, good-humored tale complete with vivid characters, multiple murders and a couple of juicy subplots."
—*The Orlando Sentinel*